Unfinished Business

LISA

A DEVON'S CAFE NOVEL
BOOK TWO

NICOLE D. MILLER

Also by Nicole D. Miller

How to Overcome Heartbreak: Recovering from Misguided Love

How to Overcome Heartbreak: Stories That Heal

Stories for the (Urban) Soul

When Love Wins

Contents

To Literary Cleveland, where Lisa was born.

Too Much of a Go-Getter

CHAPTER 1

"I cannot believe you let him get away with that. I mean, he's been doing this same back and forth for the last six months." Lisa's secretary, Danita, copped her the side eye as Lisa struggled to keep her own emotions in check.

Danita was right. Lisa's father had been giving her the run around for as long as she could remember. Six months was a drop in the bucket compared to what she had been dealing with since her parent's divorce. Instead of answering, Lisa rubbed the bulging stomach protruding from her abdomen, finding temporary comfort from the little body inside.

Danita must have noticed her tension because she added in a softer tone, "Hey. You know your peeps better than I do. I know you know how to handle it. I just hate seeing you upset. That's all." The caring secretary scooped up the papers off Lisa's desk and started scanning with her round baby browns. The files were the initial reason she came in, but when she saw the look of disappointment dressing her boss's features, she pried out of Lisa the reason for her despair. The dam broke, and Lisa's words flowed faster than the Jordan River.

"You know what?" Lisa said, "It doesn't matter how old you get,

I'm learning you always seem to need your parents." Sighing, she sank deep into her office chair, mulling over the last conversation she had with her father.

Since her parents' divorce, Hank Pedersen had been in and out of Lisa's life so long, that she knew it was easier to pinpoint the times he was actually in it than the times he wasn't. Still, this last time she thought they were really going to stay the course. And they had, for about a good two years.

Around the same time that Lisa and Michael had gotten remarried, her father popped up. His email said how sorry he was that he had missed so much of her life. He had been following her journalism career and was so proud of how far she'd come. And, more importantly, he wanted to repair the time they had lost, and finally meet his granddaughter, Michelle.

Hmm. Lisa was hesitant. She hated to potentially put her baby girl in a situation where she could be misled into thinking she was gaining another grandparent. Michelle was having such a good experience with Michael's father, and Lisa didn't want anyone to mess that up. Still, a prompting in her spirit nudged her, and she knew now by experience the voice of God. Cautiously, she agreed to reconnect, and to her surprise, Hank had been diligent about staying in touch. He even took the six-hour trip to Manhattan from his comfortable ranch-style home in Ohio. Michael was his normally courteous self during the visit, but Lisa knew her husband well enough to know, he was guarded. Knowing the history of their tumultuous relationship, Michael trusted her father about as much as she did. But Michelle, of course, was smitten and overjoyed to have "Another Papa!" which was how she referred to Michael's father.

"Lisa, I have to be here for Candace. She's in her school play and needs me. It's her first one." Hank's voice overcast Lisa's memory like cumulus clouds rolling in before the storm. Just twenty minutes prior they had spoken on video chat, where she caught the worry lines seizing his forehead. It was times like those that Lisa hated she looked just like him, adopting Hank's caramel-smooth skin and large, cocoa eyes. Her mother was a darker hue of chocolate, and too often while growing up, Lisa felt like she wasn't a part of the family. She had wished over and over she could be darker. She even went through a phase where she would sunbathe for hours during the summer, trying unsuccessfully, to achieve this particular goal.

"But, you said you would be here for Michelle's birthday. She's turning nine." Lisa couldn't keep the edge out of her voice, particularly while saying her daughter's age. She bit her lip to still it from trembling.

I hate that he affects me this way!

"Look. I didn't do it on purpose." Hank's voice turned defensive. "I double-booked myself. Novelle already got the tickets and everything. I'll make it up to Michelle. I promise."

His eyes pleaded with her to believe him but Lisa was running very low on grace. All she could think about were the numerous broken promises she'd received growing up, and now she was putting her daughter through the same thing. On top of that, over the last few months, Hank had been hard to get a hold of. It felt like he was reverting back to old behavior. Out of nowhere, he suddenly video calls her in the middle of her workday and she couldn't resist the urge to answer. Now she wished she hadn't. It only turned out to be life calling with another disappointment.

Who cares if your damn wife already got the tickets! And who cares if your stupid daughter needs you, the little girl inside Lisa's head fumed.

"Fine," was all she could muster.

Shortly after hanging up, Lisa found herself wavering in her intimate office, unable to concentrate on her article. That's when Danita had walked in.

"You want me to get you some tea or something, Lis?" Danita was sorting through the papers she had grabbed and glanced at her with concern.

Coming out of her reverie, Lisa slowly breathed, still patting her stomach. "Naw, girl. I'm ok. I just need to focus. That's all."

One swift look at her phone revealed a text from Michael confirming their appointment for the ultrasound. Baby Doris decided to pop a few kicks at that very moment, and Lisa couldn't suppress her smile. He must have known they were talking about him.

Lisa responded in text to Michael, **"Yep, babe. 6 o'clock. See you then,"** who sent a brown thumbs-up emoji in response.

It was a little after five when she glanced up from her article. She had finally made headway, burying the disappointment from her father beneath the piles of deadlines and words. It was a craft Lisa had perfected years ago.

"I'm checking out. You need anything before I go?" Danita peeked her head inside and Lisa met her with an appreciative smile.

Danita was the best. About three years ago, Lisa had hired her and hadn't been sorry since. The girl was exceptionally bright, efficient, and finishing up her B.A. in Creative Writing. It was only a matter of time before they would part ways and Lisa dreaded the day.

"No ma'am. I'll see you in the a.m. I'm gonna be heading out here soon myself."

After Danita vanished, Lisa stretched her arms over her head while leaning back in her ergonomic office chair. Fighting a yawn, she threw back her thread of curls, then started packing. Drowsiness was setting in and she knew it was the pregnancy.

"God, little boy, you are really doing a number on me," Lisa cooed to her belly. She was only 21 weeks, but it felt more like eight months. Michelle hadn't been this feisty in her womb and yet proved to be otherwise when she made it out. Lisa wondered if it would be the same for her baby boy. Would he be so much trouble now, only to be calm, cool, and collected on the outside? Losing her earlier battle, she yawned loudly then hurried to turn off her PC before fleeing the building to hail a cab.

"New York Presbyterian Hospital please," Lisa huffed to a stoic-looking Arab in the driver's seat. He grunted before they skillfully veered the streets of Manhattan in 5 o'clock traffic.

Arriving at the hospital, Lisa slipped the driver an extra five bucks. He had been gracious enough to let her out right in front of the double-door entrance, cutting off another cab that tried to take the same spot. *I guess it pays to be preggers sometimes,* she thought with humor. Even the most hardcore New Yorker didn't seem so tough with an expectant mother.

Her feet soon kissed the ground and her eyes shimmered. In the lobby, Michael stood like a Black Greek god with the most beautiful countenance Lisa had ever seen. He hit her with his light eyes, coupled with a playful smile, the epitome of sunshine on a rainy day. Lisa's tan suede high-heeled shoes lifted her as she floated towards her husband. Fortunately, the pregnancy had not stunted her ability to rock her heels. Not yet anyway.

"Baby, how was your day?" Michael smothered her with his lips and she caved inside his form, her cream scarf and Burberry trench coat crunching against his double-breasted indigo suit.

"Better, now that I'm with you," she murmured against the thick of his neck.

At that moment, Lisa didn't want to go into the details of her father and his foolishness. She didn't want to talk about the deadline she was running behind on, or that Baby Doris felt like a kicker for the San Francisco 49ers. That her ribs were aching from all the time he was putting into practice on her. No. All that mattered, right now, was that Lisa was with Michael.

Her husband rewarded her with another tight squeeze before whisking her to the elevators. The duo made their way to the seventh floor to the gynecology department, then signed in before sitting in the waiting room. As soon as Lisa's bottom hit the seat, Michael had her feet in his lap and her shoes on the floor. He wasted no time in pleasing her, running his long fingers over the nooks and crannies of her soles. She exhaled, then slid off her trench, revealing a dark button-down dress pleated at the waste that reached mid-calf.

"You check in with Aunt Sylvia?" she asked softly as Michael massaged and fondled her toes. He nodded.

"Yes ma'am. Michelle and Sylvia are doing a puzzle and will be ready when we get there. I told Sylvia about an hour to an hour and a half tops. She said, 'That's fine cuz, then we'll have time to watch *Law & Order*,'" he mocked, doing a perfect imitation of the older woman's voice.

Lisa laughed. "Michelle will be thrilled," she said facetiously, while rolling her eyes.

Michael grinned. "She don't care, as long as she's with Sylvia."

Lisa got the warm and fuzzies then. She so appreciated the volcanic rock that Sylvia had been in her life. After she and Michael had divorced, Sylvia was her lifeline, living just upstairs in the four-apartment unit Lisa and Michelle had stayed in. When Lisa didn't have parents, support, or a friend in the city, Sylvia became all three. God knew what he was doing when He made Sylvia Canton.

"Mrs. Doris?" an overset nurse announced, just when Michael was working out the kinks in her left heel. Lisa looked up.

"Dr. Swan is ready for you," the nurse advised in a friendly enough tone, though her features resembled a brick wall; stern and solid.

Obediently, Lisa and Michael gathered their things and trailed the woman to their assigned room; a standard compilation of sparse, hard furniture and a small sink to wash up in. As Michael helped her out of her clothes and fumbled with tying the thin patient robe in the back, Lisa sighed in annoyance.

"I don't know why they make these things so flimsy and difficult," she complained, and Michael chuckled.

"To give husbands a hard time," he answered. Finally, he had gotten the little ties together and helped her onto the muddy brown, high-raised bed, decorated with a slice of white paper.

"I mean, it's so thin I might as well not be wearing nothin'. And y'all 'bout to see it all anyway. They should just have us sprawl out on this fake bed butt-naked," Lisa spouted, inducing another laugh from her husband. "It'd be easier."

"Don't tempt me, girl. I don't need *no* encouragement you know." He stood in between her partially opened thighs and started caressing her face. Lisa leaned in for a kiss, but just when she was really getting into it, the door opened.

"Umm, am I interrupting?" A full-bodied, ebony woman with green eyes and jet-black robust hair stood in the doorway blanketed by a long, white coat jacket. The contrast of her skin, hair, and eyes was striking.

Lisa took a second to appreciate, once again, how fly her OBGYN was. But then, she quickly adjusted the hospital gown, closed her legs, and sat as erect as a chalkboard.

I feel like a teenager who just got caught sneaking my boyfriend into my room.

Michael took a small step from his wife, a rouge-like color flushing both cheeks. "No, Dr. Swan," he began in an embarrassed tone. "We were just uhh…"

Dr. Swan smiled, easing inside with the smoothness of a leopard and fondled her stethoscope. "Oh, I know what you were doing. And that's the reason we here in the first place," she piped in a cheeky manner. Laughing at her own humor, the doctor stood near Lisa as Michael took a seat in the corner. "So, how have you been since our last appointment?" She shot her gaze at Lisa.

Lisa shifted so that Dr. Swan could examine all the important parts.

"I've been ok. I think my son is gonna be a football player though," she joked, as her heartbeat was listened to.

Dr. Swan was gracious and had the best bedside manner of any doctor Lisa had ever seen. She was so glad to have found her, and it didn't hurt that she was a Black woman.

"Oh really? Is he keeping you on your toes?" Dr. Swan looked down at Lisa's belly. She started talking to it in a high-pitched tone while placing both hands on her hips. "I hope you keep that same energy when you get out, buddy!" She looked at the adults. "That way he can make you some money on the field," she said, before winking.

Lisa shook her head. "I don't know about that, Doc. We already have one high-strung kid. I may have to quit my job if we have two."

Everyone laughed as Dr. Swan finished her exam. "Lie on your back and we'll get you those 3D pictures you been waitin' for."

Lisa did as she was told and Michael moved to hold her hand while Dr. Swan slathered gel on her belly. She winced at the cold temperature but then eagerly looked at the monitor to see her son.

At first it was blurry, but, all of a sudden, there was a clearer picture of his form.

"Now there. Come on, Baby Doris. Show us that beautiful face of yours," Dr. Swan prompted to the screen, but the baby staunchly kept his back to his audience.

"Come on, son. Give it to us!" Michael called, but nothing.

Lisa laughed. "I guess he's as stubborn as his dad." Then, at the sound of her voice, the baby flipped over so that his front was on display.

"Well, if we had any doubts, we know for sure it's a boy," Dr. Swan exclaimed.

"Yeah. A *mama's* boy," Michael added.

"Hey! He knows who's really wearing the pants in this family." Lisa smirked while Michael swatted her hand lightly, but his face was aglow. The couple was all smiles but Dr. Swan began peering into the monitor more intently.

Swan's features grew too serious for Lisa's comfort and the doctor had become disconcertingly quiet.

"Something wrong, Doc?" Lisa asked, almost too afraid to, but knowing the question was needed. Dr. Swan remained silent and Lisa could tell the woman was choosing her words carefully.

At that moment, Lisa wanted to freeze time. She wanted everything to be perfectly ok. She wanted her baby boy and her daughter and Michael to be the happy family she grew up never having; grew up always wanting. But reality was crashing in as she studied her doctor's expression of coddled concern.

Whoever said life was supposed to be perfect anyway? It sure as hell wasn't social media. *Or was it?* Lisa thought, her mind internally pacing.

"I want to do some more tests, but I think the Placenta is attached to the wall of your uterus. When this happens, this is called Placenta Previa."

Dr. Swan's voice circled Lisa's thoughts, feeling close, but somehow still far away.

"Placenta Previa?" Lisa repeated with a frown.

"So. What does this mean?" Michael's tone was thick, and his hands tensed around Lisa's.

"It means I want to do a vaginal exam to know for sure, and then we will go from there." Swan's voice was firm, emptied out now from the light-heartedness she entered the room with.

After wiping the gel from her belly, she helped Lisa get into position. Michael was sitting down, and though she couldn't see him, Lisa heard his leather Gucci's rapidly tapping the lime-green linoleum.

Dr. Swan was her normally considerate self and made the exam as comfortable as possible. But Lisa was a bundle of nerves and fear, and had to keep taking deep breaths to loosen her body enough to be examined vaginally.

Lord, PLEASE let my baby be ok! she screamed over and over in her head like a record on repeat.

Michael must have sensed her anxiety because he slid back over and took her hand. Trying not to get in the way, he stood on the opposite end of Dr. Swan.

I will never leave you nor forsake you, Lisa heard the passage from Hebrews 13:5 as clear as day in her heart. She was so grateful for her relationship with God. For so long she didn't even know if she believed in God, but then she had her own encounter. Experiencing that kind of intimate nearness was amazing. Often, she had thought that if there *was* a God, He was posted somewhere high in the clouds, looking down on humans while they did their thing. But then, she learned by her own experience that He was so much more nearer! He was actually involved in every nuance of her being and wanted an intimate relationship with her. And even better, God became the Father that Lisa's earthly father was never able to be.

"Ok. I think we're done," Dr. Swan announced, then removed the stirrups before taking off her gloves.

Michael helped Lisa sit up while directing his gaze at the doctor.

"So?" he asked with wide eyes and Lisa stroked his arm.

"So," Swan repeated pensively. "It *is* Placenta Previa, as I was thinking." She paused. "Lisa, have you had any bleeding during this pregnancy?" Dr. Swan's stare perused Lisa in a rapid quest for answers and her stomach sank.

Had she had any bleeding?

"Umm. Only a little," Lisa admitted. "It was like spotting, then went away. So, I didn't think anything of it." Her stomach twisted into knots of guilt from minimizing the event.

Michael cast Lisa a surprised look. "What?" he asked, with a small step away from her. "When did this happen?"

"Uh. Last month? But you know, the same thing happened with Michelle. Remember? I was freaking out and we rushed to the emergency and it was nothing. I didn't want to go through all that again or worry you unnecessarily, so I didn't mention it," Lisa hurried to explain herself, then peered at the doctor. "Was I wrong to do that? I mean, isn't that common in pregnancies?"

Dr. Swan nodded, taking notes on a clipboard. "Yes. It is. But in this case, it's an indication of the issue. Basically, the Placenta is currently attached to the bottom of your uterus wall and partially covering your cervix. Although symptoms don't start until the second trimester, it would have been best had we discovered it sooner…" The doctor scribbled more notes as her voice trailed.

Lisa felt sick. Had she caused harm to their son by ignoring the bleeding?

"I…I thought…" she started, but felt herself tear up.

Michael looked upset himself but reached for her and gently rubbed her naked back. It was no longer shielded by the hospital gown as the little ties he had worked so diligently on had come undone.

"So, what caused this and what do we do now?" He was now Michael, head of the sales team, not Michael, the scared father, upset that his wife had bleeding she didn't tell him about.

"The cause could be a number of things," Swan said. "Are you a smoker?" Lisa shook her head. "Have you been pregnant several times before?"

"Only with Michelle," Lisa hurried to say and saw Michael waiting for the answer as well.

"Do you have a history of fibroids? I've only been your OBGYN for this pregnancy and will have to look at your chart for your history."

"Yes. Yes, I have. I actually had surgery to have them removed a few years ago."

"Ahh. Then that's probably it. We're going to monitor you. There's a possibility the Placenta will navigate its way to the correct position naturally. As long as there's no more bleeding, you should be fine. But please, do let me know if more bleeding occurs. That's where the real concern lies. We can't have you losing too much blood." With the expertise her degrees indicated, Swan then asked, "You had a vaginal birth with your first child, correct?"

Lisa nodded. "Yes. I did."

"Ok. Well, be prepared that we may have to do a Cesarean."

Lisa grew cold. She hadn't considered that, and preparation was her strong suit. They already had her birthing bag packed and everything and she still had 19 more weeks til her due date!

"What are the risks involved in a C-section?" Michael asked. He was still using his take charge sales executive voice. Lisa received some comfort in the fact that he was being so strong when she felt like she was crumbling inside.

"C-sections have well over a 75% success rate. But, as you know, labor in general is a risk. Mr. Doris, you have nothing additional to worry about in terms of your wife's birth than you did before we knew of this diagnosis. But," Dr. Swan squeezed her clipboard in one hand and swiped a pamphlet from a plastic tray, "here are some hard numbers and other facts for you to review concerning them."

With a grave expression, Michael took the pamphlet while muttering a soft, "Thanks."

"I do suggest you take it easy in your routine, Lisa. You don't want to do anything too strenuous like lifting weights or running. Only light walking. Oh, and you guys will need to refrain from sex for the rest of the pregnancy."

The couple nodded sullenly like two children on punishment and as Lisa caressed her abdomen the room started closing in.

"You need some water, Lis?" Ever the attentive husband,

Michael noticed her discomfort. She nodded, unable to form the words as he moved into action.

Dr. Swan gave Michael instructions to head down the hall and make a right towards the bathrooms where the water fountains were. There would be cups nearby.

For the first time since their appointment had begun, Lisa was alone with Swan. She decided she would pursue the question she was so deathly afraid to ask. But before doing so, she assessed the woman more intently.

She's probably only a few years older than me, Lisa thought, then noticed that Dr. Swan wore a wedding ring. She kicked herself for not having asked about her personal life sooner.

"Do you have children, Dr. Swan?"

Dr. Swan glanced up from her clipboard and smiled kindly. "Why, yes. I have two boys," she said proudly. "Twins actually."

"Ok. So, tell me the truth. If you were me. Or if you were in my position. Would you be worried? Mother to mother."

Lisa waited as thoughts flashed in the other woman's eyes which seemed to be the perfect hue of emerald.

"Honestly, I think any mother who wants a perfectly healthy child and a 100 percent safe birth would be concerned about any hiccups in the plan. But between you and I? Mother to mother? We have to learn to always put our children in the care of our Heavenly Father. Don't you think?"

Lisa was surprised. She hadn't expected the doctor to be a Believer. They had never once spoken of faith. Instantly consoled by her words, she responded, "Yes. Yes, you're right."

Lord, You are so good to connect me with this woman!

"And what better opportunity to start putting that into practice while they're still in the womb?" Dr. Swan winked and Lisa's heart slowed its pace. Peace flooded her then, gently lifting the burden she had been carrying.

"You're right. There's no time like now." Lisa looked down at her belly. Baby Doris was on the go again. She smiled because she knew that her son was too much of a go-getter to let anything stop him from making it into this world. Not anything at all.

How to Wait on God

CHAPTER 2

After her discussion with Dr. Swan, Lisa felt better, however, knew there would be a problem when Michael was cordial but distant as soon as they left the hospital. He helped her onto the elevator and into the car but hadn't reached for her hand once as they walked. Now he was silent as they drove to pick up Michelle.

Lisa was fighting the urge to initiate a conversation. She assumed he was pissed she hadn't told him about the bleeding. Even though she was annoyed he was giving her the silent treatment, she was glad Michael had at least kept his feelings to himself in front of the doctor.

Why should I initiate talking when he's the one with the issue? I mean, seriously. I already explained to him my logic, and yet here he is, trippin', she thought, as they whipped past a yellow convertible that had to be flying.

If we just passed that car, how fast are we actually going? Now Lisa was concerned.

"Would you please slow down?" She started trying to catch a glimpse of the speedometer over his arm.

13

"I'm fine. I'm going just over the speed limit," Michael replied, in an even tone.

But Lisa noticed that his knuckles were taut from gripping the steering wheel. *This brother is not fine.*

"Then how come we just passed that convertible with that young girl driving like she ain't got no sense? And how come I just saw your speed drop *five* miles after I said something?" She wouldn't let him off the hook that easily.

"Oh, so you make all the executive decisions in the family now, huh? You decide it all? Even how fast I should be driving?"

Michael breathed deeply and kept his gaze straight as he talked but switched over to the slow lane.

"What are you talking about? *I* make all the decisions? *You* are the breadwinner. *You* decided we move into your apartment after we got married instead of building a house in the burbs like I wanted. Even though you *knew* we were gonna try to increase our family and would need more space. *You're* the one who talked me into taking this leave after the baby, even though you *know* how important my work is to me. So please. Do tell. How am *I* the one in charge?"

Lisa had to take a deep breath. She could feel her voice starting to rise, and she wrung her hands together on top of her leather Prada bag to try and keep her cool.

"You know what I'm talking about. And don't try to pull that old, 'you giving up your work' bull. Blah. Blah. Blah," Michael spewed. "We *both* agreed this is what's best for *our* family. *You* want to breastfeed, and *you* want to be close to the baby. *And* you are *still going to* work from home. So don't go there," he threw back. But while talking, he nearly missed the exit and had to do a last-minute swerve to make it.

"Can you *please* not kill us on the way to pick up *our* daughter?" Lisa said through gritted teeth.

I am so over this mess. "If you got a problem, Michael, just say it. You can miss me with the silent treatment and passive-aggressive accusations."

But in response, her husband said nothing, and Lisa grunted in frustration.

Why does he always have to become a stone wall when something is bothering him? she seethed as the city landscape rolled by.

Cars and people painted downtown Manhattan in a perfect portrait of activity. They were nearing Lisa's old stomping grounds, and for a quick second, she longed for it all. She longed for a time where things weren't perfect, but it was a season where she was a bit more free. She only had herself and one kid to worry about back then, not a whole husband, and another baby on the way. Aunt Sylvia, the perfect shoulder to lean on, had been at her beck and call.

As they drove nearer to Sylvia's, they passed Devon's, a Black-owned cafe which Lisa had fallen entirely in love with, named after its owner. Memories of spending ample time at Devon's when it was just around the corner from her old apartment, bombarded her. She would write and drink coffee, chop it up with friends, and attend the open mic night. That's where she met Natalie. That's where she met Denise. That's where she met Joe.

Joe. Now that's a name I haven't thought of in a while.

Michael's sigh brought Lisa out of her musings. "Look. I don't want to fight. I really don't. But I am hurt that you didn't tell me about the bleeding."

Nooo. You think? Lisa thought sarcastically, but she knew better than to say it. Six months of couples therapy had taught her that much. Instead, she nodded slowly as they pulled into a space near Sylvia's building. They sat there for a few, until she finally turned to Michael, studying his profile. He was just as attractive as the day they met. The strong jawline. The chiseled chin. The light eyes that sparkled whenever she made him laugh, but were now undeniably, filled with pain. Guilt sat heavily on her chest while peering at them.

"Look," Lisa began. "I didn't intend to hurt you. I'm sorry. I really just thought the bleeding was the same thing that happened before."

Her voice became clutched by the stillness in the vehicle. She felt horrible about possibly putting their son in danger through her negligence. Didn't he know how awful she felt?

Michael clenched his jaw before finally meeting her eyes. "I just need you to consider me more, Lis. I feel like, after we split, you got even more independent. I think, sometimes, you default back to being single."

Hmm. Could that be true? Lisa sifted through his words. Even though her immediate response was to dismiss them, she slowed herself down long enough to weigh them, another tip from their counselor.

"Can you give me an example? I mean, other than the bleeding thing."

"Ok. Like, bringing your dad around. I get it. That's your dad. But you invited him to see us without even asking what I thought. I was hurt." Michael licked his lips as Lisa nodded.

"Alright. Maybe you have a point. I mean, I just thought, because you know our history, you would be supportive of me trying to reconcile with him and heal the relationship."

"Baby. Of course." Michael turned to her and placed his hands over hers. "But I still would want to be asked if I want the man at my house. I mean, honestly, I was cool with the visit, but he could have at *least* stayed at a hotel. We barely know him. *You* barely know him."

Reflecting on his words, Lisa could see his point.

""OK. I don't fully agree, but I do want to be more mindful if that's the case. But, babe, *you* need to realize that I *was* single. I was single for almost *two years* after our divorce. I was a single parent and I was *raised* by a single parent. It's going to be *work* for me to turn that all the way off."

Shifting more towards her, Michael's gaze was softer than before. "I don't want you to turn it all the way off. Don't you know your drive and self-confidence is what drew me to you in the first place? I just need you to be a little bit more…balanced."

As he caressed her hand in his, Lisa's heart grew tender. She thought about their early days.

"Really? It was my drive you were attracted to? I thought it was that white bodycon dress I was rockin' at your cousin Orlando's party?" she teased, and Michael smiled the way she knew he would.

"Heh. Yeah, that too." Michael brought her hand to his lips and teased it against his mouth. "I mean, girl, that dress was *bad*," and Lisa laughed, feeling ten times lighter.

"Well, you know. I do what I can." She fake-shrugged and knew they were back to their normally playful selves. That was one of the things she loved about them; they knew how to enjoy each other.

"Ok. I hear you. I'll try to be more considerate of you," Lisa offered. "But I need you to also share what's on your heart and not keep so much bottled inside." She looked at Michael seriously. She was so tired of having to drag things out of him.

"Girl. I done made *so* much progress and you know it. Now, if it was five years ago, you wouldn't know *why* we was drag racing that Corvette down I-81!" They both laughed.

"Yeah yeah. I guess you're right," she admitted. Michael had a point. They had both made a lot of progress with their communication.

I guess I just need to be more patient.

Softly, Lisa's hand grazed her husband's cheek, tickling it with her fingertips, until he leaned in for a kiss. Kissing Michael was like diving into the deep blue sea. It always felt like there was more, and Lisa couldn't ever get to the bottom of him.

Prying herself away from his lips, she said, "Ok. Let's go get little mama." She was starting to feel guilty that Aunt Sylvia was awaiting their arrival while they made out like teenagers.

Michael helped her out of the black-on-black X6 BMW with tinted windows that he fondly called, The Bat Mobile. The car, a leftover from his bachelor days, was Michael's work vehicle since his hours were crazy. He planned to get something more roomier for Lisa and the kids. Lisa wasn't sure exactly *when* that was going to happen, since it hadn't yet and she was already well into her 2nd trimester. But, most days, she took the train or copped a cab, so she wasn't that concerned. Lisa never had the guts to fight her way through NYC's traffic like Michael and assumed it was his Atlanta roots that gave him the edge. While he was born and raised there, she and her mom had relocated from Charlotte to ATL when she was in high school. The couple had met their sophomore year at Clark Atlanta University and were insperable soon after.

After ascending the outside stairs, Michael hit the intercom and Lisa rested against the porch in front of the vintage, once-red-turned-dull-brown, brick building. The sights and sounds of the city invaded her senses. It was quiet for a Thursday evening, but still enough movement for slight entertainment.

A block away, a rowdy bunch of teens were performing for a social media video, while Lisa whipped out her cell to use the camera for a mirror. She was glad she did too, because she clearly had lost all of her lipstick in their little makeout session. Expertly, she re-applied her NYX fetish, then patted her straw set back into place.

I need *this hair appointment,* she thought with a frown, eying her unruly tendrils. Trying to maintain her mane was its own job and Lisa already had enough on her plate as it was. Once her curls were set, her smooth caramel skin, full pink lips, and large baby browns loomed back. Though having always been the looker in her friend group, Lisa's ego wasn't sky-high due to her issues with resembling her father. Plus, she was super down-to-earth, so her beauty wasn't something she tended to lead with.

"Aunt Sylvia, we down here!" Michael boomed, after punching the buzzer to Sylvia's apartment.

"Well, come on up then!" The older woman's voice crackled back through the intercom in an upbeat tone.

Just hearing Sylvia's voice brought Lisa peace, and the pair made their way up the stairs to the small unit. Though the outside of the building was a tad run down, the inside was updated with stainless-steel appliances, hardwood floors, new windows, and central air for every tenant. It also held the luxury of having rent control, which was perfect for Lisa's retired, elderly, friend.

Lisa took her time going up the stairs, making sure to pace her breathing. Finally, they reached the top and a flood of memories entangled with warmth hugged her when Sylvia opened the door.

Sylvia's bright eyes glistened, welcoming the young couple inside. The space was clearly an older person's home, thoughtfully designed with offhand thrift store items in an eclectic taste. Little figurines of slaves sat on the wooden end table, and on top of the TV ("So we never forget!" Sylvia had stated when little Michelle had asked about them.) The TV was one of those older models that still had the back to it. When Michael tried to sweet talk her into letting him get her a new one last Christmas, Sylvia proclaimed, "This one here Richard got, works *just* fine!" Once she said that Lisa told Michael to drop it because obviously the TV was more about sentimental reasons. Richard had been the love of Sylvia's life, and her husband who passed from cancer several years prior.

Doilies were also clearly a thing because everywhere one looked, they loitered. Additionally, a deep brown carpet overlayed the beautiful apple hardwood floors, because Sylvia didn't like hardwood, even though Lisa told her it was way better than carpet. But Lisa loved every inch of her friend's home, even if it wasn't *her* style, simply because, it was Sylvia's.

"Sorry we late, Aunt Sylvia," Lisa immediately said when they entered the residence, but her apology was muffled by the bear hug she was swaddled with. White Diamonds cologne intoxicated her nostrils, as the wool from her friend's sweater scratched lovingly against her cheekbones.

"Oh, hush now, dear. You fine." Sylvia backed up, and little Michelle was at Lisa's feet.

"Mommy! Daddy! Look what I made!" Michelle held up a large picture of what Lisa assumed was a family portrait, Aunt Sylvia included, drawn meticulously in crayon.

"Oh, baby, it's *so* good!" Lisa fawned all over the drawing and held up both ends in the light, nodding her head like an art dealer. Michael then swooped up a hyper Michelle into his arms. While taking in her daughter's work the fragrance of chocolate chip cookies and an assortment of other food smells smothered Lisa's nostrils. Her stomach rumbled in response.

"My bad," Lisa blurted, but Sylvia was already moving.

"Now, honey, you know I done cooked a full meal. Y'all betta stay and have some of this food. I can't eat all this myself." The older woman motioned for them to stay before dashing to the kitchen and pulling out plates.

Lisa pitched Michael a grin with one raised brow that said, "Should we stay?"

Michael smiled easily in response and their silent conversation was settled.

"Mommy. I gave Snowball a bath today," Michelle raved proudly while Michael helped Sylvia set the table.

Lisa's eyes grew wide, "You did?" her lips sagging into a frown. "Honey, I don't think you're supposed to give cats baths." She glanced over at the white small feline snuggled in the corner of the living room, next to the faded yellow loveseat covered in plastic.

Michelle's face became confused, "Really? Auntie Sylvia said it was ok," before she hopped onto a chair and rocked her legs back and forth vehemently.

"*I* said, she could feed him some water, and *somehow* that turned into a bath," Sylvia confided, shaking her salt and pepper curls in animation. She plopped a large brown roast on the table along with her statement.

Lisa and Michael both laughed. "Oh, Lawd!" Lisa said.

"And I didn't have the heart to tell her she got it wrong," Sylvia confided with sympathetic eyes.

Michelle looked at the adults, puzzled. "I got it wrong?"

Lisa kissed the top of her daughter's forehead, then smoothed out her pigtails. "Sweetie, it's ok. We all get it wrong sometimes."

"Yes, ma'am'. We sure do," Sylvia shared. She patted Michelle's back after sitting down a large casserole bowl onto the white and grey checkered tablecloth. "But you know what?" she added, bending down and winking at her.

"What?" Michelle asked. The light brown eyes she had inherited from her father were now expanded.

"God even works *those* things for the good." Sylvia's pecan skin shone while quoting Romans 8:28, and her movements were full of joy as she hopped around, preparing a meal for her friends.

Even the way she sets the table is filled with love, Lisa marveled, but then noticed how quiet Michael was being. He had finally sat down at the small, round table after making the place settings, but hadn't responded to Sylvia's comment about God working things for the good. Instead, he was studying his nails as if they would transform into sharp, long talons at any second.

Internally, Lisa sighed. She knew his conflict with religion. Michael had been raised in the church and had seen so much hypocrisy that he was turned off from the whole thing. While he respected her views and her desire to raise their children with faith, he was pretty hands-off when it came to instilling anything of his own knowledge.

"Lis, that's cool for you, but that's not where I'm at," Michael had told her blatantly when they started dating again. She was so disheartened because she was a new Christian. Lisa thought she was going to be able to share this amazing supernatural experience with the one person she loved so dearly in the world. She thought for sure that Michael would be in agreement since God was the one leading her back to him, after all. But, instead of being met with a partner who was on one accord with her new faith, Lisa was now with someone wounded and hurt by the church. But when she was on her knees in prayer, wrestling over the fact that she had given up her ex, Joe, for Michael, and wondering if she had made the wrong decision, God responded very clearly to her spirit to, "Wait." Lisa knew God was promising her Michael's spiritual healing and salvation and that she would have to wait for it. But even more importantly, it would come through her own demonstration of faith.

But the journey to getting there is so tedious! And for the millionth time, Lisa found herself wondering, *Lord, when is he going to follow You?* But no response.

Father, please let me be as patient with Michael as You've been with me, she cried in her spirit, as Aunt Sylvia sat down and Michelle bopped around in her chair and Michael passed her the large bowl of green beans Sylvia had graciously prepared.

In the lack of an answer to her spirit, Lisa, was once again, growing deeper in her relationship with God, just as she had done nearly three years ago when a dark-skinned man named Joe with a bright smile and loving heart captivated her. Joe tought her the

Father's heart, and paved a way for her to find the road to true, eternal love. Back then Lisa had learned how to surrender and obey. She had learned how to start walking by faith. And now, she was adding "waiting" as a spiritual discipline from her journey in marriage.

Lisa was learning how to wait on God.

Before heading out, Lisa turned to give her mentor and friend a tight squeeze. "Thank you, Aunt Sylvia. You outdid yourself as always."

The older woman's hug in return held just as much vigor. "Now chil', you know I love to cook. And now that it's just me, I always seem to make too much." Stationing both hands on top of her round hips, she laughed heartily. "Sometimes I go downstairs to Mrs. Robinson's and give *her* a plate, just so I'm not eating leftovers all week."

"Oh, I'm sure she appreciates that," Michael said, and moved in to steal his own hug before Michelle reached for hers.

"Bye, Auntie Sylvia!" Michelle smiled, displaying the same dimple in her left cheek that Lisa shared, her caramel-brown features on full display.

"Now don't forget your school bag," Lisa called to her daughter who was just about to head out the doorway.

Dramatically, Michelle whipped her head back, and slapped her forehead all before marching inside, causing her knee-length dark jean skirt to twist around her small waist. "Oh! I almost forgot!" she exclaimed to no one in particular.

Lisa chuckled and met Michael's eyes that also swam with humor. *She is something else,* she thought with pride and was sure her husband was thinking the exact same thing.

"Oh yeah. How did the ultrasound go?" Sylvia asked. "Did you get those 3D pictures you been excited about? I need to see this new baby we got on the way." Sylvia looked at the couple, but her expression dimmed when she saw Lisa's grimace and Michael's gaze shift downward. "Uh. Did I say something wrong?" She frowned, moving a little out the way as Michelle bounded back to the trio.

"Umm, no. It's just. We weren't able to get the pictures," Lisa started. "We actually forgot all about 'em, because, umm," her voice faded. She was trying to be careful with her words so that Michelle didn't pick up on anything.

This girl is like a sponge.

"There's an issue we need to monitor more closely," she finished, wringing the strap to her purse and tilting all her weight to the side.

Lisa was too nervous to look at Michael. More than likely he was still sensitive about the way she had handled the bleeding.

"Oh?" Sylvia raised her thinning brows but gave Lisa a comforting smile. "Well, you know it ain't nothin' God can't handle, honey."

"What does God need to handle, Mommy?" Michelle, back at her side, peered up at Lisa. Lisa patted down some loose hairs before kissing the top of her forehead. Taking her time in answering, she adjusted the collar at the rim of Michelle's polka-dot button-down that had flipped over.

"Nothin' for you to worry about. Now, put your jacket on. It's getting chilly out. And straighten up your skirt. We can't have you out here lookin' crazy."

Finally, the group said their goodbyes and was snatched by the evening air. While Michael got Michelle's belongings situated in the backseat and listened to her ramble about her day, Lisa took in a deep breath. As she exhaled, she smiled, content and happy to have had such a good turn of events, especially after receiving that news at the hospital.

Leave it to Aunt Sylvia to make everything better, Lisa thought, as her head steered in the direction of Devon's. Out of pure habit, she rubbed her belly beneath her trench. She was just thinking about talking Michael into stopping by the beloved cafe on their next date night when she glimpsed a familiar form. In semi-disbelief Lisa's lips partially spread into a small "O." A tall man, with stark, pearly whites that were illuminated, even from this distance, and glossy skin the color of midnight, was about to cross the street nearby. Dressed to kill the way he had always been when they were acquainted, he balanced a phone glued to his ear and a leather briefcase tucked inside the other hand. Swinging it with purpose, he headed to his destination, which just so happened to be in Lisa's direction. Was she seeing a ghost? Or perhaps her mind was playing tricks on her.

"Joe?" Lisa whispered, and just as she did, his eyes met hers. Those kind, sincere eyes she used to stare into, and once in a while, dreamt about. The same ones that still sometimes caused her to struggle and wonder if she had been wrong to leave them the way she had.

Joe's own espresso browns enlarged under the streetlamps. But that was the only indication that possibly he had seen her because he didn't lose his stride. No, not one bit. A couple crossed in front of him, momentarily causing Lisa to fear that he was gone forever. But seconds later, he re-emerged, and when his foot hit the curb, was even closer than he had previously been. In fact, Joe was now closer to Lisa than he had been in years, and she found herself bombarded by a variety of emotions at the fact.

"Babe, what are you doin'?"

Michael's voice jolted Lisa out of her trance with her ex-lover, and she hurriedly dropped inside the car. The whole ordeal had only lasted a moment, but she was shaken. Even while she reached for the door handle to close it, Lisa felt *unsettled*.

I can't believe it was him. Wow, she thought, as she whipped the seatbelt over her stomach and tried to avoid sneaking another look out the tinted windows.

"Lis, what is up with you?" Michael looked at her perplexed, noticing how antsy she was, then pushed the button to start the car.

And because Lisa knew he was watching, she fought the urge

that wrestled her being to take a second look at Joe. She fought it like she was Mike Tyson in the '90s'.

"Nothin', babe," she answered, her voice surprisingly cool and steady. "Nothing at all."

But she silently repented as they pulled out the park and she craned her neck awkwardly, straining her eyes through the tinted windows, only to see the back of Joe's profile. Yes, Lisa repented because she had lied to her husband when she said that nothing had gotten into her. And it had been a long time since she had lied.

~

BREAKFAST WAS ALWAYS A BIG DEAL IN THE DORIS HOME, AND THE next morning was no exception. Michael's work schedule was typically topsy-turvy and there was no guarantee he would be home for dinner. He would, however, be there for breakfast, (if they ate early enough) so Lisa always put forth the effort to have a hot meal prepared before he was out the door and Michelle was in her carpool. Each month a few of the parents at her school chipped in for their kids to grab a rideshare together. Lisa felt better about that rather than having Michelle on the train. She preferred that she be a little older to navigate the subway alone.

Because of all of their schedules, even if it meant Lisa was up at 4 AM since Michael left at 6:30 AM, she made breakfast. This morning, she had chocolate chip pancakes, turkey sausage, turkey bacon, yogurt garnished with granola, dried fruit, and fresh cinnamon laid out from the market.

"It smells soooo good. I'm *famished*." Michelle swung into her normal seat at the large square mahogany dining room table that Lisa convinced Michael to replace his glass one with when she and Michelle moved in. He fought her on it, but she won easily after painting the picture of Michelle inevitably damaging his $1500 prized possession.

Lisa laughed at her daughter's exaggerated statement. "Thank you, but let's reserve 'famished' for people in third-world countries, shall we?" With her apron still on, she slid over and grabbed her daughter into a hearty hug, smashing her PJs in the process.

"Ok. But, what's *third world* mean?"

"It means countries that don't have the resources we do. It means they are underdeveloped."

Michelle nodded, seeming to comprehend, though Lisa suspected there would be another round of questions on this topic at some point in the near future.

"How did you sleep?" Lisa asked while backing up to peer into Michelle's eyes. The innocence there, once again, pinched her heart.

Lord, I just want to protect her from everything that hurts in this world.

Immediately, anxiety gripped Lisa the way it normally did when she obsessed over Michelle's well-being. But as her daughter babbled on about her great night of sleep, and how excited she was to get to school because her best friend Jamie and she were wearing matching shirts, and she wanted Latoya Sims (who used to be her best friend, but dropped her for Sara Thompson) to see that she had a *new* best friend (as evidenced by their matching shirts), Lisa was reminded of Dr. Swan's words.

"We have to learn to always put our children in the care of our Heavenly Father. Don't you think?"

"You're right, Lord," Lisa replied out loud in answer to her rabid thoughts.

At her mother's statement, Michelle ceased her speech of how Henry Thomas was always getting into trouble, and she couldn't *wait* to see what he was going to do *today* that would get him into trouble, and looked at her surprised.

"Mommy, what are you talking about? What's the Lord right about?" The spitting image that Lisa loved so dearly wrinkled her forehead and stared in confusion.

"Good Morning," Michael announced right when Lisa was trying to come up with a good enough answer to satisfy her inquisitive child. "How are my favorite ladies?" Her husband was already dressed and ready, decked in a Tom Ford black suit, silk gray tie, and timeless black Dior shoes.

"Daddy, Mommy was just saying 'God was right' and I was just asking what He was right about." Michelle ran over to her father and he squeezed her gently.

"Oh?" He looked at Lisa, perplexed and she blushed.

"I was just thinking out loud. That's all," she said, brushing him off.

Sweeping her hand in a grand gesture over the table, Lisa said, "Everything's ready. Let's eat," then removed her apron and landed it on the hook by the fridge.

Michael was always one to dig in and didn't need to be told twice. Michelle jumped to her chair and started telling her parents all that she wanted for her upcoming birthday. Even though she had already told them every day for the last month.

"And I really, really, *really* want a cell phone, Daddy. Plleeee-asssee!!" Michelle concluded her list of birthday items with the same thing that she always did. Only this time she begged her father while batting her long, thick lashes.

Now, where did she get that *from?* Lisa wondered, amused, but felt slightly uneasy. *I hope she ain't around no fast girls at that boogie private school she's in. They get younger and younger every year.* She buttered her pancakes and decided to let Michael handle this one.

Michael laughed before popping a piece of bacon into his mouth.

"Michelle Doris, do you work?" He looked at her, and she sighed.

"No," she said with a slight huff that indicated she already knew where this line of questioning was going.

"Then why do you feel responsible enough for a phone?" Michael cocked his head to the side as if he were having a very serious conversation, and Michelle smacked her teeth while rolling her eyes.

"Oh no, honey, we do *not* behave that way in *this* house," Lisa immediately chastised.

Michelle looked down at her plate. "Sorry," she muttered.

"Girl, you have better be on your *best* behavior, or you can forget about gifts, let alone having any kind of party Saturday for your birthday," Lisa added.

Michael shook his head and gave her a look that said, "That's *your* daughter."

"Sorry," Michelle said again. She fumbled around her plate, her face now crestfallen, her previous upbeat spirit seeped out like air from a balloon. "I will," she added.

Lisa fought a tinge of guilt. *Was I too hard on her?* She always struggled with being the "bad guy" and wished she had enough self-control to restrain herself so that Michael could discipline Michelle more often. It was one of the struggles they had when they were married the first time. Lisa had felt like she was the main disciplinarian. It was only in *this* go-round of marriage that Lisa had been able to see how she sometimes contributed to that role.

"Speaking of birthday parties, did you call the lady for the foam party?" Michael asked, before stuffing a slice of large chocolate-chip pancake into his mouth.

Lisa tilted her head, causing her silk scarf to shift and a bundle of curls to cover the right side of her face. "Umm, I thought you were doing that?"

"Lis, I promise you. We talked about this, and you told me that Danita had the hookup and you were going through *her* people." Michael's tone was a little too pacifying for Lisa's liking.

Shoot! *He's right. I did say that.* She bit her lip, and instead of responding, started typing out a text to her assistant to get the foam party contact's info. Again.

"My bad. I guess I forgot. I'll handle it today on lunch," she mumbled.

"So, I'm *not* going to have a foam party now?" Michelle looked at her mother distraught.

"You *are*, baby. We will work it out," Michael said.

Great. Bad guy again.

Lisa was now intensely chewing her bottom lip to keep from responding. Instead, she scrolled through her texts. *Yay!* Natalie was looking forward to their time together tomorrow at the hairdresser's.

Natalie Greene was the sweet young woman Devon was seeing, and Lisa's mentee. They hit it off right from the start after meeting for the first time during an interview Lisa conducted with

Devon, a close friend, about his cafe. That was before she was doing the music scene with Jazz and was still covering the lifestyle section.

Lisa predicted great things for Natalie's future. The girl had a good head on her shoulders, especially for a young 20-something. The duo usually tried to meet once a month and catch up at the salon. Lisa took a minute to send a reply that she too was in need of some girl time. Even though technically Natalie was 10 years her junior, they had a meaningful friendship and Lisa rarely got to have time with friends these days.

Lisa's eyes then narrowed at her father's text saying, "Good Morning," and that he would be sending Michelle's birthday gift ASAP. Hearing from Hank only reminded her of how pissed she was that he was missing her child's birthday. Especially when it would have been the first one he would have witnessed ever in her young life.

What's good about the morning if you're only around when you want to be around? she thought darkly, before sending him a short, "Thanks," and leaving it at that. No emoji. No "Good Morning" back. Nothing.

That's all he deserves, she decided in frustration.

But before Lisa's thoughts could spiral out of control about her wayward father, a missed text from an old number caught her eye. With growing interest, she inhaled each word:

"Lisa, it was good to see you yesterday, even from a distance. I hope I'm not intruding, but just wanted you to know, I still think of you at times and wish you the best."

She didn't have his number saved but knew without a doubt who the message was from. Knots twisted in her stomach as her heartbeat sped.

"Babe. Did you hear me?" Michael was looking at her, and Lisa's head whipped up from her phone faster than a speeding bullet. She stared at him, unable to hide her confusion. "I said, is your dad still coming to the party?" he repeated.

"Ugh. No he's not," she answered with disgust before she could think twice, then shot a quick glance at Michelle.

Shoot! I didn't mean to say it like that. But because she had been distracted, the words slipped off her tongue without consideration.

"Hmm." Michael responded, then took a long sip of coffee.

"His daughter's play is the same day, and they already bought the tickets," Lisa rushed to explain. She could tell by the look on Michael's face he was irritated, but she still felt this innate need to defend the man who had contributed to her birth. At least, with one lucky sperm.

"Papa Hank isn't coming?" Michelle's little voice pierced the room, and Lisa almost wanted to buy her that damn cell phone to erase the disappointment in her eyes. Her own heart was crushed.

"No, honey, but we'll have so much fun you won't even notice!" Lisa promised. Then she made a mental note to try to get that foam party booked during lunch today if it was the last thing she did on earth.

❧

IF HEAVEN HAD A WRITER'S ROOM, IT WOULD LOOK LIKE JAZZ magazine, Lisa was sure of it. Day-to-day productivity, mixed with a wall-to-wall ambiance of people of color, was a daytime dream. Pivoting off the elevator, clad in her Dolce & Gabbana chocolate boots, and gliding onto the ninth floor, Lisa pulled open the glass double doors. Her eyes swam in a sea of brown skin tones cascading throughout the office floor. Everyone ran to and fro in an effort to knit together next month's issue stock full of the lifestyle magazine's current highlights. Broad windows bunched in a row across the north wall facing the city, light beige carpet plastered the floors, while startling images of Black celebs ranging from Cardi B to Jay-Z, breezed along the walls.

The Jazz mag team was working hard in what appeared to be practiced synchronicity for their ultimate mission: to flood the city with the latest news on all things Black culture. Lisa specialized in the music scene as of six months ago when she received a well-earned promotion. She now had the opportunity to meet a host of stars and celebs who frequented the streets of New York City.

"Girl, if you meet Beyoncé, you have *got* to get me in the room for that interview!" her assistant, Danita gushed when she was promoted. Lisa laughed her off but made a mental note to hook her girl up should she ever have the opportunity. Danita was 'good people', and Lisa always wanted to look out for her people.

While skating towards her office amongst the flurry of bodies, Lisa's boss, Carl Miller, stopped her in her tracks.

"Morning, Lisa," Carl boomed, and Lisa offered him her best "Good Morning" smile, although inside she cringed. She dreaded the question brewing beneath his Geraldo Rivera mustache.

Though Carl was a good guy, they often bumped heads on her interview style. Lisa preferred a more laid-back, conversational approach with her guests, and sometimes Carl wanted her to, "Be a bit more, harder-edged," as he put it. Meaning, he wanted her to dig for dirt on an artist, but that just wasn't her M.O. Lisa had no problem asking the tough questions, or, if a topic came up that was uncomfortable, probing to get more info. But she was not one to "shade" another human being. Especially when there was now such a thing called "Black Twitter" and everybody's business could go viral from a few pecks on a smartphone.

"How's that piece on Alicia Keys coming?" Carl asked. "I need it in my hands, ASAP."

Yep. That was the question Lisa had been dreading. He looked at her expectantly, with dark, beady eyes that were already set too close together for her taste. And even more so when he was particularly stressed (which was often).

He looks like a bird, Lisa would frequently think, and one day, made the mistake of confessing her thoughts to Danita. Since then, Danita donned Carl "Big Bird" behind his back, and especially when he was getting on Lisa's nerves. Lisa always had to fight hard not to laugh when her assistant did this. She usually lost that fight though. What could she say? The description fit, as Carl was a fair-skinned, stocky guy, over six feet tall, with a habit of pecking the mess out of her whenever she had a deadline.

"It's great, Carl," Lisa responded in her most proficient tone, but started twisting the hem of her Kate Spade blue-grey cardigan. "You'll have it by end of day."

Underneath the cardigan lay a darling vintage off-white lace blouse that fastened all the way to her neck and smartly tucked inside her favorite A-line skirt. Lisa did have to get her skirt let out some, due to the pregnancy. It wouldn't be long before she would have to let it go altogether. But the plan was to rock it for as long as possible.

As long as I put my head to the ground, Lisa thought, regarding her article, *it'll get done.*

Carl threw her a tight smile and short nod before flying past her into his office.

Lisa exhaled. *If only I hadn't had that doctor's appointment yesterday, I could have gotten more of it done,* she admitted to herself, then made a beeline for the kitchenette. Running into Carl had made her in dire need of her one allotted cup of coffee per day.

While waiting for the Keurig to pour her fill, Lisa caressed her stomach and mulled over her situation. Being a mom sometimes hindered her performance at work, but she was determined she could do both.

I simply cannot be a stay-at-home mom like Michael wants me to be, she thought, as wrinkles gathered at the center of her forehead. *Michelle is great, but I swear we would kill each other if I didn't have work as an outlet. And who knows how rambunctious baby number two is about to be.* Her eyes dropped to her stomach.

"Girl, you 'bout to pop ain't chu'?" Renee Brush, Lisa's colleague, and number one competitor, saddled up next to her. Holding an empty mug in one hand, a fake smile lay drawn on her chunky brown face.

Though Renee wasn't one of her favorite people, Lisa still appreciated the woman's vigor and tenacity. Even still, she was definitely concerned that when she went on maternity leave, Renee was bound to go after her position. Renee had been wanting to cover the music scene for years, and Lisa's ability to snag the coveted position had left her with a target on her back.

Before responding, Lisa smothered her annoyance with a polite smile. "Yeah, girl. I definitely am getting bigger by the day."

I don't care if I am *pregnant,* Lisa fumed to herself. *Like* any *woman likes to hear they're getting fatter. Wake up people!*

"I guess you had to lose that beautiful waistline at some point, huh?" Renee pressed, teasing. She cocked her head in a mocking manner, letting arm-length sisterlocks flow seamlessly over a black blazer. Fortunately for her, it helped to minimize her bulging midsection.

"I mean, sis, who keeps a waistline that long into their 30s?" The woman's eyes sparkled with glee as she giggled, and her second chin danced in rhythm to her laugh.

No, she did not. Lisa caught the diss as soon as Renee threw it, and though she was slightly hurt, she wasn't surprised. *I always knew you were jealous of my damn waistline!*

"Well, you know, the baby weight after Michelle just slid right off, so I'm sure it'll do the same after this one," Lisa replied in a forced perky tone.

She grabbed her mug before she was tempted to really jump out of character. "But, regardless of how much my waist size changes," she paused, took a sip, then peered at her counterpart. "You can bet my stellar journalism skills ain't going nowhere, *sis.*"

Hmm, was that out of character? Lisa thought and smiled to herself.

"Oh yeah, girl. You right!" came the plastic response from Renee, but it bounced off Lisa's back because she was already heading out the door.

"Boss. You look extra dope in that outfit," Danita greeted, trailing from her cubicle when Lisa finally made it to her office.

"Thanks, ma'am," Lisa responded while turning the key to her door. "I definitely needed to hear that. Especially when folks around here are coming for my waistline," she muttered, then pushed open the door with a little too much aggression. She stumbled slightly before catching her balance.

Danita followed her inside. "Oh? Do tell," the secretary said with both hands folded in front of her. "Is Big Bird trippin'?" she added in a low tone. Her countenance was eager for gossip.

Lisa snickered while dropping her leather messenger bag onto the small microfiber couch propped against the wall. She then sat her coffee on the desk before falling into her office chair.

"Girl, you already know the haters," she said, not wanting to get into it. "But anyways, I need extra focus today. If you can field any calls until after I give you the go, I'd appreciate it." Turning on the monitor to her PC, Lisa rolled her eyes. "I have *got* to get this Alicia Keys article to Carl, or he will have my *ass*."

"Ok, boss. Umm, but you know you have that meeting with Nicki Minaj's PR manager during lunch, right?"

Ugh. This darn pregnancy brain.

"I totally forgot." Lisa huffed and looked at the ceiling. "Ok. PLEASE come get me if I am knee-deep into this article," she instructed and started opening her Word document. Danita nodded, taking her cue to go.

For hours, Lisa lost herself crafting and re-crafting all the things she wanted to say about meeting Ms. Keys. The woman was a sweet spirit and her interview was thoroughly enjoyable. Lisa loved when the artist was easy to talk to, and, even more, when their in-person conduct matched their public persona.

"I wouldn't mind interviewing her again for sure," Lisa murmured while typing her draft. By the time she got to a place where she felt comfortable stopping, Danita was at her door. It was almost time for her 12 o'clock.

"Whew! Ok. I'm coming," Lisa huffed out.

But let me check and make sure Michael hasn't reached out.

Flipping through her messages on her cell phone, there wasn't anything from her husband, but Lisa did notice that she had yet to respond to Joe Fallon. When she saw his message that morning, she didn't want to quickly say just anything. She had been really touched that he was thoughtful enough to follow up with her. Even though they had technically not even spoken yesterday.

After all this time, he didn't have to, Lisa thought.

Wanting to put forth that same care into her return message, she had waited to respond. Now, she not only had a little bit of time, but her husband and daughter weren't lurking nearby.

Joe, it's so good to hear from you! I'm doing well. Thank you so much for reaching out. I think of you at times also and pray that life is good. Thank you again for being such a great friend during a confusing time. Blessings.

After a few minutes of debating, Lisa sent the text, silently praying, "Lord, please let this be ok," before heading to her meeting.

Lisa's workday was so full that after the meeting, she went back to her office, only to once again, lose herself in her article. It wasn't until well after 4 o'clock when she emailed it to Carl.

"All done!" she shouted to no one in particular after hitting the "send" button. Sinking back into her chair, Lisa picked up her phone and pleasure squeezed her abdomen. Joe had replied!

"Lisa, you are an amazing woman and it was my honor."

Something smooth and warm flooded her insides as Lisa read and re-read that text from her old beau. It was something she couldn't quite define. And though she wasn't sure exactly what it was, it was the only thing on her mind as she finally wrapped up her workday. Her thoughts were so off track in fact, that as Lisa turned off her computer monitor and packed up her messenger bag, she didn't even realize that she had completely forgotten to book the foam party for her daughter's ninth birthday.

Doing it All

"The last few days I been stretching out my do' with headbands and buns and those colorful scarves everybody's always wearing."

Lisa had met up with Natalie the next evening for their appointment at Thelma's Hair & Style. It was the only time she rode the Amtrak to Jersey and got to see her young friend face-to-face, outside of church. Though Lisa had been a diehard client of her salon in Brooklyn, when her hairdresser of 15 years retired, she frantically searched for a safe go-to. At Natalie's referral, Lisa made the switch and learned that the monthly commute was more than worth it. Stacey, Natalie's stylist, was a master when it came to natural hair of all textures and Lisa's curls had never been happier. The duo worked it out with Stacey to get their hair done at the same time so they could catch up.

"Yeah, me too!" Natalie piped back. "I'm in *desperate* need of a trim and I know Devon is tired of this go-to bun I been doin'." She rolled her eyes but her faux-shamed expression did nothing to mask her exquisite almond-toned features.

Lisa chuckled while seated in the waiting room with her friend. "Y'all are still in the honeymoon stage, so I'm sure it's not as bad as you think." Crossing her legs, she shifted a little to get more comfortable in the oversized black leather chair that perfectly complemented the rest of the chic decor.

Natalie expelled a laugh pregnant with nervousness. "Yeah, well, honeymoon is a good word for it."

Lisa peered at her more intently. "What'd you mean by that?"

Loosening a strand of hair from her high bun, Natalie started wrapping it around a singular finger. Her eyes searched the room. Only one other woman was present, appearing decades older, and enthralled in an episode of "Family Feud" on the wall-mounted TV. When the coast seemed clear enough, Natalie spoke.

"Well... I mean. I just kinda wish we were *really* on a honeymoon. You know?" She kept on twisting that lone strand of hair but Lisa just stared at her.

"You mean you want to get *married*?" Lisa asked.

"NO! I mean——no," Natalie quickly corrected when the first "no" came out a bit too loudly. She cleared her throat and checked to see if their other attendee was paying any attention, but the woman had shouted, "Hot sauce!" just as Natalie had shouted, "No!" This indicated to Natalie that she had gone unheard.

Lisa's eyes shot to the TV screen and she read the question that the host, Steve Harvey had posed: "Name a food that goes great with anything."

Oh! Hot sauce. She snickered to herself, then drew her attention back to Natalie.

"I know we're not ready for marriage," Natalie clarified. "I just wish we could, you know, do what people *do* on their honeymoons..." Her voice trailed and now she was wrapping and re-wrapping that one strand of hair more vigorously.

"Oooohhh," Lisa said, eyes bursting with relief and intrigue. She indicated for Natalie to continue.

"It's just that, I'm really wrestling with my desires for Devon." The statement came out just above a whisper. "I mean. You know. It's been over a year and...We haven't umm, you know..." The younger woman let the sentence dangle and Lisa's mind raced.

I been wondering how they were fairing in the sex department.

Natalie was a cute young thing and Devon was fine as wine. Lisa herself had never "waited 'til marriage" and really wasn't sure if she could if she had to. She and Michael did wait the second time around but that was different. Lisa was so worried about being hurt again that she held on to 'the cookies'.

But could I have done it if I didn't have that hesitancy holding me back? She wasn't so sure.

"Mmhmm." Lisa prodded, "Ok. So, what are you saying?" She figured that if the young woman was going to be about that life, then she would need to be comfortable explicitly verbalizing it.

"Umm. Well. I just don't think I can wait anymore!" Natalie blurted and then whipped her eyes at their elderly companion. The woman was shaking her grey fro with a harsh scowl at the screen. Whatever family she was rooting for must have been losing.

At Natalie's outburst, Lisa broke into a grin that exposed her dimple. But she tried her best to sound composed and made sure to ask the right questions.

"Has Devon been pressuring you? Has he made you feel rushed?"

"No, Lis. It's not like that," Natalie stated quickly. "Devon is the *perfect* gentleman. If anything, I feel like it's the other way around. I mean, I've *never* felt like this about a guy before. I never knew a man could even make me feel like this!"

Lisa beamed. "Mmhmm. I know what you mean. I definitely felt that way with Michael. That man swept me off my feet before I even knew he had a broom." She glanced down at her 24-carat white gold wedding ring and watched it shine. Michael had saved the original but added a few diamonds to the mix to glam it up.

"So, what do I do?" Natalie's face swirled with anticipation as she twirled her lone tendril.

Poor thing. Her friend seemed lost, and Lisa felt honored that she had opened up to her. Especially when she herself didn't feel qualified to be giving anybody advice on abstinence. But then, an impression sat on her heart, so she shared what she was sensing.

"Nat, you have to be true to you. I'm not going to tell you if it's right or wrong to sleep with your boyfriend. That is a decision between you and God. But what I *will* tell you is that you have to be honest with yourself if that's the best decision for you at this time. You're finishing up school. You're looking into study abroad programs. You have a *whole life* ahead of you. Are you sure that Devon is a part of that life? Are you sure that he is a part of your destiny and calling? If he's not, will you be ok giving that part of yourself to someone who isn't? And even if he is, is this decision going to propel you both into purpose, or is it going to distract you? Devon is a good man. And I know he wants to honor you. But he is still a man. Think and use wisdom and ask God for the grace you need to continue honoring Him in your life and walking in your true identity." She took a breath and Natalie inhaled also. They were both silent for a short time.

"Thank you. I know that's what I needed to hear. It's what's in my heart and what I've been holding onto for a while now. It just gets *hard,* you know?" Natalie peered at her in distress.

"Sis, I can't imagine. The only reason I didn't sleep with Michael *this* time around, is because we didn't make it in marriage the *first* time. Sex can cloud a woman's judgment, and I didn't want my judgment clouded. You know what I mean? But clearly, we been making up for it and that's how I got baby number two on the way."

Natalie giggled and Lisa joined in. "You will have plenty of time for that, Nat. Just be led by God, and you won't regret your decision. Whatever it is."

"You're right. You're right. *Whew*! Thanks, Lis. I think I'm just ovulating or something. And the man is so *fine*."

Lisa laughed. "Yes, he is. But girl, if it's God, he's still gone' be there. And you can have *all* your fun later."

"Stupid, stupid, STUPID!"

Both ladies struck worried looks at Ms. Family Feud who shook her head furiously at the TV.

She glanced at them with a sheepish expression. "Sorry, y'all. I just hate when they can't get even the *easy* questions right!"

Natalie and Lisa wore twin grins. "Oh, it's ok," Lisa offered, "We get it."

It wasn't too long before Stacey made her debut and led the

women to her room in the back. Her cheerful countenance and steady conversation accompanied them the whole way.

"As usual y'all are my last ones tonight," Stacey chirped.

The trio made a beeline past the glass doors on both sides which normally housed hair stylists and their clients. Except, there weren't too many hair stylists remaining. It was after six o'clock and a weekday. Most workers had already left along with the receptionist. Lisa actually preferred the quiet hours to all the "rah rah" that typically escorted most conversations in beauty salons. Her old salon was chock-full of gossip and "ratchet" talk that she often tuned out with earbuds. She had only stuck it out there that long because of how amazing Patty, her stylist was.

"Now. Who's going first?" Stacey questioned once they made it to her space.

The salon oozed Chanel vibes decked in cool, classy architecture and upscale black and white decor. On the contrary, Stacey's space pulsated with highly energetic images and cascades of bright, vibrant color schemes. Black art splashed the walls portraying a spectrum of brown complexions of women. Some with fluffy, puffy hair braided down to their calves and swaddled in garments that paid homage to the motherland. One particular image was Lisa's favorite and, when asking Stacey about it, she learned that she snagged it at an art show in Cleveland, Ohio. It was from an up-and-coming artist, Anu Redway. After hearing this, Lisa hurried to buy the exact same image online. It now posed in her and Michael's shared home office.

"I believe it's Nat's turn," Lisa volunteered, plopping into the plush, burnt orange loveseat nestled to the right of the entrance. She slipped off her shoe boots, bent her knees, and tucked her feet behind her while checking her cell.

Ahh, it feels so good to get off my feet.

Lisa's soles had been killing her and her ribs were aching from the baby but she was so used to ignoring her physical ailments, she barely noticed until she settled down.

Natalie took her seat in the standard salon chair all the stylists had in their booths. The chatter from Natalie and Stacey became a soothing humdrum in the background as Lisa checked emails and sped through the latest and greatest news on her social media feed. Her eyes lit up when she saw that Angela Yee, a well-known host for the nationally syndicated radio show, The Breakfast Club, announced that she was leaving to start her own show.

Ohhh! I wonder if I can get an interview with her?

Without another thought, Lisa carved out an email to Carl to see if he would approve the exclusive. Even though Yee wasn't an artist, because she was known for covering the music scene, the article still qualified. Just to get the ball rolling, Lisa shot an email to Danita to contact Yee's PR manager.

Carl is going to love this! she thought, anticipating his approval.

It wasn't until Lisa was caught up on work stuff that she finally checked her texts. "Uh oh," she breathed, and Natalie, who had just popped up from the sink with soaking wet locks asked, "What is it?"

Shoot! Lisa bit her lip.

"I forgot to book the foam parttttttyyyy," she wailed while mulling over a text from Michael who had asked about a half hour ago if she had gotten it taken care of.

Stacey and Natalie looked at each other with questioning eyes.

"Michelle's birthday is Saturday and this girl has been *begging* for a foam party," Lisa explained. "And I *thought* Michael was booking it and then realized *I* was supposed to book it and still I forgot to do it yesterday. *Ugh!* I should have just had Danita do it but I hate asking her to take care of my personal business like that."

Lisa was rambling even as she was clicking on the link her secretary had sent for the foam party company. She zipped through their website to locate their business hours which only confirmed what she already knew. They were closed. Her stomach sank.

"Oh, Lis. I'm sure it'll be ok. Maybe Danita can look into it for you tomorrow?" Natalie peered at her with hope in her eyes, ever the optimist.

"Yeah!" Stacey chimed in while using a towel to dampen Natalie's tendrils. She began applying a tube of gooey substance Lisa assumed could only be leave-in conditioner. "You still have a whole week to get it booked."

The pit in Lisa's midsection grew. "It's *this* Saturday." Blowing a puff of air, she speedily typed a text to Danita. "As in two days from now Saturday," she added through gritted teeth. Burying her face in her phone to hide the crestfallen looks of her friends, Lisa sent the text:

Can you do me a HUGE favor and reach out to your contact at the foam company??? I totally FORGOT and I HATE asking BUT it's an EMERGENCY!

"I just wish life would slow down a little sometimes," Lisa murmured in the midst of feverishly Googling "foam party companies near me."

"Well, what all is needed for one? Maybe you and Michael can make it a fun DIY?" Natalie suggested.

"Girl. We would have to have a *whole* machine and who is trying to invest in that to use *one* time?" But Lisa's mind began running a mile a minute through her limited options.

Who do I know who has a freaking foam machine?

"I'm sorry, sis, but Michelle is just gone' have to be grateful she has a mommy and daddy who love her, who make sure she has three square meals a day with clothes on her back and a roof over her head," Stacey said. "I mean, these kids nowadays be expecting the *world*. Video games and cell phones. Puh-lease! I wish my momma would have had it like that to be getting me a foam whatever…"

Stacey went on and on about how rough she had it growing up and how what she could expect on her birthday other than a home-made birthday cake was next to nothing. But Lisa had stopped listening after the words "cell phones."

Shoot. I may just have to get this girl this phone…

By the time Natalie and Lisa were done, it was after eight o'clock and both women were waiting for their trains. Natalie was heading home to her uncle's house in South Orange, NJ while Lisa faced her typical commute to Manhattan.

During the wait, Lisa talked a little while longer with Natalie about how classes were coming and what jobs she was leaning towards. Natalie had taken an internship last year with Jazz magazine and had really enjoyed it, but wanted to weigh all of her options. From taking more writing classes, she found she had a passion for doing stories on refugees and poverty in third-world countries. She was considering a study abroad program but was concerned if she and Devon could do the distance. Lisa again advised her to think of her own purpose and calling first, and if Devon was a part of that, then he would be there when she got back.

The younger woman gripped Lisa in a tight hug before they parted, symbolic of the sisterhood knit between them.

"Thanks, Lis, for always being my rock. I'll be praying for Michelle's party, and Devon and I will be there for sure," Natalie promised as she buttoned her jean jacket over a white button-down shirtdress.

There was a chill in the air due to the changing weather and Lisa gripped her trench coat when they released each other. She knew it was a crazy notion to even be having this foam party when it would be more chilly this weekend, but Michelle always hated that her birthday was in the fall. As she put it, " I always miss out on summer birthday parties!" So, Lisa figured this party could be the exception. Plus, it was being held in the apartment complex's pool and not outdoors, so the chill wouldn't matter at all.

Guess she'll have to do a pool party instead, Lisa thought with an inward sigh.

"Thanks. I appreciate that." Lisa responded to Natalie with a brave smile, even as defeat weighed down her shoulders. She had finally managed to let go of the dread she was carrying once realizing she had forgotten to book the foam party.

I hate disappointing Michelle. I hate not being able to do it all.

Now the dread was back.

"It's all going to work out," Natalie assured once again before being whisked away on her train.

It was another hour before Lisa was riding in the building elevator to her and Michael's well-to-do three-bedroom flat. She and Michael had the master room while Michelle occupied one of the two smaller bedrooms. The third room was currently a split between their shared office and the baby's room. Michael had successfully painted one wall a calming turquoise and created space enough for a crib, though he had yet to actually build the crib. The components were still tucked in a box on the side of their shared desk, mocking Lisa every time she entered. It took everything in her not to bring it up one more time to Michael. Large alternating yellow and grey block letters spelling out the name "Lee" (the male version of "Lisa"), were tacked to the accent wall, announcing their child's arrival. Since Michelle was named after Michael it was only right that her little boy should be named after his momma.

"Isn't that right, Baby Lee?" Lisa whispered, while patting her stomach and spilling out from the elevator onto the fourth floor. In response, just as she was unlocking the front door, there was a kick in her womb. Even though the event felt like some kind of horrible civil war happening in her body, Lisa's heart warmed.

He's worth all the pain, she thought with love.

"Hey, baby," Michael greeted her when she entered, "Welcome home." Clad in joggers and no shirt, he whistled, making a show of checking out her hair.

"You lookin' good, girl."

Lisa grinned and did a little shake of her curls. As she flipped from side to side, she caught glimpses of her husband's chiseled chest. Longing emerged and she wished Doctor Swan hadn't issued a mandatory celibacy order so she could take full advantage of his half-nakedness.

"Thank you, baby."

She let Michael swoop her in his arms and welcomed the warmth of his bare torso but squeezed her legs together to cool down her hormones.

"I made lasagna. You want some?" he offered.

A rift of pleasure sailed through Lisa at the mention of dinner. It was rare for Michael to cook but he did whenever he got home early enough. And he normally did when he knew she would be home late after her monthly hair appointment.

"Yes please!" Lisa said, kicking her sneakers to the side and throwing her Burberry trench and messenger bag on a nearby coat hook. "I'm famish-I mean *hungry*." She caught herself from using a word she had chastised her daughter for using just the previous day.

I guess she got that from me, Lisa observed with a sliver of guilt.

"Michelle already in bed?"

"You know it."

Michael dashed to the oven and whipped out a large casserole dish then pulled out a glass plate. Whenever he made dinner, he looked so proud, like he was the next Van Gogh with the next Starry Night.

"Thank you!" Lisa gushed, sitting at the table and digging into her meal like it was her last one on death row.

Michael went to properly place her shoes on the shoe rack, then came and grabbed her legs to work out the kinks in her feet.

Ahh. This was heaven. Good food. A quiet home. A fine, shirtless man who cooked.

"So, what's the update about the foam party? You never responded to my text," he asked.

Crap. Of course it was all too good to be true. Lisa swallowed her current mouthful and tried to savor Michael's tender kneading in her right arch. *God, he's so good at that.* She cleared her throat.

"Well. Umm. Actually, can you grab me a drink real quick?"

Michael was on his feet. "Sure. You want water or iced tea? Or maybe hot tea?"

"Hot tea, please. Chamomile. You know I can't have too much caffeine. She patted her stomach with a tender smile, in response to more kicks from Baby Lee, but shifted to her left side to absorb some of the discomfort.

"So, about that..." Lisa chuckled and twirled the fork around and around in her left hand. "It's funny really," she started, hoping her voice sounded light and not overladen with nerves. "I had Danita look into it for me but she didn't get it done in time and..." her voice trailed. Was she really up here lying to her husband? Silently, Lisa prayed for forgiveness.

Michael stiffened while turning on the stove to heat the water.

"You asked Danita to do it?" His face scrunched in confusion. "I thought you didn't like asking her to do personal errands."

"Yeah. Right. But with everything going on I thought it would be better to hand it off, only she dropped the ball and it doesn't look like it's gonna happen." Shame flooded Lisa's gut along with some rapid kicking from Baby Lee and between the two, she was getting light-headed. "Babe, can you hurry with that tea?" she heard herself ask as a bead of sweat sprouted from her hairline.

God, I feel exhausted.

To ease her discomfort, Lisa dropped her chin into her hand and rested her elbow on the table.

At her request, Michael turned up the oven to make the water heat the teapot faster. "So, what are we gone' do?" He folded both arms over his chest, looking at her. "You know how long Michelle's been looking forward to this damn party."

"Well, we'll still have the party, it just won't be foam," Lisa replied weakly.

Why is it so hot in here?

"Baby, can you bring me cold water instead?"

Lisa had not gotten the words out of her mouth when a flood of heat swallowed her mind and then subsequently clouded her vision. She could make out Michael's shadowy figure from the kitchen. See it make its way toward her, but then, there was a ringing in her ears, until a loud thump on the ground, before there was nothing at all.

Not Out of the Woods

CHAPTER 5

"Baby! Baby! Are you ok?"

Lisa squirmed a little but her eyes were sealed shut. Michael's voice was faint and distant. Large, solid hands shook her along with it.

"Lisa. Lisa."

Michael.

Lisa couldn't tell if she had said his name out loud or in her head, but it sounded loud enough to her, so she figured it was the latter. Finally, her eyes felt less like lead and more like eyes as she pried them open. Trying to clear her vision, she squinted.

"Good. You're awake." Michael's tone oozed relief. "The ambulance is on their way. Just stay put."

Ambulance? Why is there an ambulance?

Lisa became alarmed. "Is Michelle ok?" she eked out and tried to lift herself but Michael held her down. When she raised her head, she noticed her legs propped on the dining room chair and her belt unbuckled.

"Stay down. The ambulance is coming to take you to the ER."

"What?" Lisa asked in confusion as Michael hovered over her.

"Why?" Once again, she tried to get up but Michael wouldn't allow it.

"Babe. You fainted. Don't move. Wait for the ambulance."

I fainted?

Lisa was shocked and brought her arm to her eyes to wipe it clear.

"Yeah. Let me get you a cold rag. Don't move," he reiterated.

In seconds, Michael was out of her line of vision but the thumping from his bare feet padded the wooden floor. Moments later, water from the bathroom was running before he was back and dampening her head with a cool rag.

That feels good.

Once he was done, Lisa asked, "How long have I been out?"

"A few minutes. Thank God you weren't standing or I don't know how good you would be. I don't think you hit your head because you landed on your arm." He directed his gaze to her right arm.

Must be why it's killing me. After a minute, Lisa instinctively grabbed her midsection with her unharmed arm. *The baby.*

Michael nodded quietly. "I know. We'll see what they say at the hospital."

The wait for the ambulance was endless. So much so, that Lisa was almost tempted to take the car and drive to the hospital herself. Michael insisted she ride in the ambulance so he could have time to get Michelle ready and meet her there.

"I don't want to jolt her out of bed and rush her to get dressed. She's gone' be scared enough that we have to see you at the hospital," he explained. Lisa knew he was right so she did what she almost hated doing most in the world. She waited.

Eventually, the EMT team strapped her onto a gurney, wheeled her onto the elevator and out the building. Michael promised he would see her soon with Michelle.

Riding in the ambulance, Lisa chewed her lip profusely, perpetually rubbing her stomach.

Please be ok. Please be ok. Please be ok!

The staff was nice enough, one female worker even telling her about her teenage son who went on his first date that night.

"Yes ma'am. He think he lookin' all good in some skinny jeans and a pair a Air Forces. I'm like, 'boy if you ain't decked out in a suit and tie you ain't doin' nothin'!" the woman cackled.

It took everything in Lisa not to shout, "Lady, I could care less about your safe, healthy son right now. I want *my* son to be safe. I want *my* son to be healthy!" But instead of responding, she kept chewing and rubbing.

It was after 11 PM when Lisa was planted in an open area that separated patients with white thin curtains, a sad attempt at privacy. It was another 30 minutes before a nurse moved her to an actual exam room, took her vitals, had her answer questions, and fill out paperwork. And it was close to midnight when Michael showed up with a sleepy Michelle, rumpled and fearful.

I hate that we had to wake her up.

"Mommy, are you ok?" Michelle peered at Lisa from the side of her hospital bed with worried eyes that squeezed her heartstrings.

She patted her daughter's hand. "Yes, honey. We just need to cover all our bases and hear from the doctor. That's all." Lisa signaled Michael for help and he drew Michelle to him.

"Hey, kiddo, use my iPad to play your game," he directed. She easily complied by plopping in one of the guest chairs while fondling the tablet.

Michael stood, studied Lisa, and caressed her cheek. "How you feeling?"

"More sick of waiting than anything. I just wish they would hurry up."

Grateful for his presence, Lisa caressed her hand over his. Finally, the door swung open and a tall, older, Indian man entered with a mousy-looking nurse tailing behind.

"Mrs. Doris?" he asked, half-looking at his clipboard, half-looking at her.

"Yes."

"I'm Doctor Singh, the OBGYN on duty this evening. How are you doing?"

Dr. Singh took long strides the few feet it took to get to her, and Michael sat next to Michelle to make room. The quiet nurse shadowed the entrance with a clipboard of her own and a hospital gown tucked beneath.

"Ok. I just fainted, that's all." Mindlessly, Lisa rubbed her stomach beneath her white polka dot blouse and pink wide length pants. She still had her work clothes on.

Dr. Singh turned to Michael for the first time. "Are you the spouse?" He lifted a brow and Michael nodded.

"Yes. I was with her when she fainted," Michael explained. "She was sitting at the dinner table one minute and on the floor the next. I couldn't get her in time," he admitted, dropping his eyes.

Lisa couldn't mitigate her guilt this time. "Baby, you didn't know I was gonna fall like that. You couldn't have known."

Dr. Singh agreed. "Listen to your wife. She seems like a smart woman." His wink was his first sign of life since they began their discussion, but then his face went right back to business. "I'm looking at your charts and see that we've drawn some blood but we're still waiting on the results. Your blood pressure *is* slightly elevated though." Singh's tone emanated concern. "Can you tell me if you've been eating and sleeping regularly?"

Define regularly…

"Well, I've never really needed a lot of sleep. I get about five or six hours a night," Lisa started, omitting that she had been feeling more tired with this pregnancy. "But I did that even being pregnant with my daughter, Michelle, and never had any issues."

"Five or six hours a night isn't a lot. You have to think about your being older this time around with your pregnancy, Mrs. Doris."

Lisa nodded. "Ok. I'll work on it."

"Good. I'll need to do an ultrasound along with a physical exam to learn if the baby was affected by the fall. If that's ok with you two?" Dr. Singh waited and once the couple agreed, proceeded. "I'll need you to put on the hospital gown Nurse Shannon will give you and take off everything underneath. I'm stepping out. The nurse and I will be back in a few for the exam."

Before either Lisa or Michael could respond, Singh was opening the door and Nurse Shannon was handing over the hospital gown.

"Michelle, let's give Mommy some privacy and sit outside for a minute. We'll come back after her exam, ok?" Michael coaxed. He looked at Lisa. "You ok with being by yourself or you want me here?"

"I'm ok. He seems nice and the nurse will be here." She tossed him a soft smile and watched her loved ones leave.

Lord, please let everything be ok.

Even as she stripped, Lisa started praying. But once she got her shirt and pants off and was only in her underwear, she could feel it. Something moist and sticky was sliding down her inner thigh.

No. No. No.

She inhaled, deathly afraid to look, but knowing she had to. With all the courage she could muster, she lowered a few fingers to the area where the viscous sensation was coming from. She couldn't look down and see it because her rounded belly blocked her view, but she could see it on her fingertips.

No. Lord no!

But in spite of her fervent prayers, Lisa couldn't deny her eyes. The wet substance, holding a faint scent of copper that stained the balls of her fingertips, was blood.

∾

Dr. Singh proved to be as professional as Dr. Swan sans the same friendly bedside manner. He wasn't cold per se, just more like, lukewarm. When Lisa told him about the blood, he nodded curtly but didn't seem alarmed. She went on to explain about the Placenta Previa diagnosis and he had the nurse pull her chart which confirmed it.

As her legs were raised above her head and placed in stirrups, and she lay flat on her back on the hospital bed, Lisa drew in a shaky breath. Moisture pinched the corners of her eyes.

How can this be happening? she thought frantically while being examined.

When Dr. Singh announced, "All done," she eased herself upright.

Sitting as erect as a board, Lisa dared a look into his eyes, searching for the hope she was completely void of.

"Though there is evidence of the bleeding, the baby still has a strong heartbeat," Singh explained. "I believe he'll be ok, but we're still awaiting your bloodwork. Your fall was probably broken by landing on your arm, and the bleeding is more than likely from the Placenta Previa than the fall. I do recommend you slow down your pace and not be on your feet as much. After hearing your lifestyle, I'm apt to assume you fainted from exhaustion. Losing blood can contribute, although I don't think you've lost a lot. You said none leaked through your clothes, correct?" He paused to study her face and Lisa nodded in thought.

"Right. I did see it in my underwear but not on the outside of my pants. Only the inside." She rubbed her aching arm and Nurse Shannon went to get her an ice pack as well as a maxi pad.

"Good. That means it wasn't a lot," Dr. Singh resumed. "I'm going to have them check your blood for iron deficiency and review your hemoglobin levels. We may need to increase your diet with iron depending on the results. Are you taking prenatals?"

Lisa nodded before the doctor continued.

"Good. Going forward you'll want to wear a maxi pad with your undergarments to prevent an accident. But even more, you'll want to slow down. Whatever you can do to get more rest needs to be done. If you're on your feet all day and then taking the train, you should catch an Uber instead."

Lisa sighed. *I guess my monthly hair appointment is out the window.* She was thinking of her earlier commute which had added an extra two hours to her normal schedule. Touching her newly curled hairdo, she thought, *God, I hope that didn't cause this.* Dropping her hand from her hair to her belly, she stroked it in fear.

After a beat, Lisa asked quietly, "Is that all?" and for the first time, Dr. Singh's tone softened.

"Yes. I think you'll be ok, Mrs. Doris. But you are not out of the woods."

Not out of the woods.

Lisa sat there a moment and let the sentence resonate. Nurse Shannon returned with the ice pack and maxi pad and Lisa took them both gratefully. After informing that her husband was waiting outside the room the doctor and the nurse left her to get dressed.

Lisa took her time. Everything in her dreaded seeing Michael. *I'm going to have to tell him how I'm the reason for this,* she thought while buttoning her blouse. *I'm the reason for this whole night. Me not taking care of myself is now causing this bleeding. Me needing to get my damn hair done.*

Dormant fears of rejection from her husband surfaced. It seems they were always lurking beneath the surface due to her dysfunctional childhood.

When Lisa caught a glimpse of her reflection in the mirror over the sink, her shoulders slouched. The woman reflecting back appeared put together enough. Her new do' was sparkling with bouncy coils and her skin was only slightly ashen from the late hour.

You wouldn't even know my body was going through all this.

She shook her head as she finished getting dressed. It must be the gift God gave Black women to endure all they did yet their appearance went untouched. Memories of Lisa's mother flooded her. A woman who was the queen of this Black girl magic trick. Even when addiction dug its fierce claws into her, she wore a smile and went to work every day. Her secret of popping pills was only known by a few of her closest, but especially by Lisa. Though she had been clean for years it never seemed the two could fully restore the mother-daughter bond they once shared before her habits ripped their lives to shreds.

Thinking about her mother, a longing that felt misplaced shuddered through her. It had been a while since they had spoken. Lisa glanced at her phone and started to type a text but stopped once she realized how late it was.

"I'll do it tomorrow," she murmured.

Fully dressed and ready to face the music, she flattened both shoulders and opened the door. Michael was seated nearby, his nose in his phone, with a knocked-out Michelle on his arm. He looked at her, his expression somber, his eyes questioning. It was at that moment, Lisa knew she couldn't tell him. He already had enough on his plate. She didn't want to add to it. At least, that's what she told herself. Besides, she would do what the doc said and everything would be fine.

No more hair appointments, she promised herself.

"The doc says everything's fine," she heard herself say. *Well, he did say that.*

Lisa paused, swallowed, and continued. "He says I've just been doing too much and need to scale back some. He thinks I suffered from exhaustion and that's why I fainted." Fiddling with her purse while talking, she struggled to make full eye contact, hoping Michael didn't notice.

Relief swarmed her husband's face and a small upturn appeared at the corners of his mouth. "Whew." He visibly exhaled. "Good. I'm glad it's something we can easily rectify."

As he woke up Michelle and the trio strolled to the car, Lisa told herself over and over that she was right to not worry Michael. Calming peace that he was still beside her hugged her.

It was only a little blood. Even Doctor Singh had said it wasn't a lot.

Plus, was it really a lie if she just didn't mention it?

By the time the crew was settled at home, it was almost 1:30 in the morning. Lisa had already decided she would work from home the next day and let Michelle sleep in, telling the school she was ill. But because it was the day before her party, Michelle begged to still go. She wanted to remind everyone to be at her party, so Lisa agreed she could do a half a day.

"But only if you go straight to bed when we get home," she admonished.

As soon as they were home, Michelle bounded into her bedroom, declaring, "I'm going *right* to bed so I'll get *plenty* of sleep!"

A chuckle slipped from Lisa's lips and she glanced at Michael. "That's *your* daughter."

He grabbed her by the waist and squeezed her like he hadn't seen her in years. "Nope, she's all you."

When the two hopped into bed Michael kept a firm grip on her.

Lisa knew he was grateful she was ok. She too was thankful he was by her side, that ever-present fear of him leaving, momentarily satiated. Still, a sharp ball sat in her throat, even as she lay in her husband's arms. No matter how many times she swallowed, it just wouldn't dissipate. It wasn't until right before she finally sailed off to sleep that Lisa realized what the thing was that was stuck in her throat. It was guilt.

No Harm at All

CHAPTER 6

The next morning the Doris household drummed to a slower beat. Being at the hospital all night had everyone grumpy. Even little Michelle, normally the life of the party, moved with uncharacteristic irritability.

"But I don't want to go, Mommy!" She had fought Lisa when she woke her up at 9 am and Lisa shook her silk bonnet at her.

"Now, *you* said you wanted to go to school to remind everybody about your party, little girl and so that's what you gone' do."

It was like pulling teeth getting her ready. All Lisa had in herself was to dish up a hot bowl of oatmeal, fruit, and toast. There would be no fancy spread today.

Michael yawned with a vengeance and dragged himself into the kitchen, a 5 o'clock shadow accompanying his business suit.

"Morning," he muttered and Lisa kissed him on the cheek. Her heart ached to see him so tired.

"I made oatmeal," she proclaimed in a forced, bubbly tone. Everyone seemed to be in slow motion, bobbing silverware and clanging glasses. Lisa eyed the two as they munched on their food, searching for telltale signs.

Do they blame me that they're so tired?

The plan was for Michael to drop off Michelle at school on his way to work. Since he was going in later, that meant he would be home later.

"Don't forget to verify the caterer for tomorrow," he uttered, before inhaling his second cup of coffee.

"I got it." Lisa absently nodded.

Michael's statement about the party reminded her of her father not being there, which in turn reminded her of her desire to connect with her mother last night. She had forgotten all about her almost-attempt to text her until just now.

"Lis."

Lisa glanced up from her phone mid-text. "Huh?"

"Do you want Michelle to let the kids know it'll be a pool party instead?" Michael asked.

Ugh. Lisa stared daggers at him. *You couldn't have run that by me in private first?*

"Whaaaatttt? A *pool* party?" Michelle shrieked. "I'm not having a *foam* party?" Her mouth dropped in horror while clasping an oatmeal-smothered spoon midair.

Inwardly, Lisa smacked her teeth. *Too late.* This is exactly what she did *not* want.

Michael cleared his throat while lowering his gaze.

Lisa rushed in. "Baby, we couldn't get the foam party but we're still going to have the *best* pool party. It's gone' be just as fun and you won't even miss not having a foam party." Lisa tried to make her voice exuberant but even *she* was a bit disappointed.

"All your friends will be there," she continued. "Auntie Sylvia will be there. Oh, and Jamie is definitely gonna be there. I already confirmed with her mom." Lisa hoped that last tidbit would smooth things over since Jamie was Michelle's new bestie. "Her mom even said she could spend the night," she added as a last-ditched effort.

Michael's head lifted in surprise but Lisa only had eyes for Michelle.

Now I just need to confirm with Jamie's mom, she thought and steam-rolled ahead.

"*And* we have a very *very* special birthday gift for you!"

Michelle perked up.

Michael cast a look Lisa's way that she chose to ignore.

"Really? What is it? Is it my phone? What is it, Mommy?"

Roaming her gaze around the room, Lisa pretended like she couldn't hear or see her daughter. "Michael, do you know where Michelle went? Suddenly I don't see her. I think she disappeared. I guess she doesn't want to be at her really fun pool party tomorrow and get her gifts from all her friends." Lisa even made a show of peeking under the table.

Normally Michael would jump in, as he was the king of games, but this time he didn't participate. Lisa chose to believe he was just too tired, not that he was upset she was alluding to a special gift, which of course, in Michelle's mind, was a cell phone. Truth be told, their big gift for Michelle was a trip to Disney World. The vacation was actually a reward from Michael's job for leading the team with the highest sales numbers three quarters in a row. So, it was a win-win. They had a full week, all expenses paid, and decided they would book it for Christmas. That way Michelle could have a Disney Christmas, something Lisa could never have even fathomed in her childhood.

"Mommy! I'm right here," Michelle cried in mock frustration and giddiness, even standing and waving her arms across the table. She loved this game.

Even if she *was* getting older, Lisa relished the fact that her daughter was still a kid at heart.

"Ohh, *there* you are." Lisa smacked her palm against her forehead. "Man, for a minute you disappeared and I didn't think you would be back for your birthday party."

Lisa grinned and Michelle cheesed back. Even Michael cracked a small smile. Michelle's joy was always contagious and she was the only person that brought out Lisa's goofy side.

"You're so silly sometimes." Michelle shook her head while grabbing her toast and taking a huge bite.

A wave of relief clothed Lisa. *All is right in the world.*

Michael checked his Rolex, "Michelle, grab your things. We

need to head out," then redirected his focus to Lisa. "We'll talk later."

Welp. Almost all was right. Lisa nodded, barely meeting his eyes, and finished her text to her mother.

"Hey, Mom. Just checking in. Hope you're well. Let me know if you have time to talk soon..."

After a few minutes of debate, she pressed "send." Lisa's mother was retired and tended to sleep in but she figured she could expect to hear from her by noon. Still, they were so out of touch she wasn't completely sure of her mother's schedule.

When her husband and daughter made their exit, with Michael only giving her a quick peck on the cheek, Lisa sighed.

Why is it I always feel like I need to keep a million plates spinning at once?

Sometimes trying to keep both Michelle and Michael happy felt like two very different full-time jobs that often conflicted.

I know he's annoyed I didn't run that Jamie thing by him, but tough luck. He shouldn't have announced to Michelle about the foam party without checking with me first. That was a definite rookie move.

After clearing the table and still in her terry cloth robe, Lisa gripped a steaming cup of hot water and slid into her ergonomic office chair. This time around in her pregnancy, she had discovered plain old hot water as a soothing substitute for coffee. Sometimes she would plop in a slice of lemon if she was feeling jazzy.

While taking a sip, anxious thoughts surrounded her, ranging from both her children to her husband, to her parents, to her job. To fight anxiety, she started checking off her to-do list. Getting things done had always been a stellar coping mechanism.

Confirm the caterer. Check. *Text Jamie's mom about her spending the night.* Check. *Make sure the DJ will be on time and not late like he was last time.* Double check.

It was around the time that Lisa sent a group text to the decoration team consisting of Natalie, Danita, and Sylvia, that a text rolled through.

"Hey, Lis. It's good to hear from you. I'm glad you reached out. I know you're busy with the family but I'd love if we could chat sometime. Even video chat would be

great, especially since Michelle's birthday is coming up. Let me know your availability." It was her mother.

Wow. She was surprised. Lisa didn't even know her mother *knew* how to video chat. Before she could lose her nerve she responded.

"Sure. How about we do a call in the morning? I know Michelle would love to talk to you on her birthday."

A calming sensation perched on the tip of Lisa's heart. She recognized it as God's presence.

"That sounds wonderful. Let's talk then," came the immediate response.

Leaning back in her chair, a smile smothered Lisa's face. She couldn't think of the last time her daughter had a call with her mother, and never a video chat. Usually, there was only a Happy Birthday card that would surface in the mail.

But she wants a call. Wow. Then a sudden tightening in Lisa's belly appeared and she frowned. *I hope everything's ok with her.*

Another text came through. It was the DJ saying, yes, he would be on time and asking if he could get a ride. Lisa shook her head and rolled her eyes. *This is what happens when you hire family for business.* She hammered out a text stating that they would include a tip for Uber.

Lisa then texted Michael, **"This is the LAST time we use Brandon for DJing. I'm sick of his extraness."** She included three rolling eyes emojis.

Michael responded, **"You know he fire. Just chill."** A GIF of Michael Jackson doing the moonwalk masked her screen.

Lisa smirked. **"This is the LAST time!"** But she knew it wasn't. Brandon was Michael's homeboy and one of the top DJs in Brooklyn. The fact that they had the connect for such a hot DJ was in and of itself a blessing. But still, he acted like they were too much like family, strolling in late. That mess got under Lisa's skin.

I mean, if you gone' act like we fam then we need to be getting the family discount, is all I'm sayin'.

But Michael and Brandon had been boys forever and Michael always wanted to bless him with funds.

"You know he got the girls," Michael would argue back, "and he doin' his thing full-time."

Puh. That brotha on DJ Khaled's mixtape. He 'bout to blow any second.

But Lisa couldn't be mad. She was genuinely proud of Brandon and was keeping a close watch on him so she could get first dibs on an interview for *Jazz*. Thinking of *Jazz*, she flipped open her laptop. Now that she had handled her personal items, it was time for business.

Working from home was always a treat. No kid hounding her every thirty minutes for a cell phone. No boss cornering her in the hallway, demanding her latest submission. No jealous coworker gunning for her job at every chance she got. Nope. It was just Lisa, her tunes, and her steaming cup of hot water.

That afternoon it was smooth sailing as she began a new article. This one covering Esteban Serrano and his new book, "The Ten Dad Commandments: Fatherhood Through the Lens of Hip-Hop." In addition to her interview, Lisa had listened to it on Audible and found it a delightful read. She loved how the author wove his passion for hip-hop with his passion for fatherhood, and in a lot of ways Esteban reminded her of Michael.

Michael was truly the first up-close and personal demonstration of positive fatherhood Lisa had seen. Then, when observing the dynamic between him and his father, who Michelle had immediately favored, she became enlightened. It finally made sense to Lisa why Michael excelled so well at being a dad. It was because he had a dad. It was then she understood that so many Black men had lost their identities because they lacked the teachings and examples in their households of positive masculinity. As a result, it seemed toxic masculinity was slaughtering Black families at a rate that rivaled the crack epidemic in the 1980s.

Ding. Lisa's phone alarm chirped as she churned out her article. It was her one-hour reminder to walk. Even though she often had it set when working from home as a reminder to not sit all day, after reading the article, "Sitting is the New Smoking," she hardly heeded it. But after last night, Dr Singh's warning rang in her head: *"You are not out of the woods.*" Since both doctors said light walking would be ok, she suddenly felt motivated.

"Ok, Baby Lee!" Lisa chimed to her belly. "We about to walk on this treadmill."

After changing into some yoga pants and ditching her robe and bonnet, Lisa's ride down the mahogany and glass-laced elevator to the gym was accompanied by her Lauryn Hill playlist. She just loved her some Lauryn Hill and would go to blows with anyone about her being the greatest lyricist of all time. Well, at least one of them. The Queen and MC Lyte were definite contenders.

Lisa's hips shook from side to side. She was vibing out without a care in the world when the doors suddenly popped open. Her eyes were still closed while dancing, so she didn't know she had an audience until she was jarred by the elevator stopping. Blinking them open, a Caucasian woman with glossy, brown curly hair in her mid-30s, filled her vision. Though Lisa had seen her around, the two had never spoken. The woman eyed her with open intrigue frosting icy blue irises. She too was decked in workout gear and clasping a water bottle. Lisa made the quick assumption they were heading in the same direction.

"Sorry." She gave a lofty, embarrassed grin, and the woman joined her.

"Oh, no worries. Keep at it. I'm about to get my groove on too."

Lisa cringed. *Groove on. Lady, please don't try to use slang. Especially when it's outdated.*

It was one of Lisa's pet peeves when white people tried to appear hip just because they were in the presence of a person of color. Lisa just nodded politely and stared at the closed doors. It was suddenly about to be a long three floors down.

"I see you often in the building. My name's Carol." Lisa's elevator companion reached out her hand and Lisa took it.

"Lisa."

It was true they had seen each other before, but Lisa usually had a million things going on. She was either on a work call or Michelle was gabbing her ear off or Michael was jabbering about their schedules, and all she could normally afford the woman was a quick smile.

"Yeah, I live on the fourth floor," Lisa revealed. "How about you?"

"I'm on the third. It's a beautiful building. My husband Robbie and I just moved from Seattle. We're here for his job." Carol's pear-shaped frame shuffled a little. "I'm still looking for work," she admitted with a nervous chuckle and a wave of guilt swiped her features.

A pang of sympathy nabbed Lisa. She had moved to NYC to follow Michael and his career and it had taken her a while to get her bearings too.

"I know that feeling. It was the same with me when I first came here with *my* husband," Lisa offered with an empathetic smile. Carol's smile back was grateful as the elevator halted with a loud bell announcing their arrival.

"You heading to the gym?" Lisa asked. Her eyes ran over Carol's outfit. There weren't too many options on this floor. It was either the gym, the sauna, or the pool. There were a few smaller recreation rooms that residents could rent, which Lisa and Michael had done for Michelle's party the next day. They figured it would be easier to get the caterer and cake into one of those rooms rather than navigate the pool area.

"Yep. You?"

"Yep. I'm gonna hit the treadmill to give this baby some exercise." Lisa smoothed a hand over her belly as they exited the elevator and started down the hallway. The movement made her baby bump more prominent under her t-shirt but she noticed Carol's eyes lower and her shoulders slump a little.

Did I say something wrong?

"*Oh. I see,*" was all Carol said. Her earlier eagerness for connection seemed to have dwindled.

"Umm, do you guys have any kids?" was all Lisa could think to say. She felt totally caught off guard by Carol's change in behavior. They had reached the gym and by the time Carol responded, Lisa was holding the door open.

"No. No, we don't," her new companion answered quietly.

When Carol slid inside, Lisa followed suit. There weren't too many folks in the gym at this time of day, which Lisa had expected. Most were at work, not working from home or searching for work like her new friend here.

"Well, trust me, girl, you not missing a thing. The one I got is a handful by herself and this one is already tearing up my insides with his kicking." Lisa tried to make light of her blessings. She knew she was blessed and no matter how much Michelle worked her nerves she was one of the best things that had ever happened to her. Especially after the divorce.

Carol nodded, a thoughtful expression hiding in her eyes, but her mouth remained grim. "We've had a few setbacks," she stated, then looked around to see if she could be heard. Lisa doubted it because the few folks that were there wore earbuds and there was a speaker blasting some random song by Smashing Pumpkins. This was exactly why Lisa always brought her earbuds to the gym, because, wasn't nobody trying to workout to some Smashing Pumpkins.

"Oh. I see," Lisa replied softly. She was saddened by what she could already discern was loss from the woman.

The two strolled to the treadmills in sync and Lisa plopped her phone down, waiting. She felt led not to turn on her music but to provide space for Carol to open up more. Which she did.

"We had a few miscarriages…I don't know what's *wrong*," Carol unleashed with pain strangling her last word. The women had both gotten their machines moving and were strolling at a mirrored pace. "We've seen doctors but everything seems to be working fine on both our ends." Her shoulders met her ear lobes as she threw up her hands.

Wow. Lisa was at a loss for words. She had never had one miscarriage let alone three and didn't want to make any presumptions on what to say, so she just listened.

"I'm sorry. You don't even know me and here I am pouring out all my junk." Carol gave a sad smile and Lisa hurried to assure her.

"No. I definitely get it. I haven't been through anything like that and I wish I could offer more than just a listening ear." She tucked a loose, curly strand behind her ear. There were a slew of mirrors facing their treadmills and Lisa caught her movement in the reflection. Her hair was strapped into a high bun and her workout pants were solidly held up by her round stomach. She suddenly felt embarrassed by her belly.

How could I have so much and this woman is struggling?

"It's ok. Just you listening helps. It's been hard being here and not knowing anyone. Robbie is always working and I don't have any family in the city." Carol paused. "I'm also looking for a church home."

Lisa's eyes brightened. *Now* that *I can help with!*

"Well, I go to *New Life Fellowship*. It's nondenominational and all inclusive," she eagerly shared. "I love it because it has a new school vibe and is very diverse. My friend Natalie got me hip. I'm going Sunday if you're interested."

For the first time since their discussion on pregnancy, Carol beamed. "Yes. Yes, I would *love* that! I've been watching some services online but haven't felt—*connected,* you know? It would be great to be there in person *and* to actually know someone."

"I feel you. I mean it's a huge church but they have a lot of small groups you can be a part of. I was in a devotional group but fell off with my schedule." Lisa's eyes dropped a little. "But maybe I'll pick it back up if I have a partner in crime," she said, alluding to Carol's potential attendance.

"Oh yeah? That sounds great! Do they read devotionals every morning? What else does it consist of?"

"Yep. They have different devotionals that they study and discuss every year. It's usually early in the morning. But like I said, I fell off, so I'm not sure what lessons they're discussing right now. But we can view them online to catch up." Lisa popped open her phone and pulled up the church website.

"What's your phone number? I'll text you their link and you can check out the site."

Carol rattled off some numbers and Lisa sent her the link.

"Great," Lisa replied. "I'll let you know when I'm ready for service on Sunday. It's at 11:15 am. It'll just be me and Michelle though. My husband doesn't go." It was at that moment that Lisa was reminded of her own burden to carry. Michael's lack of a relationship with God had always been at the top of her prayer list, but with everything going on, she hadn't been as fervent in prayer as she used to be.

I definitely need to get back into that *habit.*

"Sounds good. I'm looking forward to it!" Carol's countenance looked ten times brighter and Lisa was happy she had contributed to it.

Thank You, Lord, for using me.

Carol sped up her pace then to a light jog. She was curvy for a white girl and Lisa appreciated her shape.

These white women are getting thicker and thicker every day.

She laughed to herself while resuming her Lauren Hill playlist. Just as she hit the play button, a notification from her social media account flooded her screen.

It was a friend request from Joe Fallon. Lisa took a few pensive bites of her lower lip. She had successfully forgotten about her random contact with Joe earlier that week and was finally feeling like the past was the past. But now, the past was suddenly creeping into her present. Should she accept the friend request?

She waited until the end of her 15-minute walk to decide. Lisa didn't want to do something rash, but in the end, figured, why not? Joe was just a friend. Isn't that what she had told him in her text the other day? And really, what could be the harm in connecting online? It wasn't like they were texting each other, which was way more personal. No, Lisa decided. There was no harm at all. And, after having that little internal dialogue with herself, she swiped open the notification, clicked on accept, and befriended her ex on social media.

Unfinished Business

CHAPTER 7

Lisa and Michael woke up to a hyper Michelle tugging and screaming, "It's my **BIRTHDAY!!!!**"

Well, maybe she wasn't actually screaming, but it sounded like it to Lisa.

"Ugh." Michael's grunt accompanied his body shifting and pulling their shared blanket away from Lisa in his effort to roll over.

Ugh is right, Lisa thought. *What time is it?* She darted an eye at the blurry red numbers on the nightstand glowing: 6:15 am.

"Michelle, baby, if you go to bed and wake up in a few hours it will *still* be your birthday," she muttered, the tail end of her statement hugged by a deep yawn.

"But, Mommy, you said I could open my gifts on my birthday and it's my birthday *now.*"

Though she was tired as all get out after staying up late putting together the party favors with Michael, Lisa could not deny the reasoning of her child.

Maybe she'll be a lawyer one day?

"Ok. Ok. You're right. I did say that. But, since it's so early you can only open one," Lisa said, thinking that would shorten this whole ordeal and she could get back to bed.

"But, that wasn't the agreement. You didn't say just one. You said giftsssss," Michelle responded, dragging out the "s" sound to enunciate that the word was plural.

Mmhmm. Definitely a lawyer.

Lisa sighed while stretching and Michael murmured, "That's *your* daughter."

"Ok. Ok. Let's go." Succumbing to her child's anticipation, she intentionally kneaded Michael in the back on her way out of bed. Removing the 800-count silk white sheets and tossing back the mustard-colored quilted duvet, Lisa scrounged up all her strength to wake up.

"Coffee," Michael croaked. She nodded as Michelle gripped her hand, leading the way to the dining room where her gifts sat waiting.

This child acts like her birthday is freaking Christmas, Lisa thought, but smiled anyway.

It was nice to be able to give Michelle this type of experience when she barely had it herself. Lisa's mother worked hard to provide but there were no huge family vacations that stood out in her memory. And certainly no trips to Disney.

At the thought of her mother, Lisa's heart lifted. *I'm so glad she's calling today. She'll get to see how big Michelle has gotten.*

They had scheduled the call for 10 AM which would be perfect since the party started at 1 PM and the girls were arriving at noon to set up.

As Michelle hopped around shaking each present, trying to guess what it was and pontificating about who said they were coming to her party, Lisa started the coffee. Michael liked his black with only a splash of cream. She figured she deserved a cup herself since there was a long day ahead.

"Mommy, this one is from Papa Hank! Can I open it first?"

Lisa eyed the medium-sized present that had arrived in the mail in a random Amazon box just yesterday, along with a card. Despite herself, she had wrapped it with gift wrap, happy her father made do on his promise, even if he couldn't attend.

"Don't you want to open Mommy and Daddy's gifts first?" Lisa suggested, feeling a little put-off. How was it that her father was the gift forerunner, yet had barely been in Michelle's life two minutes?

After examining the boxes beneath the card from Lisa and Michael, Michelle frowned. Lisa figured she could guess most of the gifts were clothes but the girl was growing like a weed and needed clothes.

I wish my wardrobe was a quarter of her wardrobe when I was growing up!

Rolling her eyes, Lisa tied her robe. "Fine. You can open Hank's. But wait for your dad. He's still in bed."

"Daddy!" Michelle jetted to their bedroom and Lisa chuckled.

It was like this every year and she wondered when Michelle's only child syndrome would be cured to where she wasn't so gung-ho about her birthday. But her eyes dropped to her swollen belly, a stark reminder that Michelle's only-child days were fastly dwindling. A cluster of knots then began forming in Lisa's chest as she fought concern about how Michelle would respond to the baby. Right now, she seemed fine and even excited to be a "big sister," but the truth would reveal itself when Baby Lee was here in real time.

This girl is so spoiled, I don't know if she's really ready to share her attention.

"I'm here," Michael announced while being tugged forward by his little girl.

They were a sight and looked so cute the image tugged at Lisa's heartstrings. Michael was in a pair of pajama pants and his black terry cloth robe hung partially open, while Michelle, hair barely in her scarf, pulled him forward in her Barbie nightgown.

Lisa stole a couple of mugs from the cupboard, "I got you, baby," she assured her husband.

Michael took a few steps toward her and pecked her lips as Michelle shimmied to the gifts. Lisa knew Michael hated waking up early on the weekend. Saturdays and Sundays were his only real days to rest as he worked nearly 50 hours a week. He needed his coffee to even pull that off.

"And whose idea was it to have a high-strung, feisty, inquisitive child?" Michael asked, receiving the mug that said, "Best Dad Ever" from Lisa.

"Well, I definitely didn't get myself pregnant, Mr. Doris." She smirked and patted her belly. "But umm, let's just hope *this* kid is a late sleeper, shall we?"

"Are you guys ready now?" Michelle was on pins and needles, dancing in her bare feet and holding up her first present.

"She wants to open Hank's first," Lisa murmured, giving Michael the heads up.

"I see," he replied, before taking a sip.

The two glided from the kitchen into the living room which faced the dining room table. Making themselves comfortable side-by-side on the plush auburn sofa, they tossed the dark grey throw over their laps.

Steam masked Lisa's face and she breathed in the warmth, not just from her coffee but from her family. Her husband was truly a good man and she loved his rock steadiness. Even if they argued at times and couldn't see eye-to-eye on certain things, such as religion, Michael always showed up for her. Lisa didn't want to ever take that for granted.

"What?" Michael lowered his questioning gaze at her.

Lisa hadn't realized she was staring. "Nothing. Just grateful for you. That's all."

Smiling, Michael took her hand with his free one and stroked it with his thumb a few times, but their intimate moment was broken by Michelle's shriek of glee.

When Lisa turned her head to see the present her daughter had opened she almost dropped her cup of coffee. Both her eyes bulged, but before she could even get out the words, Michelle beat her to it.

"It's a cell phone!!!"

It's a damn cell phone. He got her an F-ing cell phone!

Michelle was bursting as she jiggled up and down. "Daddy. Daddy, can you open it for me? Pleeeassee???" The shiny, silvery model still in its plastic container waived above her head like a prize won in a contest.

Michael looked at Lisa with a confused face. "Did you?—"

Lisa cut him off. "No. No, I did not tell Hank he could get her a freaking cell phone." She was gripping her bottom lip with her teeth to keep all the four-letter words swimming through her mind from splashing out of her mouth.

Michael went to get the scissors with Michelle in tow.

"Don't open that. It's going back." Lisa was livid.

How in the hell is he gone' do something like this and he didn't even run this by me!

Michael stopped dead in his tracks, and, only inches behind, Michelle smacked into him.

"What? No, Mommy! Whyyy????" Michelle whined and Lisa braced herself for the tears.

"Because, honey, Papa Hank did not ask Mommy *or* Daddy if it was ok to get this gift. And if he had we would have told him you're not old enough for a phone yet."

Lisa managed to contain her tone enough so that her rage was not aimed at her daughter and for that she was grateful.

Oh, but when I talk to Hank, he is getting it all!

"But I am! I am, I am, I *am*! Jamie has one and Shannon *and* Brittany!" The tears were pouring now as Michelle hyperventilated.

Michael just stood there looking helpless.

Lisa sighed. *Why? Why am I always the bad guy?*

"Michelle, go to your room," she said quietly.

"What? Why? It's my birthday! I haven't opened all my gifts!"

"Because you're being a brat. You need to *earn* the right to open your gifts. You don't just get gifts because it's your birthday. You get gifts because people spend their hard-earned money to do something *nice* for you. But when you are *ungrateful,* like when you don't open gifts *first* from the people who love you the most, like Mommy and Daddy, then you don't deserve those gifts!"

Lisa was yelling and she hadn't meant to but her own emotions were now fully invested. She knew it was her stupid father. Her stupid father who was never there for her and had bought her daughter a damn cell phone.

Michelle stalked to her room, still crying, and Michael started towards Lisa, but she held up her hands.

"Don't. Don't because you said nothing, Michael. You said nothing when your daughter was out of pocket and now she hates me and not you. She hates me and looooovesss her Papa Hank and looooovesss her father, but the woman in her life who gave birth to her, she hates!"Tears strangled Lisa's eyes as her body trembled.

"You didn't give me time. I was going to but you didn't give me time," Michael refuted.

But Lisa didn't want to hear it. "You said nothing. And now I'm the one who looks bad in her eyes."

She gripped her robe and inhaled. *Why is it always like this?*

Instead of responding Michael left the room, reappearing moments later in gym shorts and a t-shirt. "I'm going for a run," he muttered, lunging for the front door.

Lisa kept quiet. Instead of responding, she sipped her coffee and prayed. When the door closed she grabbed her cell phone and dialed her father. It was 7 AM and more than likely he wouldn't answer but she didn't care. He would get a nasty voicemail instead. To her surprise, Hank picked up on the first ring.

"Lisa, everything ok?" Hank's voice dripping concern only irked Lisa more.

You have the nerve to act like you care when you're the cause for my damn pain.

"No. Everything is not ok, Hank." Lisa said the words calmly although her mind was reeling. It was rare that she called her father Hank to his face. She normally reserved that for when she referred to him indirectly. It was a rare occasion for her to call him "Dad" too. She usually just spoke to him like he was someone she knew but wasn't close to, kind of like a distant relative. So she typically didn't call him anything. Except today. Today he was Hank.

"What's wrong?" Hank's voice resounded alarm. "Is Michelle ok?"

Is Michelle ok? Lisa scoffed.

"Yeah, *my* baby is ok. Or at least she was. She was *overjoyed* by the cell phone you purchased but is now sulking in her bedroom because I had to tell her we're sending it back because you never asked our permission to even buy it." Lisa's tone was hard and she had to keep balling and unballing her fingers to contain her emotions.

"Ohh. Well, every time I talked to that girl all she talked about was wanting a phone and I just figured I would be doing you guys a favor by getting it for her. So many kids nowadays have them, you know. Candace had one when she was Michelle's age."

"I do *not* want to hear about what *your* daughter had at that age! Or *any* age!"

Whatever ability Lisa had to contain herself had flown out the window.

"Do you think Michael and I are struggling financially, Hank? Do you think we couldn't have *afforded* to buy Michelle a cell phone? There were no *favors* done for us when you bought that cell phone. There was only your desire to be viewed in a good light from not being there for so many years and then *flaking* at the first chance you got to actually be there. And then you don't even consult *me*, like my authority over my own child isn't a thing. I don't give a damn if Candace, *your daughter* had a cell phone because I would rather *die* than follow in *your* footsteps when it comes to parenting!" And with that, Lisa hung up.

She sat, chest heaving, tears streaming, heartbeat thumping in her chest. Baby Lee started kicking which reminded her she needed to be careful. She couldn't have another episode and end up in the hospital. Taking deep breaths, she attempted to calm herself.

Lord, what do I do?

The vibration from her phone tickled her palm and she glanced at it. The caller ID glowed her father's name. There was no way Lisa was going to answer. She had *never* spoken to Hank that way and had *no idea* how he would respond. No idea if their relationship could even survive that type of brutal honesty. Her mother had gotten plenty of it, though. Lisa had rarely held back her words with her mother, especially during her teenage years.

A voicemail notification popped up but instead of listening to it, Lisa called a different number entirely.

"Honey, you ok?" When Sylvia answered on the other end Lisa started sobbing.

"No. No, I'm not," she cried, and filled in the gaps for Sylvia. Sylvia already knew her background with her father and listened with a sympathetic ear. She too had grown up without a father ever since her dad was murdered when she was three.

"I know it's hard, sweetie. He was definitely wrong for not asking your permission, but you know your response was about more than that, right?"

Lisa breathed and nodded, then realized she hadn't said anything. "Yes, I know." She moved from the couch to get tissue from the master bathroom while answering. "Ugh. I just can't believe I'm 34 years old and still have daddy issues!"

After snatching Kleenex from atop the toilet, Lisa cascaded onto their bed. When she landed, Michael's PJs stared at her in accusation and she knew they were a sign of his expedient departure. Her husband was a neat freak and normally the one to put their clothes in their proper place and make the bed each morning. Neither of which were done. As Sylvia's soothing tone washed over her, Lisa started folding.

"You have every right to feel the way you do and it's probably good you even let it out for once since you normally suppress it," the older woman consoled. "But you have to process it so you don't do it at the wrong time." Sylvia paused, then added gently. "Or with the wrong people."

Lisa thought of Michelle. While it was true her daughter *was* acting like a brat, it was more true that she had unleashed 34 years of pain that had nothing to do with Michelle.

She finished folding Michael's PJ's and placed them on their dresser before starting to make the bed. "You're right. I do," Lisa breathed into the phone. "I'm gonna to talk to Michelle and explain why I responded the way I did. More calmly this time."

"Good. And we all gone' have a blast at that pool party today! I got a new suit just for the occasion." Sylvia guffawed and Lisa grinned.

"Aunt Sylvia, you do not own a swimsuit."

"I sure do, honey. I ain't too old to dip in the pool. Shoot. I do my senior's water aerobics twice a week at the YMCA. I'm ready to show off these moves I done learnt. Especially since y'all got that DJ there."

Lisa's heart soared in gratitude. Finishing up the bed, she said, "Well excuuusssee me. Now, I'm gone' be taking pictures so make sure you are rea-dy."

"Oh, Mama, I *been* ready!"

Talking with Sylvia had been exactly what Lisa needed. By the time they ended their call, the weight on her shoulders had vanished.

Thank you, Lord for Sylvia, she prayed, not for the first time.

From her position on the bed, Lisa placed both hands on her thighs to push herself upward. It was almost 8 AM, and when she opened Michelle's bedroom door, her daughter was passed out, face down, scarf completely off her head.

"Michelle." She rubbed her back and Michelle stirred a little before blinking and fluttering her eyes open.

"I wanted to apologize to you for yelling," Lisa said when her daughter seemed awake enough to comprehend. "I hate communicating that way with you because it's not a healthy way to get your point across."

Michelle eased up as Lisa perched beside her on the bed, ducking beneath the lacy canopy. The room was fit for a princess, everything frills, lace, and pink. So much pink. They had even gotten her a glow-in-the-dark mosquito net to go over the canopy so Michelle could play pretend with her little friends when they spent the night. But she wouldn't know that yet since she hadn't opened their gifts.

"Mommy, I didn't mean to be ungrateful. I just knew Papa Hank said he might send me a phone, so I really wanted to open his first."

Michelle's eyes were red from crying and Lisa's heart plummeted at her daughter's confession.

"Oh, he did, did he? Well, the problem is that Papa Hank did not run that by me first. Me or your dad." She corrected herself, remembering not to be too independent. "Do you understand why that's wrong?" She stroked her daughter's baby face and licked her finger to remove a tear stain.

And where was I when he made this promise? Lisa thought, thinking back on the phone calls she let Michelle have with Hank. *I must have been in the bathroom or something.*

Michelle slowly bobbed her head. "Because I'm you and Daddy's responsibility and you have the authority." Her face was so solemn that Lisa had to try not to laugh. Michelle was obviously repeating comments she and Michael had made in conversations with other adults.

"Yes. Something like that," Lisa replied. "You are ours to steward, baby, but God's to own. So, we have to make sure we do what's best for you so you can be the woman someday God wants you to be. Ok?" Lisa repeated a phrase she had said several times to engrave it into Michelle's mind.

"Yes. I understand. Mommy, I'm sorry I was a brat," Michelle said with large, sincere eyes.

Now Lisa had to laugh. "Well. Sometimes you can't help it. You're a very privileged little girl. Especially since Mommy and Daddy got back together and now you have the world at your feet. But that's not all your fault. I need to come up with ways to help balance you out." Lisa moved her hand from Michelle's cheek to her daughter's hair and started patting down the wild poofy tendrils.

"But thank you for the apology. Just know that Mommy has her own stuff to work through and sometimes your relationship with Papa Hank will be a hard thing for me."

Michelle scrunched her forehead. "Hard? Why?"

"Because, uh, Papa Hank and I haven't always had the best relationship. And in a sense, we have, er, some, um…unfinished business."

"Oh. Ok. If you want me to help you finish your business I can," Michelle eagerly volunteered.

Unable to resist the urge, Lisa pulled her daughter in for a hug.

"Sweetie, I appreciate you saying that but that's not your responsibility. All you need to be worried about is opening your presents and getting ready for your party."

At the mention of presents Michelle's eyes brightened. "I can open the rest of my gifts?"

Lisa nodded. "Yep. As soon as your dad gets home." The words were barely out of her mouth when the front door opened and closed.

Michelle leapt from Lisa's arms and was on her feet running to her father. "Daddy! Mommy said I can open my presents!"

Lisa chuckled but then sighed.

Here we go for convo number two.

But before facing the music with Michael, she muddled over her words to her daughter. It wasn't until she had said them out loud that Lisa realized how true they were. She and her father surely had some unfinished business.

Good to Go

CHAPTER 8

It didn't matter how many times they argued, the experience left Lisa feeling terrible, regardless of who's fault it was.

But it was definitely his fault, she told herself as she and Michael took turns ooh'ing and ahh'ing over Michelle opening birthday presents.

When Michael returned from his run, he zoomed straight to the shower. After he successfully dressed, Michelle hurried him to the dining room. They still hadn't spoken with their mouths but Lisa could read her husband better than a Jazz magazine article. He was sorry. She was just waiting for him to say it. Truth be told she was sorry too. Not because what she said was wrong, because she knew he should have handled the situation with Michelle better, but because she realized she was projecting unhealed pain onto her relationship.

While Michael was showering, Lisa spent time journaling and in prayer and let God minister to her spirit. Sylvia's pointing out that her response was to a greater issue helped her see that she hadn't just taken old pain out on Michelle. She had taken it out on Michael too.

"You wanna talk?" Michael initiated when Michelle finished

opening all her gifts. The child thanked her parents profusely for every single item, which Lisa knew was Michelle's attempt at being grateful. And she had leapt with joy when they showed her the tickets for Disney.

"I can't wait, I can't wait, I can't *wait!*" Michelle jumped up and down while rattling off everything she wanted to see and take pictures of.

Lisa nodded in reply and followed Michael into the bedroom where they closed the door and left Michelle to play with her new toys.

"Lis, I'm sorry. I should have taken the initiative and not given in to Michelle." Michael sat on the edge of the bed next to her and took her hand in his. She turned to him.

"Yeah. You didn't step in when you should have." Lisa sighed. "I know we've had these situations happen before and I need you to be more proactive with disciplining her."

"I know. I really wanted to say something but I wasn't sure what my role should be. I mean, your dad bought her the phone and I figured since it was your dad I'd let you handle it."

"I get that, but then she starts throwing a tantrum and you just stand there like a dear in headlights."

Michael went quiet as his forehead creased. "I know. I think it's because I struggle with emotionalism. I know my therapist said this when I was in therapy. My mom sometimes got super emotional if something set her off. She would start hyperventilating and crying over the smallest stuff. My dad would just leave the house or go for a walk, or, take me for a drive. We'd come back and she'd act like nothing happened."

"Wow. Baby, you never told me that."

"Yeah. I didn't even make the connection until I went on my run."

"Well, that makes a lot of sense." Lisa nodded her head with a thoughtful expression.

"I might need to get back into therapy," Michael stated. "Might do me some good." He stroked her fingers between his, pensive deep lines framing his forehead.

"You're not the only one. I realized I was taking out my pain and fear from my father onto you two," Lisa volunteered. She felt inspired by his transparency. "You're the first man I ever felt secure with. Truly safe with. But when you don't show up for me the way I need you to with Michelle, I feel deserted. You check out and I'm left with the hard parts of parenting."

"I get it. I'm gonna do better. And I'm going to see Dr. Roland again because I do want to help with the emotional aspect of raising Michelle."

Lisa let her cheek drop onto Michael's shoulder and nuzzled her nose deep into the pocket of his neck. His jaw was smooth from a fresh shave and his skin smelled like something sweet and edible.

"Thank you, baby. I appreciate that. And I'm gone' look into some therapy too," she said. "Cuz now that my dad is back, and Michelle seems determined to keep him, I can't run from our issues anymore."

When Michael drew her close and wrapped his muscular arm around her, Lisa felt herself becoming aroused. Making up always did that to her.

"Baby," Michael breathed in her ear, his lips fondling the insides of her drum.

"Hmm?"

"I know the doc said no sex, but…" Michael began kneading her lower back and Lisa's pregnant hormones started to skyrocket.

"But what?"

"Maybe…other stuff?"

And before Lisa could respond, Michael's mouth was covering hers, her blood was pulsing in her chest and the tingling sensation between her thighs was on ten.

Yes, she thought. *Give me* all *the other stuff…*

~

THE MORNING FLEW WITH LISA MAKING SPECIAL BIRTHDAY PANCAKES and Michelle bouncing around in her PJs with her new Barbies.

"Girl, get in the tub and put on your suit. Everyone will be here in an hour to decorate," Lisa charged while clearing the table.

Michael started loading the dishwasher. "I got it. I'm already dressed. You go ahead and get ready." She thanked him with a smile.

I love when we make up.

Lisa then eyed her daughter still prancing around with her toys. "Michelle."

"I'm going!" Freezing, Michelle took off to her bedroom.

Lisa shared a grin with Michael. "I'll be right out. Let me know if anyone shows up before I'm ready," she added.

The plan was for the decoration committee (Sylvia, Natalie, and Danita) to come to the apartment and they would all go to the rec room together.

As she hummed, the rainfall shower head did its thing over Lisa's soft caramel skin. Her face was aglow from her time with Michael, and also, knowing that she was at peace with Michelle. Even having the breakthrough revelation about her father had provided peace.

Ugh.

Her mood dimmed a little and she frowned, thinking about Hank. In the midst of everything, Lisa had forgotten about him. And then, another related thought *really* caused her alarm.

Mom!

"Shoot, shoot, *shoot!*" Lisa muttered and sped up bathing.

Without a doubt she and Michelle had missed the call with her mother because it was definitely after 11 am. Grunting, she turned off the water and snatched a fluffy white towel from the shiny chrome rack. The rest of the bathroom stood bathed in white and scented with lavender oils. Semi-dripping, Lisa half-toweled, half-shimmied to her bed, and dove for her phone. Sure enough, there was a missed video chat from her mother. Her fingers drilled out a swift text.

Mom I'm so sorry. Things got crazy around here this morning and we missed the call! Can we call you tonight or even tomorrow?"

Hoping for a speedy response, she waited on her bed, but there was nothing, and the chasm between Lisa and her mother seemed to be widening by the minute. Dropping the phone, Lisa munched on her lower lip.

I need to hurry to be ready for the girls, she finally decided.

Moving like lightning, she threw on a pair of maternity skinny jeans and a loose blue tank over a loud orange sports bra. There was no way she was getting in the pool in a bathing suit in this body. After whipping off her bonnet and fluffing her curls, Lisa ran a handful of defining cream through them. Using an old tooth brush she slathered some jam on her baby hair and tied down an edge scarf for the final touch. Now that she was good, her next order of business was her daughter.

"Michelle!"

"I'm ready!" Michelle shrieked from the living room.

Relief flooded Lisa, seeing Michelle in her new Barbie swimsuit they had gotten for her birthday. This one depicted the President Barbie from the Barbie movie whose character Issa Rae played oh so well.

"Honey, grab your comb and brush," Lisa directed and was grateful when Michelle spun into action.

"Brandon is on his way and the caterer too," Michael informed.

"Thank you!" Lisa figured Michael was updating her on the slew of group texts she had ignored when she texted her mother. She was so glad to have a partner who helped her get stuff done. She knew other women didn't have that luxury.

"Here you go, Mommy." Michelle handed her the comb and brush and Lisa guided her to their normal spot on the couch.

"Michael, can you—" but Lisa didn't even have to finish. Michael manifested like a vision, grasping an already full spray bottle. He smiled.

"Thank you, my king!" she gushed, cupping the spray bottle.

Michelle propped herself on the floor between Lisa's knees and in record time Lisa separated her locks into two long French braids. She made sure to create a zig-zag part in the middle just the way Michelle liked it.

"All done," Lisa announced and gave Michelle a hand mirror. "Go look at your part and then grab the jam so I can lay down your edges."

Michelle took off with the hand mirror so she could see the back of her head in the bathroom mirror. Lisa had taught her that the trick was to turn her back to the larger mirror and hold up the hand mirror in front of her face. Pivoting at the right angle, she would be able to see the back of her head.

"Looks good," Michelle piped, reappearing and handing Lisa the container of jam along with a thumbs up.

Lisa chuckled at her daughter's approval while completing her remaining touches. *This girl is too much sometimes.* But it warmed her heart. Doing Michelle's hair always reminded Lisa of when her mother did her hair growing up. It was such a moment of bonding for them and one of the highlights of Lisa's childhood.

Another pang from missing her mother's call hit her heart but just as Lisa was grabbing her phone to see if her mother had responded, the intercom rang.

"I got it," Michael shouted as Lisa jumped from her spot on the couch.

"Baby, go to your room and play unless you want to help us with decorating. Oh, and make sure to get your beach towel and swim toys when you come down."

Lisa knew Michelle was not about to help with decorating and would much rather play, so she added that last part.

Within seconds, Sylvia with Natalie in tow, made a grand entrance.

"Who's ready to partayyyyy???!!!"

Michelle immediately deviated from her initial course to her bedroom.

"Auntie Sylvia!!" The child sped through the living room and into the older woman's arms.

Sylvia grabbed her and held her close. "Now is it just me or do she look like a nine-year-old, y'all? Last time I seen't you, you was looking like a teeny little eight-year-old. But now I definitely think you lookin' like a big ol' nine-year-old!" Sylvia howled and everyone laughed.

Michelle's large smile and round eyes soaked up all the adoration.

"Let me get those for you," Michael offered, stepping forward to take the bags off Natalie's hands. He peeked behind her. "No Devon?" he said, his tone disappointed.

"Thanks. He'll be here later," Natalie informed. "He got held up at the cafe." She handed over the gifts before capturing Michelle into a warm hug. "Happy Birthday, Michelle!"

Lisa motioned for her guests to come inside. "Thank you, ladies, so much for coming. We just waiting on Danita and then we'll go downstairs. Make yourselves comfortable."

"OOO, good! I need a minute cuz' my feet is definitely tired. I had to stand on my first train and then Nat here was on my second train, so she gave me *her* seat so that did help some, but I sure do need a break," Sylvia recounted while waddling inside. She was donned in a large, oversized jacket with a hood and a bulky handbag. Looking completely worn out, she plopped into the large suede chair in the corner of the living room and tossed her handbag on her lap in one fluid motion.

Natalie selected a dining room chair then eagerly cupped the bottled water Lisa had handed out. The women were chatting about the latest urban literature read by Kimberla Lawson Roby, and how things were going in their lives, when Danita arrived wearing a smile. Her long box braids with blue hair woven throughout, swung from side to side as she greeted the group.

"Sorry, I'm late y'all! My train was late." Danita offered a round of hugs to everyone except Michelle who was playing in her bedroom, and Michael who was taking a work call.

Lisa clapped both hands. "Ladies, thank you all so much for being here and for being willing to tackle this day with me. Michael already took the decorations downstairs so all we have to do is put them up. I'm ready when y'all are."

In response, the women bunched together in a herd and

marched out the door. As they walked and talked, Lisa made sure she had her phone and the key to the rec room.

"I see you got yo' hair did, Danita," Lisa chirped. "It's super cute."

Danita flipped her box braids to one side. "Thanks, boss. I had to since I knew I was about to be in this pool today. Ain't nobody tryna jack up their hair with that chlorine."

The women laughed and chimed in on the hardship of maintenancing their hair when swimming. That's what they were discussing when the elevator burst open on the third floor.

"Carol!" Lisa greeted.

Carol was in workout gear again but this time her curly brown hair was swooped into a high ponytail. Both sapphire eyes widened in pleasure upon seeing Lisa before she took in the rest of the crew.

"Hey!" she replied and slid inside as everyone shifted to make room.

Lisa made the introductions, letting everyone know Carol was a new friend who was attending church with her the next day.

"Oh, you're going to *love* it," Natalie affirmed and the conversation morphed from hair to the need of a good church and finding a spiritual community. By the time they hit the basement, it felt like Carol had been sewn into the group, so Lisa did the thing that was pressing on her heart.

"Would you like to join us for Michelle's party? It's a pool party but we not about to be swimmin'," she paused then eyed Sylvia, then Danita. "Well, *some* of us won't be." The women giggled. "So you can hang with the adults," she finished.

Carol beamed and shook her head in eager agreement. "I would *love* that." An expression of relief followed, dressing her round, peach pie face. "I literally was only going to the gym, because I was bored," she admitted.

"Well, honey you ain't gotta be bored because we need a hand with these decorations," Sylvia spouted.

Parading down the hall, the women followed Lisa into the rec room where everyone jumped into action hanging streamers and unfolding tablecloths. The caterers arrived shortly after and started setting out sandwiches, bowls of chips, bottles of juice, and plates of chocolate chip cookies. Michael appeared with an excited Michelle glued to his hip.

"Mommy, people are coming so I'm going to the pool!" Michelle announced before giving Lisa a kiss on the cheek and speeding off.

Lisa smiled. *My little roadrunner.*

"Brandon is setting up, so I'll be at the pool too," Michael informed. "You good here?" He did a swift one over all the moving bodies.

"Yep." Lisa advised. "We're all good." She pecked him on the lips then checked the time: 11:50am.

Whew! We are good to go, she thought, as Michael and Michelle vanished, and the caterers finished setting everything up and the ladies bonded over their individual tasks.

Taking in the scene, the events from early that morning briefly straddled Lisa's mind. How upset she had been at her father and her husband and her daughter. But then, how God had used Sylvia and showed her the healing she still needed from Hank. And after, how, once she humbled herself and apologized to her daughter, everything seemed to flow seamlessly. It was like all her prayers were being answered. Even ones she hadn't realized she needed to pray.

Lord, thank You for moving.

And peace hugged Lisa's heart. And she knew God had heard her.

Blind Faith

CHAPTER 9

The pool party was in full effect with kids splashing, and screams reverberating their little energetic lungs before bouncing off the walls. Michelle had opened her best friend, Jamie's gift, and was proudly sporting her new tiara.

"I'm only going to open Jamie's right now, Mommy because she's my bestie!" Michelle had declared. Lisa had complied, though she kept worrying the thing was going to slide off Michelle's head at any moment. Thus far the trusty bobby pins she had used to secure it seemed to be doing their job.

Brandon, the DJ was blaring teeny bopper tunes which Lisa always got a kick out of. It was so funny to her that there was a market for remixed pop songs with little kids singing them.

Carol exclaimed to Lisa, "This is such a fun party."

They were seated at a table in the pool area, watching the show from a safe, dry distance. Just as Carol had spoken, Aunt Sylvia picked up an elated Michelle and dunked her in the pool. Lisa shook her head.

"It is. I just hope we don't have to take Sylvia to the emergency messing around with these kids."

"Right. She seems to be having a ball, though!" Carol said.

The ladies fell into easy chit chat about their lives and Lisa learned Carol had two best friends back home that she missed terribly. She described them as her "ride or dies" and admitted how hard it had been to catch them with the time difference in Seattle.

"I'm so glad I met you, Lisa. Thank you for inviting me." Carol looked at Lisa in appreciation and Lisa was touched.

"Definitely. Like I said, I've been there. Sylvia was my very first friend in New York. We met when Michael and I got divorced and Michelle and I moved into her building."

Carol's light brown eyebrows stood up. "I didn't know you guys got divorced."

Lisa nodded. "Yeah, girl. It's a whole testimony. I seriously didn't think we would get back together. But God does miraculous things!"

Carol smiled and agreed. "That I know. I just *know* He's going to give me the desire of my heart with this child. I can't tell you how I can even possibly believe that because I haven't had *any* success. But I just believe in my heart. You know?"

She looked to Lisa for confirmation and Lisa nodded. "Yeah. That's how it is with God. It's faith. Shoot. It's like blind faith. It's like you can't explain it but you just know in your heart of hearts, *this* is what the Father said."

Lisa hesitated, then licked her lips, stealing a look at Michael. He was at the DJ station with Devon and Brandon, cracking up about whatever it is men talked about at children's birthday parties. Natalie and Danita were being sweethearts and manning the food in the rec room.

After her initial hesitation, Lisa added, "I feel the same way about Michael's relationship with God."

Carol seemed surprised. "Oh? Is Michael not a Believer?"

Lisa paused again, but, feeling like Carol was a safe space to vent, she continued. "He's been wounded by the church."

Carol's eyes dimmed with understanding which encouraged Lisa to speak her heart.

"I know many have this experience. They see the hypocrisy of a church leader who ain't right and is living foul while preaching something different in the pulpit. I know it can be hard to separate men's folly from God's goodness."

"Yeah. Robbie has his own story of faith. I didn't even know he *wasn't* a Believer until *after* we got married."

Lisa's mouth parted in surprise and Carol continued.

"Yep. We went to the same church and everything, but he never had a personal encounter. For Robbie, it was just about the works. As long as he was a good person and went to church, he thought that was all that was needed. And I wasn't as strong spiritually, so I didn't realize how important it would be to have a partner that was equally yoked." She gave a sheepish look.

Lisa meditated on that. "I know. I really had to hear God for me to go back into this marriage with Michael, knowing we wouldn't be on the same page spiritually. And when I kept wrestling with God about it, the passage that kept coming to me was when Esther married King Ahasuerus. It was her marriage to him that saved her people. I feel like God said it would be our marriage that would save Michael."

"Whew! Now *that's* a word. I will definitely keep you in prayer about Michael. I know firsthand how hard it can be not having a husband who is spiritually led."

Baby Lee chose that particular moment to start his normal workout routine and Lisa rubbed her belly, pressing the loose material.

Carol's eyes dropped to her baby bulge. She tried to cover her sadness with a smile.

Seeing her pain, Lisa reached over and patted her hand.

"And I will be in agreement for you too," she said, to comfort her new friend. "That God's promised child will come!"

Carol wove her fingers beneath Lisa's in response. "Thank you so much. I know we'll both have testimonies soon!"

Lisa beamed, grateful to have met another kindred spirit, especially when she had felt some kind of way by their first interaction.

Who knew this woman was such a powerhouse of faith?

But Lisa knew the answer to that question. God knew. And it was just like Him to remind her not to judge a book by its cover by bringing Carol into her life. As a writer you would think she would know this by now. But it was always just like the Father to keep teaching her things.

"Ladies, what ch'all over here doin'?" Aunt Sylvia stood, dripping wet in a lime green one-piece with a tutu glued to her midsection. She was a sight. Salt and pepper kinky coils matted the top of her head as she patted herself with a striped beach towel.

"Oh, nothing. Just bonding over how good God is," Lisa filled in.

Sylvia's face brightened. "Now you know I love them kind a conversations!" The older woman plopped down in a seat. "I can always benefit from a good praise break." She tossed her head back and laughed.

The rest of the party flowed nicely as the adults indulged in adult time and the kids splashed about 'til their heart's content. When the festivities sailed into the rec room and everyone sang, "Happy Birthday," Lisa's heart swelled with emotion.

She's getting older, she realized when Michelle was adamant that she didn't want any help serving her guests cake. Michael had to insist that he would be cutting and that she was too young to be holding a large cake knife. Thankfully he won that argument but Lisa knew there weren't too many years left when he would. Taking her time, Michelle successfully placed each slice on the small round plates and handed them to her friends.

It wasn't long before the sugar kicked in and the kids transformed into Bebe's kids, running around ragged. Another hour and they were slumping in corners and on sections of carpet looking as if the wind was knocked out of them. They had successfully crashed and burned.

One by one parents stopped by to collect their offspring, and, after cleaning, Lisa's crew moved upstairs to her apartment. Only Jamie, Michelle's bestie, came with them. True to her word, Lisa let Jamie spend the night for Michelle's birthday. The girls were playing in Michelle's bedroom, using her new glow-in-the-dark mosquito net to pretend they were ballerinas turned forest park rangers hunting deer in the woods. Never mind that forest park rangers didn't hunt. Every now and then Lisa would peek her head inside to make sure they were still alive.

Devon and Natalie had stayed to catch up while Danita headed out, stating she had a hot date to get ready for. Carol too had made her exit since Robbie was taking her to dinner. But Sylvia had topped them all with her horse and carriage date in Central Park.

"Y'all know me and Clifford been goin' strong for a year now, so we celebrating our anniversary," Sylvia boasted and everyone offered their congratulations.

It was still too early for wine, so Michael fixed his famous lattes and cappuccinos with his fancy expresso machine.

"Now, Nat, what were you saying?" Lisa asked. She had just returned to the living room after checking on the girls and caught the tail end of Natalie's statement.

"That you need communication to build a sustaining relationship," Natalie said.

Somehow the topic of conversation had flowed from travel, to best eating spots in NYC, to relationships.

Lisa nodded, "Definitely," then took her seat next to Michael on the couch and looked at her friends.

Devon leaned back, his white Polo shirt and jeans, a cool complement to his crisp fade. The only giveaway of his age was the premature sliver of grey slicing through it. Natalie had settled onto his lap in her white three-quarter sleeve blouse and ripped blue jeans.

They're matching, Lisa thought with a fond smile. *I remember those days.*

"I would have to agree," Michael chimed in. He had thrown his arm around Lisa and she let her neck caress it after taking a sip of hot water.

"I wouldn't have known actual ways to better communicate though if we hadn't gone to counseling," Lisa revealed with a small frown. "It's like the stuff people don't tell you about marriage."

"Or they tell you, but you don't have a grid for it until you're in it," Michael added.

Devon asked, "So, what would you guys say are vital tools that help your relationship thrive?"

Lisa smiled. It was so nice that she and Michael could share their life-taught wisdom with Devon and Natalie. There had been a handful of times when the foursome had hung out, but those moments were rare with having a kid, Devon's business, and Natalie being in school. Lisa was thankful for this impromptu time of bonding.

"Well, let's see. I would say, outside of communication, we have to be intentional to move toward each other," Lisa replied. She thought about her argument with Michael just that morning. If he hadn't come to her after his run and initiated the conversation, it may have never happened. Or, it would have happened much later. She could think of the first time around in their marriage when those types of disagreements had went on for days.

Thank you, Lord, that's over!

"Yeah. And we have to try to see the other person's perspective, even when we don't agree with it," Michael said. He looked at Lisa and all the love in her heart spun to the surface. His eyes mirrored what she was experiencing as she rubbed his thigh with her free hand.

"I can say that's been a hard one," Natalie admitted. "Devon and I have a tendency to have different views, which is fine, but if it's something I feel passionate about," she paused and gave him a teasing smile, "or he feels passionate about, that's when things can get wonky."

Devon stroked her back with his hand. "Yeah. I think we struggle when our emotions get involved with certain topics, like politics. Nat and I definitely have different views there."

"Like this war in the Middle East for example. Our stupid commander-in-chief feels we have a bone in this fight, yet all *our* people are losing their loved ones. It's casualty after casualty." Natalie's voice increased an octave with every word and Devon shifted uncomfortably beneath her.

"Yeah. But we need to *be* an ally for when we *need* an ally. And we need to combat this war on terrorism. We have the artillery to help win this thing," Devon dove in with a frustrated tone.

Lisa chuckled internally. She could see the electric dynamic between the young couple. It would be up to them to either let their energy fuel them into a common purpose, or allow it to shoot them in different directions entirely.

Then, suddenly, Devon's face softened and his demeanor relaxed. He rubbed Natalie's shoulder and her expression calmed, the unspoken message received.

Natalie laughed softly. "Like I said. Two different perspectives."

"But still the same common goal," Devon added. "We both want to help people."

Lisa loved seeing them resolve their conflict. Or at least, put a pin in it.

There's hope for them yet.

She also appreciated how eager they were to grow in their relationship and be healthy, especially since Natalie was so much younger. She was a good ten years Devon's junior but Lisa felt it worked because the girl was so mature for her age. She had been through a lot with the loss of her mother and her father's abandonment. When she moved to Jersey from Philly to be with extended family, it was in an effort to heal from grief. Lisa could see the changes that had taken place as a result of Natalie's healing. There was no doubt, Devon had been a key part of those changes.

The conversation eventually ended with Devon and Natalie calling it a night around 10 PM. By then Michelle and Jamie were tucked in deep inside the mosquito net, and the coffee had turned to wine. Well, for everyone except Lisa who wasn't doing alcohol due to her pregnancy. But she made up for that by having an extra portion of their Vietnamese takeout.

Breathing in contentment, Lisa closed the door after seeing out their guests. "That was nice that we got to spend time with them." She let out a huge yawn while raising her hands in praise. She was eager to fall into bed herself. It had been a long day and she had church in the morning.

Michael stood in front of her and braced her on each side, wrinkling her tank. "Yeah. I love them. I hope they push through this next season. I know Devon said Natalie was thinking of studying abroad."

Lisa dropped her arms and lightly rubbed Michael's biceps, taking a step closer so they would be intertwined. His basketball shorts and blue and yellow KD's were always a nice change of pace from his work suits. The weekends were a break from everything, including dressing up. When Lisa lifted her chin for a kiss, Michael obliged. Her lips pressed to his, she counted her blessings. Her husband was the reliable solid rock she always needed. God had given her good friends in the city, even adding to her collection with Carol as a bonus. Her daughter was momentarily satiated, even though she didn't get the cell phone or the foam party she had been desperate for. But Lisa's face suddenly scrunched when she thought about her parents. Stepping back, she reached into her pocket.

"What?" Michael looked at her, surprised she was breaking their moment of intimacy. "What is it?"

Knots formed in Lisa's stomach as she swiped through her text messages. No. Her mother had never responded. Trying to diminish the disappointment, her shoulders deflated. Today had been such a lovely day and she didn't want it to be ruined.

"Nothing. It's just the stuff it always is. That's all."

Pulling her to him, Michael caressed her arms. He then gripped her fallen chin and peered into her eyes, his own heavy with concern.

"Now, didn't we just get done telling these two how communication is vital for a good relationship? How you not gone' open up to me?"

Her husband was right. Lisa just hated that her family stuff was so much worse than his. Michael grew up with two loving parents. He had the ideal background. Even if it wasn't perfect, as he alluded to just that morning, it was still way better than what she had had.

"I just wish my mom was more involved, you know?" Lisa finally said. "I just wish we didn't always seem to miss each other."

Having spoken the words out loud, she felt a little lighter. Lisa wasn't sure the last time she had said them.

"We were supposed to do a video chat this morning for Michelle's birthday, which she initiated, but then with our argument and Michelle throwing her tantrum, the call got lost in the sauce." Lisa shrugged. "I asked if we could reschedule, but no response."

"Oh. I see." Michael murmured with a pensive frown. "Well, maybe she didn't get the text? Try her again in the a.m."

Her husband's response was reasonable and Lisa's own was probably steeped in her projecting her past into her present. Still, it was difficult not to believe her mother had left her hanging. Once Lisa graduated from Clark Atlanta University, she and Michael moved to Houston for their careers, and she didn't look back. She could count the number of times she and her mother had talked back then. Traumatized by the brokenness between them, it just seemed easier to keep the emotional distance. After she and Michael got married, Lisa's focus became building her own family. It wasn't until the last few years, when she started therapy, that she realized how important reconnecting with her mother truly was.

After a beat, Lisa said, "You're right," to her husband. Biting her lip, she added, "I'm gonna just text now while I have the courage and you're next to me."

Michael smiled in assurance. "That's right, babe. You got this."

Such the motivator. She couldn't help but smile back.

"Hey, Mom. Just following up on this. Michelle and I would love to talk to you in the morning before church if you're free."

After typing the message, Lisa tried to ignore the fear of rejection embedded in her belly, and instead, focus on Michael. His ease at life was one of the things that drew her to him. No matter what was going on, Michael had this self-assuredness about him which made him a fantastic sales exec. It also was a great balance to Lisa's constant struggle with anxiety. She had to make her checklists and do her breathing exercises and talk to Sylvia and pray and journal to establish the level of ease Michael exuded.

A few moments later, the vibration from Lisa's phone shifted her attention. She pulled back a little to view the message. A sad expression stained her face.

"What is it?" Michael asked, "What's wrong?"

While staring at the stove, Lisa shook her head, unable to meet his gaze. For all of his well-meaning intent, the truth was because Michael didn't have the issues with his parents that she had, his advice simply wasn't applicable. When Lisa hurriedly went to read her mother's response, she saw that her mother had declined her invitation. But it wasn't just a decline to a call. It was a decline to reconnecting ever again.

Let it Out

CHAPTER 10

Pastor Luis' gentle tone blared from the podium. It was Sunday morning and New Life bursted with church attendees. Every aisle was stuffed with people of all races and nationalities, their single commonality, their love for God.

In the process of Lisa crossing her legs, her upper arm bumped Natalie, who glanced over and smiled. She smiled back. It was good to be with friends. It was good to hear the Word.

I feel like it's been forever.

Eyes closed, and tilting her chin upward, the message saturated her heart. Gently, it massaged the inner chambers, then kneaded God's truth into her spirit. Seated between Carol and Natalie, Lisa waded in love.

Father, thank You for a new day. Your mercies are new each morning.

Pastor Luis dove into the scripture he was preaching from, stirring Lisa to attention.

"There comes a time when we must go through the tests of life," the young Puerto Rican stated. "I know we hate going through tests and trials but these thorns are what grow us. We never grow being on life's mountains." Pastor Luis resumed in his endearing accent, "It is always when we're in the valleys."

Thinking of how true that was, Lisa bobbed her head in agreement. Her divorce from Michael was the heart-wrenching pain that opened her to establishing a relationship with God. For years, she thought she could white-knuckle life as her parents had. But just as Sylvia said, she needed someone stronger than herself to lean on.

"It's when we come out on the other side that our faith shines as gold," the pastor said.

Pastor Luis went on to provide scripture references—1 Peter 1:7 being one of them—and Lisa eagerly jotted notes. She knew she needed to get back to her morning time in devotion and snuck a peak at Carol highlighting on her phone. They were both using their Bible apps. Devon, perched on the other side of Natalie, was the only one with a traditional leather-bound paper copy. The rest of the service was jam-packed with more encouragement to withstand the storms of life. Lisa absorbed it all, once again grateful to have found a spiritual home.

"That was so good," Carol remarked as the trio spilled into the foyer after service.

Natalie informed that Devon had to help with things at church and that she was free to leave without him.

"I'm so glad you liked it." Lisa smiled and hugged her Burberry tan tote closer to her double-breasted feather-grey peacoat. She was thankful she had rooted the coat out of the back of the closet that morning because the weather had dipped into the 50s.

Natalie echoed in agreement, "Yeah. I definitely resonated with that word," her face aglow with sincerity.

"Mommy. Mommy, can I go to Tracy's house? Plleeeassseee?" Michelle was a ball of energy burning at Lisa's side, somehow mystifying from the hallway that led to the room for children's church.

Peering down at her daughter's pleading expression, Lisa's eyes waded in humor. "What did her mother say?" She searched in the direction Michelle was pointing, to see Tracy and her mother at the entrance.

"She said 'yes'! She said she would drop me off later." Michelle's words flew from her mouth faster than she could pronounce them.

Lisa shared a look with Tracy's mom, Lauren, whose ebony skin glowed and full figure bounced with joy. Lauren broke their silent discussion with a wink, confiming that her daughter told no lie. Though she came off hesitant in her reply, Lisa was secretly pleased. She normally wanted Michelle to play with Tracy because her daughter didn't have too many friends who looked like her. Being at that boogie private school had its benefits, but diversity wasn't one of them.

"Ok. But be on your *best* behavior," she relinquished. "I don't want to hear anything about y'all putting gum in each other's hair to see who has thicker hair."

Michelle let out an exasperated noise. "Mommy. That only happened *once*."

Lisa shook her head. "Once is enough. It took me forever to get that gum out!"

After pecking Lisa on the cheek, Michelle did an about-face, fought the moving crowd and made her way safely to her friend.

"She's too adorable," Carol commented, having witnessed the entire interaction. "*How* do you stand it?"

"Girl. She is getting more and more like me every day, I'll tell you that much. My mother—" Lisa stopped herself and quickly retracted her statement. "I knew one day I'd have to pay for how hyper I was as a kid is all I'll say," she finished, her tone dipping some.

"Yeah. My mom always said," Natalie quoted, as the three women moved in step, "'You'll have one just like you one day'."

The truth was that what Natalie said was exactly what Lisa was going to say, but after her mother's text last night she couldn't bring herself to.

How is it that my relationships with both *my parents are a mess? Thank God for Michael. And Michelle. And this one.*

Lisa rubbed her belly before the women hopped a train to a nearby cafe they frequented after church. Since Devon's was closed on Sundays it was the next best thing.

When they entered inside, Lisa asked, "Y'all want to sit in the back?"

The aroma of coffee teased her nostrils and she took a strong whiff.

I may just have to get a cup today. Life is too hectic. Who in their right mind can do it without coffee?

"That sounds good. Is our normal table open?" Natalie asked. She stood on her tiptoes to see but the after-church crowd was blocking her view.

"I think so," Lisa replied, then took the lead, bulldozing through until she reached a corner table. The threesome scurried to claim it.

"Ahh. It feels so good to get off my feet," Lisa chirped nonchalantly. Whipping up her foot she re-tied her black and white Nikes. They went horribly with her midnight cashmere pants suit but she was trying to make some changes for the sake of Baby Lee. Getting rid of her heels was one of those changes.

Carol announced, "I think I'm going to get the gravy and biscuits," but the sentence was cloaked by the menu that buried her face.

The other ladies volunteered their orders when the waitress arrived, a short, round woman with loud eyeshadow inappropriate for daywear. She chucked her head at each one in memorization.

"So, how are you settling in, Carol?" Natalie turned to Carol while swinging her jean jacket over the back of her chair.

Carol smiled. "It's gotten so much better since I met Lisa." She looked at Lisa fondly and Lisa's face grew warm.

"Oh, girl. It works both ways. It's been great to have a new friend in the building. I definitely don't have it in me to keep up with my people like I should. I'm grateful when y'all can work with me." Bashfully, Lisa sipped her water.

Natalie came to the rescue. "Lis, you do a great job. You got a lot going on and yet still make time for our girl talks at our monthly hair appointments."

"Uh. Yeah. About those." Fighting guilt, Lisa tossed her eyes to her stomach and then back at Natalie. "I'm actually gonna to have to put a pin in those for a while. At least, until this baby comes."

"Oh? Ok. Everything good, though?" Natalie's eyes shined with concern. She knew Lisa wasn't one to open up easily and needed some nudging every now and then.

Shifting a little in her seat, Lisa started playing with her Chanel black and gold studded cuff, a birthday gift from Michael. "I been having some bleeding…" she said quietly.

Immediately, the ladies' faces wore worry like it was in style.

"But it's gonna be ok," Lisa assured. "The doc says I just need to take it easy." She half shrugged. "Not do too much."

Carol was the first to respond. "Oh, hon, I'm sure you're right. Everything is going to work out."

Lisa was appreciative of the encouragment, especially coming from Carol who had struggled so much in this area.

Natalie co-signed. "Yeah, sis. You know God got chu'!"

"Thanks, y'all. I know. I'm not worried. I just had a couple of scares. But other than that, the pregnancy has been pretty smooth sailing. Except for Baby Lee going in on my ribs," she joked to lighten the mood.

Carol's eyes lit up. "Aww, that's his name? Lee?'

"Yep. After his mama." Lisa grinned and felt better just having gotten the issue of the bleeding off her chest.

When the waitress brought their orders, the women chatted between bites about everything from romantic partners, to work, to the political climate that was sweeping the nation with election day fast approaching.

"Ugh. I hate election day. Me and Devon just can't seem to get on the same page with politics," Natalie vented. "I mean, we're pretty good on the local stuff but the national stuff is always an issue." She paused. "And it's not like we don't see eye-to-eye on the big picture, we just have different views on how to get there."

"Yeah. Me and Michael are cool with politics, but you know, we struggle with spiritual stuff," Lisa said, her eyes downcast.

And just like that, they were back to relationships.

"Well, you know how long it took for me and Robbie. I told you it was three years before he figured it out," Carol said.

"Three years?" Natalie's eyes ballooned. "Whew. How did you make it?"

Carol replied, "Lots of prayer," her vision aimed at the ceiling to indicate that her prayers were heard.

"Man. I guess you just never know what people have been through." Natalie commented, caressing her coffee. "I mean, we can look so good on the outside but have the world spinning out of control on the inside."

Discomfort poked at Lisa. Was her world spinning out of control?

I mean, it's not like I'm struggling with miscarriages, she thought when reflecting on Carol's situation. *Or grieving the loss of a parent*, she then thought, thinking of Natalie's mom's death less than two years ago. But was being at odds with your parents still considered a loss? The pinch in Lisa's spirit wouldn't let go and suddenly she blurted, "I hate my dad and my mom hates me."

Both women jerked their heads toward her in shock.

"I thought you and your dad were getting along?" Natalie asked in surprise. "Wasn't he even sending Michelle a birthday gift?"

Lisa sighed. "Yeah. The *wrong* birthday gift. He got the girl a cell phone."

"Uh oh," Natalie said. "I know how much you didn't want her to have a cell phone."

"Right. And on top of that he didn't even ask me and Michael." Lisa filled the ladies in on the rest of her conversation with her father yesterday morning. She still hadn't listened to his voicemail.

"I'm sorry to hear that." Carol reached over and rubbed her shoulder. "I know that can be hard, even though I can't imagine. I've always been closer to my dad than my mom."

"Thanks. Yeah. It was a risk letting him back in after being so flaky all these years. And the only reason I did is because I really wanted him to have a solid relationship with Michelle." But that wasn't fully the case. Lisa also wanted that relationship for herself but she wasn't comfortable saying it out loud.

"I'm sorry, Lis." Natalie offered a sympathetic look. "But why do you think your mom hates you?" Her lips puckered in confusion.

Lisa nibbled at her thumb and took a sip of hot water before answering. "My mom and I have always been at odds. Well, not always. But definitely since junior high. She had a um…" Lisa's voice faded. It was so hard to share because she hated exposing her mom's weakness. But Natalie's sweet eyes and Carol's innocent face double-teamed her. "She had a drug addiction, so growing up we weren't on the best of terms. Then when I got older it just seemed easier to keep my distance." There. She had said it.

"Oh, wow. I had no idea your mom was an addict." Natalie covered Lisa's hand with one of her own.

Lisa nodded quietly.

"But why do you think she hates you?" Carol asked with an enigmatic expression.

"I was supposed to call her on Michelle's birthday yesterday," Lisa explained. "We were supposed to do a video call. It was like the first one ever. And *she* even initiated it. But then things got crazy and I forgot the call." Lisa rolled her eyes at herself, her chest heavy with the weight of her mistake. "And when I reached out to reschedule, it was too late. Then she said she felt it would be better if we didn't have the call at all." Moisture squeezed Lisa's right eye and before she could stop it, rolled rebelliously down her cheek.

"Oh, honey!" Both Natalie and Carol had moved toward her and before she even knew what was happening, caved her into their arms.

Lisa felt entirely foolish having a breakdown in the middle of a cafe but even as she dried her eye with the napkin she was handed, and felt their hands rubbing her back, and their heartfelt words consoling her ears, she knew that this was exactly what she needed. Lisa needed to let it out.

THE ESSENCE OF JAZZ WAS LIKE THE ESSENCE OF LISA. METTLED, classy and polished. Each issue went out like clockwork and only the best of the best were featured. That included the journalists. Jazz was so competitive that a journalist could get approval for a piece, set out to do their research, interviews, and write-ups, but if the editors didn't feel an article made the cut, their work was easily replaced. Or, their words re-arranged so much it felt like a totally different writer wrote it. So far Lisa had not gotten replaced or her words too re-arranged, but she was certain her colleague, Renee Brush, was eager for the former to occur. Even though Lisa had proven her worth by landing the position as a music journalist, everyone's job was always teetering on the brink of the next best writer. As a result, she was never completely comfortable.

Which is how I like it, Lisa thought while hammering out her piece on the one and only Angela Yee. When Carl approved her pitch, Lisa was elated. She had half expected him to decline since they weren't the first with the news, but, since it was early, they were still in the window to be viewed as an "in the know mag."

Lookout Essence! We comin' for you.

Lisa's fingers threaded invisible needles over the keyboard as Lofi jazz hip-hop sprinkled her office airwaves. With every tap, the source of creativity and deftness drizzled from her fingertips. The deadline for the article and the precarious balance of her position only pumped adrenaline harder through Lisa's veins. That double major in journalism and communications from Clark had never let her down. She was made for this.

A sudden knock at the door broke Lisa's momentum. At the same time, a reminder for their writer's meeting flushed her screen.

Danita's long braids draped the door frame, a questioning brow complementing them. "Ready, boss?"

Already standing in her gray Asics running shoes, Lisa piped back, "Yep!"

The two bobbed and weaved through the ocean of Jazz workers until Renee's bulky figure bumped Lisa's side.

"Oh. Lisa. Sorry, girl. I didn't see you!" Renee loudly proclaimed as they slid into the large conference room. This was a "writer's only" meeting, so there would only be about 20 in attendance. More than half were freelancers who worked offsite.

Lisa shot Renee a polite smile. "It's all good." She waved off her comment while following Danita to their usual spot at the long oval table. Though Lisa had the distinct feeling Renee had bumped her on purpose, she decided to put on her Michelle Obama hat and take the high road.

"Yeah, sis. Normally you're a little bit taller. I guess you lost some height, huh?" Renee said, following her. She chuckled and then had the nerve to plop down in the seat right next to Lisa.

This B!

Lisa fought to ignore the rush of emotion choking her throat and to not remove her MB hat. She knew Renee was referring to the fact that she wasn't wearing her heels.

Expelling a light laugh, Lisa responded, "I guess so. But thankfully height isn't a requirement to keep churning out amazing articles. Did you happen to catch the one I did on Ms. Keys?"

Lisa couldn't keep herself from saying it and just as Renee's gaze widened with some snappy comeback looming in her eyes, Carl's voice rang above the chatter filling the room.

For the first time ever Lisa was gratefully distracted by Carl's incessantness. The man was one long soliloquy away from being a narcissist. Except, he didn't really talk about himself. He only talked about the job. Every time Lisa had any type of dialogue with Carl, he never alluded to an outside life. No family. No kids. Nothing. She was convinced he went home just to do more work. If there was such a thing as a work narcissist, he was it.

I guess that would be a workaholic.

"Did you catch that?" Danita whispered next to Lisa and she hurried to attention.

Clicking her inner playback button, Lisa re-ran Carl's last sentence in her thoughts.

"I'll be partnering you in teams for this upcoming issue."

Lisa nodded to Danita and scribbled notes on her notepad. She was old-schooling it but loved the roll of the pen between her fingertips. Danita was normally great at notetaking, but, just in case, Lisa liked to back her up.

"Renee Brush and Lisa Doris," Carl announced.

Lisa's head whipped up faster than a speeding bullet. *What?!*

Her eyes darted to Renee. The same shock she felt was mirrored in her colleague's eyes coupled by a subtle downturn to the corners of her mouth. It took everything in Lisa to pay attention the rest of the meeting. Carl was announcing other pairs and explaining that this was a time to get the writers out of their comfort zones. He wanted the piece each pair worked on to sound like one voice. One style.

Lisa could just hear Leonard Roberts in the movie Drumline. "One band. One sound!"

"We're taking Jazz to the next level folks!" Carl continued. "And that means a deeper level of commitment to your colleagues. I know we have a competitive atmosphere here, but we all have the same mission. The same goal. We want that goal to be delivered in our articles at Jazz. We want you to do that with this issue."

Carl advised that if your partner worked in a different section, the two of you would write two pieces, combining your writing styles and voices into one. A sinking feeling of dread kept Lisa stitched to her seat as Carl dismissed everyone.

Ugh. This is going to be just the open door Renee probably wants to take my position, Lisa thought.

"Uh. Well. This is gonna be fun," Renee offered weakly, while slowly standing.

Lisa nodded and put on her best Colgate smile. "Right. I guess we'll be working together."

That was all she could say. Danita's presence moved around beside her but Lisa wouldn't dare make eye contact with her assistant. She was sure that if she did Renee would read every look between the two and know they were talking about her. Even while not using words.

"So, I'll shoot you an email with some ideas, er, and have Danita send my schedule. And, uh… you do the same. And we'll connect. On some things…" Lisa tried to save her stilted words with another cordial smile.

Renee nodded, "Yeah. Sounds good. Talk soon," and shuffled quickly behind the other staff members.

"Bathroom?" Danita asked, as soon as Renee was out of earshot.

"Please," Lisa muttered.

The two were in the women's stall in no time but had taken the elevator ride to the twelfth floor because they didn't want anyone else to hear their conversation. This was a common occurrence if either Lisa or Danita was going through something that required an emergency venting session.

"Girlll, can you believe this?" Danita let out once they checked the stalls and made sure they were alone.

Lisa shook her 4B tendrils. "Not at all! What are the odds? And how in the world did Carl pick those damn names?" She was dancing from side to side and it wasn't until the end of their venting session that she realized it was because she had to pee really bad.

"Hang on D. Let me use the restroom real quick and we can get back to work."

"Ok." Danita was primping in the mirror and reapplying her lipstick.

Lisa hopped into the nearest stall and swiftly started removing her work pants. Danita's voice was a humdrum from behind the door as she went on and on about Big Bird having a bird brain.

"The fact that that man can't see that y'all can't stand each other…" floated underneath the door.

But the yammering from her friend was shoved to the back of her thoughts as Lisa's eyes inhaled the cotton soaked in blood. It wasn't just in her underwear, it was in her pants too. It was, in fact, everywhere. It took her a minute to realize what was happening, but when she did, she cried out in fear.

"Danita! Call 911! I'm hemorrhaging!"

Even in the Storm

CHAPTER 11

A buzzing startled the insides of her ears as Lisa's eyes fluttered open. Blurry movements launched before her and though the outline of a body was the best she could see, she made out Michael's voice as clear as day.

"Baby. Baby. I got you." He was there, beside her, stroking her.

She gripped his fingers with her right hand until finally, he came into focus; a disheveled, wrought version of himself. His eyes—bloodshot red, his face caked with exhaustion and worry, and, something else. She didn't know what though.

"Michael," Lisa said in a croaked, whispery sort of way.

"Baby, let me get you some water." Michael dissapeared from view but then returned. He began feeding Lisa water with a paper cup and helping her sit up to swallow.

Finally, the hospital room was in vivid focus. Turns out the buzzing was from the GED overhead lighting.

"Thank you," Lisa mustered, her voice stronger, but still soft. It wasn't until she sat back with the bed propped in a slanted position, curtesy of Michael hitting the little lever on the side, that she understood. Something was wrong.

"Michael?" Lisa began, but his eyes said it all. That's when she realized what it was she had seen in them before. Grief.

An overwhelming sense of horror suffocated her then. It was like a veil thicker than any blackout curtain ever created. In an instant, it draped her mind, her eyes, and lastly, her heart. A pitch-black inky lens now covered everything she had previously known.

Doctor Swan arrived shortly after. Michael had alerted the nurse that Lisa was awake, who in turn, alerted the doctor. They both stood near her bedside next to Michael.

Dr. Swan had done an emergency C-section and put her under anesthesia. As Lisa awakened from it, the ride in the ambulance flooded her memory. Danita holding her hand the whole way. Danita calling Michael on their way to the hospital. There was so much blood. It was gushing from her. Baby Lee was gushing from her. So, they did the C-section.

"He didn't make it," Michael whispered, confirming her inner suspicions. Extinguishing what last bit of hope remained in her heart.

"Noooooooo!!"

It was a painful wail. The wail of the mothers in the Bible who had lost their children to the ugliness of war. The women who knew suffering like none other. There simply was no suffering like losing a child.

"Nooooo!!"

The word convulsed Lisa's entire being. It slashed through her mind, raced through her veins, and slaughtered the most tender parts of her heart. Lisa didn't even know she was yelling. All she knew was that Michael had her. He had jumped on the bed and shielded her body with his as if trying to absorb her pain.

Doctor Swan's words were a reverberating muffle through Michael's torso. Lisa's own body was shaking relentlessly. She couldn't stop it. Agony took turns with dread clawing her insides.

But Michael was there. He was rocking her and she could feel his tears rolling onto her neckline as his own sobs beat his body.

"I got you, baby," he kept saying over and over again. "I got you."

Lisa buried her head into his being, pressing and pressing as if the act could hide her from this unspeakable nightmare. They were like that for however long until finally, the shaking had ceased. A deep moan dragged from her lips. She peered at Doctor Swan behind Michael's head. The woman looked sincerely sorry but all Lisa felt was rage.

You liar! she screamed in her mind at the memory of Swan telling her to trust that her baby would be ok. To trust *God*.

You liar!!! Lisa screamed over and over. And it took everything in her not to say the words out loud.

❧

DAYS LATER, LISA LAY BURIED IN A LAYER OF BLANKETS AND PILLOWS. Michael had wrapped her with so many she wondered if he thought blankets had a superpower to snap her out of her state. And truly she was in a state. She hadn't said a word since they left the hospital. Not one.

"Baby, I'm going to get Michelle from Sylvia's," Michael uttered but all Lisa could do was nod into the pillow with her back to the door. When she heard him leave, she re-entered another round of silent crying. After the wailing in the hospital, her cries had turned silent.

It was another hour before murmuring kissed the other side of the door. Someone else was in the house. Quiet speaking, some padded footsteps, and then Michelle's little voice, but Lisa couldn't decipher actual words.

My baby, she thought and longed for Michelle but was too heavy to dig out of the covers. And then, God forbid, lift herself off the bed.

The bedroom door squeaked open and arms were enfolding her. A familiar fragrance that didn't belong to her daughter, slid beneath the top layer of covers. Arms much too long for a nine-year-old, enclosed Lisa's body and warmth began to spoon her from behind. Curiosity joined the darkness in her mind and Lisa turned her head, peering into the dimness of the room. Sylvia's angelic face shone from above and her crying morphed into bellows.

"I know, baby," the older woman said and tightened her hold around Lisa's frame. "I know."

"He-he's gone," was all she could get out before the words were snuffed by pain.

"I know," Sylvia repeated and the two stayed like that until Lisa finally fell asleep.

～

THE ALARM CLOCK READ 2:33 AM. LISA SQUINTED IN THE darkness. She wasn't sure how long she had slept but it felt like forever. A faint snoring resounded on the other side of the bed. Sylvia.

Where was Michael?

She carefully slid from beneath the covers and the limp arm that Sylvia had straddled over her body. Tiptoeing to the door, Lisa risked creaking it open, and looked back at the shadow on the bed. It hadn't moved.

The night light from the kitchen was on. They normally kept it lit for Michelle in case she had to make a middle-of-the-night run to the bathroom. Lisa peered into the living room but the couch was empty. No Michael.

He must be with Michelle.

Lisa couldn't imagine Michael's large frame on her daughter's canopy bed but maybe he was on the floor? Then her mind remembered. Gathering all of her courage, she veered to the office. Her eyes studied the closed door in the darkness, sizing it up. Immediately, she shut them at its foreboding image.

Lord, help me.

It was the first time Lisa had prayed since everything and it felt odd. Praying was like a foreign language she had learned years ago. Only a remnant of what she once knew remained.

Touching the door, Lisa pried it open, and sure as she suspected, her husband lay crumpled on the floor. He was hugging one of the stuffed bears they had gotten their son. It was the one Michelle picked out. Her heart melted at the endearing image.

Lord, how are we going to get through this?

There she was praying again. It seemed to be happening without her even trying. Lisa sighed and traipsed back into the living room to grab the one remaining fleece from the couch. It had to be the only one left in the whole house, the rest, sprawled on her bed. She wrapped it around herself, threw the rest over Michael, laid next to her husband, and ignored the crib he had finished last week. She let her mind run itself into the ground, until finally, darkness enclosed her.

THE WEEK WAS A HAZE OF BLEEDING, CHANGING BANDAGES, THE cremation of their son's body, memorial service arrangements, loved ones reaching out with condolences, and Lisa trying to manage her emotions through it all. She felt like she had been hit by a Mack truck. Not just from her emotional loss but from the surgery itself. Sylvia, bless her heart, had packed a bag and stayed. After the first night, she slept in Michelle's room, and Lisa and Michael stayed in theirs. But Lisa wasn't able to sleep, so she just lay there all-night watching Michael. She envied his ability to find rest.

The girls had coordinated meals, so Lisa was off duty for cooking. Each night they ate something Natalie, Danita or Carol whipped up. Except, Lisa couldn't eat either. She mainly picked at her food and drank hot water. The thick veil over her mind seemed immovable and not even Michelle's tender hugs and Sylvia's beautiful spirit were doing the trick. Michael appeared to be forcing food down his throat, and outside of common greetings, they had said very little to each other.

Danita related the news at Jazz that Lisa was recovering, and Carl was so understanding he gave her two weeks of family leave time. It made Lisa feel bad about all the times she had made fun of him. She also felt bad about missing so much work and was hoping to at least start working from home next week.

A ragged sigh escaped her as Lisa and Sylvia sat in the living room. Michael was at work. She told him to take off but he said it helped him to keep going. Michelle was doing homework at the dining room table on Lisa's laptop. The TV was on and Lisa was pretending to watch Sylvia's favorite show, "Law & Order".

At the sound of her sigh, Sylvia patted Lisa's lap and scooted closer. "You want more tea?" the kind, older woman asked.

Remains of Lisa's peppermint tea cradled the bottom of her mug. Silently, she tilted her chin in a yes motion and Sylvia went to put on water, before returning with a fresh fill.

"Why does He allow these things?" Lisa finally whispered. She had been wrestling with the question all week. Her eyes slid to Michelle, concerned that her withering faith would seep into her daughter. But Michelle had her headphones on while feverishly working out a math problem.

Sylvia spoke in such a gentle tone, it seemed to swirl around Lisa's question and hug it with care.

"He's with us, even in the storm."

Lisa wondered at her lack of faith. *Why is it that I can't seem to trust Him?* she thought, until an image of her father assaulted her mind. And then it became clear. Lisa's father was the root of her distrust. The one person with the power to heal her had withheld that gift *for years*. Her phone was somewhere in her room and suddenly, she was wracked with an urge to retrieve it.

"I'll be back," Lisa mumbled and though Sylvia looked startled by her abruptness, she didn't try to stop her.

In moments, Lisa was in her bedroom digging through the clutter. Michael was the neat freak but wasn't on his A-game and as a result, their bedroom, like their current mental state, was in shambles. She flipped over some bills thrown on her nightstand and tossed away this week's PJs from her side of the bed. But it was only after lifting the duvet that the shiny metal sleeping between it and the fitted sheet revealed itself. Snatching the phone as if it would grow legs and run, Lisa plopped onto the bed. 24 unread texts and 10 voicemails.

Don't.

It was but a faint whisper to her spirit but she knew the voice of God, even when He whispered.

"Why?!"

She glared at the ceiling with her cry. "Why shouldn't he be held accountable for all he's done?!"

Awaiting a response, she stared, but all she felt was an impression on her soul that God did not want her to act in anger. Still, anger was all Lisa felt. A blind, roaring, anger.

"You *liar*!!!" she screamed and threw the phone against the wall.

"You liar! You said you would never leave or forsake me!!! You *left* me!!" Lisa didn't know who she was talking to, her father, or God. Maybe it was both.

Sylvia was on the bed, sheltering her as her body convulsed with pain.

"It's ok, baby. Just let it out." Sylvia's soothing voice sang over Lisa's form a song of deliverance from one of the Psalms. Each word lulling and caressing the inner chambers of her heart.

"Why did he leave me, Sylvia?" Lisa whimpered in the tiniest voice. "Why did he leave?"

But instead of answering, Sylvia cradled her even more and kissed the tops of her disheveled curls. And that was enough.

THE SERVICE IN MEMORY OF LEE MICHAEL DORIS WAS HELD IN A corner of Riverside Park, not too far from the bridge and next to a beautiful Red Maple. It was the perfect fall day if there could ever be a perfect day for honoring a lost loved one. There were only two handfuls in attendance. Lisa didn't want it to be a huge ordeal. She understood her son's life had been short. Non-existent even, to some, and yet knew the importance of remembering her child.

Michael rubbed her shoulders when a crisp, cutting wind shook them all. "You ready?" he asked gruffly, his cold breath tickling the outside of her earlobe. There was a hint of alcohol, but Lisa wasn't sure, so she brushed it off.

Taking a few steps forward, she did an about-face toward the intimate crowd in front of the Maple. "Thank you all for being here," Lisa started, though struggled to maintain eye contact. "I know we don't have any memories with Lee but I do want to still honor who he was to us."

The friends that had shown were a cohesive unit of sympathetic nods and comforting smiles. She was so loved.

"I always wanted a son," Lisa confessed over the lump in her throat. "I know typically women want girls, and I love me some Michelle," her eyes dipped to her daughter who seemed to be taking everything ok but was more quiet than normal. Her daughter had lost her spunk. "But I wanted a son because I knew he was going to be just like his dad."

Lisa's eyes lingered on Michael's and the connection between them seemed unbreakable. Her heart swelled. She breathed in deep and counted to five, then let it out slow.

"I'm so thankful for the time we were given to steward Baby Lee. Even though it was short, it was so sweet." Her voice trembled and the weight of her head became greater, but she pushed on. "I know we will see him again."

Ending on a note of bravery, chin slightly lifted, eyes to the heavens, Lisa's heart was full. Not just with the love of her community, but with the ethereal hope that she would see her child again.

Michael gathered everyone around the tree and they put their items down. Michelle had brought a one-of-a-kind hand-crafted family picture of the four of them secured in a silver frame. Baby Lee was in the middle. Michael brought the stuffed teddy Lisa found him with that night when she discovered him in the office on the floor. They had left the box with their child's ashes safely at home. This memorial was only symbolic, intended to give some kind of closure. The other attendees held small candles they struggled to, but successfully, lit. It seemed, even the winds knew this was a sacred moment, and ceased their fretful howling.

Lisa was last. Slowly crouching at the root of the trunk, her large, thick plaid scarf rose to her mouth. She bent on her knees while Michael and Michelle hovered over her. Their friends formed a shelter around the trio. Lisa reached inside her peacoat, smoothing the fabric between the balls of her gloves. The small, fitted cloth that she had intended to bring her son home in, revealed itself. Bright red letters were stitched over a white onesie reading "Momma's Boy." Her hands clung to the letters before finally letting them go. Michael moved Michelle's picture frame so that it secured the onesie.

Goodnight, sweet boy, Lisa thought, while nestled in the center of her loved ones.

THE WARMTH OF FRIENDS DISSIPATED ONE BY ONE AND TWO BY TWO. After the memorial service, they exited the Doris residence until the couple was, for the first time in two weeks, alone. During that time Lisa had caught glimpses of Michael, but they hadn't had any real conversation. Sylvia had been a much-needed presence that balanced their family of three in ways Lisa was eternally grateful for. Especially when it came to Michelle. Michelle was overjoyed to have shared her bed with Auntie Sylvia. She cried when Sylvia explained she had to leave. Lisa's heart broke and she knew her child was demonstrating her own grief. Sylvia promised that Michelle could come over during her normally scheduled times of babysitting and that seemed to pacify the child. But still, Lisa worried. She had been able to take a semi-break from parenting but now would be back on the clock full-time. Could she do it?

It was Sunday night. Michael was showering and Lisa was sifting through emails, preparing for her first day back in the office. She had managed to work from home the last few days but knew it was time.

Michael asked, "You ready for tomorrow?" He was toweling off while standing stark naked in their bedroom. He had started picking up after them again so there was less of a mess at least.

Lisa offered him a small smile while glancing up from her phone. "As ready as I'll ever be." She let her eyes admire his physique as her husband rummaged through the drawers, pulling out a pair of pajama pants that looked amazing against his butt. A stirring between her legs began but she reminded herself to wait. She was still bleeding and had up to six weeks before sex was on the table.

"Your dad has been trying to get in touch with you," Michael informed.

Lisa looked up startled.

"He called a few times and texted. I let him know what happened," Michael finished.

"What? When?"

"Yesterday. I figured he should know *something* since you've been ignoring him."

"Well, I wish you would have told *me* first before you did that." Lisa couldn't keep the bite out of her voice.

"I wish you would have let *me* know a lot of things," Michael said. He had his own bite to his voice.

Huh? Lisa looked at him in confusion, "What do you mean?"

He sighed. "At the hospital, Dr. Swan mentioned the notes from the other doctor, Dr. Singh."

A sinking discomfort began to settle in Lisa's stomach. "Ok," she said slowly. She looked back at her phone. "And?"

"And, why didn't you tell me you were bleeding during that visit?" Michael was staring at Lisa intensely, his eyes not menacing, but still slightly accusing.

"I-I was handling it," she stammered. "I didn't want you to worry."

"You were handling it? How?" Disbelief mounted Michael's voice and the disappointment in his eyes was tormenting.

"I-I did what he said to do. I cut out my long commutes to Jersey for my hair appointments. I switched out my heels for sneakers. I started taking naps when working from home." Lisa could hear her own voice resounding in defensiveness. Why was she on the defensive? She didn't do anything wrong.

"You did all that and didn't talk to me. You did all that and knew what he said and didn't let me in."

Her husband paced as he spewed the words, Lisa realized, that he had probably been mulling over since the hospital.

"Baby, I wasn't trying to keep you out. I just didn't think you needed to worry." She softened her expression, seeing his pain and trying to fix it.

Michael's head flew up as he suddenly stood still. "Yeah? And how well did that turn out?" His voice was cold, his shoulders straight, his jaw clenched.

Lisa was quiet, her heart jolted by the switch in his stance. Was he blaming her for losing their child?

Michael began grabbing a pillow and an extra throw on the bed. "I'm sleeping on the couch," he stated flatly.

"What? Don't do that," she called, but he was already heading to the door.

"I'll see you in the morning," he threw back, before disappearing.

Sorry for Your Loss

CHAPTER 12

The morning came, but Michael didn't stay for breakfast, vanishing quickly and muttering about an early meeting. Lisa was too consumed with preparing for her first day back to spend any time worrying about it. She plopped a bowl of cereal in front of Michelle, along with some toast.

"No eggs?" Michelle asked in a sullen voice.

Lisa said, "Don't start," in her best no-nonsense tone. "Daddy has a meeting and Mommy has to prepare for her first day back to work." There was no time for her daughter's extraness today.

After successfully managing to get Michelle ready before her rideshare arrived, Lisa was on the A-train to Jazz. Sliding in at the 8 o'clock hour, the excited buzzing of mission-minded worker bees was a welcomed distraction from the suffocating pain of the last two weeks. Between herself, Michael and Michelle, Lisa needed a break.

"Welcome back, boss," Danita chirped as Lisa charged to her office. Her secretary's cubicle was pitched right outside and in easy access.

Lisa threw an appreciative smile, "Thanks, D," before stuffing the key into her office door and popping it open. Danita trailed behind.

The stuffiness in the room was a sign that it hadn't been occupied, along with the darkness from closed blinds. But when Danita started raising them, Lisa stopped her.

"Only halfway," she advised, with a slight grimace. She couldn't take too much light.

Danita nodded, "Gotcha," and slowed her roll.

The two coordinated the day's events, and Lisa spit out her marching orders. She was all business and it felt good to wear this hat again. Maybe life's tragic obstacles had blindsided her, but she was a straight badass when it came to journalism.

"Did you connect with Renee about finalizing her article for women's health?" Lisa asked. She had assigned Danita this task and cc'd her on emails with Renee while she was out.

"Yep. She's free today at 1 PM to meet if you're up for it." Danita didn't miss a beat and Lisa was once again, grateful for her assiduousness.

Lisa made the appointment with Renee for 1:30 PM because she had a virtual call with her counselor at noon. She didn't like virtual sessions but it was the earliest available, so she took it.

"Can you pick up a salad for me at lunch and drop it off? I'll be on a call and won't make it out." It took everything in Lisa to make this request. She hardly asked Danita for personal runs, even if it was just lunch, but she would need to adjust her Black-girl-magic-cape to get through this season.

"Of course," Danita assured with a hearty smile. "I got you."

At those words, the inner chamber of Lisa's heart shook. She fought back tears at the reminder of Michael's response in the hospital.

The look on Lisa's face must have made her inner angst apparent because Danita was at her side in an instant, warming her with a love-packed hug; one that Lisa hadn't even realized she was in need of.

"Thanks, D," she murmured into her friend's neckline.

The rest of the day was less eventful emotionally, for which Lisa was relieved. Her literary talents flourished while tackling the article Renee sent over. Renee had started the fibroids article and they had agreed via email that Lisa would add to it with her research. The two would then finalize it together. They would do the same for Lisa's piece for the music section. Lisa still had butterflies in her stomach about Renee being in such nearness to her precious position but decided this was a minute issue given what she was dealing with in her personal life. It wasn't until nearly noon that she took a breather before her counseling appointment and scrolled through social media.

Pictures of Michelle's birthday cruised by. They were her very last post. Lisa glowered. That event seemed light years away. Her daughter's smiling face while dripping wet in Sylvia's arms was a dream that Lisa wanted to last forever.

But nothing does, she thought bitterly.

Then a pleasant sensation smacked her when several notifications from Joe glowed on the screen. He had liked every single picture from the party, including the ones with Michael, which semi-surprised her. He even commented on one in particular.

"Looks just like her beautiful momma!" read beneath a photo of Lisa and Michelle in front of the pool. They were literally "twinning," which is what Lisa had written as the caption. The Doris girls cheesed so that both identical dimples made their debut.

Faster than her brain could process, Lisa's fingers flew as she sent Joe a direct message:

"Hey, it's so good to have reconnected with you. How are things?"

Only a slight hesitation slowed her but when she saw it was 11:59, and there was literally only a minute to spare, Lisa hit "send."

It's cool. I mean, he even liked the pics with Michael, so it's not like we aren't really *friends.*

Focusing on the video chat helped to swallow Lisa's concerns. It was almost time to deal with her loss. At exactly noon, Dr. Celia Johnson's inviting face flooded the screen.

"Lisa! How are things?" Celia's voice oozed care which was one of the reasons Lisa stuck with her after Natalie had given the referral. The woman was a delightful blend of authenticity, kindness and wisdom.

In response, Lisa licked her lips before braving a fragile smile. "It's ok. Thank you so much for fitting me in. I know you were booked." She fidgeted with the container of chicken cobb salad that Danita had sat on her desk ten minutes prior.

"Of course, dear. Now, you said it was an emergency. What's happening? Trouble in paradise?"

Lisa figured Dr. Celia was referring to her marriage. Dr. Celia had been her and Michael's go-to marriage counselor after a year of trying it on their own. Turns out, re-marrying your spouse can be even more difficult if there are old issues triggering you from the previously failed marriage. She and Michael had greatly benefited from Dr. Celia helping them sort through unhealthy ways of functioning.

Lisa started, "Well…a little this. A little that," and filled her in on all that had happened since their last meeting over a year ago. Dr. Celia hadn't even known Lisa was pregnant.

Celia frowned at the news. "I'm so sorry to hear that. I've had a miscarriage, so I know the loss of a child on some level. Though it wasn't all that you endured."

Lisa's brows rose. "Wow. I didn't know that."

Understanding wading in her eyes, Celia nodded. "Yes. Too many women have been through these experiences on varying levels. You would probably do well to be involved in a group where you can receive assistance in your healing. I'll recommend one that helped me. They actually have a virtual meeting, so you don't have to go in person."

For the first time since everything, Lisa felt encouraged. There were *groups* of women who understood this type of loss? Outside of Carol, she hadn't known any. Or, maybe they just hadn't told her?

"Thank you! That would be so helpful."

"Of course, dear. One of the things you'll have to keep in mind is that when you grieve, you'll also need to grieve the hope you attached to your child's future. I'm sure you had dreams and plans connected to Baby Lee, correct?"

Lisa nodded in earnest, digging into her salad and popping in a mouthful. "I'm sorry. I'm just really hungry," she explained.

Probably from all the bleeding. She was now taking iron pills to restore her hemoglobin levels.

"Oh, no worries. I'm waiting for my pizza to be delivered as we speak." The doctor laughed, her down-to-earth style a needed comfort.

"But yeah, there was so much planning involved," Lisa resumed. "Part of it is because I am, by nature a planner, and part of it is because Michael is too." Images of the crib lurking in their shared office gripped her mind. Hurt pinged her heart.

"Those are the things to keep in mind. The college he would have attended. The spouse he would have chosen. You would have experienced all of those things with Baby Lee, and as a result, will have to lay those to rest too."

Lisa sighed. She hadn't thought of that, but it made perfect sense. She knew she felt this huge loss and figured it was because she had carried Lee for almost six months, which was longer than people who went through miscarriages. Some babies were even born in that time. She also had the extra physical burden of having the C-section and waking up to receive the horrible news that he didn't make it. As a result, there was an actual fetus they had to cremate. Lisa had a literal visual of her child's life that didn't come to fruition. Now, she had to process that there was a future he didn't get to manifest. She would have to grieve Lee's future. She would have to grieve her own.

"The other thing to keep in mind is that Michael's grief and Michelle's grief may look different than yours," Dr. Celia advised. "In fact, it probably will. You were Lee's mother and felt him in your womb, so your grief is going to be from that standpoint. Michael is a man. After working with him personally, I can say, he probably feels a sense of letting you down. He takes his job of protecting his family seriously."

Lisa chewed her salad in thought. "You know my husband."

It felt like her therapist had simultaneously nailed his description on the head *and* given her insight as to how Michael would grieve.

Up until this point, Lisa hadn't realized that their roles as man and woman would influence *how* they grieved.

"I'm going to recommend you encourage Michael to do counseling. I know men are typically not thought of when there's a miscarriage or similar death of a child, but they go through the loss too. They just tend to deal with it differently."

"Yeah. He had mentioned counseling prior to all this." Lisa frowned. "So, I know he's open. I just don't know if he's made the connection that he needs it for *this*." She thought about how Michael had been pushing forward with work and hadn't slowed down at all. Was diving into work projects his way to fill the void of losing their son?

The rest of the hour flew by as Lisa took notes and tried to remember all that Celia had shared.

"Let's schedule another session in two weeks. I want to monitor your progress in healing," Celia said with a sincere smile. She dropped her calendar link in the chat box and informed that she would email some resources.

"Sounds good." Lisa ended the call, lighter and encouraged. She had a ways to go in her healing but now there seemed to be hope that she could get there.

A nagging in her stomach tugged at her though. She realized she had failed to mention to Celia the reason for her emergency C-section. The Placenta Previa that had been discovered, that had caused her to faint, that had caused excessive bleeding and that ultimately ended her son's existence. Lisa wrestled with why this didn't come up. But there was no time to even process it because her meeting with Renee was upon her.

Huffing in exhaustion, she gathered her things. Her body was still in recovery and it was taking all of Lisa's energy to carry out her normal work duties.

I just hope this girl isn't trippin'. I seriously don't know if I have it in me to deal with Renee's shenanigans today.

When Lisa emailed Renee, she only said that she was ill. As far as Lisa knew, Renee didn't know what caused an illness that made her MIA for two weeks. Bowing her head to her loose cashmere cream sweater, it was clear she was no longer pregnant, though her belly was still swollen. But even with the sweater being loose, Lisa's previous belly would have bulged through the material.

Well, I guess she'll know now, she thought, regarding Renee, while heading to one of the smaller meeting rooms.

Danita was already waiting with Renee and her eyes searched Lisa's, asking a question only Lisa could decipher: *You ok?* To which Lisa gave a slight nod before slipping on her work smile.

"Hey Renee, thanks so much for your flexibility, in handling this article. My apologies that I couldn't work with you in person." The rehearsed sentences rolled off Lisa's tongue, but even on the tail-end of them, she caught the rapid flutter of Renee's eyelids lower to her abdomen. Slapping away the rush of pain, she jumped into their meeting.

The two women, surprisingly, worked well together and Lisa was thankful for Renee's pertinacious work ethic and straightforward writing style. She was succinct, yet considerate when tackling the issue on fibroids. Since Lisa had navigated her own issue with fibroids, which seemed to have led to her diagnosis of Placenta Previa, which in turn caused her emergency C-section, she felt she had a bone in this fight.

"I'd like to add my personal interview as a source," Lisa heard herself volunteering. The surprise in Renee and Danita's faces reflected her own. It was then when Lisa heard as clear as day:

I work all things for the good, Beloved.

The passage of scripture referenced from Romans 8:28 was a gentle reminder of the Father's goodness. A goodness that Lisa had grappled with since that traumatic day. She had barely attempted to talk to God after the memorial for her Lee. Though without a doubt, God was the one who had given her the strength to cremate her child and stand before her loved ones. Still, it confused her that He allowed it to happen. Especially since she had prayed so vehemently for it not to.

"Ok. That can happen," Renee responded to Lisa's offer to be interviewed. She flipped her sisterlocks onto one beefy shoulder. "When do you want it done?"

"How about now?" Lisa shoved her things out of the way so that Renee was closer in proximity.

Danita, sitting inches from Renee, hopped to her feet, "I'll get a recorder," and was out the door.

Renee switched a little in her seat, hips flirting with the sturdy chair arms. "Umm. You sure about this?" Her round face took on an uncharacteristic softness that Lisa didn't know how to receive, so she discarded it. The last thing she wanted was anyone's pity.

"I've got it," Lisa answered in an incontestable tone.

Danita was back in no time, handing the recorder to Renee and grasping a pen and pad for backup. The interview was thorough, efficient and smooth. Lisa had to give it to Renee, she was an excellent interviewer. She literally was conducting it on the spot but delivered as if she had been preparing all week.

"Thanks, Lisa. I'll type it up and shoot it over for you to tweak," Renee informed, finishing up her notes.

Lisa shook her head in agreement. "Ok. I'll have my feedback to you by tomorrow, depending on when I receive it. We should be able to start the music article on Swizz Beatz. You can sit in my meeting with his PR team tomorrow morning if you're free."

Lisa was thankful to Alicia Keys for the connect with her hubby. Apparently, their interview had gone so well that she gave him the referral and Swizz Beatz' manager reached out to Lisa. That's when you knew you were making moves. When the artist reached out to *you*.

A slight tug appeared at the corner of Renee's mouth at the opportunity to be in the room with the artist and his team. But the woman at least had the decency not to give in to it. Instead, she dipped her head in acknowledgment and kept her professionalism.

Still, Lisa's gut bubbled. *Lord, please don't let this woman take my job.*

The prayer sprouted from out of nowhere. But then, Lisa buried it, because, you just never knew what God would allow to be taken.

Danita shuffled her notes. "You need anything? I'm gonna type these up and shoot 'em over."

"Nope, you're good," Lisa replied. "Thanks, D."

Danita exited the room as Lisa started packing her messenger bag. Though she had brought her laptop, she had never even needed it. When she was done packing, she caught up with Renee at the entrance, but while attempting to walk by, Renee stuck a hand to her back. Turning in confusion, Lisa faced her, thinking that maybe she had left something on the table. But when she looked into her colleague's eyes, all she saw was sympathy. The hand she felt gently transformed into a sincere rub.

"Lisa," Renee paused and swayed in her stark black Mary Jane's, looking uncertain.

Lisa slanted her head slightly. "Yes?"

"I just wanted to say," Renee cleared her throat, paused again, then rushed on. "I'm sorry for your loss."

Mind wrought with shock, Lisa's eyes widened. Wow. Her arch enemy, her toughest rival, her meanest competitor, was, *sorry for her loss?* And in that moment, she knew her circumstances must be very dire indeed.

"Umm. Thank you." Lisa shifted her gaze downward and mindlessly rubbed her stomach. "That means a lot." And the crazy thing was, she meant it.

With that, the two women walked out, in sync, for the first time ever in their careers.

~

"The nuttiest thing about the day was how well Renee and I got along."

That evening Lisa was stirring the pot of stew that Carol had brought upstairs. It was a hearty concoction of steak strips, seasoning and veggies. The aroma flooded the house with much-needed warmth.

"And you say you guys have *never* gotten along?" Carol asked, while leaning on the counter and sipping a goblet glass of Merlot.

Lisa nodded in response, eyeing the delicious red hue. There *was* one solitary benefit to no longer being pregnant. She could drink.

Stirring the stainless-steel pot a little more, Lisa set the label on the counter before joining her friend with her own glass. They drifted to the living room where Michelle quietly played a game on Michael's tablet. He had texted Lisa that he would be late and that they should eat without him. This wasn't a surprise as he had been working late since last week. Lisa couldn't remember them eating together that week at all as a family. Not even for breakfast.

"You would be surprised at how people respond to miscarriages and similar losses," Carol advised. "It could be that Renee's lost a child."

"It trips me out how common miscarriages are and how many women have endured losing children in different ways," Lisa marveled. She folded her legs behind her while taking a swig and a rush of pleasure sewn into the silky substance slid down her throat.

Mmmm.

"I agree," Carol responded. "I didn't know the measure of support that was out there until my second miscarriage when I finally talked to my mom about it. She told me all my aunts had them. I have four aunts."

Lisa's jaw dropped. "Four?" she repeated in disbelief.

Carol agreed with sad eyes. "Only two of them have had children since. One of them even had to deliver a stillborn."

A shutter of heartbreak racked Lisa's body. She related to that kind of loss. Even though she was asleep it felt like something had been ripped from her body after she realized Lee had died. Still, being awake and delivering him would have been its own nightmare on Elm Street.

The conversation, as heavy as it was, was a hug to Lisa's heart. She so appreciated the timing of her friendship with Carol, who provided an empathetic ear. She had become a helpful guide in navigating this unwanted path. Nearing the end of their time together, Lisa mentioned the virtual group Dr. Celia told her about, and Carol eagerly agreed to tap in. Carol also brought up the morning devotionals New Life was doing.

"I know you've had a lot going on, so I didn't want to press, but, I've been doing the morning devotional from your church. I really think it could help during this time," Carol said. Her blue eyes sparkled with care.

"Oh yeah?" A splinter of fear pricked Lisa's heart. Doing a devotional would be a step toward reconnecting with God. Right now, it felt like she and God were standing on opposite ends of a room. God was beckoning her to come, and Lisa was looking at Him side-eyed while weighing her options.

"Umm, I guess it couldn't hurt," Lisa finally managed before sipping. Her stomach turned over and she needed something to calm her. This wine seemed to be doing the trick.

"Great!" Carol's voice was a basket of love. "The devotional we're reading is *Jesus Calling* by Sarah Young. So far it's been a life-giver. Every devotion seems to be jam-packed with encouragement for hard things."

Hmm, Jesus Calling. Well, I guess this is Jesus calling me, Lisa thought, then chuckled at herself. Carol gave her a strange look. "Sorry, girl," she blurted. "I'm just trippin' on this wine." Carol giggled in response. "But, I'm in."

Lisa knew she needed to do *something* to activate her faith and she was going to need all the help she could get. This *Jesus Calling* thing may just be it.

Carol ended their discussion, agreeing to call Lisa in the morning to make sure she was awake. The devotional started at 4:30 am and ended at 5 am. That would give Lisa enough time to start breakfast.

"Thanks again for the soup," Lisa said, leading Carol out the door. "You sure you don't want to take some for you and Robbie?"

"Nah. We're eating green bean casserole. But I do need to hurry because we have our show to watch at eight o' clock."

Carol ducked to slip on her all-white Sperry's ankle boots. When she popped back up, she caged Lisa into a bear hug. Lisa inhaled deeply and let out her breath over her friend's shoulder. Her heart swelled before releasing her and showing her the door.

"I'll talk to you in the morning," Carol turned to say.

Lisa was just about to respond, but after opening the door and peering out, she suddenly lost all of her words. Because right in front of Carol, stood a tall, wide-shouldered figure whose face Lisa hadn't seen in person in months, but would recognize in any crowded room. The tightly wound curls, debonair, clean-shaven appearance, round large button brown eyes that were a screaming resemblance to her own, all blasted alarm bells.

"Dad?" Lisa heard herself whisper in utter shock. She was so shocked in fact, that she didn't even realize she hadn't called her father by his first name.

Now You Know How it Feels

CHAPTER 13

Hank Pedersen fiddled outside the apartment door standing ominously closed. It had taken every last one of his nerves for this trip, but the incessant back and forth between his inner dialogue had become too great a burden. When the third phone call made to his daughter had gone unrequited, and Michael finally filled him in on Baby Lee's death, Hank knew. It was time. It was finally time to repair what was lost. But in the past, every time he tried, things seemed to go left. Several provocative conversations with his wife, Novelle, who kept urging him to go, forced Hank to congregate every last bit of bravery. Relinquishing all hesitancy, he made the six-hour drive to Manhattan.

Figuring that calling Lisa would mean another ignored attempt, Hank texted Michael instead, letting him know he was getting on the road. Michael informed he would be home late, but Lisa would be there and gave Hank the building code.

When the apartment door swung open, it was as much a surprise to Hank as it clearly was for Lisa. Hank had gotten so tangled in his fears that hesitation had him rooted in the same spot. For the last fifteen minutes he hadn't been able to knock.

Lisa gasped, eyes big, mouth flailed open. It was only when Hank saw her visitor that he realized, *This could be bad timing.*

"Uhh. Oh. I didn't know you had company," tumbled out of Hank's mouth before he could snatch back the words.

Lord. Help, please!

God's inner peace became a satchel enclosing Hank's heart. Still, he worked his lower lip, his eyes laser-beaming Lisa around her friend's helmet of curls.

"Oh!" the friend cried in surprise. "I'm sorry. I'm Carol." Carol extended her hand with a sweet round face, both blue eyes staring curiously at him. "And you are..." she abandoned the question for a stealthy look at Lisa, who was standing beside her.

"He was just leaving," Lisa responded through tight lips and a placid face. Her beautiful browns glinted in anger.

Hank winced. Her statement had slapped him.

"Papa Hank!" Michelle's voice screeched from across the living room as she hurled her little body toward the adults. But before she could make it to him, Lisa stood, a planted fortress between them.

"Michelle, go back to your game."

The sentence was an order, not a statement, and Hank's hope, which had soared at his granddaughter's eagerness, came crashing down.

Lord, how am I gonna do this?

You can do all things through Christ who strengthens you (Phil 4:13) said the still, small voice that Hank was still getting used to.

For nearly thirty years, Hank had been out of church, but that didn't matter to God. When he suddenly cried out after learning Novelle had been diagnosed with cancer, the faith he'd run from most of his life flooded him in an instant. God walked them through chemo, hair loss, and the subsequent removal of one of her breasts. Hank had experienced firsthand a divine miracle. He still had his Novelle, but what he didn't have was his daughter. That longing for Lisa seemed to grow in congruency to his faith. He hated that he had to leave her as a child. Hated that he had to go his own way. But her mother rarely let him see Lisa when he reached out. Sighing inwardly, Hank's eyes searched Lisa's, pleading for a chance to rectify his wrongs.

Carol awkwardly moved out of the way, intending to slide through the little opening that separated Hank from the rest of his family.

"Well, umm. I'm going to go and let you guys…er…visit." Nervous laughter punctuated Carol's announcement, but then she thought about it, turned around, and swooped Lisa into another hug.

Care squeezed Hank's heart. *It's good to know she has friends,* he thought, comforted by at least that fact.

Though it seemed like an endless amount of time, it was probably only a few moments, when Carol made her exit.

Michelle stared at him from the halfway point between the kitchen and the living room, her face a fusion of excitement, confusion, and intrigue. "You came to visit me, Papa Hank?" She braved the question from a distance.

"Michelle."

Who knew one word could contain a whole sentence? Lisa had said it without flinching, eyes glued to Hank, mouth drawn in a firm line.

Heeding the implied warning, Michelle scurried to her prior position on the living room floor.

"I came a long way, Lisa."

"I didn't ask you to come."

"I told Michael I was coming." The look on Lisa's face told Hank everything he needed to know. She blinked. "Michael didn't tell you?"

The hardened armor of his daughter's expression melted into disbelief, and Hank was at a loss for words. How could Michael not tell her?

"I-I wouldn't have come had I not thought I shouldn't…" he trailed off, fumbling for the right words. "I'm sorry about Lee."

The comment seemed to jolt his daughter because the incredulousness in her eyes swiftly morphed into stinging fury.

"Don't say his name." Her words were ice and Hank could sense the winter storm brewing beneath them.

Lisa was so much like him. They were cut from the same cloth. It was his stubbornness, his tenaciousness, his bullheadedness that had brought down his first marriage. It was Novelle's oozing patience and easy-going style that had won Hank to Christ. Lisa's mother, Vanessa, was too much like him too. That's why they couldn't work. That, and the pills she was popping. He had to leave.

Hank shook his head at the memories that haunted him. If there was one thing he had learned while journeying in his new faith it was that God made everything new (Rev 21:5).

"I'm staying at The Four Seasons. I'll be there all week. I want to see you." His eyes skidded past her to the living room where Michelle was. "I want to see Michelle."

"I wanted a lot of things growing up, but I didn't get them. Did I, Hank?" Lisa had both arms covering her chest. Her voice was steel. Her chin jutted.

The scolding in the usage of his first name stung. Hank tried to keep it from making him flee all the way back to Ohio.

"I'll be waiting," he said with a crack in his tone.

Shoulders drooping in his tan Kenneth Cole peacoat, Hank turned to leave, hands in his pockets, head crisply bowed. But then, suddenly, he stopped in his tracks and whipped back around.

"I love you."

Not awaiting a response, he pivoted on his patent leather Oxford heels, praying to God the whole time that he had done the right thing in coming.

THE HOUR AFTER HANK LEFT WAS A STIFLING ONE, MUDDLED WITH inner turmoil. Lisa set the bowl of soup on the table for Michelle but she held no appetite of her own. So she did what she hardly ever did and allowed Michelle to play her game while eating.

Screen time be damned.

Part of Lisa's logic in doing this was due to her own lack of appetite. This, coupled with Michael's absence, meant that her daughter would be eating alone. The other part was to cut Michelle's string of questions that began as soon as Lisa dismissed her father. One stare from Lisa did shut Michelle up, but then Lisa felt bad. Letting her daughter continue with her game was a peace offering.

In the wake of this sudden surprise visit, and as Michelle ate dinner, Lisa curled on the couch, stunned out of her mind. Neo Soul floated in the room, as she was using it to calm her nerves, along with another glass of wine. She took a long sip.

This is some straight bull. My father is so freaking selfish and inconsiderate. Who just pops up at someone's door like that expecting to be catered to?

But then, she flashed back to his words: *"Michael didn't tell you?"*

Michael.

Michael knew and didn't tell me? What the hell is that about?

The nervous jitter in her foot see-sawed it back and forth as Lisa stared at her phone toggled on the edge of her kneecap. She wanted so badly to call Sylvia but when she went to pick up Michelle earlier, Sylvia mentioned it was Bingo night at church. Lisa thought of Carol but it was enough that Carol saw the man in the flesh she had just broken down about weeks ago. As much as she appreciated their budding friendship, it was still new and unpacking the decades of trauma with her father didn't bid well. Natalie and Danita were both options but the former was still her junior. Lisa always felt a little weird leaning on Natalie as a result, even though, out of her friend group, Natalie would probably relate the most. Danita was a great listening ear but didn't really offer the mentoring guidance she received from Sylvia. She was more of a sista-friend and would give something of a "Yeah, girl, me too," response or, "You wanna go slash his tires?" suggestion, especially if heartbreak was involved. It was while Lisa weighed these possibilities that she had popped open her social media account. Her eyes glistened.

Joe! I forgot I reached out to him.

Flicking open her DM's, she read his message fast.

Lisa, it's been a ride for sure. Life has its surprises and yet God has been faithful. I've been making some changes in my career and hoping to launch my own business in the next six months. I've been pretty focused as a result. I can see you and the fam are doing well. That Michelle has grown up so fast! I remember when she was a little thing. But she is still your spitting image. Looks like you have another one on the way. Congrats! I'm sure Michael is happy to be having a boy :-)

A bitter smile stole Lisa's lips. It warmed her soul that Joe was still the same caring, kind individual she remembered from years ago, but his mention of Lee was a stabbing reminder of her remorse. Before she could chicken out, her fingers started pecking.

Joe, thank you for your beautiful words. You're still the amazing man I remembered. I'm sad to share, I actually lost our precious baby boy. I wish I had better news, but it's the reality we're all trying to cope with. I'm still in the midst of grappling with it as it was only a couple of weeks ago. I know you're a praying man. If you remember, say a prayer for me. I have no doubt God hears your pure heart.

After re-reading the message, Lisa hit send, the act soon followed by a sip of Merlot. It was so good to say those words: "I know you are a praying man."

Why can't Michael be a praying man?

At that moment, a memory of being with Joe crept from the basement of Lisa's mind. They were at a worship service at Joe's church, and for some reason, Michelle wasn't with them. Maybe because it was being held all night. Joe had invited Lisa, and although she was still on the fence about religion, she went. That service was a breadcrumb leading to the promised land. Lisa couldn't deny that whatever Joe was experiencing was something she craved. His face, tilted to the sky, shone with peace and love. She had never witnessed a man who was so masculine cry unabashedly before. She figured his display of emotion was a reaction to what he was experiencing spiritually and she couldn't stop her heart from being drawn to him. There was just something attractive about a man who openly shared his feelings without needing a crowbar to pry them loose.

"Mommy, I'm done." Michelle stood, waving an empty bowl from the table, ripping Lisa from her trip down memory lane. She nearly jumped out of her skin.

"Ok. Put it in the sink and start your bath," Lisa advised from her position on the couch. This was their nightly routine. Since Michael's work hours were topsy-turvy, he was hit or miss for dinner but usually home by story time. Lisa and Michael rotated on who Michelle would read to. Tonight, it was her turn.

As the bath water ran, Lisa's phone dinged. She looked down, thinking it could be Michael informing her he was on his way, but instead, she found a notification on her social media account. Apparently, Joe was online.

"I'm so sorry to hear that, Lisa. I can't imagine what you're going through. Being a man, I commend women for everything they sacrifice for the human life experience to exist. You will certainly be in my prayers. My sis actually lost a child a few years ago. It wasn't during birth but still a tragedy. Would you like me to ask her for resources to assist in your healing?"

Lisa's heart swelled with sorrow. Joe's sister lost a child? There were just too many hard things in this life. But her waywardness in responding lasted a bit. Should she take Joe up on his offer? Lisa couldn't deny the fondness that burst in her heart at the memory of his church. Would her response prolong the contact between them she wasn't even sure they should be having? Instead of making a definitive decision, she closed her social media app and started scrolling through emails. Renee had sent her the interview she did for the fibroids article. As adeptly as if she hadn't had two glasses of wine, Lisa edited it, the work sharpening her focus. But then, afterward, she was reminded of Joe's message again. She had left him unread.

"Mommy, I'm ready!"

Lisa nearly dropped the phone. She had just been about to respond.

"Ok, baby," she half-called, half-shrieked to her daughter. "I'm coming."

The sight of Michelle snuggled in a lace-pink nightgown with a glittery crown stamped on the front warmed Lisa. "Grab your comb and brush," she directed and waited for Michelle to comply.

As Michelle chatted about her new friend, Gabby, Lisa worked on her tresses. It was much easier to do Michelle's hair the night before school rather than in the morning when they were bustling about, trying not to be late. In the morning, she could just touch things up.

"Mommy, are you going to see Papa Hank?"

The question was inevitable, but it still jarred Lisa from her thoughts of Joe.

"I haven't decided," she replied honestly. The drawl in her speech indicated that that last glass of wine may have been one too many. Lisa narrowed her concentration on the thick braid clutched in her hand.

"Well, if you decide, can I go too?"

Michelle was such a determined child and under normal circumstances, Lisa would have been proud of her tenacity. But right now, her persistence was only irritating.

Instead of answering, Lisa said, "Turn your head," and pushed down Michelle's head to the side a little too roughly.

"Ow!"

"I'm sorry," Lisa replied, but continued the job of braiding. The sooner she could finish this girl's hair and hear her bedtime story, the better.

An hour later, Michelle dozed off after a Jerry Craft fan favorite and just as Lisa was peering at her phone to check the time, the door clicked open.

Finally, she thought. Frustrated, she gripped her phone while standing up from the canopy. *This brotha better have a good reason for bringing this ridiculousness to my doorstep.*

The conglomerate of emotions Lisa had been swimming in

sloshed and lapped the rim of her mind, but anger won out, shooting to the surface. White. Searing. Anger.

After Hank left, Lisa considered calling her husband but decided against it. She wanted to see Michael's face when she confronted him. The audacity to keep something like that from her!

"You're home late," she greeted, slanting against the wall that led to the kitchen. Her arms sat crossed, both hands choking her elbows to control her mounting fury.

Michael had his back to her as he slipped off his shoes and placed them on the shoe rack.

"Yeah. We're working on end of year, so you know how it is." He kept his voice neutral, though his head peeked in her direction.

"Carol brought soup. You want some?" she offered. Her voice sounded a little too thick, so she made an extra effort to sober up by clearing her throat.

"I already ate." Michael had half-turned toward her after putting his coat on the rack. "But thanks," he added, seemingly as an afterthought.

He was in his usual dress shirt and slacks and Lisa could see the weariness in his expression. Her resolve caved a little at the discovery. She had to remind herself, she was tired too.

"Hank came by," Lisa said, deciding to just lay it out right there. To her surprise, her husband didn't make any adjustments to his expression. He just placed his suitcase on the counter and headed to the fridge.

"Did you hear me?" she asked.

"Yep. I heard you." Michael grabbed a glass from the cupboard and she was now in his peripheral.

"You not gone' ask me how it went?" Lisa was astounded.

I can't believe he is being so damn nonchalant about this.

"How did it go?" Michael's voice was robotic as he pressed the glass against the water dispenser on the stainless-steel machine. The silence between them was only broken by the streaming liquid.

Instead of answering his question, Lisa pounced on him. His, *I don't care demeanor* was pissing her off.

"He said you told him to come. He said you *gave* him the building code? Is that true?"

Michael sighed and turned to look her straight in the eyes for the first time that evening. "Yeah. I gave him the code. I told him you would be here."

Hurt pierced Lisa. The fact that this man had the balls to look her in the eye while telling her that he intentionally defied her wishes was insanity. But after the hurt, there was only outrage.

"Sooo," she dragged out. "Even though you *know* I'm not ready to talk to him, you *know* I'm still working through the pain and letdowns of how he's moved my *whole* entire life, and what I've been through just trying to restore myself from that man, you keep something like this from me? *And* encourage his ass to come down here?"

Each word climbed in something mixed with shock and hysteria. Maybe it was the wine from earlier, maybe it was the grief, but Lisa could feel herself becoming *unhinged.* In fact, she had stepped towards Michael, her neck rolling, her face full of malice, her finger in his face.

But Michael didn't back down. Instead, he scoffed and shook his head in disgust. "You you you," he spat. "It's always about chu', huh? You march around this house, charging orders and dictating everyone's every move to carry out *your* vision for this family."

"What? What in the hell are you talking about, Michael? I'm up every morning at 4 am *slaving* and serving this damn family. I'm not the one who has the luxury of sleeping in and rolling over when it's time to get Michelle ready for school. Get her hair done. Make sure she makes her carpool."

Lisa was livid. How dare he accuse her of dictatorship! If this was her way of dictating, why the hell was she exhausted from all the sacrifices she was making?

If I was a freaking dictator, I would be propped up with my feet somewhere chillin' on a damn beach with a Mai Tai.

Michael charged past her to the living room. Pillows were thrown out of the way before he started removing his shirt. "I'm sleeping on the couch," he muttered.

Lisa was flabbergasted. "So, that's all you have to say? You tell my father to come down here, *knowing* I wouldn't be on board, *intentionally* keeping it from me, and you not even gone' apologize?" Her heart was hammering in her ears. Her mind raced like a corvette.

Is this the man you told me to marry, Lord? The question sprouted amidst the intensity of Lisa's feelings.

Instead of answering, Michael gestured at the empty wine glass and bottle sitting atop the dinner table. "Have you been drinking?"

He said it accusingly, as if their current topic of conversation paled in comparison to her having a glass of wine. Or two.

Lisa huffed a defensive sigh. "Yes, Michael. I had a *couple* of glasses of wine *with Carol*. Is that a problem?" she asked in a hardened tone, daring him to disagree.

"Just two?" he asked and Lisa knew why. Since her mother was an addict, she had to keep a close eye on all things substance-use related. She hardly ever had more than two glasses of wine at a time. But that was even before she met Michael.

"I don't need you keeping count of my drinks. I'm a dictator, remember? I can dictate myself."

Michael just stared at her and Lisa glared back. Finally, he strangled his pillow while lying down, and flipped his back to her.

Pathetic, Lisa thought in disgust.

Once again, her husband was Fort Knox and she was iced out. It was then that the similarities between Michael and her father became apparent. Arguments from when her parents were married bombarded Lisa's mind. The ice storm coldness between them. The suffocating silences that lagged for days, even weeks at a time. The divorce was actually a relief. Then, she only had to deal with one ridiculous parent.

Just as Lisa was about to leave and head to their bedroom, Michael's voice stopped her in her tracks.

"Now you know how it feels," he grumbled against the stillness of their home.

Lisa's skin crawled. *What is he talking about?*

Turning back around, she asked, "Know how what feels?"

"Now you know how it feels to not be told something important and be kept out of the loop," he spat. This time he shifted his head to face her and she saw the grievous expression that masked his features.

Her heart squeezed. It was then that Lisa knew for certain. Michael was punishing her for their child's death.

Waiving a White Flag

CHAPTER 14

The ear-splitting ringing was a necessary, yet unwelcomed greeting to the morning. Every day for the past week, Lisa had been missing the *Jesus Calling* devotional meetings. Partly because her phone had been on Do Not Disturb out of habit and Carol's calls were missed, and partly because, subconsciously, and maybe not so subconsciously, she had been wrestling with God. Wrestling with God wasn't the wisest thing, since, as the saying went, He always won. Still, Lisa was going to drag out this match for as long as it took for her to stop feeling so angry.

"Ugh," she groaned while slapping the alarm clock on the night-stand. The clock glared back. 4:15 am.

It wasn't like Lisa wasn't used to getting up early. It was more like, her motivation for getting up early had vanished. After her fight with Michael earlier in the week where he accused her of being a dictator, Lisa decided that her service to her family wasn't appreci-ated. As a result, there were no bougie breakfasts. Michelle had been living off oatmeal, toast and an occasional turkey sausage for the last few days. Michael had been smart enough to not even eat at home. Lisa hadn't seen him at a meal all week.

Well, that's his problem, she mused while sitting up and stretching.

Fumbling to the bathroom, she washed the dried tear stains from her cheeks. The night before, Lisa had cried herself to sleep. In fact, she had cried herself to sleep every night for the past week. Her family was a mess and she was tangled in the weeds of grief. Michael had stuck to his guns by sleeping on the couch. Obviously he was sending her a message by not taking responsibility and apologizing for his role in the Hank situation. He blamed her for losing their child, and this was his payback. On top of that, Lisa's window of seeing Hank was closing. If her father meant what he said, today would be his last at The Four Seasons.

After digging crust from her eyes and running her toothbrush through her mouth, Lisa drummed out a closed-mouth sigh.

What the hell am I going to do about Hank?

But the gentle quiet of the early morning was its own soothing melody. The achiness of Lisa's heart somehow seemed less achy in its wake as she plopped on her bed, folded her legs, and reached for her Bible. It had been a while since she'd flipped open its pages, preferring her Bible app at church over lugging around a huge book. But the thin paper did bring a comforting vintage feel.

The meetings started at 4:30 am on the dot. At least, that's what Carol had said, so Lisa hurried to locate the Zoom link in her texts.

Lord, if You could just give me a sign that things will get better.

The prayer shot up from the depths of her core, bringing with it confusion. If she was supposed to be wrestling with God, then this prayer may just be a white flag. But Lisa drop-kicked the thought of surrender to the side before hopping on the Zoom call.

An Italian woman with long wavy hair, full red lips, and an easy smile was leading the meeting. You wouldn't even know it was the crack of dawn by looking at her.

Some people are just made for this hour, Lisa thought, with slight humor.

The woman welcomed everyone and thanked them for joining. Carol's name popped up shortly after Lisa entered the chat room. The virtual meeting settings didn't allow the attendees to speak but they could use their video. Lisa opted out of that one. She wasn't camera-ready, as evidenced by her puffy red eyes and silky hair bonnet.

The meeting began with the leader, Sofia, reading from the devotional. Although Lisa didn't have a copy, she was able to pull it online on her laptop. When she saw that the topic was forgiveness, her heart jumped a little. Luke 17:4, the NIV version, was the referenced verse.

"Even if they sin against you seven times in a day and seven times come back to you saying, 'I repent,' you must forgive them."

A picture of Lisa's father standing at the doorway from earlier that week flashed before her eyes.

Sofia finished the reading before expounding on her personal life and how the devotional pertained to her.

"I grew up in a single-parent home. My mom was a great mom but my longing for my dad just never seemed to go away. I struggled so much in my relationships with men as a result. I kept trying to find acceptance and approval from men but it was really the acceptance I wanted from my dad. Finally, when I was older and came to Christ, I was able to receive healing. God became my Father. But even in that experience, I still desired my earthly father."

Lisa's stomach started doing somersaults. This woman's story was too close to home. With each word she shared, goosebumps inched up Lisa's forearms.

"I finally worked up enough nerve to reach out to my dad," Sofia continued. "We actually lived in the same city. It was crazy we never saw each other, or that I never saw my half-siblings."

Thoughts of Lisa's two half-sisters, Candace and Gina, flooded her mind's eye. Gina was the oldest and a sophomore in college. Ironically, she attended Lisa's alma mater, Clark Atlanta University. Lisa was 14 years older than her. Hank married their mother, Novelle, only a year after he divorced her mom and then out popped Gina. It was like he couldn't wait to start a new family. At least, that's how it felt to Lisa. Then, five years later, Candace was on the scene. By the time the child could speak a full sentence, Lisa was in her mid-twenties, married to Michael and working on starting her own family. She was in a whole different life stage. What was she going to even talk to the girl about? Plus, Lisa barely had a stable relationship with her father, so she'd never once considered trying to establish one with her half-sisters. As far as she was concerned, she was an only child.

"It was so wild to get to know them because I saw how many similarities we had, even though we hadn't grown up together," Sofia shared and peace hugged her face.

Envy tugged at Lisa. *She looks—happy.*

Memories of that same exhilaration from when Lisa first came to Christ surfaced. It was like discovering this newfound love that she had never known existed. Could it be that restoring her relationship with her father could create the same euphoria? It seemed to have done so for Sofia.

"It hasn't been easy," Sofia went on, "but we're making it work. One day at a time. And it all started with forgiveness. I had to forgive my dad for the choices of his past. I had to forgive him for not being there. For being human."

For being human.

Lisa let the statement bake in her mind. It was true that as an adult, and now a parent, she could see how easy it was to blame a parent for falling short. She thought of how she had been treating Michelle this week, not giving her a fancy meal because of her fight with Michael. Michelle didn't know she was caught in the crossfires. She could very well take the change in treatment personally and think *she* did something wrong.

A settling resided in Lisa's gut, and she shifted her position. As Sofia went on in closing, Lisa's heart unthawed. A single tear streamed its way down her face and the presence of God enveloped her.

Father, why is it so hard for me to forgive him? she asked quietly, capitalizing on the supernatural moment.

As I have forgiven you, forgive him.

The response in her heart seemed to caress the early morning hour that fondled the room.

When the meeting ended, and just when Lisa was going to close out the Zoom call, her screen was interrupted by a call from

Carol. Tapping the accept button, she flung the lone tear from her eye.

"Good Morning!" Carol bubbled, clearly a morning person. "I saw you caught the meeting."

A watery smile dressed Lisa's lips. "Yeah," she answered quietly. "I did."

Carol's face collapsed in concern. "You ok, hon? I know that was a tough one," she added, ever so thoughtful.

"Yeah. It was."

Lisa's shoulders deflated and something swirled in her heart that she couldn't put her finger on. But after she confided in Carol all that she had gotten out of the devotional and how she felt God wanted her to forgive her father, she realized what that swirling settled feeling was. She felt—surrendered.

～

CARL MILLER WAS IN HIS BAG, CHARGING DIRECTIVES AND delegating tasks to each worker like a pro. Lisa had to give it to him, he was good at what he did. They all were. Scanning the writer's meeting, she realized, once again, Jazz had le crême de la crême. Each person's unparalleled talent and uncanny knack for delivering excellence buoyed the ten-year magazine. This enabled them to swim the shores of the shark tank of New York City. No other independent magazine had lasted that long. The original owners, the Bowman Brothers, were still in charge and kept their offices on the tenth floor. The other execs were stationed on that floor as well. Lisa only caught glimpses of the men in suits and wondered if they would ever hire a woman. As much as she loved that her people had their own mag, the need for female equality was still a thing. Even within the Black community. Maybe especially so.

"Lisa, can I see you for a sec?" Carl called after her just as Lisa was packing up her laptop. The meeting had ended, and everyone scattered the room like ants at a picnic.

She glanced at Danita. "I'll see you in a few. Tell Renee I'm on my way," she advised.

When the coast was clear, Carl made a feeble attempt at a smile. At least, Lisa thought it was an attempt. She had never actually seen the man smile or be happy. Or, friendly for that matter. Their interactions were mostly him barking orders or henpecking her about deadlines.

"Anything I can do for you, Carl?" Lisa's work voice was sharply dressed in politeness. She always kept it polite and professional with Carl. The fewer words she said to him, the quicker she could meet his objectives and get back to what she loved: journalism.

Carl hefted his six-foot, lumpy frame against the U-shaped conference table that furnished the room. Other than the row of windows stamped across the east wing, there was nothing snazzy about the room. It was proficient in doing its job. Lisa liked to think of herself the same way.

As Carl fiddled with his bushy black mustache, she realized with a tad bit of horror, *He's nervous.*

Her boss's unease ignited her own, and butterflies began fluttering rapidly in Lisa's midsection.

"Lisa, you're one of our brightest and best, you know," Carl started.

Uh oh. Is this man about to fire me? Queasiness latched around her stomach like a belt.

"I know things haven't been easy for you lately," he added, glancing down at Lisa's silk blouse stuffed inside her navy-blue pencil skirt. She had her pre-pregnancy wasteline back, as evidenced by the form-fitting outfit, and figured Carl's lowered gaze was implying the miscarriage.

Confirming her suspicions, Carl cleared his throat and ventured, "How are things in that department, by the way?"

If Lisa hadn't been so worried about his gearing up to fire her, she would have been stunned by the care in her boss's tone *and* the uncharacteristic personal line of questioning.

"I-I" she stuttered and needed to take a breath to re-compose herself. The man had completely caught her off guard. "I'm working through things," Lisa finally managed. "Thank you for asking," she finished lamely, trying to digest the oddness of the whole ordeal with one deep swallow.

"Good," he said and the relief in his tone was evident. Carl twisted his neck behind him, hesitated a second, then made an executive decision to shut the door. This move *really* threw Lisa and she wondered if she should be sitting for this conversation.

If he fires me, I don't want to accidentally faint and knock myself unconscious.

Her boss returned to his former spot and took the same stance, but his tone suddenly turned conspiratorial.

"Look. You've been here, what five, six years?"

Carl's beady eyes drilled into her and Lisa feared she was about to fail some kind of exam if she answered incorrectly.

She shook her head up and down, the pesky lump in her throat refusing to disintegrate no matter how many times she swallowed. Finally, she found her voice.

"Six. I've been here almost six years."

"Then you know how intense the climate at Jazz can be." It was more of a statement than a question, so Lisa just let him continue. "I value your hard work and effort, so I wanted to give you a heads up on some changes that are about to occur."

The flipping in Lisa's stomach went double-time. "Changes?" she asked stupidly.

For as long as she had worked at Jazz there had been a rhythm. Yes, it was intense, but you kind of knew that's what you were signing up for. Working in media was not for the weak.

"The men upstairs are getting antsy. They're trying to compete with the mainstream mags, and they're tired of coming in last. The Bowman Brothers—" Carl suddenly stopped and his gaze darted to the closed door.

Spikes of angst protruded from Lisa's back, and she just wished he would spit it out already.

Once assured no one was eavesdropping, Carl continued. "They want to make some cuts with the staffers and replace them with more freelancers."

Ugh. There it was. Lisa was a goner.

She had been in her position a few years, and in a sense, grand-fathered in. Jazz was doing really well and had dumped their resources into hiring full-timers before they started beefing up with contributing writers and editors. The cut-off for full-time hires happened right after Lisa's arrival. It seems she'd slid in at just the right time. Carl himself was doing double duty, working as music editor *and* health & wellness editor. Jazz had already been dwindling down full-time workers the last few years due to a decrease in adver-tisement funds. Now this.

Carl inhaled and spoke in a hushed tone, even though they were alone. "That's why they paired you guys off the way they did. They ran the numbers and saw who each other's greatest competitors were."

Ohhh. Understanding flooded Lisa's mind. "So... *you* didn't put me with Renee?" She repeated her inner question out loud.

Carl looked surprised. "Hell no. I know how much you two hate each other."

Lisa couldn't help herself. She burst out laughing.

I guess he's more aware of his staff than I thought.

At her reaction, a full-blown smile unleashed on Carl's face and his beady eyes lit up. Yes. There was no doubt. Carl was smiling.

"I'm sorry. I just didn't expect you to say that!" Lisa explained, but her face was still beaming. She took a minute to try and gather herself.

Man, I needed that laugh.

When they regained their composure, Carl continued. "So, they paired you guys off to see who would sink or swim. They don't know your writing styles, so they're leaning on the editors to high-light the weak parts in the articles, and we'll tell them the author. But it's not just you against your partner, it's you against the other teams. Because this is a team effort, if the articles don't come out polished, they'll make whole team cuts."

The reality of what Carl was saying soaked her brain and sobered Lisa. Whatever joy she had found in her boss's covert sense of humor was now buried beneath sheer turmoil.

Lord, what is happening? What am I going to do if I lose my job?

"So, you're saying my job's in jeopardy?" Lisa asked for clarity's sake.

Carl looked at her grimly. "I'm saying, everyone's is."

THOUGHTS IN LISA'S MIND SPUN FASTER THAN A BALLERINA IN A Julliard School's ballet. Though she was successfully able to carry out her meeting with Renee and Danita about the Swizz Beatz article, it took everything in her to not blurt the news that they were all under tight scrutiny. Her newfound alliance with Renee was more work-based than personal, and Lisa didn't really know how much she could trust her associate. As a result, she wasn't ready to confide something so monumental. But she definitely had to tell Danita.

Once they were safely inside Lisa's office and she had unloaded the mission impossible secret that Carl had disclosed, Danita busted out, "Girl, this is insane! I can't believe they would be so. So..." Her voice ceased as her eyes grappled wildly with the ceiling.

"So ruthless?" Lisa finished dryly, her comment accented with a bitter snort as she reclined in her ergonomic chair. "I mean, why wouldn't they be? The higher ups aren't in touch with their workers. They hide on the tenth floor, and we never even *see* them. It's not like they're personally invested in our lives."

Not like Carl, she couldn't help thinking. Lisa had pegged him all wrong. When it came down to it, Carl had demonstrated ample care for her as an employee.

"I think we need to retire Carl's nickname," she remarked absently.

Danita looked at Lisa from her position on the couch, puzzled. "Where did that come from?"

Lisa shrugged. "It's just that—he isn't the oger I thought he was."

Danita made a noncommittal sound. "I mean, I get it. He looked out for you with this intel, but the man *has* Big Bird tendencies."

Lisa couldn't stifle a smile. Leave it to Danita...

"And why did he tell you all this anyway?" Danita's face became suspicious as strands from her long black ponytail, cascaded it. Wide-rimmed streaked platinum bangs lay across plump twin microbladed brows to contrast.

Lisa had wondered the same thing until she was on her way out of their little pow-wow and Carl revealed that *she* was his favorite journalist. That's why he was always on her so tough. Shocked relief absorbed her at his confession. Who knew?

But Lisa didn't feel comfortable tooting her own horn so she just lifted a shoulder and slid her eyes to her phone. It was time to leave.

"I need to head to another important meeting. Say a prayer for me will you?"

Still slouched on the couch, Danita dropped her chin and stared into space, processing the whole work-cut thing. "What am I praying for again?" she asked, finally flitting her eyes across the room at her superior.

Lisa's lips were sewn into a flat line as she started packing her messenger bag.

"Pray for me and my father. I'm about to go see him."

She Started After Her Loss

CHAPTER 15

The rideshare Lisa caught to The Four Seasons was a vintage black Mercedes Benz. She hadn't even selected the luxury vehicle option so the fact that that's what she received was a pleasant surprise. The young, fine, ebony-toned brotha offered a nice view as well. Lisa couldn't help but think of Joe.

I never did get back to him.

While Joe was on her mind, she popped open her social media account and started a message.

"Joe, so sorry for the delay. Lots going on. Apparently my job is on the rocks (rolled eye emoji) but that's life. Sure, please do ask your sis for resources on grief recovery. I've joined an online group and am now in counseling but I can use all the help I can get. Thank you so much for your kindness and always being a great friend. Let me know if there's any way I can pray for you. I'm sorry I was all about me and didn't ask you this before."

Feeling pleased for reiterating their friendship and offering prayer, Lisa hit send. It was at that moment that a stirring churned in her gut. She and Michael had been on the outs and she hadn't even told *him* yet about her job.

I just found out!

Lisa refuted the feeling and dismissed it. She had other things to worry about. More *immediate* things.

"The Four Seasons," the young Hershey's chocolate brotha sang out. He looked back at Lisa and gifted her with a wide-tooth smile. She had to remind herself she was married.

"Thanks, sir." When Lisa grinned back, his face brightened.

"Ma, I'm nobody's sir. Especially with a woman as fine as you."

Oooo! Let me get out this car right *now*.

Snatching her things, Lisa nervous-chuckled, *"Umm, well thank you for the compliment,"* making sure to display her fat diamond in the process.

But either he didn't see her rock or didn't care. The driver boldly fondled her left hand resting atop the passenger's seat.

"Yo, I'm serious. Call me anytime." He winked and Lisa sped up her pace.

"Now, I don't think my hubby would like that very much. But, thank you for the offer."

Disappointment swept across his features and he shrugged. Lisa didn't stay long enough to see any other reaction. She escaped the vehicle with her belongings and set her mind on meeting her father. But still, there was a flutter of appreciation from the driver's efforts.

At least somebody *is checking for me*. The thought accompanied Lisa into the large double-glass doors. Apprehension then met her along with the affluent mahogany counter, marble floors, and chandelier dripping from the ceiling.

What the heck am I doing here? The frantic question leapt from her mind but God's peace squashed it.

"Umm, excuse me?"—The blond receptionist presented Lisa with a practiced perky smile—"Can you tell me where the bar is?" Lisa asked. She had agreed to meet Hank at the bar when she texted him earlier on lunch. Though she was pleasantly surprised that he responded so fast, she was also scared to death.

"Right over there, sweetie." The blond tipped her chin to Lisa's left and Lisa couldn't help being tickled by the term of endearment. The girl couldn't be more than 25.

Strangling her Prada purse, Lisa's high-heeled boots started pumping. During the short trip, a messenger bag loosely straddled her peacoat, the strap smooshing down a fluffy white scarf.

With each step, she muttered, "God, just give me the words to say," eventually sliding past the clutters of round tables and chairs that decorated the entrance to the bar.

This whole experience was a faith walk. If it wasn't for hearing Sofia's testimony that morning during the *Jesus Calling* devotional, Lisa would never have considered reaching out to her father. She was truly tired of the back-and-forth ping pong game between them. Other than the last month he had been reaching out, over the years it had felt like *she* was pursuing *him. Not* the other way around.

The fact that Hank showed up at her door unannounced stirred a concoction of emotions. While it was touching that, for the first time ever in their relationship, he sacrificed to pursue her, it was still audacious as hell.

He totally crossed boundaries. I never gave him permission to come. Just like he crossed boundaries with that damn phone...

Slowing, when her father's figure emerged sitting on a bar stool, head low, peering at his phone, Lisa's resolve strengthened.

"Hey," she greeted moments later, unloading her things on the immaculate bar counter.

The look on Hank's face was a blend of pleasure, fear and love. In the split second of his gaze, she wondered, how the two, fear and love, could simultaneously exist.

"Hey," Hank responded, his eyes seeming to inhale everything about her.

Though she kept her voice steady, internally, Lisa was that 12-year-old kid he had walked out on.

"Did you want something?" Hank asked. It was then that she noticed his glass of what she presumed was bourbon, kept him company on the counter next to him.

Against her better judgment—there was still a long day ahead and she had to pick up Michelle—Lisa nodded. She would need *something* to help her get through this mess.

The bartender, a dirty blond with a chisel in his chin—The Four Seasons sure knew how to pick 'em—plopped a glass of Cabernet before her once Hank had gotten his attention.

I guess you pay for prompt service.

Impressed, Lisa sipped as her eyes shifted. It was somewhere between 5:30 and 6 pm and the bustle of hotel guests was prime-time. Furs, jewels, leathers, and all types of swanky name brands, languished at tables and chatted loudly from one too many Happy Hour drinks.

"So. How was work?" Hank asked.

Ok. So that's the route we're going?

But Lisa couldn't necessarily *blame* Hank for the small talk. How *does* one start a conversation built upon decades of unhealed pain?

She shrugged, still standing, and began to undo the wide brown buttons on her peacoat. "Work is work." When she struggled with a button, Hank bent in a little to help. She flinched.

"Oh. I'm sorry," he uttered, looking sheepish.

"No. It's fine. I-I overreacted." Lisa breathed a deep sigh while finishing opening her coat.

Get a grip, Lis!

That's when the pain in her father's eyes protruded. It made him look older somehow. Additionally, extra lines were plowing into his forehead, slight shadows sat beneath his eyes, and a family of grays had moved in on the crown of his head.

Well, at least he still has all his hair.

"I. I just want to say… I'm sorry, Lisa." Hank took a breath, played with his blood-red scarf that draped his neck, and pushed on. "I know I wasn't there for you. I know I missed a lot." His head drooped and Lisa felt a smidge of sympathy. But only a smidge.

"You're right. You weren't. You weren't when I needed you and that's the part that's hard." The vulnerability in Lisa's voice shocked even her. She had never really admitted her need to Hank. Or maybe, to herself.

Hank's face reflected her surprise. "I tried to be, honey. Believe me, there were times I tried."

"Not hard enough." Lisa spit out the words, cutting him off from whatever bologna he was about to feed her. To keep herself composed, she drank some wine.

"Your mother and I. We—we had our issues."

The statement from Hank dug up memories from this week of Lisa and Michael fighting and poor Michelle quicksand-stuck in the middle. The hypocrisy of her own behavior as a parent did not escape her, so Lisa held her tongue.

"And I didn't know that she wouldn't let me see you whenever I wanted. That when I moved on and got married, that meant she would keep you from me." Hank added this last bit while rubbing his palms over his face, his shoulders hunched, his sorrow evident, his regret, even more.

"So you're blaming this on mom?" Lisa said, her voice soaked with disgust. "You're not taking *any* responsibility?"

Hank's head jerked up, his eyes two round soggy chocolate chips. "No. No not at all! I definitely know I should have been more on it with getting you and trying to see you. The fact is, I—I was…" he dropped his head again and before he spoke, the word pinched Lisa's heart. They said it at the exact same time.

"Ashamed."

Hank looked at her, his gaze blooming at their synchronicity. "Yes. I was ashamed," he echoed. "As time rolled by and the years kept on I just felt like a failure trying to reach out. You seemed to be doing so well without me. Going to college. Getting married. Starting your family. I would read all of your articles at Jazz. I would stalk you on social media, once Novelle showed me how to use it."

"You're on social media?" Lisa couldn't help but ask.

A proud grin split Hank's face. "Yep! Though I don't have anything posted. I actually follow you. I'm MustangRich2.0." He puffed out his chest when he said it.

Lisa laughed. "That would be you. I know how much you love cars."

"Yep. Got my first Mustang when I was 19 and I been chasin' em' ever since."

Hank peered at her, youth now oozing from his eyeballs and suddenly, Lisa could envision her father at 19. He was an attractive man, she knew, but her abandonment issues often kept her from thinking of him in any positive light.

"I'm sure you got all the ladies with your Mustang," she kidded with a knowing smile.

"You know it! My boys were so jealous. My cousin Earnie would steal that thing and lie to his little dates that it was his. We had a few fist fights cuz he kept hot-wiring my ride."

Hank sat back, lost in memory lane and Lisa couldn't help it. She was enjoying herself. Her father was a smooth one and it was easy to see how her mother had fallen for him.

"Why didn't you and mom work out?" Lisa interrupted his speech on Betty, his first vehicle.

Her dad's expression soured slightly. "Oh, baby, there were so many reasons. First and foremost, we were just so young," Hank started, but Lisa cut him off. She wanted the real answer and for the first time in her adulthood, felt brazen enough to ask.

"I mean, for real, Dad. Young people get married and have babies all the time and some of them *still* make it. Or older people get married and they still *don't* make it. So, it's not just about age. What was it?" Lisa propped her chin in one hand as shadows of thoughts danced across her father's features.

Finally, Hank took a sip of his bourbon, before letting out, "It was the pills, Lisa."

His voice was barely above a whisper and she had to strain her ears to even hear it. The crowded bar had become more crowded and the noise level increased with the number of folks being crammed into the same amount of square footage.

But still, Lisa did hear it, and in a sense, it was a comforting answer. All these years she had wondered if her father knew. They had never talked about her mother's addiction but the evidence was there. Her childhood memories were mostly of fights and arguments and hardly of the two of them together, happy. Most of the happy memories she did have consisted of her parents spending time with her individually.

"When did it start?" Lisa wanted to get his side because for her, her mother's habit had been there since she could remember.

"You weren't our first child, Lisa," Hank revealed and Lisa gasped.

What? "Are you saying I have another sibling?"

It was as if the floor had just been removed. Or, that the earth was no longer spinning and rotating around the sun. Like, she was caught in the Upside Down in Stranger Things. But Hank rushed on.

"No. No, honey. I mean, we lost a child before you."

Reality set in and while absorbing her father's sad expression, Lisa felt the loss as if it had happened to *her*.

But it did happen to me.

She had to remind herself of Baby Lee and maybe that was why this fantom older sibling felt almost real. Like he, or she, was at some point, *alive*.

"How far along was she?" It took everything in Lisa to ask, but she was on a roll and knew this was a prime opportunity to get some answers. Her journalism Spidey senses were in full throttle.

Hank shifted on his stool, stretching one long leg against the red-brown hardwood flooring. He sank a little and it was clear by his hesitancy he was still affected by the loss and everything it entailed.

"Your mom was about six months along…about as long as you —" he stopped and Lisa imagined he was probably scared she would flip out on him like she had at her doorway. But she finished the sentence for him.

"About as far along as I was with Lee."

For some reason, it felt good to say it. Like there was some type of control and freedom in saying it, and not just this consuming pain she had been bogged down by for the past month. It was Lisa's to share, and so she shared it.

"Yes," Hank repeated carefully, "About as far as you with Lee."

They both fell silent, imprisoned by their thoughts. Only the chatter and occasional eruption of happy laughter from intoxicated rich people filled the space.

I can't believe my mother lost a child before me. I can't believe she was as far along as me.

And then, after letting these truths sink in, Lisa was finally able to fit the puzzle pieces together.

Steering her gaze to her father, her mouth slightly parted in revelation. He was studying her, it seemed, prodding her along to the truth.

"She started using after the baby?" Lisa asked, even already knowing the answer. Hank nodded, so she continued. "She started after her loss."

This time, when Hank moved in, and placed his hand over Lisa's, and rubbed it gently, calmly, she didn't stop him. She didn't stop him at all.

~

SITTING AT THE FOUR SEASONS' BAR WAS A SLICE OF HEAVEN. HANK couldn't remember when he had this kind of time with his daughter without anyone else around. It had to have been at least ten years. His mind rewound to one of those times.

Lisa was in college. It was one of the few moments he'd managed to stay in communication with her before messing it up, i.e., dropping the ball by not keeping contact. It seemed there was always a distraction. Something would happen with Candace. Or Gina. Or Novelle. Something would turn up and Lisa would be put on the back burner. But this time he pushed through and visited her on campus at Clark.

It was a stifling hot day, which wasn't a surprise. It was Atlanta after all. The heat in and of itself was one of Hank's main reasons for leaving. He had picked Lisa up, taken her to lunch, and afterward, they walked the campus. He met her friends. Saw her dorm room. He was so proud of her.

Hank hadn't been to college himself. He was a smart man but working on cars was his thing. He ended up owning a successful mechanic shop and then used the money to make more money in investments. Investing had substituted his love for gambling. Hank had a nasty habit that he finally kicked when he met Novelle. But he was still a hustler through and through and loved the risk-taking high that gambling fed him. Diving into entrepreneurship and stocks helped satiate that craving. It also helped him keep money in his pockets that he kept losing to the racetrack all those years. Even after his wealth came, he still worked on cars. Hank loved his cars more than he loved anything in the world. But that was before Lisa was born. He couldn't remember being happier on any day more than on Lisa's born day. Especially after they lost that first baby.

The memory of visiting Lisa at college dissipated as Hank returned to the present. His daughter was opening up about Lee. His revealing the loss of he and Vanessa's first child seemed to have broken her emotional dam.

Lord, thank you so much for giving me this time with her.

I make all things new. (Rev 21:5)

Hank heard the Spirit of the Most High as clearly as if God had spoken out loud.

Suddenly, his daughter looked at him in concern. She stopped chatting and said, "Dad?" while reaching for his cheek.

"Oh!" Hank uttered a small gasp and Lisa grabbed for a napkin to dab at his face. He hadn't realized he was crying.

"I'm sorry." Hank chuckled at himself, embarrassed. "I guess I just got caught up in the moment." Lisa's lips spread into a sweet smile. The smile reminded him of her mother.

"Have you talked to Vanessa?" he ventured. The topic of her mother rarely came up between them, but since this was a moment like none other, Lisa being vulnerable and all, Hank figured he would take a stab at it.

Lisa stiffened. Leaning back, she set the napkin used to wipe his face atop the bar counter, then took a sip from her almost depleted wine glass.

Uh Oh. Hank feared he had stepped over the line. That the emotional door that Lisa had finally crept open was now slammed shut in his face.

But after his daughter swallowed, her eyelids downcast, a quiet, "No," escaped her lips.

But there was something there. She had reverted back to the little girl Hank had known and loved, not the successful spitfire of a woman she tackled the world as. Her body language was tight, inward, as if she had somehow—shrunk. His heart broke. Hank had very little contact with Vanessa, but every now and then, he thought about her. She was his first love and the mother of his first born. As rough as it had been between them, there would always be care there.

Instead of responding, Hank reached over and patted his daughter's hand. She didn't move but she didn't push him away either. He took that as a good sign. They weren't where he wanted to be. He wanted to crush her in his arms and swaddle her with love. But they weren't where they had been either.

We'll get there, Hank pacified himself to ease his mind. They would have to because God had promised him this and God always delivered on His promises.

By 7:30 pm Lisa explained she had to pick up Michelle from her friend Sylvia's.

Steeling his heart for the letdown, Hank asked, "Do you think I could see her?"

His voice tip-toed on cautious-hope. His eyes glowed with sincerity. Since everything between him and Lisa was so fresh, he had to keep his guard up. There was no telling how she would even feel about him in the morning.

To Hank's relief, there was only a slight pause before Lisa replied, "Yes. But don't make her any promises about the future. I don't want to get her hopes up."

His daughter rose, and started putting her coat on, then after a second, added, "And no more cell phones." Her stern voice indicated she was back to the bulldog of a woman her mother had raised her to be.

Hank bobbed his head, eagerly falling in line. "Yep. Of course. From now on, I'll run everything through you and Michael!"

"*And* no more surprise visits," she added and Hank couldn't help but grin. She was so fiery!

"Got it. I'll DM you first!"

Hank winked and the smile he was aiming for lit up Lisa's face. She was beautiful.

The car ride in Hank's rental was a quiet one but it was an easy quiet, like two old friends who had just caught up. It *was* a little strange that Lisa was with him, but strange in a good way. Hank loved this kind of strange.

The city was a blur of horrible back-to-back bumper traffic and Hank realized why most New Yorkers didn't drive.

"I definitely don't think I could do this kind of traffic on the regular," he commented and Lisa chuckled.

"Yeah. Michael does most of the driving in The Bat Mobile. I don't know how he has the patience."

"The Bat Mobile?" Hank's forehead crinkled.

"Mmhmm. The name of his car." Lisa paused and looked at him. "He loves cars too."

"I knew I liked that brotha."

Lisa laughed and Hank made it his new goal in life to make that happen as often as possible.

Finally, after what seemed like one too many near collisions, they arrived at the old run-down building in Harlem. Lisa led them up the short stairs to the porch and Hank waited patiently as she hit the outside buzzer. Butterflies flapped in the cocoon of his stomach. He was so excited to see his granddaughter. Other than the sneak peek he had gotten when he first arrived, Hank had only seen Michelle one other time in person.

The intercom gurgled with a muffled child's voice on the other end. "Mommy?" It was Michelle.

Hank's face burst into a wide smile, but his smile dimmed when he saw his daughter's expression.

"Honey? Where is Aunt Sylvia?" Lisa asked. A frown tugged on the corners of her mouth but Hank wasn't sure why.

"She's asleep," Michelle crackled back.

"Baby, hit the button to let me up. I have a surprise for you."

After a few seconds, Lisa pulled the entrance door ajar. She looked back at Hank, her face swamped in confusion. "She's never sleep at this time," Lisa explained about her friend Sylvia. "I hope she's feeling ok."

"Hmmm." Hank took the door and tried to keep Lisa's pace as she scaled the stairs like an Olympic Mountain Climber, even in heels.

When they reached the apartment Hank was a little winded but his eagerness to see Michelle out won any shortness of breath. With a smile of her own, Lisa turned to him, her eyes matching his excitement. She gripped the knob and the door opened to reveal the perfect replica of his daughter on the other side.

"Papa Hank!"

Michelle was already in his arms before he officially crossed the threshold. Her love brought Hank to his knees. Her little limbs gripping his neck, her cheek pressing so dearly against his. It was the best feeling in the world.

"Michelle!" was all he could choke out. Hank was stooped on the floor, entangled in her affection. Tears, once again, rolled down his cheeks but he didn't bother removing them. They were his reward for the long road there.

After moments of basking in the scent of his grandchild's love, Hank hobbled to his feet with Michelle still clutching his hand. His eyes searched for Lisa but what he found made him grow cold. Her back was to him. She was kneeled, her curls hovering over the couch. No. Wait. Over a figure on the couch. He could only see bits and pieces because now his daughter had strewn herself across the image. *The body*, he realized. Finally, Hank saw her face. It was a woman. She looked—at peace. She looked—asleep.

Lisa was shuddering, her body wracking with quiet sobs. The icy coldness circling Hank was now suffocating, as dread enshrouded his understanding.

Lisa looked up at him, her eyes pools of tears, her face caked with sorrow.

"She's gone," she whispered. "She's dead."

Let Her Go

CHAPTER 16

"There are some people in this life who have a knack for living on purpose. It's like their spirit is so in tune with the Almighty that they come out of the womb beaming His light. Sylvia Canton is such a person. Every person in this room, I have no doubt, has been touched by her light," the minister said.

They were gathered at St. Ebenezer's Church where Sylvia's funeral was being held. There were young and old, Black and white, men and women. The assortment of people that Sylvia had impacted left no stone unturned. Lisa knew this firsthand. As she sat in the second row of the service listening, her expression could have rivaled any top-shelf MAC concealer. It was almost stoic. The remaining members of Sylvia's family filled the first row. Sylvia left one surviving sister, a niece from out of town, and a distant cousin. Lisa understood upon meeting them, that Sylvia had adopted *her* as a daughter. They each raved about her and "little Michelle." How much Sylvia had talked about them during long-distance phone calls and emails. How she had treasured their relationships after Richard passed. They were so worried about her because she never had children.

"But she had you," Sylvia's older sister, Bernadette, affirmed Lisa when they had embraced.

Lisa let the compliment wash her. Hug her. Hold her. She gripped Michelle's hand tighter when the older woman enfolded them. Bernadette had such a sweet resemblance to her sister that Lisa was tempted to pretend for just one moment that this lovely woman was her beloved spiritual mother, life mentor, and confidant. The very woman who had served as a shining guide in her life when Lisa was cloaked in a dark standstill. When there was no one she could lean on. When Michael was no longer there. When her parents weren't there. When the hardship of single motherhood and the heartbreak from divorce proved to be overwhelming. When she lost her child.

"There was you," Lisa whispered and felt Michael's arm immediately slip around her. She couldn't look his way though. She feared, if she did, she would break. And she couldn't break.

Michelle.

The child was a stone wall now but oh how she had wailed and cried in the apartment when Lisa discovered Sylvia had died. Slumped together in the middle of the living room, Lisa had Michelle tucked in her arms. It was Lisa's father who had called the ambulance. Hank had been their rock. Hank had stayed until they moved the body. Hank was with them now, seated in the back row. Keeping watch.

"Mommy?" Michelle looked up at her and Lisa realized she missed something. She gave her daughter a questioning gaze. "Can I say something?"

It must be time for remarks. Lisa scanned the program before responding.

"Ok."

Seeing the two rise, Michael did as well. The Dorises bundled together, nearing the podium, a solid brigade of three. The perfect portrait of the happy Black family. Only, there had been more pain than happiness as of late. As a result, they were glued together more as a survival tactic than an act of affection. Minister Jeffery smiled encouragement when they arrived, shuffling over and making room. Michael took the lead.

"We want to say how important Sylvia was to us." He cleared his throat, his tone gentle, yet firm. "Our family benefited greatly from Sylvia's hospitality. Her faith and love have been nourishment to our souls." He paused and Lisa could see the muscle in his jaw working, which happened when he was emotional. She touched his tightened grip around the podium. "We just want to say, Sylvia, thank you for loving us so well. Now we can love others just as well."

Lisa thought she would certainly break then. Pierced by her husband's genuineness, and vulnerability, it almost shattered her. But Michelle was clutching her. Holding her.

Michelle.

"Mommy?" Michelle peered up, tawny eyes swimming with sadness and fear. She was looking for approval to speak.

"Go on, baby." Lisa lowered the mic and Michelle hopped on the stoop. Michael rested his hands on Lisa's shoulders as she hovered behind their child.

"Auntie Sylvia made every day a good day. When I was sad because I didn't get picked for the soccer team and the girls who got picked went out for ice cream, she said, 'You never mind those girls. We'll start our own team, and she played soccer with me in the park, then took me out for ice cream."

The attendees who had previously been silent made "aww" sounds.

"And when I cut my knee while riding my bike, she put medicine on it and the hurting stopped. She always made the hurting stop."

Michelle paused and Lisa's heart wrenched.

Lord, please help my baby.

Michelle's little body drew in a breath and she continued. "I'm going to miss you, Auntie Sylvia." She looked over at the corpse that previously housed their friend for 73 remarkable years. "But I know I'll see you in my dreams."

Michelle stepped back, indicating she was done and Lisa had never been more proud. She marveled at her child's boldness and strength to speak in such a grievous state. It was truly an honor to be called her mother.

~

On Saturdays, Riley's Chicken and Soul was a normally jam-packed bustling onslaught of hangry customers. But it was Sylvia's favorite eating spot, so Lisa rented out the only room in the back to dine in. Thankfully, it was a quieter closed-in space from the rest of the rowdiness that clawed its walls. Lisa was grateful for the semi-peaceful area. She needed a reprieve, drained from the intended kindness of strangers and their 'Sorry for your losses.' Since she was the only one of Sylvia's loved ones who lived in the same city, Lisa had been a vital part of the repass and funeral-planning. Sylvia's sister, Bernadette, still resided in their hometown Chicago.

"I told Syl when Richard got that job in New York she was never comin' back," Bernadette cackled and the jovial sound echoed memories of Sylvia in Lisa's broken heart. "I knew she would fall in love with the city, and I was right!" While viciously tearing into a patch of collard greens limp from hot sauce, Bernadette's head bounced up and down.

The spread was exactly what Sylvia would have wanted. The Soul Food and love made with it by the Black small business owners, adequately paid homage to the woman who had offered the same to so many.

Clifford, Sylvia's one-year-beau, spoke up. "I'm so glad she did. That woman was the best thing that happened to me!"

The older gentleman beamed before diving in to their love story. They met at St. Ebenezer's when Clifford couldn't get enough of Sylvia's teasing him about his horrible Bingo game skills. She bragged and bragged that he needed a new card and that every one that she touched was a winner.

"But do you know that woman was right? She gave me a new card, and I won!" Clifford exclaimed, with the happiest expression Lisa had ever seen on any Bingo winner.

It went on like that for a while. People at the table popped up with stories of how Sylvia had oozed the same vigorous love for life that had enchanted Lisa. When the topic turned to her times of travel and the cruise she and Bernadette went on to Jamaica, Lisa's eyes fell to Michelle. Her plate of sweet potatoes, greens, and fried chicken lay, barely touched.

"Baby, you want to eat so you can honor Sylvia," Lisa prompted. "You know she always wanted you to finish your plate."

Even though Lisa didn't adhere to that old-school rule (she felt it caused kids to develop unhealthy relationships with food) she allowed it at Sylvia's. Because, well, it was Sylvia, and who was going to argue with *her*?

At a snail's pace, Michelle lifted her fork and her little arm angled slightly under its weight. She stabbed one singular sweet potato, dragged it to her mouth, bit a small portion, painstakingly chewed, and ignored the remnant.

Sighing inwardly, Lisa wondered, not for the first time, *How are we going to get through this?*

"Michelle. Can you show me how you and Sylvia used to collect leaves? There's some amazing fall leaves that I saw that are perfect for collecting," Hank suggested on the other side of Michelle. Lisa peered at him gratefully.

For the first time that day, Michelle brightened. "Yes! I'll show you," then looked at her mom, "Can I go?"

Those eyes, the same light brown shade as Michael's, vacuumed all the love in Lisa's heart. She happily gave consent. As their child left, the exuding warmth of Michael's palm caressing Lisa's thigh became a small comfort.

"It's good to see Hank here," he murmured and all she could do was nod.

It was the most unlikely scenario in the world. The woman Lisa was closest to on the planet was gone and the man she was the least closest to was here?

Lord, what are You doing?

The prayer was a repetitive one. Since they had discovered Sylvia's body, that prayer had become an A-train circling the track of Lisa's mind nonstop.

When the ambulance arrived and pronounced her dead.

Lord, what are You doing?

When Lisa held her baby in her arms while Michelle cried herself to sleep each night this week.

Lord, what are You doing?

When she committed to be a part of the funeral and repass planning and made executive decisions concerning the woman who had guided her for the last five years.

Lord, what are You doing?

But no response. Only the legacy Sylvia survived that exuded her faith and the principles she stood firm on until the end. All the joy, the quality time, the service Sylvia had lavished upon Lisa had prepared her to do what she needed to do on this particular day.

Each had ultimately prepared Lisa to let her friend go.

After the repass, the group dispersed to get ready to return to their individual lives. Bernadette gave Lisa permission to clean out Sylvia's apartment. The woman was 80 years old, so Lisa denied her requests to assist. Clifford, not too shy of 80 himself, was adamant, though, and said he would meet the Dorises in the morning to help.

"I couldn't let Sylvia go knowing I didn't offer a hand." He chuckled and the dear old man shuffled out the door with his hands in his pockets and his head bowed from grief.

As they prepared to walk outside the restaurant, Lisa looked at Michael. "Ready?" she said, but she was asking more than one question.

Are you ready to start this new chapter without this rock-solid woman in our lives? Are you ready to begin grieving the loss of her when we're still grieving the loss of our child?

And, most importantly, *Are you ready to help with Michelle?*

Uncertain if he fully understood her meaning but accepting her husband's "Yes" as agreement to all three questions, Lisa grabbed Michelle. The three of them headed home with Hank tailing behind in his rental. Hank had stayed the whole week, extending his trip to be what Lisa needed. What Michelle needed. Michael had moved back to their bedroom and Hank had taken over the couch, even with Lisa offering to pay his hotel bill. But he refused, saying he felt like it would help Michelle if he was nearby, especially since he was able to watch her after school until Lisa came home from work. He was doing the job that Sylvia had done. Lisa wasn't going to argue. She wasn't able to take any more time off and was too scared to work from home unnecessarily with the work cuts looming over everyone. She pitched Hank a grateful smile and made sure he had extra pillows.

Other than soft jazz, there was silence during the ride home. Lisa kept pivoting her neck around but finally stopped when Michelle lay slumped over, knocked out.

"She's sleep," she half-whispered, half-mimed to Michael. He reached over and stroked her gloved hand. It was getting colder every day.

When they arrived, Michael, bless his heart, carried Michelle into the building as Lisa and Hank followed suit. It was so odd how easily Hank seemed to have been woven into their little nucleus, as if he had been there all along. Part of Lisa was frightened of how Michelle would react once he left. The other part was afraid of how she would. They had agreed Hank would leave Monday while Michelle was at school. Lisa braced herself for it.

Thank you, Lord, for giving us time with him.

Lisa now understood just how short life truly was. Whether it was six months or 73 years, there never seemed to be enough time.

When Michael slid Michelle into the canopy, Lisa took over by removing her shoes and coat and tucking her in. The child was flat on her back, mouth adjacent, snores ricocheting. Envy of her rest sat on Lisa's chest. She had barely slept all week and was running on fumes.

A small "Meow" escaped from beneath the bed before Snowball revealed himself. Lisa had almost forgotten about Sylvia's cat. She stooped to pet him as he rubbed against her hand in desperate need of affection.

Poor thing. Well, I guess you're ours now. That was one silver lining in all this. Michelle had been overjoyed to inherit Snowball.

The all-white feline hopped onto Michelle's bed and Lisa took that as her cue to go. But when she cracked open the door a, "Mommy?" materialized in the room.

She jolted from the sound and turned. "I thought you were asleep, honey."

Michelle lifted her head and Lisa stumbled to her in the semi-darkness. "Did I kill Aunt Sylvia?" The question sliced through Lisa as if her daughter had used a real knife.

"Baby, *no*! Why would you say that?" Her face exuding horror, Lisa tossed Michelle's clothes onto the bed and cradled her cheek in one palm. A startled Snowball crawled to the edge and repositioned himself.

"I didn't call 911. I didn't call you." Michelle's small voice was wrapped in guilt and Lisa's stomach became a twisted pretzel.

"Auntie Sylvia told you she was going to sleep. That she was tired. You didn't know she had—died. You couldn't have known. If you had known, you would have called me."

Michelle nodded slowly but her eyes remained unsure.

"Baby, Auntie Sylvia had a beautiful, purposeful, long life. Yes, we wanted more time with her but she had finished her work. God called her home. And she went in a beautiful way. She didn't suffer. She was at peace. And, she got to do what she loved to do and that was being with you."

Michelle seemed to receive that last statement because she rolled over and curled on her side. Without a word, Lisa lay with her and waited until she drifted back to sleep with Snowball snuggled at her feet.

But even then, Lisa knew, *It's going to be a long road.*

It was well after 8 o'clock when Lisa removed herself from her daughter's bedroom. The men in her life were chatting in the living room and she took a moment to observe them from the hallway. Michael was pulling up something on his laptop and Hank sat back marveling, eyes shining, mouth almost salivating. They were two peas in a pod and had not just negative traits in common but positive ones too. Both men were ambitious, intelligent, and smooth. Their shared passion for work and cars was just icing on the cake.

As she leaned forward, Lisa could make out a few words. Something about corvettes and Mustangs.

"Well, I hate to interrupt this male bonding," Lisa finally said after getting her fill.

The men looked up. "Michelle good?" Michael asked first and Hank's expression echoed his sentiments. Lisa was so thankful for their support.

"Yes." She frowned then, thinking about her daughter's statements. "She's finally asleep."

"You good?" Michael asked, moving toward her and lightly touching her arms. "You want some tea?"

Suddenly, Lisa was exhausted. The heaviness of the past week weighed on her shoulders and she was finally coming down off the adrenaline rush.

"I appreciate that but I think I'm just gonna go to bed."

Hank started stuttering. "Umm…Y-you sure?" He stood also. "I was thinking we could hang out a little. You know, since I'm leaving Monday."

Guilt straddled Lisa's heart but she couldn't deny the tapped-out feeling. "I'm sorry, I just don't think I can. How about an early morning breakfast? My treat?"

"Sure. Sure. I understand. Yep. That'll work!"

Hank met her, and before Lisa could even register what was happening, "Get some rest," he whispered, enfolding her and dropping a kiss on her forehead. She allowed herself to awkwardly lean into his embrace. It was probably the first one they'd shared in years.

Michael was next. "I love you," he said before squeezing her in his arms. Returning the favor, Lisa melted beneath his affection. Again, she was thankful.

"The girls are coming over to help us tomorrow," she mentioned as a last-minute thought. Both Carol and Natalie had volunteered. Danita wasn't free but said she could come the next day if they still needed her. All three had sent flowers to the church at the service. A bold, beautiful display of white lilies that now sat perched on the kitchen island.

"Gotcha. Sounds good." Michael's reply was their last words exchanged before she made her exit.

Shutting their bedroom door, Lisa's undressing was accompanied by muffled murmurs. She let the sounds massage her heart, reminding her that she wasn't alone. It was at that moment, that she realized, there was a piece of her that did feel that way. Alone. Sylvia had been the nurturing, mothering, north star Lisa had needed these five years.

How will I make it without you?

But to keep her mind from going there, she decided to jump in the shower. The hot steam and tantalizing liquid became a world-class sauna, massaging and rubbing all the right places. Lisa didn't know how long she took, but she took her time, letting it run its course.

By the time she was in her PJs and hidden beneath the covers, the murmurs continued through the closed door. There seemed to be a lot of discussion going on and she took heart that her loved ones were bonding before her mind drifted back to Sylvia. The constant effervescent encouragement. The bubbly joy that spilled over every conversation. The magnanimous zest for life.

Aching pierced Lisa's core. Yearning with it.

For what seemed like another hour, she lay trying to sleep. But sleep was elusive. Instead, pain became her companion. It seeped in without asking permission, joining her under the covers, stroking her mind and heart. The go-go-go of this past week was at a sudden standstill. The onset of loneliness began consuming her in its place. It felt dark. It felt hard. It felt like everywhere Lisa turned a loved one died.

A click from the bedroom door disturbed her grievous musings. *Michael.*

Lisa could feel herself slipping away mentally, emotionally, and maybe even, again, spiritually. The hurt was now overshadowing her mind as footsteps approached. The bed sagged and shifted next to her. Her breaths were now coming out rapid and short. Tears stung her eyes but stubbornly clung to her eyelids, refusing to fall. It was then that arms enclosed her, spooning her.

Maybe Michael could save her?

Lisa lifted and turned over, straining to see through tears and darkness. Her chest was sunken and heavy; heartbreak threatening explosion. But instead of Michael, there appeared a different shadow. A different outline. A woman. A beautiful, chocolate woman whom she hadn't seen in so long.

"*Mommy?*" Lisa whispered.

And that's when she broke.

Life is Too Short

CHAPTER 17

Vanessa Pedersen sat on the airplane; stomach contorted into a messy assortment of figure eights. She folded and unfolded her hands so many times on the airplane tray she feared her neighbor would complain. Every time she did her right upper arm shoved against his meaty left one. Thankfully, he was out like a light, his fervent snoring a dead give-away.

Lord, what am I doing?

Vanessa had asked herself this every step of the journey. From the time Hank called and told her about Sylvia's passing, his voice asking, no, *begging* her to come. It was the shock of a lifetime. Vanessa hadn't spoken to Hank in at least a decade. Once Lisa was grown and on her own, there was really no need to. When his unsaved number flashed on her cell phone, she answered, thinking it was the new girl she was sponsoring in Narcotics Anonymous. She hadn't saved her number, had just left a message, and was expecting a callback. But Hank's worried voice flooded the line instead.

"Vanessa, our daughter needs you."

The sentence rang and rang in her mind, providing a melody to the beat of her folding and unfolding her hands.

Ending the call with Hank, Vanessa sighed. "Lord, what should I do?" The answer was clear.

Go.

For years Vanessa had run from God, turned off by her poor mother being shammed by the church. She grew up seeing through the faux prophets who manipulated desperate souls into piling more money into the offering plate; her mother, their most devout contributor.

If I'm going to give my money to something, I want a return on my investment, Vanessa decided.

And so, she had picked up gambling. The lottery tickets she had purchased gave an incomparable thrill, even when she didn't win, but especially when she did. There was always this rush at the possibility that: *This could be it!*

When Vanessa met Hank, she graduated to the casino and they became some gambling fools together. Only, Hank loved horses. He would work on cars and then spend the weekends at the racetrack. Vanessa was his lucky charm and most times she went with him he would win. They were young and free back then, using their winnings to shop and travel. It felt like they hadn't a care in the world. But then, Vanessa got pregnant. Hank was old-school and wasn't going to let her, "have a baby out of wedlock," as he put it. So, he put a ring on it and when she was about three months along, they got married.

Their love seemed to unravel fast, though. When they lost the baby, it felt like they had each lost a piece of themselves. Vanessa kept trying to find her piece in gambling, but then, she found it in pills. Or so she had thought. After her failed C-section the doctor prescribed Oxytocin to treat the excessive bleeding. The rush she had been chasing in gambling was attached to that same euphoric feeling of getting high. Her marriage was already shaky, but between the financial setbacks from gambling losses and trying to support her addiction, it inevitably steamrolled downhill. The only time Vanessa was able to stop using was during her pregnancy with Lisa. It took fifteen years to kick the habit. Sadly, it seemed, the damage to her relationships had already been done.

Vanessa shook her head from the memories, flinging away the shame and grief associated with her past.

Change the things you can, she reminded herself, reciting the long-standing mantra of Narcotics Anonymous. It was at those meetings she found something she lost after losing her child, and again, when she and Hank divorced. She found hope. And somewhere along the way when repeating that prayer, "God grant me the serenity..." God shape-shifted from an abstract idea into a real Person.

Now Vanessa was seatbelt-buckled in to a two-hour flight to New York, hoping to God she was right. That He was in fact real and not abstract. But she knew in her heart of hearts, if not for Him, she could never have gotten clean. Taking those pills was how she coped with life. She just needed a more effective way of coping.

"Our daughter needs you."

That one simple sentence was gift-wrapped in surprise. Since when had Lisa ever needed her? It seemed Lisa came out of the womb a self-sufficient ball of fire. Vanessa knew that part of the reason was because she had to be. When her parents were going at it (sometimes even physically) and Vanessa herself was out of it due to the drugs, Lisa was left with the thing that most kids of substance-abuse users are left with: parenting themselves.

But now she needs me, Vanessa reminded herself, trying to stifle the angst constricting her midsection. The plane was descending and she imagined God's hands massaging her anxiety-wracked heart. The beating growing slower. Her breathing following. Her therapist had taught her that trick. Visualization had been a great tool in Vanessa's recovery.

Before she knew it, she was stampeding amongst the herd of travelers, fighting for her suitcase and copping a rideshare. Hank's voice was a bucket of shocked delight when she called him back and said she was on her way. He explained he didn't think it would be wise to let Lisa know ahead of time and shared her response to him when he had come.

"But she needs you and I don't want her to refuse you. If she knows ahead of time she just might," he added. "So come."

Vanessa was stunned by his role in all this.

Since when is Hank trying to help me with my relationship with Lisa?

But the proof was in the pudding. He had transferred her money to aid with the plane ticket and given Vanessa the address. "We'll be waiting."

But even as she fidgeted in the back of the red Hyundai that picked her up, Vanessa's frazzled brain sprinted at top speed.

What really is the plan here, God? What *am I doing?*

But all she had was this certainty that she had to get there.

Within the hour, a large white-on-white upscale building loomed ahead, towering like a skyscraper. The inside was just as stylish. All vault-like ceilings, bright shiny mirrors, and red velvet drapes swaddled in fall apparel.

These people sure love fall.

Vanessa snorted while making her way to the sparkling elevators. A woman was waiting with a lavish crown of dark curls on her head. A few bags from a HomeGoods store swaddled her grip, but she smiled with kind sweet blue eyes. This put Vanessa at ease. You just never knew how these folks were going to act.

"You going up?" the woman asked and Vanessa nodded, a little uncertain.

"Umm. Four please?" Vanessa waddled in four-inch heels near her luggage as her elevator companion pressed the button.

"Visiting loved ones?" The woman's baby blues fondled Vanessa's singular black Coach suitcase trimmed in gold.

A little deterred by her friendliness but liking the sound of what she had said, Vanessa's chin tilted slowly.

"Umm, sure. Yeah... I'm—visiting *loved ones.*"

Her voice kind of choked on the words as she tried them out and the woman looked understanding.

"Well, enjoy your time. Life is too short," she replied before she got off on the third floor, shopping bags still clutched.

Vanessa agreed. Life was much too short. When she exited the elevator, she called and Hank answered on the first half ring.

"You here?"

"Yeah. I'm coming off the elevator." He had given Vanessa the building code but now that she was nearing her destination those pesky figure-eight knots were back.

Lord, help!

But then, Hank was in front of her with the door wide open and Michael next to him. They swarmed her with hugs and pulled her inside. The chatter started. Hank asking how her flight was and Michael taking her coat and putting water on for tea. It was as if this wasn't her very first time in Michael's home and the very first time she had seen Hank in over a decade. But instead of fear, there was only love. It was a little awkward when the excitement of Vanessa's appearance died down. Hank's eyes then moistened.

"She's in the bed. I tried to keep her up for you but she was too tired." He shrugged, looking a little deflated.

They must be exhausted, Vanessa realized, thinking about what they had all been through in the past 24 hours.

Seated in the living room, she sipped her herbal tea. It was a beautiful home and Vanessa wouldn't have expected anything less. But the realization that the walls and tables were decked with only family pictures including the three of them, bruised her heart. Even a few, she presumed, included Michael's parents, but nothing of her or Hank.

"No problem," Vanessa responded to her ex. But something was tugging in her gut. This nagging urge that she *had* to see Lisa.

"Maybe I'll just peek in on her and take a look?" She hoisted a brow to Michael who seemed like a very accommodating man in the 20 minutes she had been there. They had only met a handful of times and had never had any lengthy conversations.

"That's fine," he obliged, his face peppered with concern. "Anything you can do to help."

And with that, Vanessa breathed out silently. She envisioned herself wrapping her arms around her daughter. Her heart ached for it.

But Lord, what if she rejects me?

But the feeling wouldn't go away. So, she caved, easing into the room, cracking the door ajar. It was pretty dark and she could only see the outline of a shadow in the bed, the form vacuuming all of her love.

Lisa.

It was as if a force had taken Vanessa over. Mindlessly, she made her way to the bed, laid down, opened her arms, and embraced her daughter.

~

THE PAINFUL CRIES AND CRUSHING SOBS CAME IN WAVES. BLANKETED beneath her mother, Lisa lay shivering as each one rolled through her like water gushing from a waterfall.

Lord, when will it end? she wondered as her mother rubbed, patted, and soothed with comforting words that sounded so familiar.

"Just let it out."

And so, she did. Balled beneath the covers, nostrils dripping snot and stuffed with the faint smell of Vanessa's perfume.

Must be Chanel, Lisa wondered fleetingly before another involuntary round of tears erupted.

Finally exhausted, eyes puffy, throat sore, she choked out, "Can you get me some water?"

Her mother didn't hesitate. Vanessa was on her feet and had the door swung open in no time.

Lisa exhaled long and hard. She still felt bad, just not as bad.

"Here."

Vanessa re-appeared with a glass and Lisa sat up to take it. The lamp turned on as she drank. Though Lisa's eyes fluttered against the brightness, she didn't stop drinking.

Vanessa sat on the bed. Lisa could feel her eyes digesting every morsel of her. She tried not to stare herself when she was done drinking.

"Thank you," she murmured, handing back the glass.

Quiet clung to the room as Vanessa stroked her hair, coddling her head against her chest. Lisa was in stark disbelief that A, her mother was there, and B, she was crying on her bosom.

When was the last time I cried in front of her?

"I can't remember either," Vanessa whispered.

That's when Lisa realized she had said the words out loud.

"I—I'm sorry. I—I didn't mean to say that," she stumbled out, trying to undo what may have been done.

"No, baby. *I'm* sorry. I'm sorry it took me so long to get here."

They sat a little longer as Lisa's clarity was restored.

"How—how *did you* get here? How did you know?" was all she could muster.

Lisa's body was achy. Being in her mother's arms sent a swarm of emotions through her limbs. It was hard to know even how to feel. *Sad* that her spiritual mother was gone? *Elated* that her real mother was here? *Confused* by her presence?

"Your father called—"

"*Hank* called you?" *Now* Lisa *knew* how she felt.

Bewildered.

Lifting a little, she cocked her neck back to view her mother's face. Those charcoal almond-shaped eyes that slanted perfectly upward. The full pouty lips, smooth glowing skin, and voluminous threads of locks that poured over each shoulder blade. Everything was the same. Her mother, unlike her father, seemed to have barely aged.

"Yes," Vanessa responded and her locks shook with her head. "I'm as surprised as you. But he filled me in on Sylvia. Said it was urgent." Her hand waved in the air like a magician's. "So here I am."

Lines digging into her forehead, Lisa frowned. Looking off into the distance she recalled their last text. "But. But you said you didn't want to communicate anymore."

"What?" Vanessa cried in surprise. "When did I say that?"

"Your last text." Lisa popped up.

I know I'm not crazy. This woman said she didn't want any more contact with me.

"You must have misunderstood. Let me get my phone." Vanessa vanished again and reappeared, phone in hand.

Lisa waited, muddled and curious, watching her stroke a few keys and opening up their text thread.

"You said," Vanessa recited, **"Hey, mom. Just following up on this. Michelle and I would love to talk to you in the morning before church if you're free."** She paused, then read, "And I said, **'Ok. Let's not worry about Sunday.'** And then I never heard from you. Here I am thinking you were going to shoot out another day and time that worked because I wasn't trying to take up your Sunday since you had church and I knew I was busy afterward."

Lisa blinked. "Mom, I thought you were blowing me off. Like you were really saying never mind then about the whole thing. That this was your way of getting out of the call. Especially since you didn't answer the initial text," Lisa reminded her.

"I was wondering why you never got back to me," Vanessa shared, her face hinting at a smile and Lisa could see the humor hiding in her eyes. "I just missed it the first time that's why I didn't respond. See, that's why I don't like this whole text thing. It's too many miscommunications!"

"Yeah. But why didn't you just reach out when you didn't hear from me?" Lisa prodded. She leaned against the headboard with a puzzled expression.

"Well, honestly, honey. I thought *you* were rejecting *me*. I thought you didn't really want the call and you were too busy and didn't really want to be bothered."

Lisa shot her mother a look of unbelief. "How could you think that? I was so excited to have that video chat with you!"

"Now, you always have a million and one things going on. And the fact that you missed the call in the first place was evidence of that."

Lisa couldn't deny what Vanessa had said. In that moment, she visually stepped back and looked at her life from her mother's perspective.

"I guess, it could seem that way. But, Mom, I always want to connect with you. I know our past has been rocky…" Lisa let her voice trail and Vanessa's eyes fell to the duvet. She seemed to be fighting her own internal battle but then steeled herself and met Lisa's direct gaze.

"But I don't want to waste any more time dwelling on the past. Life is too short," Lisa stated.

Vanessa's eyes widened. "That seems to be the word of the evening," she murmured, then brushed off Lisa's questioning expression. "Never mind. I'm just glad I made it!"

"Me too. I can't believe you're here!" Lisa exclaimed, her eyes wide as a child's on Christmas morning. Love raced through her from head to foot.

"I'm sorry about Sylvia." Vanessa paused and inched closer before grabbing Lisa's hands in hers. "And I'm sorry about Lee."

The last sentiment sent another painful rift through Lisa. "I appreciate that. And I'm sorry I didn't even tell you about Lee. I assume Hank—I mean, Dad did?"

"Yeah. He did. I just want you to know, I'm here and I'm not going anywhere." Vanessa scooted closer and pulled Lisa into a hug.

Lisa whiffed the space between her mother's neck and the rich, robust ropes of hair, inhaling all the love.

And that's when she knew for certain. *She is definitely wearing Chanel.*

~

FOR THE FIRST TIME IN A LONG TIME, LISA AWOKE WITH A SMILE. The flood of memories from last night gushed her mind.

Mom's here!

Rolling over, she faced her mother's back reverberating with snores beneath the covers. After their conversation last night, Michael had volunteered to make a pallet in the office. Weeks prior he had successfully removed the remnants of the crib, taken down Lee's name from the wall, and reverted it to their home office. Now there was space for him to sleep there. Of course, Vanessa had fought him on his offer, saying she would be fine in a hotel. But Michael was adamant she would stay with them, at least for the night. It was midnight by then and he didn't want her wandering the city.

Vanessa's yawn alerted Lisa that she was awake, disturbing her musings. "Good Morning." She flipped over and smiled, catching the last of Lisa staring at her.

"Good Morning," Lisa whispered, eyes shining, unable to conceal the awe in her voice.

"Breakfast?" Vanessa asked with a half-smile and sat up to stretch.

Lisa's stomach growled in response. "Definitely."

The two escaped the Doris bedroom and found Hank propped on the couch, drinking a cup of something and watching the Stock Market.

"Morning ladies!" His eyes sparkled and Lisa couldn't contain herself. Her face broke into a joyous grin.

I can't believe both *my parents are here.*

"Morning, Hank," her mother responded, which sent another flurry of wonder through Lisa's mind.

And they're being nice *to each other.*

Michelle entered the room which sent its own rush of emotions. Suddenly, her grandparents were fawning all over her, exclaiming over her growth and stark beauty.

"Gramma V?" Michelle's eyes bulged as she embraced her grandmother and Lisa thought she herself might faint from incredulousness. Vanessa stooped and squeezed the child into her arms.

"You came to see me?" Michelle asked and Vanessa wordlessly bobbed her locks up and down.

Lisa knew by the shuttering of her mother's head that she was crying. Wiping her eyes and hopping to her feet, Vanessa said, "Ok. Ok. Y'all not 'bout to have me up here in tears all day. Let's get breakfast started!"

Lisa had to laugh. It was just like her mother to take charge.

The two navigated the kitchen with Lisa telling Vanessa where everything was, Michelle determining to help but getting in the way more than helping, and Lisa soaking it all up with a smile.

Michael finally appeared, "Good Morning," and smooshed her lips to his.

Holding onto him a little longer, Lisa asked in a low tone, "How did you sleep?" She felt bad he had to sleep on the floor.

"Like I was on a cloud."

Michael leaned his forehead against hers and she warmed at the words. He was such a good husband.

Before long, the table was set with a lavish spread of grits with cheese, scrambled eggs, buttermilk biscuits, turkey bacon, fresh fruit, and syrup to top it off.

"My God, woman, you outdid yourself!" Hank beamed and Vanessa winked.

"You know I know how to throw down in the kitchen." She propped her hands on her swollen hips. "Ain't nothin' changed."

"I helped too!" Michelle chimed in.

Vanessa immediately patted the crown of her granddaughter's head. "You sure did, baby."

Michael went and got the ergonomic office chair as the dining room table only seated four. It was the perfect fit as far as Lisa was concerned. She eyed her loved ones draping the table and thought her heart would explode. Hank volunteered to say grace and it was then that she heard his intimacy with God.

It just keeps getting better, Lisa thought in sheer amazement.

Everyone started passing plates. It was then that the answer she had been waiting on to that question she kept asking, *Lord, what are you doing?* settled in her heart.

I am doing this, *Beloved.*

I am doing this.

Life of the Party

CHAPTER 18

Since they had woken up so early, Lisa's clan was able to successfully get dressed and head to Sylvia's by 8:30 am. One benefit of having so many hands was that the whole event of packing the apartment only lasted a couple of hours. Michael had the smarts to contact Habitat for Humanity and workers came by and hauled off all the furniture before Good Will grabbed the rest. Lisa couldn't deny it broke her heart watching it all traipse out the door. Especially when Sylvia's precious TV, her beloved gift from Richard, was lugged away. Lisa had to remind herself, it had served its purpose.

A funny thing happened though when Carol arrived. Vanessa said, "Hey, I know you!" and the two explained how they met at the elevator.

God is always working, Lisa marveled while alone with Vanessa in Sylvia's bedroom. They were packing when her mother shared what Carol had said at the elevator.

"You've got a good friend there," Vanessa admonished regarding Carol, and Lisa knew in her heart of hearts how true that statement was.

"Babe, look at these." Michael approached as Lisa was stuffing the last box with books in the living room.

I'm definitely going to keep these. Lisa eyed the collection of Toni Morrison, Maya Angelou, and Angela Davis, before peering up at her husband.

In Michael's hand was three letters with Sylvia's distinct handwriting on each one. Her brow lifted when she saw *Lisa* written in beautiful cursive.

"She made one for each of us," he murmured, "and for her sister and Clifford," he shifted toward the elderly man hunched on the floor with a cane. There wasn't a lot he could do but his presence still felt comforting.

"Wow. Of course she did," Lisa said. "She was so on top of things."

Once again admiration for her friend gripped her heart. Sylvia had crossed every "T" and dotted every "I." All of her insurance paperwork had been in safekeeping, making it easy for her loved ones to bury her properly.

"You can put them in my bag and we can read them later." Lisa chucked her chin towards her purse in the corner by the door.

The group worked diligently until every room was empty, and the former life of Sylvia Canton was neatly stored in boxes and bins.

"Lis, we can come back tomorrow, if need be, but church is starting and we'd like to catch what we can," Natalie said. Carol stood next to her, nodding in agreement.

"Oh. Yes. Of course. Thank you, guys, so much for coming and helping!" Lisa bubbled, reaching for her friends and pulling them into hugs.

"Did somebody say church?" Vanessa asked. The whole group was now congregated in the living room, having cleared everything. The remaining boxes sat stacked along the north wall. The only real thing left to do was clean.

"Umm, yeah. We have service at New Life. It starts at 11:15," Natalie answered.

Dumbfounded, Lisa slanted her neck to the side, squinting at her mother. "Mom, you don't go to church. *Do you?*"

She had never known her mother to attend one service. Her whole life all she heard was how corrupt ministers were. That they were nothing more than pimps with pulpits.

"I do when it's right. I been going for about three years now," Vanessa revealed.

Hank jumped in. "I'd like a service myself. It would be great to visit your church, Lisa!"

Clifford hobbled up from his spot on the floor. "Yep. No way I'm going to make Ebenezer. We start at 10. Might as well get the Word in somewhere. As long as it's good and sound," he added with a firm nod.

Suddenly, Lisa found herself the nucleus of an atom of dichard churchgoers. Her vision darted to Michael. But instead of finding that closed off look he always had whenever religion or church became a topic, his eyes seemed uncloudy. Sharp even. And then, out of all of them, he blew her away the most.

"Let's go then," he said.

And Lisa, though she had never known for sure before, knew at that exact moment that aliens, were in fact, real. Because they had definitely usurped her husband's body.

"Unless a grain of wheat falls into the earth and dies it remains alone, but if it dies it bears much fruit," Minister Luis read. "John 12:24."

Riveted, Lisa sat, squeezed between Hank and Vanessa. Little Michelle was on the other side of Vanessa and Michael was perched on her right. Then Natalie, Devon, Carol, and Clifford filled in the rest of the row. The crew arrived right after worship and were in the balcony as a result. But Lisa couldn't care less.

I'm at church with my parents. And *my husband!* It was a dream come true.

"Death can seem unbearable at times, but in this passage, Christ teaches us that when we're Believers we do not face death for the sake of facing death. There is life on the other side of death. There is resurrection on the other side."

A chorus of "amens" echoed throughout the atmosphere in response to Minister Luis, sending chills up Lisa's spine. She thought of Sylvia and her baby boy, then looked at her family surrounding her. Their presence that day was a clear result of these losses. These hardships.

Lord, I'm so thankful that You've brought my family together, but why do these good things have to come out of such hard *things?* Lisa's inner dialogue was interrupted by the slew of words shooting from the podium.

"But he shall receive a hundredfold now in this time, houses and brethren and sisters and mothers and children and lands, with persecutions, and in the world to come, eternal life. Mark 10:30," Pastor Luis used another verse to follow up his points. "That's Jesus telling his disciples, telling *us* that we will reap good things but we can also expect persecution while reaping. In both verses, there are good things happening but there are hard things too. Sometimes we want just the good, but in this life, we need to expect both."

Lisa nodded, pecking notes on her phone. *Ok, Father. I hear You.* That's when she could sense Hank looking at her. She peered up. The smile on his face stretched to his eyes.

It is truly a miracle to have my dad by my side.

Then, Lisa glanced at her mother whose gaze remained steadfast over the balcony onto the large screen that featured Pastor Luis. A giddy feeling bubbled up inside.

And *to have my mother in* church *of all places!*

The rest of the sermon was just as meaty and nourishing and Lisa was thankful her friends had insisted on coming. But no, not just her friends. Her *husband. Her husband* had insisted on coming. When everyone stood to leave, she eagerly tried to lock eyes, but Michael was too busy engaging with Michelle. By the time he was done, it was Lisa's turn to trail her father out of the row.

"Ohhh that was so good!" Vanessa gushed and Lisa had to simmer her shocked expression. Her mother being a Believer was still taking some getting used to.

"It sure was!" the crew co-signed while Michael and Hank went to get the cars. Since there were eight of them, they had to split into two groups driving there. Lisa, Vanessa, Michael, and Michelle were in one car and Natalie, Carol, Clifford, and Hank were in the other. Now they had Devon who was hand-in-hand with Natalie as they all braved the brutal cold air. Clifford bid his farewell, saying he was due for a nap but that he enjoyed the service. Lisa gave him an extra-long squeeze and told him to keep in touch.

Natalie and Devon said they would catch the train and they all agreed to meet at the cafe.

"I want to bless y'all and open the cafe just for us!" Devon beamed with a boyish grin.

"Aww thanks, Devon! That means a lot." Lisa knew Devon never worked on Sundays so him opening the cafe was a special treat.

She turned to Vanessa, "Mom, I can't wait for you to see how cute Devon's spot is. I've had some great memories there," she shared. But then her heart skipped a little. *Joe.* She had great memories with Joe there. Lisa had been so consumed with everything with Sylvia that she had never gotten back to his last message. Had in fact, completely forgotten about it until just now when thinking about her past at Devon's.

"You don't say? Well, I can't wait to see it!" Vanessa cheesed and grabbed hold of Michelle. "Come on, kiddo. Let's see who can jump up and down the fastest to fight off this cold," and proceeded jumping in her three-inch shoe boots right outside the church entrance. Michelle giggled and followed suit, but jumped at a much faster rate.

Lisa exploded with laughter. "Really, Ma? You 'bout to be out here jumpin' around?" Though passersby did look, nobody stopped to say anything. New Yorkers were once again, on their grind. Even on Sunday.

Regardless of the foot traffic, her mother and daughter joyously bounced, puffing out smoke like chimneys, scarves twisting around their little necks. But they looked like they were having so much fun that Lisa caved and joined in. And that's what they were doing when

Hank and Michael pulled up bumper to bumper; jumping around like some lunatics.

"What in the world are y'all doin'?" Michael called out the window but he was wearing a huge grin.

"Jumping!" Lisa puffed out, chest light-weight heaving, voice semi-muffled by her scarf. "Would you like to join us, my love?"

"Yeah, Daddy, come on!" Michelle urged. She was doing a little shimmy with her jump and Lisa couldn't help but be impressed.

I think this girl may be a dancer.

Hank beeped the horn. "Ya'll betta get in this car. We gotta go!" But his expression was clothed in amusement.

"Daddy, I thought you were the life of the party, but now you're just being a party pooper!" Lisa sang out in a teasing tone. "I bet you won't get out that car and jump with us," she added.

Her father's brows shot to the roof.

"Ooooo, those are fighting words!" Vanessa instigated while high in the air, locks slapping her face on the way down. "Your dad NEVER turns down a bet!"

Lisa laughed and taunted her father with a daring look. She kept on jumping but cocked her head. "I guess he's too—"

"Uhh, little girl! You bet not say it!" Hank yelled, still a sitting duck in the car.

"*Scared!*" Lisa screamed at the top of her lungs and before she knew it Hank had abandoned the vehicle and was jumping with the rest of them.

Michael just shook his head, unbuckled his seatbelt, strolled from the car, and started jumping.

THE ETHEREAL SOUNDS OF SABRINA CLAUDIO SHADOWED THE conversations that morphed from sports to war & terrorism, to religion. The bunch was a smorgasbord of beliefs holding one thing in common: Lisa.

Lisa gazed at her loved ones around the table at Devon's Cafe.

They had to smoosh two tables together to fit them all. Lucky for them, they knew the owner.

"Natalie said she's got about ten more minutes on those paninis," Devon announced from behind the bar. "And I'm almost done with these drinks."

"Thanks, Devon. We are doing just fine!" Lisa assured, her hands clutching the hot mug of water he had provided. It was odd to be back at Devon's for multiple reasons. One, because she didn't have Sylvia around the corner to visit after she was done, and two because Michelle was with her. Lisa had spent so many times in this very cafe, writing an article for *Jazz* or catching an open mic night. Usually, Michelle was with Sylvia when she did.

I'm gonna miss you, dear woman. Tears started building behind her eyelids.

"Remember when you used to wear that teeny tiny fro, Vanessa?" Hank was saying. The comment snatched Lisa's attention. Apparently, her parents had traveled from sports, down to memory lane.

"Mom had a fro?" Lisa leaned in and looked at her mother who sat across from her. Examining her long thick locs, she tried to picture it.

Hank feverishly nodded while Vanessa rolled her eyes. "Now, why you gotta bring that up, Hank? Ain't nobody talkin' about that *dirt* you used to wear on your upper lip that you *thought* was a mustache," she dissed back.

Lisa giggled. Her parents were a trip.

Who knew how cool and fun they could be when they're not at each other's throats?

"Alright. Drinks are ready!" Devon appeared with a tray and named off the items. "Mocha latte, cappuccino, green tea latte, chai, coffee..." When he sat down the tray everyone reached for theirs.

"Oh, and this one is a special hot chocolate with large puffy marshmallows for a special little lady," Devon added and bent down next to Michelle, who eyed the mug as if she were about to dive in and take a swim.

"Now, Devon, that mug is about as big as her head!" Lisa exclaimed.

"I know. *That's* why it's only for special occasions," Devon replied and Lisa couldn't be mad. She knew he was trying to treat Michelle. Under normal circumstances, she wouldn't have let Michelle consume half that amount of chocolate. Her daughter was going to be *jumping outside* the rest of the evening.

"Mommy, I'll drink all of it. I promise!" Michelle manhandled the mug with both palms and started going in on the marshmallows.

Lisa chuckled, "I'm sure you will," but let her daughter indulge.

"Did somebody say paninis and fries?" Natalie popped in from the kitchen in the back with an apron tied around her waist and her chef's hat on. Literally. There was a tall, white lopsided hat decorating her flat twist out. Devon quickly swiped the large tray from her hands.

"Thanks, Nat." He took over and started serving while she hopped in an open seat next to Carol.

"Nat, thanks so much for cooking," Lisa said.

"Yeah," everyone chimed in.

"Oh, it was nothing. I love cooking. When I'm not doing admin for Devon I actually work in the kitchen," she revealed.

Everyone made "mmm" noises while devouring their meals, the conversation meeting its death to the delicious taste of paninis.

Watching them, Lisa was overcome with emotion. *Lord, thank you so much again for bringing us together.*

The vibe at Devon's was the buttercream icing on the cake for this little reunion. The charming bar stools, glazed mahogany counter, and whispering neo soul ballads curated the perfect ambiance.

"So, did we talk about how you guys met already?" Devon asked.

Lisa's stomach churned when she realized he was directing the question to her parents. She knew that Devon didn't mean any harm by it. More than likely Natalie hadn't filled him in on her rocky relationships with them, *or* their rocky relationship with each other. To Lisa's relief, her parents seemed ready with an answer.

"Yeah, I was working on cars and this one here decided she had an issue. But personally, I think she sabotaged her Honda so she could talk to me," Hank revealed, looking smug.

Vanessa smacked her teeth. "Brotha, *nobody* was thinkin' about chu'. I just couldn't get you to stop sweatin' me so I gave you my number out of pity," Vanessa refuted, swinging her locks in his direction. The whole table laughed.

"Sooo, I guess the truth is somewhere in the middle then, huh?" Devon stated with humorous eyes.

Lisa's brain combed over his statement. In her mind, her relationship with her parents had always been black and white. One-sided even. They had dropped the ball and missed the mark and she was a casualty of their war-torn love. At least, that's how it had felt. But now that they were all adults, and she could see how lively and fun they were when they were sober and saved, it seemed like they could have actually been her *friends*. It also seemed like things weren't as black and white as she had perceived as a child.

"But seriously, we were in love. We were each other's first loves," Vanessa said and her frankness was startling.

Lisa's ears perked up. She had never heard her mother sound so sincere about her love for her father. After the divorce, Hank had been a dead-bolted topic for Vanessa.

Hank agreed, "Yeah. We had some good times before…before we didn't. But we were young, and really didn't know ourselves," he finished and took a sip from his mug.

Wow. Look at the grace.

"It helps to know yourself. And to know the Lord. Neither of us was walking with God back then," Vanessa added.

Again, Lisa had to reconcile this new version of her mother as a holy roller. The very woman who had drilled in her mind never to be taken advantage of by any lurking minister. The woman who preferred to put her faith in pills and slot machines was now a Believer.

"So…how *did* you come to faith?" Lisa couldn't help but ask. She tried to smother the incredulousness from her tone. In the hours-long conversation last night that they'd shared, her mother's faith had never come up.

Vanessa smiled and her dark browns met Lisa's questioning gaze. "In my 12-step program," she stated proudly. "I met God one step at a time. Or should I say, He met me."

Lisa nodded. *That makes sense. It's still crazy she never talked to me about this before.* But then Lisa had to remind herself how much she had kept her mother at bay once she hit college. *I guess I never gave her much of a chance to share.* Shifting in her seat, she tried to snuff the guilt.

"And what about you?" Vanessa asked.

And, in that moment, Lisa realized, she had never brought up *her* faith either. She cleared her throat.

"Sylvia. Sylvia was a big part of my faith journey."

And then, she remembered again. *And Joe.*

"Umm, excuse me. I have to use the bathroom," Lisa muttered. "I'll be right back."

When Lisa reached for her purse, Michael looked at her and she could read him loud and clear.

You ok? His light browns were asking. She rubbed his shoulder but avoided his stare while swiping her purse and turned to leave.

Once she hit the bathroom, Lisa locked it to make sure no one would enter. Pulling out her phone, she checked her social media and saw that Joe had indeed responded to her last message about a week ago.

She re-read her DM:

"Joe, so sorry for the delay. Lots going on. Apparently, my job is on the rocks (rolled eye emoji) but that's life. Sure, please do ask your sis for resources on grief recovery. I've joined an online group and am now in counseling but I can use all the help I can get. Thank you so much for your kindness and always being a great friend. Please let me know if there's any way I can pray for you? I'm sorry I was all about me and didn't ask you this before."

She read his reply:

Trust me Lisa there is no need to apologize. So sorry to

hear about your job. I totally get where you're at grief-wise. It can leave you shell-shocked and scattered, though I haven't been there myself. But I did get a glimpse walking with my sis through my nephew's death. It was a doozy and her and her husband are still navigating it. I'm going to send you these links that she referenced once I told her about you. There is also a book I have that can really help with the Christian grief experience. It's called "A Grief Observed" by C.S Lewis. It helped me through my uncle's death. I have a copy on me if you want to borrow it. Would be great to see you again also. I'll of course be keeping you lifted. As for me, you can pray I trust God to be my provider with this new business. I'm scared to death. LOL!"

Breathing deep, Lisa crafted her response, then hit send. When she returned to the table, Michael looked at her, his gaze probing. But there was too much happening. Everyone was high on sugar and caffeine and the lively discussion was bouncing off the cafe walls. In response to his unasked question, Lisa slid her arm around her husband's shoulder, leaned in, and kissed his cheek.

Someone suggested they take a group picture and everyone moved into place. Devon set his phone down with the lens facing the bunch and clicked the timer. Lisa basked in the nearness of her loved ones and smiled for the camera.

Body Snatchers

❧

CHAPTER 19

The next morning the Doris-Pedersen clan gathered for their last meal. That day Hank would be traveling back to Ohio and Vanessa would be staying another week. "So I can help with Michelle," she advised.

"Yay!" At the news, Michelle reached for her grandmother and buckled her waist like a belt.

A rush of gratefulness hugged Lisa as she drank in their easy affection with one another. Children were so resilient. It was as if her mother had been an incremental part of Michelle's whole life and not just distantly watching from the sidelines.

"Thank you. I really appreciate that," Lisa told her mother.

And she did. But fear and angst tag-teamed her mind. Lisa couldn't help brooding on what she would be faced with emotionally once the dust settled and her parents were gone and she was left with the task of picking up the shipwrecked parts of their lives. That was one of the reasons why she had agreed to meet with Joe. In her last response to him on social media, she made sure to tell him to text her so she wouldn't miss his messages. She simply wasn't on social media enough and wanted to make sure they connected. Lisa needed all the support she could get and was so moved by his insightful response as to all that grief entailed. She was too nervous to admit the other reason she wanted to meet with Joe. It was then that another flashback surfaced.

Lisa and Joe were at Devon's and he was reciting a poem he was working on. Lisa sat, drinking in the sultry tone of his voice along with a latte. Joe caressed her with his words, sending chills up her forearms. It was as if they were the only ones in the cafe. Joe had this way of creating a world using vernacular that captivated Lisa, causing their surroundings to fade and drawing her to their own mental reclusive enclave.

"Lisa?"

"Huh?" Lisa's head jerked toward her dad sitting across from her.

"You wanna pass me the butter, baby?"

She hurried to oblige.

"I'm gonna head out around noon if that's ok," Hank announced while slathering butter onto a piece of toast. The group nodded.

"Drive safe," Lisa said returning to the present from her daydream. *Girl get it together.* "We're supposed to be getting snow soon," she added, forcing normalcy into her tone.

"See, that's why I couldn't do it up north. It's the snow for me!" Vanessa piped. She swung her folded arms while raising her shoulders to her earlobes. Exaggerated shivering noises oozed out of her.

"I love snow, Gramma V! Can we make snow angels if it snows?" Michelle begged. The conversation then settled on fun things to do in the snow.

"Oooo, remember that one year we went to Canada, V? We took Lisa and she was able to play in the snow?" Hank said.

Lisa almost dropped her mug. "Canada? I don't remember this."

And since when is my mother, V?

Vanessa looked off, a happy expression shading her expresso features. "Yeah. You were probably around three or four." Her face scrunched while thinking, "Ahhh! That was a good trip," her eyes shining with nostalgia.

Flabbergasted, Lisa sat back. "We had a family trip together?"

Both Pedersen's nodded.

"Yep. We went to Niagara Falls and stayed in a little cabin. It was cold as all get out!" Vanessa said. "But it was a lot of fun."

Lisa let that marinate. They had *fun*. As a *family*. So much of her childhood was stung with memories of fighting and drama. Her parents, each dealing with their own demons had left her to fend for herself. But now the missing pieces were being filled and she was learning there was more to the story.

"What was Lisa like as a kid?" Michael asked.

Lisa met her husband's eyes with a smile. With everything happening they had had little alone time. The last couple of nights he slept in the office, giving her time with her mother.

I need to make that up to him, she decided, thinking of her lace black lingerie from Victoria's Secret. It was his favorite.

That's probably why I'm having these damn flashbacks. We haven't had our alone time.

"You know Lisa. She 'bout the same as she was as a kid," Hank replied.

"Yeah, headstrong, sharp, and feisty as all get out!" Vanessa finished and both parents laughed. "Whew! Those fire signs," she added.

"Well, I got it honest!" Lisa said, pretending offense.

"You sure did. From yo mom," Hank teased and Vanessa rolled her eyes.

"From us *both*!" she exclaimed.

Lisa shoveled in a mouthful of eggs, swimming in the euphoria of it all. The brokenness of her family was being repaired before her very eyes.

Before Michael could jet for work, Vanessa said, "Hey! Let's take a family picture. Since Hank is leaving, we don't know when the next time will be when we'll get the chance."

"Ohh, that's a good idea," Hank concurred.

Lisa touched her bonnet while looking at her mother; the only woman on the planet she knew who woke up stunning. "Uh, you gone' have to at least let me get myself together," she said.

"Foolishness! You're gorgeous."

But Lisa removed her bonnet and used her phone to primp her curls anyway. When it was all said and done, she would just have to ignore the frizziness of her hair and the paleness of her skin.

After Michael placed the phone and set the timer, they bunched together at the table and he got them all in one shot.

"Great. Now let's Hank and I do one with Michelle!" Vanessa said.

And it went on like that for a good ten minutes, concluding with the last picture where Lisa was propped between her mother and father.

Lord, this is nuts*!* she thought, but her heart was smiling wide.

"Girl, it is like invasion of the body snatchers at my house." Lisa cackled, her head dipping back while laughing. Shiny, bouncy black coils dangled over the ergonomic chair and she had to grip the desk to keep from rolling backward.

"Lis, I can't believe God has moved liked that in your family!" Danita shook her long wavy purple streaked tresses in wonder and amazement.

The two were having lunch in-between meetings and Lisa's one o'clock with Renee was up next. The duo was finalizing the music article on Swizz Beatz before turning it in to Carl. This would be their last meeting before the deadline. They had successfully worked together without killing each other, and for that, Lisa was proud.

"Yeah. It is *wild,* to say the least. I never thought I would see the day my mom would step inside of a church building." Lisa added, "Then she had the nerve to say, 'Now *that* was a *good* word.' Like she been goin' to church her whole life!"

"It just goes to show, *anything* is possible with God." Danita crossed her legs on Lisa's office couch, wagging her rose-gold heels, eyes pumped with wonder. "I mean, how long have you been praying for this? For reconciliation I mean."

Sitting straighter in her chair, Lisa thought about it. "I gave up praying a while ago about my dad, but my mom...well...it's definitely been on my heart since I first came to Christ. I wanted so badly to experience that closeness with her that I had with Michelle. But it felt like we were just trying to be too careful with one another. Like if we talked too much or hung out too often it would inevitably hurt the other, so we played nice and kept our distance. It's crazy when I think of the timeframe of us both coming to faith. She said it's been three years of her going to church and five years since she came to faith. For me it's been about five years also," Lisa realized in awe.

"Wow. And what about your dad? What's his testimony?"

Danita's intrigue reminded Lisa of the power of her family's reconciliation. Pressing a finger to her lips, she thought about it.

"He said it was when his wife got breast cancer. So, yeah…I guess that was about five years ago."

"Wow! That's crazy," the younger woman exclaimed, she then took a huge bite of her roast beef sandwich.

"I know. I hadn't even put the time frames together until you asked the question." Lisa sat frozen, pondering the Father's hand on her family's life.

"You would think my parents were besties the way they crushed being around each other this weekend," she added after a beat. "I'm not gone' lie, I was on pins and needles that at any moment a fight would break out. But it was like they had never had beef." Lisa shook her head in utter amazement.

"It really shows how much they love you, Lis. They did all that for you." Danita added, "They showed up for you."

"Yeah. I know. It's just wild because for so many years they hadn't. I'm so used to having to push through life myself. It was truly a miracle to have so much support to bury Sylvia." The words caught a little in her throat and Lisa had to take a swig from her water bottle to get them down.

"And how *is* everything going with the grief journey?" Seeing the opening, Danita smoothly pivoted the conversation to a more serious note. "So sorry I couldn't be there yesterday to help pack up." She made a guilty look but Lisa waved her hand. "I had to help my sister get ready for my nephew's 13th birthday party."

"Sis, you were there in spirit." Letting out a pensive sigh, Lisa fiddled with her fork in her left hand. "But to be honest, it's been amazing. I couldn't have crafted a better experience to deal with something so difficult. I'm just terrified of what's going to happen when everyone leaves. When it's just us. Especially concerning Michelle." Biting her lip, Lisa sank deeper into her chair.

Danita slid her food to the side and stood. "You know it's not just gone' be you. Your parents may leave, but you still have us." She walked over to her friend and bent to give her a hug. "And most importantly, you have God."

Lisa buried her face in Danita's neck. "Thanks. You're right." She released her and cleared her throat. "Sometimes I forget that though because Sylvia was such a strong pillar in my life. But I know it was the God in her that was the strength."

"Christ has not been a crutch for me, but instead, a strong arm to fight with." Lisa's mentor's words reverberated in her mind, and she took comfort in their proclamation.

"You know you can call me anytime. I'm only a train ride away. I will roll up on you if I do not hear from you or have eyes on you at work." Danita stepped back, resting her palms on her shapely hips. Her snug grey pencil skirt, stretched to capacity, was doing its job complementing her figure.

Lisa laughed. "I know. I know." She hesitated, then decided, *Somebody needs to know what my plans are.* "I may need you on *another* account though…"

Danita sat down again to snag her roast beef sandwhich. "What's up?" she asked, before stuffing her face, and Lisa filled her in.

She explained how she reconnected with her ex. That he was the very one who had influenced her faith along with Sylvia. He was also the one she turned down for Michael. With every word, Danita's eyes grew bigger and bigger. She nearly spit out her Pepsi when Lisa got to the part where they were meeting on Thursday.

"Girl. I don't know if you should be doin' all that. I mean, is he *safe?*" Danita asked.

"That's the thing. Joe is one of the safest people I know. He's super safe. He has a genuine heart and truly cares."

"Okkkaayyy. Is he *married? Engaged. Dating?* I mean, this brotha, regardless of how safe he is, still needs some insurance." Danita then went in, sharing about an ex she had who she thought was "safe" but was actually gay and wanted to see if she was down for a threesome.

"I wouldn't have *ever* thought that brotha was freaky like that but you just never know the other sides that people have."

Lisa was shocked and immediately wanted to refute Danita's concern. But she didn't want to be a fool, so she ran over her instincts in her mind. Licking her lips and looking at the ceiling, she replied slowly. "I mean, honestly, I don't know. But what I *do* know is, Joe is super respectful. He barely even *kissed* me when we dated."

"Yeah, but, Lis, you're in a *super* sensitive space right now. You and Michael still have a lot to work through. Plus, Michael's not spiritually where you want him to be and you believe Joe is. This just sounds like a recipe for disaster to me."

Danita's worried frown zipped confusion through Lisa's stomach.

But I know I can trust Joe. And I know he is definitely not gay!

But then, another thought sprouted up.

But can I trust myself?

The memory of her recent flashbacks of Joe snaked its way to the forefront of Lisa's mind. But just when she was about to respond, her phone alarm went off. She peered down at the reminder for her work meeting.

"Let's talk about this later. We need to meet Renee."

WHEN THE LADIES ARRIVED FIVE MINUTES 'TIL 1:00 PM, RENEE WAS already seated in the small conference room. Her yellow t-shirt dress flowing over tan leggings roped with a wide belt was a nice change of pace, Lisa decided.

She's normally in more somber colors, she realized about her coworker.

This time of working with Renee helped Lisa to grow in respect for her associate. She still wouldn't have called the woman a friend but she could appreciate her hustle and ability to consistently deliver great content. When Lisa saw what they had achieved together on the fibroids article, she was thoroughly impressed.

Well, sis, let's do it again, she thought, getting seated and whipping out her laptop.

There was no need to be there more than thirty minutes because the meeting was more housekeeping and checking off all the things to make sure Carl didn't respond with 21 questions.

"I thought it would be good if we included the collab Swizz is doing with Timbaland," Renee said.

Lisa frowned. "What collab?" She scanned the article they'd drafted then looked at her notes.

"Exactly. It's not even leaked yet. I was in the bathroom after our meeting when Swizz's manager started making small talk. She loved my sisterlocks but has been too scared to take the leap, so I started hyping her up and telling her to go for it. I gave her my hair-dresser's info and she let it slip that Swizz was doing this collab called *Beatz & Barz.*" It sounds pretty groundbreaking. Like folks are gonna be able to view *free* concerts online."

Lisa's jaw nearly dropped. "Yeah. I'll say," she managed. "Groundbreaking indeed."

Renee's eyes danced as her voice bubbled over in excitement. "She didn't say *not* to share it, so I'm pretty sure it's cool if we do."

A mixture of being impressed and a tad jealous battled in Lisa, but she stifled the latter.

This is for both of us, she reminded herself.

"Okayyy," Lisa answered cautiously. "But let's double-check with her first. I don't want *Jazz* to get sued or anything. We don't know what paperwork they have on file for their agreement for this *Beatz & Barz.*"

Renee looked a little surprised. "Oh. Ok. I didn't think about that."

"But that was dope that you were on the lookout for a sneak peek. That's smart journalism. We just have to make sure we cover all our bases," Lisa added. She wanted to affirm Renee and school her at the same time.

Still, she was treading lightly. The more Renee knew about writing for the music column, the more of an advantage she would have to take Lisa's position.

Who's to say Jazz *won't fire me and* still *give her my job?*

After they reviewed the entire article, dissected it, and had Danita read it out loud, Lisa said, "Well, I don't see anything else we may want to change. Do you?"

"Nope," Renee replied. "It looks good. I'll reach out to the manager and let you know if I get a response in the next hour. If not, we can just move forward with what we have. Better safe than sorry."

"Agreed. I'll hold off on the email for another hour. Danita, can you send me a reminder in an hour to email Carl?" She looked over and Danita nodded.

Lisa replied, "Good. I guess we're all set! It was great working with you, Renee." She then added, and actually meant, "Oh, and that yellow looks good on you."

A cloud of hesitancy overcast Renee's features like the woman was battling internally.

"I appreciate that. Umm. Do you think we could talk for a sec?" As her eyes lowered, she fiddled with her dress, flicking a piece of lent off of it.

Lisa was caught off guard.

Is Renee, insecure?

"I'll be at my desk if you need me," Danita announced, taking the opportunity to exit.

"What's up? Everything ok?" The check-in tasted odd on Lisa's tongue so, trying to normalize it, she scraped it against the roof of her mouth.

"Yeah. I just. I just wanted to apologize for how I know I've acted toward you," Renee rushed out.

If the alien abduction hadn't just hit her whole household, Lisa would have been floored. But right now, she was only mildly surprised. She let the woman continue.

"I know I've probably hit below the belt…" Renee's gaze drifted but then found Lisa's eyes, "and that wasn't cool. The last few weeks working together showed me the power of teamwork." She paused. "And sisterhood."

"Wow. I definitely didn't expect you to say that. I appreciate you sharing and it does mean a lot that you apologized."

"I just come from a really competitive background with women and honestly, I-I struggled with…with jealousy." Renee's gaze lowered.

Lisa raised her chin. *You don't say?*

"You just seemed to have *everything*. The husband. The kids. The job. The waistline." Renee chuckled. "But then, when you lost your…you know. And then hearing your story about the fibroids. Well, it opened my eyes to how people just don't always know what others are going through."

Inwardly, Lisa smirked. *Lady, you have no idea.*

But instead of spilling out her woes to her colleague, Lisa replied, "Yeah. I think Black women especially have this tendency to appear like everything is ok. We really have a grace to endure a lot and not wear it. I can attest to growing up and seeing my mother as an example of this. I think sisterhood is vital in our community for us to really succeed, instead of being pitted against each other. But, we need to be healed for that to happen. That healing begins with being transparent, especially with each other." Lisa reached over and patted Renee's arm.

Lord, please let my discernment be on point, and don't let this woman play me for a fool.

"I appreciate your transparency. And I want to be transparent with you," Lisa began. She took a deep breath. "I want to let you in on something Carl told me."

Renee's face crinkled in surprise, and Lisa did a nosedive into everything her boss had told her, holding nothing back. She just hoped to God she wouldn't regret it.

See You in My Dreams

CHAPTER 20

Five degrees and frost were the first words Lisa read when she checked her weather app on her phone after rolling over the next morning. Both irises enlarged at the next word.

"*Snow!*" Muffled as it was, Michelle's voice on the other side of the door, tickled Lisa's ear.

Easing up in bed, phone still in hand and Michael moving around beside her, she walked over to peer out the bedroom window for confirmation. White was *everywhere*.

"Baby, I don't think we're going to work today," Lisa murmured to the window, painting a fog with her words that evaporated in seconds.

Her husband's grunt fought through the covers. "Yeah," he croaked, "Your daughter just made the weather announcement."

Within moments, Michelle's inevitable knock on the door resounded. After Lisa gave her the ok, she burst in, eyes wild and head bobbing like it was going to fall off her neck.

"Mommy! Mommy! It *snowed*!!!" Michelle was a flurry of excitement and Lisa couldn't resist some excitment herself.

"Yes. I see. Why don't you go share your news with Gramma V and I'll be out in a sec?"

"Gramma V is already up and making breakfast. And she already *knows*!" Michelle cried but spun on her heels to flee the room anyway.

A flood of gratefulness washed over Lisa. She could get used to her mom's breakfast.

Maybe we can hire a cook when she leaves?

She glanced at Michael who was yawning deeply, still flat on his back. His six-pack was on full display. He looked so good, she wanted to eat *him*.

"Babe. I'm gonna see if I can work from home today. It looks like we got about 12 inches, and it's *still* coming."

"Ok. Me too." Michael swiped crust from his face. Then his eye gleamed. "Guess we'll get some much-needed alone time," and Lisa knew what that meant.

Anticipation clutched her as she tossed him a seductive smile. "Looking forward to it, Mr. Doris."

But first, breakfast.

As if bringing confirmation, the aroma of bacon, and something else exquisite, wafted through their open bedroom door. That's when Lisa decided, *it's going to be a good day.*

The morning was a conglomerate of chatter over the delicious ensemble that Vanessa concocted—"Mom, thank you so much for treating us with your amazing meals," Lisa chirpedand—and Lisa and Michael splitting the office to work. Somehow, Vanessa got wrangled into making snow angels with Michelle. The poor woman had to wear Lisa's winter gear which was a size smaller and a few inches shorter than her own physique. But she made it work.

It was so nice being side-by-side with Michael, or maybe the more accurate term was back-to-back, since they carried out their work duties facing opposite walls. Lisa and Michael hardly ever worked together. In the space of Lee's crib, Michael had retrieved their other desk out of the basement's storage and slabbed it against the wall. Lisa's heart wrenched when he did it and she had to schedule a much-needed therapy session with Dr. Celia. It seemed many milestones triggered her grief and Celia had to remind her, there was a long road ahead.

"Think of grief as a journey and that you're taking one step at a time on this journey. Your end goal is healing, *not* perfection."

The woman's wise words buoyed Lisa's ability to make it through another day. Another amazing resource was "The Thanksgiver's Podcast," by J. Lewis. It was included in the bundle of websites that Joe's sister had forwarded. One of the seasons featured a topic of heavy-hitting testimonies about dealing with grief from powerful women of faith. The podcast had been a life-giving indulgence during Lisa's work commutes each morning.

Churning out the last of her emails, Lisa checked the time: 4:03 pm. Puffing a sigh, she whipped around. Michael sat hunched over his work computer, face bearded with concentration.

"Babe."

Michael raised his head but kept typing. "Huh?"

"I'm finishing up. When will you be done?"

"Uhh, probably another hour," he murmured at the screen.

"Ok. Make it a quick hour," she said and Michael turned his neck, the smile on his face reaching his eyeballs.

Lisa grinned before hitting "send" on her email to Renee, CC-ing Danita.

Renee and Lisa were able to get the exclusive from Swizz's manager and her stomach danced in joy.

This is gonna be so dope!

The leak of *Beatz & Barz* could be a game-changer and even though it caused Lisa conflicting feelings—*What if this put Renee on the map since she was the source?* —she had to do what she *always* had to do. Trust God. Over the last few months, this one fact had become starkly apparent.

Sitting and waiting for Michael to finish, Lisa's spirit stirred. *This would be a good time to journal and pray*, she thought and decided to make it happen.

"Let me know when you're done," Lisa told her husband before leaving the room.

Conversation from her daughter and mother kissed her ears as she peeked in from the hallway to check on them. Michelle and Vanessa were *coloring* of all things. Lisa smiled as her mother gave Michelle tips on shading to make certain pictures stand out and add depth. As if her mother knew anything about drawing. Tickled, Lisa shook her head while ambling to her bedroom, giving them their alone time.

After crossing the bed to pull out her journal, her eyes lightened. Sylvia's letter was tucked in between its pages, the top sticking out.

I forgot about this, Lisa thought, flipping open the book and revealing the crisp white envelope. It looked *fresh*.

It was a whirlwind after they had cleaned Sylvia's apartment. The group went back the next day and removed the rest of the boxes, dropping them off at various shelters, churches, and thrift stores. Danita made good on her word and helped, along with Devon and Natalie, so it was a rather quick process. Upon arriving home Sunday evening, Lisa had stuffed the letter in her journal, thinking she would read it then, but life kept moving. Finally, she had a moment.

Breathing deeply, she drew in all her courage and opened the letter.

My dearest, Lisa, if you're reading this it's because I was right and my time was nearing to an end. I started having dreams of loved ones who had transitioned, and when I saw Richard, I knew. I was being called home. I don't know when, or even how, I just know its SOON. So, I want to make sure my loved ones know how much you all mean to me with these letters.

Lisa had to take another breath. Her lip trembled as tears moistened her eyes, but she forged ahead.

I've so appreciated our time together, and our connection. You may not know this but I never had a child, though I was pregnant. I had a miscarriage. Similar to you. So when you went through what you went through, I grieved in a unique way. I knew exactly how hard it was. While you had six months to prepare for Baby Lee and become attached, I had three. But then Richard and I never conceived again. We had to find love and fulfillment outside of bearing children. I know it's hard, baby, but know that all of these hard things do work for the good. I spent decades not having that desire fulfilled. But then, guess what? I met you.

At that, Lisa didn't even try and stop the river of tears streaming down her cheeks.

You became the daughter I never had. I found so much joy and fulfillment in being your surrogate mother. And then, I got to be a grandmother to my baby Michelle! Oh, it was such a highlight, especially after losing Richard. We can't always know why God allows things, or why He does things the way He does, but we can know at the end of the day, He is good. Good things don't always happen, but there is a good outcome for those of us who believe.

You were my good outcome, Lisa. You and your family. Thank you for engrafting me into your heart and into your life. You have served me as much as I know you feel I served you.

My greatest takeaway from this life is to love hard. Love is truly what lasts eternally. Because our Maker is Love, and we are made in His image, we can be assured that we will always last.

Know that I'm always with you, even when you can't see me. And, that we will surely meet again. Even in your dreams.

Love, Sylvia

Lisa was a puddle, curled in a fetal position, the letter clutched carefully in her hand. Moisture saturated her face, her palms, rolled down her neckline. She couldn't stop crying. And all she could think, was, *Lord, thank You for Sylvia Canton.*

A TICKLING SENSATION CREPT ALONG HER NECK FROM A GENTLE nuzzling, and Lisa's eyes fluttered open to Michael kissing her. A slow, Cheshire-cat smile spread across her lips as she realized what was happening.

"Your mom's making dinner," he whispered against the tip of her earlobe, "Let's take a shower."

"Ok," she murmured, still trying to come to, but knowing enough that she should say yes.

Michael gripped her hand and the water was already going when Lisa entered the bathroom.

How long have I been out? she wondered. But then, her husband started peeling off layers and she realized she no longer cared.

Following his lead, anticipation mounted at the reality of being near his chiseled, naked physique. It had been too long.

Michael held out his hand, leading Lisa beneath the shower head. Wasting no time, he swallowed her mouth in his as the steaming liquid engulfed them. Lisa was so into it, she wasn't even concerned about her hair getting wet.

It needed a wash, she thought with a small smile beneath Michael's probing tongue.

His arms were all over, soothing and rubbing and stroking. She let out a small cry bursting with pleasure when his hand stroked further down. His fingers danced between her thighs. Ecstasy consumed her, and every part of her gave in to it.

An hour later the clan was seated for another luscious meal prepared by Vanessa.

"Mom, you outdid yourself," Lisa gushed, offering her mother a gentle squeeze on the shoulder while getting seated. "I'm thinking we gone' have to hire a chef when you leave," she half-joked.

"Oh, it's nothin'." Vanessa whipped a hand at the turkey chops smothered in gravy, stuffed sweet potatoes, sauteed green beans in green onions, mouth-watering buttered rolls, and pecan pie. "I just want to make sure ya'll are fed, that's all."

Lisa rolled her eyes at her mom's minimizations. "I know. And we appreciate you!"

"Yeah, Vanessa, you killed it," Michael concurred then stuffed a whole half roll into his mouth.

Michelle laughed. "Da-ddy, you almost ate the whole thing in one bite!"

Michael looked sheepish. "Heh. I guess I'm hungry!" He caught eyes with Lisa and they shared an intimate gaze.

"So, did y'all get all your work done?" Vanessa asked kicking off the quiet evening dinner conversation.

Lisa updated them on her team effort with Renee and how they were finalizing everything. "It's been pretty dope to work with her which is *crazy* given I couldn't stand her just a month ago," Lisa said before ramming a spoonful of green beans into her mouth.

"That's awesome, baby," Michael and Vanessa both said at the same time and Lisa's heart squeezed. Her loved ones looked at each other and shared a laugh.

"Yeah. I was in utter shock when she apologized for being such a jerk all these years."

Lisa related to her family about the silent competition she had had with Renee and how Renee confessed jealousy.

"Sounds like she admired you and just didn't know how to respond appropriately," Vanessa diagnosed. "So many of us women genuinely esteem each other but because of our own insecurities, it turns into jealousy."

"Mhmm. It's a shame. But I do feel like Black women are doing better these days about establishing real sisterhood with the Black Girl Magic Movement. Mom, do you feel like you have sisters in your life?"

As an adult, Lisa had always wondered about her mother's friends because growing up there weren't too many around. Lots of associates, but not actual "ride or dies."

Vanessa took a minute to respond, swallowing a bit of turkey. "Well, I honestly feel like the deepest relationships I've formed are the ones in my NA group. Those women and I have really bonded because we've experienced the hardship of overcoming addiction. I feel like once you go through something with someone, that bonds you. Even in marriage. If you go through hard things in your marriage and you're able to come out together, you can grow even closer."

Wow. Lisa was surprised at her mother's view since her own love story had ended in a tragic divorce.

"I can agree to that." She peeked at Michael and he winked at her, his mouth hectically chewing.

When Lisa thought of the younger years with her husband there was so much excitement and hope about the future, but then, during their first marriage, reality set it. Marriage was hard. Becoming one with someone was hard. But her love for Michael never disappeared, even after they divorced. She remembered the constant yearning she would talk about with Sylvia and Sylvia's subsequent response.

"Let God show you how to heal your heart. He has the key."

Lisa learned that her healing came from God. But then, He restored her back to Michael. This round of marriage proved to be even harder, whereas it wasn't necessarily their internal struggles that threatened them, it was their outside circumstances.

Lisa went on to share about the work cuts that Carl warned her about and it felt so good to build this time of intimacy with her mother and rebuild it with Michael.

"So, I assume they plan on hiring a whole bunch of replacements if they let y'all go?" Vanessa asked while clearing the table and preparing for dessert.

"They're going to use more freelancers. There will probably be an option for staffers to go the freelance route but that would mean no benefits—,"

"No insurance," Vanessa cut in at the same time, and Lisa nodded, biting her lip.

"I'm grateful I had the coverage after everything with Lee. And even that paid time off that Carl gave me. Now, knowing all this was in the making I can see how much he went out on a limb for me."

"Well, you know we have our savings," Michael volunteered, "and I can carry us if need be. Push comes to shove you can stay home with Michelle—"

But Lisa interrupted, "I'll find something if they fire me." Her voice rattled with annoyance.

Michael knew how much Lisa did not want to stay home. Being a stay-at-home mom was simply not her calling. On top of his lack of understanding about her need to work, it frustrated her that he couldn't have had a spiritual response, like, *Baby, don't worry. God has us.* That was the painful reminder that her husband, as amazing as he was, and as much as he loved her, was still unable to cover her in prayer.

"Well, baby, don't worry. God has you," Vanessa said. "You know He's the ultimate provider."

Lisa's mouth fell open as she stared at her mother.

Ok, Jesus. I see you!

"Thanks, Ma. I know that's what God is saying." She threw her a grateful look. "We don't need to worry."

Even though worry had been Lisa's best friend since she was growing up in her uber-dysfunctional home environment. But on her path of faith, Lisa was unlearning so many things. Worry and anxiety were rooted in a survival mindset. She no longer needed to survive. Now, she could thrive.

"Ok, y'all. Tell me how this pie came out!" Vanessa carried on about all she put in it and everyone had the proper responses; "mmm-ing" and smacking their lips at just the right moments.

The pie was exquisite and reminded Lisa of a sweet Thanksgiving Day. Peering at her family, she got the warm and fuzzies, thankfulness swelling her heart.

"So, what did y'all do today?" Lisa asked, devouring another bite.

"I had a conference call for quarter-end. The team is still delivering, so it looks like we'll reach our projected goals," Michael spouted.

Lisa reached over to pat him on the hand. "That's great!" She knew how important it was to support her husband, even when she didn't feel supported from him in the way *she* needed.

Once again, Lisa prayed that familiar prayer, *Lord, please help me to be patient.*

"Gramma V and I made the BEST snow angels in the world!" Michelle declared, kicking her legs beneath the table in excitement.

"In the whole world?" Lisa asked, eyes ballooning as if incredibly impressed.

Michelle hopped up and down in her seat. "Yep! Wanna see?"

Lisa frowned. "Michelle, it's been snowing for hours since you made those angels." She glanced out the window blanketed by snow. "We've gotten *at least* another foot since then."

Michelle shook her head. "Gramma V took pictures!"

Oh. Of course.

Lisa captured the phone from her mother's extended hand. Swiping at the photos of their snow angels and Michelle toppled in snow, she cracked up at their happy faces masked in scarves, earmuffs and hats. Eyes red and watering, and their faces only partially revealed, their joy was still evident.

Hmmm.

When the pictures changed from their snow party to drawings and colored images, Lisa asked, "What's this one, honey?" Her eyes narrowed more intently at one particular photo.

Michelle leaned in to get a better view. "Oh. That's the picture I drew."

Lisa studied the drawing more closely, her spirit becoming instantly alert. "Is that—?"

Michelle was shaking her head in excitement. "Yep. That's Auntie Sylvia and that's Baby Lee!" She pointed, now standing over her mother's shoulder.

Lisa took in a breath and then looked at Michael who had a brow cocked. Her eyes shifted to her mother whose face held a warm small smile.

"But, Michelle. Baby Lee isn't a baby in this picture. He looks to be about..." Lisa slanted her head to the side, "three or four," she finished slowly. She used her fingers to pinch the image and make it larger.

"I know, Mommy," Michelle said as if this were the most obvious thing in the world. "But that's how he looked in my dream."

Lisa's stomach dropped.

Dream?

She drew her eyes from the picture and looked at Michelle.

"You had a dream?"

Michelle smiled brightly. "Yep! I saw Auntie Sylvia and she was with Baby Lee and he looked like *that*. Older." She pointed to the screen. "And Auntie Sylvia said, 'I'm keeping him company'."

Michelle went back to her seat and started munching on her pie as if nothing extraordinary had just happened.

Lisa sat back mulling over this information then felt the Father's presence ripple through her. That's when she remembered what Michelle had said at Sylvia's funeral.

I know I'll see you in my dreams.

And at that moment, Lisa looked at her daughter through a whole new lens.

My baby is a prophet!

Like a Miracle

CHAPTER 21

Dessert morphed into conversation drizzled over a puzzle that Michelle begged the family to put together. It was only 500 pieces, so everyone agreed, underestimating how advanced this puzzle was.

I mean, did they make this for kids, or adults? Lisa thought, fighting to find a piece that complemented the one in her hand. It was shaded in blue on the left, white on the right and contained a hint of teal blended in the middle. She was working on the sky, but then, stared enviously at Michael who had more pieces fitted on the board than anyone.

"I feel like you're cheating," she accused, with a glint in her eye.

"Now, how am I supposed to cheat with a puzzle?" Michael smirked and hovered back over his board, shoulders taut, eyes laser-focused. He looked like he was reviewing a sales report at work.

"By peeking at the letters on the back," Lisa replied in a smug tone.

Michael rolled his eyes and flipped over the piece, reflecting a blank slate of cardboard.

Oh. Guess I should have checked to see if these had the letters, Lisa thought. Sheepishly, her eyes dropped back to her puzzle piece.

A victory grin dashed across Michael's face.

Vanessa scoffed, "I been trying to connect this same piece *forever*." Her gaze shifted to Michael's area. "I think you stole my piece!"

Michael's grin fell. "Now, why is everybody comin' for *me* all of a sudden? I'm over here mindin' my business. Doin' my *job* and making this thing happen. Just because I'm a *master* puzzler..."

Michelle laughed, her head falling backward as she folded her legs beneath her. The gesture caused a startled Snowball to "Meow" since her movement disturbed his nap. The poor feline had been using her leg as a pillow.

Petting Snowball, Michelle responded to her father, "Daddy, you made that up!"

"Tell me you didn't take that piece that belonged to me?" Vanessa eyed Michael, serious as a heart attack. Leaning over on her forearms, she homed in on his area. The group had the puzzle sprawled on cardboard across the living room floor so they could move it easily.

Lisa couldn't help but laugh. "Mom. I think you been in this house too long."

Vanessa's face curved into a rueful smile and she backed off, "Well. Maybe you right," then eyed her phone. "I need to get my tail in the bed. It's almost 11 o'clock. *That's* why I'm trippin'."

Lisa hadn't realized it was that late. She figured Michelle wouldn't have school the next day. They had accumulated over two feet of snow and the temperature had fallen to -1 degrees.

"Michelle, you should turn in too. We don't know if you'll have school tomorrow but you've still had a long day. Get some rest."

Right on time, Michelle yawned and didn't even fight to try to stay up longer; a telltale sign of her exhaustion.

"Can we finish tomorrow?" she asked, a little sullen, shoulders shrinking in surrender.

"Yep. Unless I complete the rest when you go to bed," Michael teased.

The little girl's jaw dropped. "Daddy! You're gonna finish my puzzle without me?"

Michael hopped to his feet, then swooped her from the floor and squeezed her tight. "You'll see when you wake up." Pretending to bite her, he buried his face into her neck, and she giggled.

Lisa joined them for a group hug. It was this moment right here that she wanted to hold onto forever.

Since Hank left, Vanessa had been sleeping with Michelle in her room. It was a great arrangement because Lisa knew Michelle needed the comfort from Sylvia's passing. Catching her mom stretch and yawn, Lisa realized, she did too.

When she was done, Lisa pulled Vanessa in for a hug. "Thanks for coming."

Tears clung to Vanessa's eyes.

"Of course," she whispered, and smoothed Lisa's tendrils with a loving hand. "I'm just glad your dad told me to."

Lisa agreed, "Me too. *And* that he left when he did. It's a *mess* out there." They both looked out the window in horror, still intertwined.

Lord, thank You for keeping the rest of my loved ones safe, Lisa had prayed right after Hank had texted that he made it home.

When Vanessa and Michelle exited with Snowball safely locked in Michelle's arms, Lisa and Michael snuggled on the couch beneath a fleece. Michael had a bottle of Soban Estate Cabernet popped open and two glasses poured. The wine was so good only one glass was needed to feel it, yet Michael was already on his second. Ari Lennox resounded from the Bluetooth speaker, completing the ambiance.

"I feel like we needed this," Lisa murmured against his chest, referring to their snow day. His scratchy crew-neck auburn sweater pressed deeper into her cheek as she dug in closer.

Michael's nod ruffled her bed of kinky coils. "Yeah. I definitely needed it," he replied in a husky-seductive way.

Lisa elbowed him as best she could while straddled in between his legs.

"I'm just joking," he added, then raised her lips to his. The kiss was slow and deep. Not like earlier in the shower when he had devoured her.

In a low tone, Lisa asked, "So, I guess this means you forgive me?"

She had barely said the words above a whisper, using all her bravery to muster them. A beat later, a swirl of fear swam in her gut and she washed it down with a swig of wine. When she lowered her glass, Michael lifted her chin and peered into her eyes.

"Forgive you for what?"

He seemed genuine, though Lisa was confused as to how he could be.

"You know."

She tried to gulp down the ickiness in her throat and force the burning sensation behind her eyes to the back of her head.

"For Lee," she finally managed, but the burning didn't go away.

Michael's eyes dawned in understanding. "You think I blamed you for Lee?"

He sounded surprised and Lisa sat up a little to discern if he was being completely honest.

"You didn't? *You—don't?*"

"Baby, how could I blame you for that? Dr. Swan said Placenta Previa isn't something that can even be prevented or reversed. I was just upset because you didn't keep me in the loop. Not that you had necessarily *done something* to cause the bleeding."

Care swam in Michael's eyes and Lisa hadn't been privy to the burden she was lugging around until he released her from it. The burning behind her eyes, however, increased, until tears streamed over her frowning lips.

"I thought. I thought you did. I thought, that's why you were mad." She bowed her head and snuggled her stemless glass between her folded legs, both shoulders shaking a little.

Michael pulled her closer and caressed her back.

"No. I *was* mad. I mean, I was *angry* that you didn't let me in. That you didn't trust me enough to lean on me. But for the most part, I was more mad at myself. And. And God," he let out.

God?

Michael huffed a breath, the outward protrusion of his chest lifting her head. "I was mad that I couldn't keep you from it," he continued. "Sometimes, I still hear you screaming at the hospital when you woke up and found out," he whispered. He looked off into a daze.

A cold shiver sliced through Lisa. "You couldn't have done anything either. How can you blame yourself and not me?" she asked. "If anything, I should have slowed down more." She bit her lip and sat back up, wiping the moisture from her face with the back of her sleeve. "Maybe, worked from home like you were begging me to."

It was then when Lisa remembered that she hadn't shared about the Placenta Previa with Dr. Celia during their first call. If she had, it would have been like admitting she could have prevented the outcome with Baby Lee by slowing down more. The weight of this revelation pierced her.

I blame myself.

"Look at me." Michael cupped Lisa's face, lifting it and she had no choice but to stare into his earnest expression. "I don't blame you. I don't even blame God. Anymore."

Realizing that this was the second time her husband had mentioned God in less than a minute, which was more than he had mentioned Him all year, Lisa's ears stood up.

"So. So *why* don't you blame God?" she asked carefully, her journalism degree now working overtime.

Ask open-ended questions. Handle the interview with care.

Michael sighed before taking a long sip. "I honestly can't really explain it. I just know how hurt and angry I was when we lost Lee. I couldn't understand how that could happen. How *God* could *let* that happen. Then Sylvia died and I thought for sure you was gone' fall to pieces and hide in a dark hole and we would never see you again. Anybody would have. Nobody would have blamed you. It was all too much. But you didn't. You held on. And you kept talking about God, even though you were so hurt. And then, your parents came and I started seeing something I had never seen before..." He looked off as if searching for the words.

Lisa was witnessing a miracle. Right here. Right now. A full-blown, genuine miracle was happening with Michael Doris.

"And then your dad was talking about how his wife almost lost her life to breast cancer, and I realized how blessed I was to still have you. Even when we lost Baby Lee." He paused, looking at her and wiped a tear from her face, even though his own eyes were watering.

"And then, your mom was talking about God delivering her from 15 years of addiction. That blew me away because…" his voice trailed and he stared at his wine glass for a second. "Because I can't imagine how hard it would be to stop an addiction you've had that long," he finished while gently caressing Lisa's hand covering her glass. "And knowing how estranged you guys had been, and seeing how they showed up, and put all of that stuff in the past…"

Wow. This is nuts, Lisa thought, processing everything Michael was sharing. All *that* had been building up inside of him since Sylvia's passing? No. Since they lost Baby Lee.

Sure, Lisa had known how impactful her parents' visit had been for Michelle. Even how much encouragement and healing she had received personally, but she never stopped to think as to what it would do for Michael. Out of everyone in the world, except probably Sylvia, Michael knew how Lisa's upbringing had resulted in her brokenness. Especially when it came to trusting others. He saw her at her lowest. He saw when her father's abandonment and her mother's distance would bring her to her knees. Now he got to witness them being there. He got to witness them *healing* her.

"It was like, everything you had ever wanted with them was happening," Michael finally finished. He looked at Lisa, his light brown eyes magnifying every feeling flowing in her heart.

She set her glass on the floor and grabbed his hands.

"It was like." Michael paused, seeming to be fearful of sounding foolish, so Lisa finished the sentence for him.

"Like a miracle," she breathed.

"Yeah," he said, his voice thickened with emotion and awe.

The tears that were now spilling over his face showed Lisa exactly what she had suspected. Michael was coming to faith.

~

MICHAEL SAT AT LISA'S BEDSIDE IN THE HOSPITAL ROOM, KNEE rocking profusely, head cradled in his hands, waiting. He was waiting for Lisa to come to after Dr. Swan rushed her for an emergency C-section. Her body had dispelled so much blood.

Trying to wrap his brain around everything, he rubbed his head, both hands still masking his face. The horror of hearing the news from Danita that they were taking Lisa to the hospital still echoed in his ears. Relief emerged that Lisa was ok, only to be quenched by the loss of their son.

"Lisa pulled through, but the baby didn't make it," Dr. Swan said with a grim expression.

Michael couldn't hold back his pain. *I can't believe it.* His mind was bundled with shock. His baby boy was gone. Tears emasculated his cheeks and with trembling fingers, he rubbed them away.

I've got to get myself together before she wakes up, he thought, shooting Lisa a determined look. Her face was ashen but she was still so beautiful, and the magnet of their shared love drew him to her.

"Baby. Baby. I got you," Michael whispered while gripping her hand. He hadn't expected her to respond but to his surprise, she started moving.

"Michael?" Lisa said in a raspy tone.

"Lisa."

Michael squeezed her hand, momentarily grateful she was alive. Momentarily grateful that she was ok. But then, her wailing started, and all he wanted to do was crawl into that dark hole with her. But he couldn't. He was her husband. It was his duty to protect her. So even though he couldn't keep her from the loss of their son, he laid over her on the hospital bed, attempting to shield her the best way he knew how.

That evening was horrendous. Michael wasn't a drinker but found an old bottle of Vodka in the cabinet and drank it straight. It was the only way he could sleep. When Lisa came home, he let Sylvia sleep with her and ended up on the floor by Baby Lee's crib. At his wife's incessant nagging, he had finally finished it. And for what?

Curled on bare hardwood and clutching his son's stuffed animal was the first time in Michael's life he had ever felt *devastated*.

Why?!

His soul cried, grasping at straws. Anything to make sense of it. He and Lisa were good people. Lisa was this devout Christian. How could the God she serves take their son? Take *her* son?

The question, "Why?" was as surprising to Michael as he was sure it was to God. Michael had never cried out to God. He had never needed to. He came from a safe, loving home. It wasn't Cosby Show-perfect, but he had all his needs met. His father was an upstanding role model, training him to be a good man. His mother was the gentle loving soul that nurtured him in the ways all children required. His intelligence, good looks and charm had consistently been at his beck and call, aiding him to climb the heights of corporate America. Being a Black male in America carried its own weighty bag of micro-aggressions, stereotypes, and blatant racism, yet Michael had never encountered anything that brought him to his knees. Until now.

Pain threatened to burst his heart in his chest. All the months of planning. All the dreams about to be realized. And then this.

Lisa doesn't deserve this.

There he was, talking to God again. Not that God was talking back. That was the thing that got Michael. How did people talk to an invisible Being who didn't respond? He never understood it. But even though there was no audible voice in answer, somewhere inside himself, Michael knew, *something* was happening. Because, he had never needed to talk to God before, and, though he wasn't fully ready to admit it, now he did.

The day to cremate his son arrived too soon. Michael was floored by the strength Lisa was exuding. On the outside he was keeping it together but on the inside, he was a tangled mess. Each night he needed Vodka to sleep. Having finished the old bottle, he purchased a new one. The day of the memorial was the first time Michael drank in the middle of the day. That's when he knew, *Houston, we have a problem.*

It's cool. I'll stop once we get through this.

But then, Sylvia died.

He couldn't believe this amazing, spirited, sweet, vivacious human being *died*. And his daughter was there!

God. What are you doing?

That's when Michael became more direct in his line of questioning. But still, no response. Only anger. Anger that Lisa kept him out of the loop from Dr. Singh's full report and didn't tell him she had been bleeding even during that visit. Anger that after all these years she didn't trust him enough to lean on him, share with him. Anger that God allowed tragedy after tragedy to touch their household. Anger that he couldn't save his family from any of it.

Poor Michelle, who was so close to Sylvia, had witnessed her beloved Auntie Sylvia dead, and now held some type of responsibility about it. Lisa had told him about Michelle's question, *Did she kill Sylvia?*

While on his knees, in his son's old room, with the bottle strangled between his fingers, Michael's heart caved. Since Hank was on the couch, Michael was hiding in the office. He couldn't drink so openly at night anymore after Lisa went to bed.

Looking at the ceiling, another prayer escaped. *What are you doing?*

But no answer, so he took a sip. Thankfully, Hank had shown up out of nowhere, filling the space Michael was struggling to fill. Giving Lisa peace and healing in a way he had never witnessed before. Hank told him about Novelle. How her life-threatening diagnosis had brought him to his knees. That God had saved her. That her diagnosis made him realize how short life really was.

Michael's heart started to unthaw upon heraing this. God was good. He had heard it so many times from Lisa and Sylvia but now he was hearing it from another man. A Black man. A Black father. A man who clearly had been changed from his spiritual encounter.

Then, Vanessa showed up, testifying about her deliverance from addiction. Michael didn't know the stinging feeling in his heart was conviction, but he knew enough to know, God was speaking to him. It was the first time in his life he felt it. Goosebumps eroded his arms as Vanessa shared her faith. Shared her resilience. *God's* resilience.

Lord, I don't want to be an alcoholic, Michael stated, simply. He was a fantastic sales exec and though no one knew his struggle, he knew enough about addiction to know, that wouldn't last. Eventually, he would start slipping.

Then they went to church. Part of the reason Michael said they should go was because the whole group was down and he didn't want to be the one holding them back. Another part of that reason was because he knew Lisa needed it and wanted to make sure she got what she needed. But another part, a more pressing part, was this ferocious curiosity and insatiable desire mounting his spirit.

He *needed* to know, "*Why?*"

After the service Michael felt the eyes of his heart start to become enlightened. It was like he had been fumbling around a dark room, hands smacking the walls, body ramming into furniture, trying to find his way. But now, there were glimpses of light in answer to his questions. Hank was a glimmer of light. Vanessa was a glimmer of light. Sylvia was a glimmer of light. Lisa was a glimmer of light.

The minister said hard things happen in our faith. That we should expect both hard things and good things, Michael ruminated.

In the midst of all their pain and struggles, he couldn't deny the good things. He still had Lisa. He still had Michelle. And now, they had Hank and Vanessa.

As he looked across the table sharing their meal, Michael watched Lisa basking in the love of her parents for the first time ever in the 14 years he had known her. It was then that he finally heard a clear, small voice in answer to his question, *Lord, what are you doing?*

I am doing this, Beloved.

I am doing this.

Answered Prayers

CHAPTER 22

The next morning, Lisa and her tribe tackled another day indoors. They managed to finish the puzzle—with minimal accusations toward Michael—before all four ventured outside to play in the snow. Michael helped Michelle build the snowman while Vanessa "supervised" and Lisa caught it all on her phone.

"Ya'll, that head is lookin' raaa-*ther* lumpy." Vanessa frowned while stooping to the side, her cheek paralleled to the ground, locks dangling. "You need to pack it in more."

Michael shot Vanessa a look and Lisa cracked up.

"You *are* on my live, Mr. Doris! Bruh, fix your face."

"*Good*. Then the folks who see this will be witness that Mr. Black's head is just fine!" he barked back.

Lisa zoomed in on the snowman's head to show her viewers while recording live on her social media account.

"And why are y'all namin' him Mr. Black?" Vanessa asked. "Looks white as snow to me!" She laughed at her own humor.

"Cuz, we got this black scarf to put on him." Michelle waved the scarf in the air as evidence.

Just when Lisa was zooming out to capture Mr. Black's future scarf, Joe popped in on her live feed. Lisa hurried to end the live, not wanting her husband to all of a sudden desire to view the footage. She hurriedly exited her account and switched to her video setting. Discomfort tickled her abdomen.

Lisa and Joe were initially supposed to meet today for her to get the book he promised, but due to the weather, decided to re-schedule. Still, her uncertainty about them even meeting is what prompted her to end the live. Now that things were back on track with Michael, her mind felt more clear.

How would Michael feel if he knew I was meeting Joe?

But her concerns were snuffed by a flying snowball smacking her square in the jaw. The act caused Lisa's phone to fall from her hand.

"Oh no you did not, Michael Doris!" she huffed, vigorously shaking her white beanie hat, snow flying everywhere. "You better watch yo back!" Working quickly, she began creating a snowball in retaliation. This marked the onset of an hour-long snowball fight between the foursome.

That evening, Carol invited them down for hot chocolate and chocolate chip cookies, "Because it's the perfect treat for a snow day!" she gushed. When Michelle overheard Lisa telling Michael about the invite, her alternate pleading and begging to go, solidified their plans.

Later that evening, while leaning on the kitchen counter, Lisa admired the elegant decor of Carol's home. "I love your space," she commented. It was all whites, soft greys, and nudes. Clearly her friend did not have children.

Michelle's crayons and dirty hands would be all over every inch of white in this house.

Lisa grimaced, thinking about it. But then, sadness emerged because she knew how much Carol wanted children. More pain followed at the remembrance of her own loss.

"Thanks," Carol replied. "It took me *forever* to get the exact hue of pearl for the curtains and we had to measure and cut the shades to fit the windows."

The perfect hostess, Carol fluttered around the living room, making sure everyone was taken care of by setting out a fresh plate of cookies and refilling mugs. The aroma of sugar entwined with chocolate clung to the atmosphere.

Inhaling, Lisa eyed the plate of goodies. *Homemade*, of all things.

She couldn't remember the last time she'd baked something. *It would have been when Michelle was way smaller.* Between work, being a mom and wife, and making breakfast each morning, when did she have time to bake?

But still, it would be nice if I tried my hand at a pie sometime.

Lisa glanced around the home. The layout was the same but opposite of the Dorises. Their home entry came in from the west and opened into the kitchen but the Johnson's entrance was on the east.

After making her rounds, Carol returned to the kitchen. "I'm glad you guys could come down. What happened to your mom?" She was adorable, swaddled in a large oversized blue turtleneck sweater that matched her ocean-colored eyes.

"Oh, she had a virtual NA meeting she needed to hop on," Lisa replied.

Carol nodded, compassion imprinting her face. "Gotcha. Make sure to bag up some cookies for her. We don't need them all! And I'm not expecting anyone else. I haven't had any visitors since we moved here. You guys are the first." As she spoke, she tossed her head at the corner nook near the kitchen, and Lisa followed.

Though Lisa's home didn't have a nook, it did have an island in the kitchen, in lieu of the nook. While trailing her friend, Lisa peeked at Michael bonding in front of the 72-inch TV with Robbie, a tall friendly man with glasses. He was exactly the type of guy Lisa could see Carol with and seemed to harbor the same sweet spirit, although more introverted.

A football game was in action and the husbands were yelling randomly at players. Michelle was spread eagle on the floor just about to use Michael's tablet with her chocolate-smeared fingers.

"Uh unh! Wash your hands before you touch that thing," Lisa called from her vantage point and Michelle spewed a robust eye roll. But before Lisa could check her, Michael was on it.

"Do you want to go back upstairs and go to bed early?" he immediately asked.

Michelle's face morphed into alarm and the two high puffs on her head toggled from side to side.

"Then apologize to your mom and go wash your hands."

Lisa didn't know if she was more impressed that Michael had chastised their daughter, or that he had done so in the middle of a freaking football game.

Eyes drilling the floor, Michelle muttered, "Sorry," on her way into the restroom.

Lisa decided she was more impressed by the latter. Michael winked before being glued back to the screen and her heart smiled.

We are definitely back on track.

"So, what's new?" Carol asked. She had folded her legs while perched on the little bench and slouched against the crisscross-pained picture window. Though the blizzard outside had finally calmed, there was little hope of a school day tomorrow.

Another indoor saga with this girl, Lisa thought, wondering how they would fare with Michelle the next day. *Thank God mom is here.*

Before answering Carol, Lisa took a sip from her hot chocolate. "Girl, what's *not* new," she said, and proceeded to update her on work stuff, starting with the lightest topic first.

"What are you gonna do if the work cuts happen?" Carol looked concerned while munching on a cookie.

"I honestly don't know. It really is a walk-by-faith situation. I mean, if they give me the option to be a freelancer that probably means less hours, losing my office, maybe losing Danita, and definitely losing health insurance."

Carol's face looked puzzled. "But don't you get health insurance through Michael's job?"

Lisa sighed. "Yeah. It really is just me needing to provide for myself. I know it sounds crazy and maybe there's something wrong with it but I have this innate thing that just does not feel comfortable being solely dependent on someone else. Even if it is my husband," she added with a rueful glance toward Michael. He hi-fived Robbie after somebody put some important point on the board.

I'm glad he found a friend. She chuckled to herself. Sports was not Lisa's thing, so Robbie and Michael could get that all day as far as she was concerned.

"Well, I certainly understand that," Carol agreed. "It's been sooo uncomfortable being out of work after moving here. *And,* thanks to HGTV, I've got this new habit of decorating. But I simply can't add any more home decor to this house!" she exclaimed. "I swear if I bring one more piece of home decor home, Robbie is going to *kill* me."

They both laughed, but Lisa felt a wave of guilt afterward. "I'm sorry, girl. I haven't even asked how the job hunt was going for you."

Carol shooed Lisa off. "You've had the *most* going on. But, I honestly feel like God just has me in a rest season, you know? I've been frustrated and anxious but He just keeps on providing. Besides, it's probably best that I slow down right now." Hesitating, she placed her hand gently over her stomach. "I'm pregnant," she revealed.

"What!" Lisa's excitement seemed to swallow the entire word. As she grinned, her face was a lightbulb. "That's *great!*"

Carol held a small smile. "It is. I'm sorry for not seeming more excited. It's just, after so many failed attempts, it gets hard to be."

Lisa nodded, thinking that she wasn't even sure how she would feel if *she* got pregnant again.

Going through that was so traumatic, Lord. Please give me at least a year. I simply can't even think about another baby.

Lisa reached over and rubbed her friend's hand. "I haven't been through what you've been through, but now, I can imagine." She offered sympathetic eyes. "Still, I have news that may provide some encouragement with our faith."

Carol sat up straighter, "Do tell. I always need encouragement," then chuckled.

Pitching a gaze at her husband, Lisa confided in a low tone, "I think Michael has come to Christ." She then shared about their conversation from last night.

Carol's icy blue eyes were frosted with wonder then skated toward Michael. It was now *her* time to reach for her friend. "Oh, I'm so happy for you. I know it's been a long time coming."

"Yep. It sure has. I honestly *never* thought I would see the day," Lisa admitted, shame hidden in her eyes.

"Yeah. But you know what this means?"

"Mmhmm. That aliens have abducted my husband," Lisa joked.

Carol laughed, then patted her stomach with a dreamy look. "Well, *maybe*. But I was gonna say, it means—if this baby comes to fruition of course," she paused, dropping her eyes to her stomach, then lifted them again, "that *both* of our prayers have been answered."

Lisa smiled, placed her hand over her friend's stomach, and rubbed it.

"Yeah. That sounds much better than aliens."

***

"How was your time with Carol and Robbie?" Vanessa asked. She and Lisa languidly lounged on the couch while Michael listened to Michelle's bedtime story. It was his turn tonight.

Lisa smiled. "Carol is pregnant," she shared.

"Oh. Well, that's nice."

Lisa then realized her mother's understated reaction was predicated on the fact that she didn't know the whole story.

"It is. It's her *fourth* pregnancy. She's had *three* miscarriages." Lisa held up three fingers to confirm.

Vanessa stopped chewing the chocolate chip cookie filling her mouth, "Oh!" dropping crumbs everywhere. "Well then, this is *really* a blessing." She hurried to grasp the crumbs and swept them onto her saucer.

"Yeah. I pray this one is it." Lisa got comfortable, rubbing her hands on her lap and folding her calves beneath her, her yoga black pants sliding along the microfiber fabric.

"And how are you doing with that?" Vanessa studied her daughter.

Somewhat caught off guard, Lisa wondered, *How* do *I feel?*

"Well, honestly, I have a few different thoughts." She took a sip of hot water while trying to pin down her emotions.

"Disheartened because it makes me miss Baby Lee. If he was born, our kids would only be five months apart. But hopeful for Carol because she's had such a hard journey and I just want this to be *it* for her."

Vanessa leaned in and patted Lisa's kneecap. "I can understand that. If there's one thing I've learned in this life, it's that no matter how solid your plan is, there's always surprises."

Intrigue sparked in Lisa about her mother's journey. "Mom, what were some of the things you hoped for when you were younger?" For some reason, it never dawned on Lisa to ask her this, probably because, like most children, it was hard to think her parents had a life before her.

Vanessa caught a faraway gaze while swallowing her milk. "I wanted to be a designer. I loved putting fits together. I even had an internship with this fly boutique in Atlanta and thought *that* was gonna be my ticket."

"Wow. I can totally see that."

Lisa's eyes ran over her mother's large netted emerald sweater that dipped below her butt, covering a black tank that hung fabulously over black jeggings. Her shimmering pink lip only slightly faded by eating, was the ideal accent. Vanessa was always put together on the outside, even when she wasn't so put together on the inside.

"So, what happened?" Lisa asked.

"I got pregnant."

"Oh." Lisa lowered her eyes.

"But not with you, honey. By the time you came along, we were already married and those plans were put on the top shelf."

"So, it was with the other baby then?"

It felt so odd to reference this mysterious being that had come before Lisa. Up until a few weeks ago, in her mind, she was an only child. Even if on some secret psychological level, she threw her dad's kids in the mix, she was still the oldest. There was never *anyone* before her.

"Yeah. It was the other baby." Vanessa gulped her drink and silence sat between them.

Lisa had so many questions and was trying to choose which one was best.

"How did you…how did you get over it?" she finally asked and waited on the edge of her seat.

Vanessa smiled sadly. "Honestly, that's the issue. I didn't." Heaving a heavy sigh, pain was breathed into each word. "That's why I turned to the drugs. My doctor had prescribed OxyContin to help with the bleeding and then I was hooked."

Lisa's jaw dropped. "You got turned out because of a doctor?" That was the last thing she had expected to hear.

Vanessa nodded. "Back then they didn't know how addictive it was. They did what they knew to do." She shrugged but Lisa was in shock.

"That's unbelievable. I can't believe you were basically a victim and yet our society treated you like a…" She let her voice die, not wanting to hurt her mother.

"Like a feen? Yeah. But it ain't the first time. Imagine what happened to our people during the crack epidemic. All this political rhetoric about cracking down on crack and making America great again and *they* were the ones dumping it into our communities." Vanessa's mouth set into a thin line, eyes transforming into steal.

"It's so sickening that those with drug-abuse histories are the very ones that get demonized and stumped on. Especially when it's the government who were the real dealers," Lisa spit out. Her anger was starting to boil. It was at that moment, the darkness that had covered her childhood received some light. It wasn't that her mother had *tried* to be cruel, or mean, or negligent during those years. It was that she too was a victim.

And I never knew it was because of the lost baby. Lisa patted her mother's leg in empathy. *That could have easily been me.*

"Mom, I'm sorry. I never even asked your story as to how you started doing drugs."

"Sweetie, that is not your responsibility. I had my own demons I was battling. It wouldn't have even been right to share something like that with you. If anything, I just wish I could have been the mother you deserved." A tear slipped over Vanessa's cheek and she hurried to wipe it.

"What I'm learning is, as parents, we really are just doing the best we can," Lisa said, thinking of her own mistakes in parenting. She also thought of how easily it could have been for her to take up drinking or drugs after all the pain she experienced losing Lee, and then Sylvia.

Well, I'm not out of the woods yet.

A sinking feeling hit her insides as she thought about her recent connection with Joe.

"Baby girl has safely landed into dreamland." Michael materialized at the hallway entry, startling the mess out of Lisa.

He laughed when she jumped, "Did I scare you?" then slid over and planted a kiss on her cheek with a big smile. But his smile simmered once he noticed how thick the air was. "Oh. My bad. Didn't mean to interrupt."

Vanessa was trying to get her face together, dabbing a napkin over tears and Lisa was trying to make it seem like she hadn't been thinking of another man.

"No, it's cool." Lisa cleared her throat. "We were just uhh,"

"Just having a very serious conversation that I interrupted." Michael chuckled and straightened up from his kiss. "It's all good. I'm a go bond with myself and catch up on the NFL highlights. Yo boy Robbie thinks the Cowboys are a shoo-in for the playoffs." He smirked, "Shooot. Yeah *right*," then disappeared into their bedroom.

Relief circled Lisa and she couldn't deny that that wasn't the proper response to her husband leaving the room. When the click to their bedroom door solidified that it was closed she snuck a peak at her mom. Vanessa was again munching on her cookie.

"Ma. Can I…can I tell you something?"

Vanessa looked up, her face filled with so much peace that Lisa now understood came from the grace of God.

"Sure. What's up?"

Lisa hesitated, Danita's reaction ringing in her mind, but knew after all that her mother had shared and been through, there would surely be no judgment on her part. So, she poured out, informing her about Joe's sudden appearance. Who he had been to her back then. The beautiful man that he was and how he seemed to genuinely be offering a friendship in a season that had been so difficult.

Throughout the confession, her mother lacked any type of response except for when Lisa admitted they were supposed to meet that very day. Vanessa had taken a swig of the remaining milk in her cup. Lisa wondered if it was to hide her frown.

"But the storm happened, so we re-scheduled," Lisa finished.

Telling her mother everything in her heart felt somehow freeing and she realized it was normally something she would have shared with Sylvia. Sylvia's wisdom had been her north star for a whole five years. Lisa had to remind herself it was the Father's Spirit that was really guiding her. Still, she was so used to His spirit being packaged in the older woman's joyous physical being.

After Lisa was done, she waited, thinking Vanessa was probably going to tell her she was crazy for considering meeting up with her ex.

To her surprise, Vanessa replied, "Well, what is God saying?"

Hmm. Now that was a good question. What *was* God saying?

"I-I'm not sure." Lisa breathed a long exhale as her shoulders sagged. "Everything's been so murky lately. I only know how refreshing it was to reconnect with Joe. I realized I've felt burdened by leaving him like that and ending things how I did. Like—I'm responsible if he isn't happy. If he hasn't found someone…" She let her voice drift along with her vision, staring at the hardwood flooring. Little thin lines appeared on her forehead while she tried to verbalize her feelings. "And it seems like there's just still something…" Lisa struggled for the words, "*unfinished* about us."

There. That's what it was. It felt like Lisa and Joe had unfinished business.

"It's like I left him *hanging* and just kept it movin'," she added, thinking about her last moment with Joe.

They were outside his church where she had received spiritual revelation that she was supposed to choose Michael. Lisa was a new Believer and it was such a big deal because she hadn't ever heard

God that clearly before. It was also her first experience letting go of something good with the blind hope of receiving something better.

"Well, timing is everything." Vanessa's eyes shifted to the frosted windows that clothed their home, indicating the storm that interrupted the planned meet-up. "If this is something that needs to be resolved between the two of you, then God's timing will allow for it. Have you prayed about it?"

This shiny new spiritual version of her mother was blowing Lisa away. It was truly a miracle. Eyes downcast, she shook her Bantu knot-out. "No. No, I haven't."

Vanessa set her empty mug and saucer onto the floor next to her pedicured feet. She scooted over and held out her hands, white part upward. "Ok. Let's do it now then."

Encouragement and gratitude group hugged Lisa's heart. It was the same experience she often had with Sylvia, but now she was having it with her mother.

I never thought I'd see the day.

Lisa extended her hands and placed them into Vanessa's soft palms. Both women bowed their heads to pray together, for the first time ever.

Honesty Breeds Healing

CHAPTER 23

The flurry of the Jazz mag team rivaled the snow coming down in droves. Everyone was trying to tie the final knots on their work assignments before the holiday break. Thanksgiving was a mere three days away and today was the last day in the office. Folks would, of course, be working from home but Lisa wasn't sure if she would be one of them. Knowing what she knew about the impending work cuts had her rethinking her position at Jazz and how much blood, sweat, and tears she had been giving them. Should she cease the grueling combative fight she had been doing the last six years to hold on to her position, or take her chances with freelance? Working freelance wasn't ideal at all as it wasn't consistent, didn't give her health benefits, and meant being at home more, where she would inevitably meet her demise. If boredom didn't take her out, Michelle's Energizer-Bunny-hyperness surely would.

All these thoughts reeled in Lisa's mind when Danita popped in saying Carl wanted to see her.

Lisa glanced from her work desk. "Did he say what it was about?" Her eyes scurried to the clock. 4:17 pm. She was trying to leave on time for her and Michael's counseling appointment with Dr. Celia. They were re-starting marriage counseling, both agreeing it would be a great tune-up after this heavy-hitting season.

Danita shrugged, "Not a clue," before vanishing as suddenly as she had appeared.

With an annoyed frown, Lisa finished chiseling out her sentence.

This man wants me to turn this article in by this freaking deadline but then wants to take up the time I need to do it.

That freelance option was looking better and better. Continuing to ruminate, she pushed herself away from her desk and grabbed her phone.

In case I have to tell Michael I'll be late.

Moments later, Lisa rounded the hall in her Dolce & Gabbana black pumps and was surprised to see Renee coming from the opposite direction.

She smiled. "Hey. You heading to Carl?" Lisa's eyes bloomed curiously.

"Yeah, you?" Renee sounded just as curious.

Lisa nodded as they fell into step. "You know what this is about?" She dared the question, mumbling as people zipped by. You never could know who was eavesdropping and plotting to usurp your position with any malicious gossip.

"Not at all," Renee murmured back with a short chuckle. "I guess we 'bout to find out."

Trying to discern if they were true, Lisa weighed her associate's words. Was Renee as really in the dark as much as she was? They had been cool since working together last month but people could easily revert to their old ways. Lisa *had* managed to get her previous pregnancy waistline back, which, for all she knew, sparked more jealousy from her colleague.

When they reached the meeting room, Lisa let Renee go first. Peeking over Renee's shoulder she tried to get a read on how Carl responded when she walked in, but all Lisa saw was his cordial greeting. Yet, when his eyes met hers, there was something more.

As Carl shut the door, the two took their seats side-by-side and waited.

Lisa's stomach sank .

Oh God. Is this it? Are we 'bout to get the drop? Or maybe I am? Or maybe Renee is?

"Ladies, we're making some upcoming changes around here at Jazz." Carl cleared his throat, clasping his hands in front of him and looking as professional as ever.

Neither woman spoke. They just stared.

Well, if Renee is in on this she's doing a good job hiding it.

Lisa couldn't help assessing her peer out of her peripheral. Renee sat as rigid as a board, but Lisa could tell the woman was as stressed as she was. Her right finger kept tapping over her left hand.

"I want to thank the two of you for working together," Carl said. "I know it wasn't easy but I want you to know your persistence and talent have impressed even the higher-ups."

Lisa leaned in, wondering where this was going.

"That article you guys did on fibroids has resulted in over *seventy* emails from women who can relate. And the emails are *still* pouring in!" Carl's gaze zeroed in on Lisa. "Lisa, your authentic testimonial *blew* our readers away. Thank you so much for opening up about your experience."

For the first time during the meeting, Lisa cracked a smile. "Thanks. It's really good to know so many others were helped by it."

That's why he was looking at me like that. He was pleased.

"Yes. They were. And then the article on Swizz Beats!" Carl made a chef's kiss in the air but it was the huge beaming smile that almost knocked Lisa over. "The leak on the *Beatz & Barz?*! *Insane!* Our numbers *skyrocketed!*"

Lisa quickly spoke, "That was all Renee. *She* was the one who got the intel."

Renee tossed a grateful smile to Lisa. "Yeah. It was me but Lisa's the one who made sure our bases were covered, so we didn't get sued!"

"Regardless, you both did a fantastic job. There will be a couple of bonuses in your next checks as a result. We want to keep you on as staffers and be on the lookout for other paired assignments. Not everyone was so lucky to get this type of news, so you two should feel *exceptional*." Carl's face shone like a proud father and Lisa felt overwhelmed with the good news.

Bonuses? Emails for her fibroids story?

And here I was thinking I was about to get fired!

Basking in the rare praise from her superior, Lisa silently prayed, *Thank you, Father for your goodness.*

❧

SWIMMING ON THE HIGH FROM HER WORK PICK-ME-UP, LISA RUSHED into the building that housed Dr. Celia's office on Madison and 34th Street. She hadn't had a physical visit in a while and hadn't had one with Michael in over a year, so even though it was a familiar space, it took some getting used to. Upon entering, she discovered Michael already seated and Dr. Celia serving him something from the Keurig.

Coffee?

"So sorry I'm late!" accompanied Lisa's dashing into the intimate office space. She flung her bag and peacoat on a nearby coat hook. "I had a really good reason," she said, grinning.

"No worries. We've only been here a few minutes." Dr. Celia looked at her watch as Lisa snuck her husband a quick hug.

"Hey you." Michael's murmur against her forehead caused butterflies. It was good to know he still had that affect on her.

"Let's get started, shall we?" Dr. Celia indicated for the couple to sit in the plush comfy chairs that faced hers. They were stationed perpendicular to the fluffy chic sofa against the east wall.

The space held an amazing ambiance that drew in all the senses with lavender gracing the windowsill and floating along the premises. It was the perfect homey, soothing interior for Lisa to unwind in after a hectic workday. Plopping back into her seat, she got comfortable.

"Let's do a quick check-in. On a scale of 1-5, one being the worst, five being the best, how are you guys doing?" Dr. Celia dipped her eyes over her gold-trimmed rims and peered at the couple. Her long, wavy hair that normally dangled to her shoulders was carefully swept into a grand knot on the top.

"You mean today, or in general?" Michael asked. He had loosened his tie and was cradling his mug of, what Lisa could finally see, was hot tea.

"Both," Dr. Celia answered and smiled with encouragement.

"Alrighty." Lisa offered, "I'll say I'm at a three generally and a five today." Lisa figured if she went first it would break the ice for Michael. Even though he was open to counseling, like most men, he wasn't thrilled to be sitting around, discussing his feelings for an hour.

Dr. Celia nodded. "Good. How about you, Michael?"

Michael sipped before answering, his brows furrowed. "I guess five for both."

Lisa was surprised and glanced at Dr. Celia but the woman didn't look put off. She just kept digging.

"Ok. What makes it a five for you on both accounts?"

"Well, me and Lisa are in a good place. I have my job. I have my health and family. I feel really good about us coming out of some hard things. I feel like things are looking up." Michael explained all of this as if his outlook was the most normal thing in the world.

"But as I recall it's only been a couple of months since Baby Lee," Dr. Celia started delicately. "And then you had *another* loss, correct?" She looked through her notes and then at Lisa for confirmation.

Lisa nodded. Sylvia's passing had been a topic in her one-on-one grief counseling with Dr. Celia.

"Yeah. But, like I said, we aren't wallowing in it. Those were hard things but we got through em'." Michael paused to correct himself. "I mean, we're getting through them." He shrugged.

Dr. Celia replied, "Ok. But *how* are you getting through them? Are you coping in ways that are healthy?"

That's when Michael went quiet. He took another sip of his tea before finally answering, "I've been working a lot." He shrugged. "Work helps me get through."

"Lisa. What about you? How are you coping?"

"I've been in a group therapy for mothers who lost their children," Lisa started. "The one you told me about. I've also been doing these morning devotionals with my friend Carol. Carol had several miscarriages, so it's been a blessing to have someone who gets it. Plus, I've been listening to podcasts on grief…" Lisa let her voice trail, thinking about the podcasts Joe had referenced, but not wanting to mention him.

"Good. It sounds like you're on track with processing your feelings. The need for doing so is vital to move through the stages of grief." Dr. Celia dipped her eyes to her pen and pad and scribbled some notes. "The stages of grief are doubt, anger, bargaining, depression, and acceptance. Where do you feel like you two are on that spectrum?"

"I'm sorry, but I thought we were here to talk about our marriage. Yet you keep talking about grief?" Michael's tone was slightly irritated. He fidgeted some in his chair and Lisa raised a brow.

"You're right, Michael. We are here to talk about your marriage. Your marriage has been hugely tested in this season with these losses and deaths. We need to see where you're at individually to adequately measure how your marriage is doing in total. A marriage is two individual parts coming together, but if those individual parts aren't solid, then the marriage isn't solid." Dr. Celia's voice resounded strong and steady in the intimate setting. She was clearly undeterred by her client's anxious response.

Michael didn't say anything but his silence said it all.

Lisa wasn't sure if she should feel relieved at Dr. Celia's thorough explanation or nervous that her husband seeemed ready to bolt any minute now. For some reason, he appeared to be growing more uncomfortable by the moment.

"Ok," Michael eventually answered, now slightly slouching in his chair with a nonchalant air. "I guess I'm at acceptance."

"And what about you, Lisa?" the doctor asked.

Hmmm. Where was she in her processing?

"Well, I was mad as hell after Lee. I was so angry at God and then even at my dad. But when Sylvia transitioned, I couldn't afford to go into that dark pit again. Sylvia was one of my main ways of climbing out of it. I guess a part of me felt like if I fell into that dark angry hole again, I wouldn't make it out. Because she couldn't help me this time." Lisa shifted, stretching her turquoise skirt down to her knees and adjusting her chevron printed blouse. "I was also able to let go of the anger when my dad and mom came to visit. That helped a lot."

"That's great, Lisa," Dr. Celia affirmed while jotting more notes.

"So, I guess I would say, I'm at acceptance. But it's still really hard. Sometimes I feel shame, like it's my fault and I should have taken better care of myself, and Lee wouldn't have died," Lisa's tone caught on her words but she bravely continued. "So maybe there's some bargaining there. Every day I fight the sadness and depression. I just can't afford to let it consume me. Especially for Michelle's sake."

Dr. Celia tilted her chin. "It does sound like you've been able to move through some of those difficult emotions. It's even ok to feel multiple emotions at the same time like it sounds like you're doing."

Her eyes drifted over to Michael. "Michael, Lisa said she was angry after losing the baby. Did you ever feel angry during your processing?"

Michael frowned. "Yeah. Of course. Who wouldn't be?"

"What helped you stop feeling angry?"

"I would say Lisa's parents coming helped. Then I was able to see good come from the deaths. I was able to see—God."

Lisa smiled. She hadn't had any more God-conversations with Michael. It was great to hear him reference faith.

"Yeah? How so?" Dr. Celia prompted. She reached for her mug and took a sip, but her eyes stayed pinned on him.

For the first time, Michael seemed to loosen up, his face brightening.

"I mean, it was like a miracle seeing Lisa's parents be there the way they had never been. I knew it was something she had been waiting for, probably most of her life. And then I got to know them and bond with them. It was like, we were all becoming a family.

And it happened so *fast*. You can't deny something like that isn't God,"

The certainty of Michael's tone caused Lisa's heart to skyrocket. *That's right, baby!*

"Awesome. It sounds like you've developed more in your faith," Celia said. "Would you say you've been depending on God to help you process your loved ones' deaths?"

Michael looked at the ground, then at his hands, then at the ceiling. "I don't know."

What is happening with my husband? Lisa wondered, watching him.

Gruffly, Michael added, "I don't think so."

"That's quite alright. It may be that you just don't know how. Especially if you're faith is new. When we come to God we don't always know we have access to everything He offers," Dr. Celia said in a caring tone. "Not just salvation, but restoration of relationships, as you witnessed with Lisa's family. And healing, whether it's emotionally, mentally or physically."

Dr. Celia turned to Lisa. "Have you been depending on God for your processing, Lisa?"

Lisa licked her lips and thought for a moment. "I think so. It took me a minute to get there because I was so mad at Him. I just couldn't believe He would allow us to lose Lee when I kept praying against it. Then after Sylvia, it was hard because I used to go to Sylvia for so much and God would use her. But now, often, I have to go directly to Him. It's been a transition for sure."

Celia took more notes. "And what about going to each other? Have you guys been leaning on each other in processing?"

This time both Lisa *and* Michael were silent.

Dr. Celia spoke in a serious tone. "It's vital for you two to make sure you're connecting and leaning on one another. I can see that you're in different places in your grief journeys *and* in your faith journeys. We don't need you on the same sentence because you're two people who are wired differently, but we at least want you on the same page. I'm going to give you guys an exercise. I want you to write down things you've been using to cope outside of God and your relationship. Sometimes when grieving we fall into what we call in the counseling world "short term energy relieving behaviors." These are usually unhealthy behaviors we turn to that give us a temperary escape from our pain but they're normally destructive and don't last. Some examples can be overeating, over shopping, even overworking. After you make your list I want you to write down things you can do to lean on each other and God. Things that are not short term. Then I want you both to share your lists out loud."

Before either could respond, Dr. Celia was ripping out pages of notebook paper and tossing ink pens at them.

Lisa swallowed hard with the pen tip pressing her lip. What had she been leaning on outside of Michael and God? What were short term behaviors?

There was her counseling with Celia, her friends, her podcasts that Joe had given her… And there it was.

Joe.

Lisa had been leaning on Joe. Joe was the first person she had told about the work cuts to. Joe was the first man she asked for prayer from. Joe was the one who offered her support for grief in ways that Michael hadn't, by giving resources, prayer, and a listening ear. Michael was busy hiding at work, and even, hiding from God. There was even presently a text thread sitting in her phone where she and Joe were going back-and-forth trying to reschedule their missed snowstorm meeting.

How would Michael feel about this thread?

Lisa was terrified of the answer. It was clear as day that she was moving towards an unhealthy dependency on a man who was not her husband. As she sat, hovering over her list, the paper became blurry from the tears muddying her eyes.

"Lisa?" Celia was peering at her in concern. "Do you need Kleenex?"

Keeping her head low, Lisa's coils bobbed while covering her face. The tears were now falling, drenching the paper.

Michael's hand suddenly appeared on her back. "Baby. It's ok. I'm here." He rubbed her and though she appreciated his comfort, Lisa wondered how he was going to take her brutal honesty.

After wiping her face and getting herself together, she looked up.

Dr. Celia advised she wanted them each to share one thing off their list that they were using to cope outside of each other and God.

"That one thing needs to be the most important thing. Don't cheat yourself. Admitting the greatest ways we miss the mark brings the most healing. I guarantee, if you want your marriage to truly thrive, it needs to be built on honesty. Honesty breeds healing."

Honesty breeds healing.

The words ran laps around Lisa's mind as she glared at the three-letter name written on her paper.

Joe.

She tried to talk herself out of it but knew the Spirit of God was nudging her to be open. To be honest. That was going to be the key to her healing.

"Lisa, why don't you go first?" Dr. Celia said and her eyes were full of compassion.

Lisa cleared her throat and musterd her courage; head shadowing her list, shoulders hunched. "I've been…I've been talking to an old friend. An old lover."

Michael sat up. Lisa could feel his eyes even though she was too afraid to look at them.

"Not a lot. Not even on the phone. Just…just through social media mainly. Only a little through text." Lisa finally looked up to see Michael staring at her. "A few times, I guess…"

The hurt was evident when Michael asked, "Did you see him?"

She shook her head. "No. I mean…" *Be honest Lisa.* "I was going to. But I didn't," she rushed to say. "I haven't."

But you would have.

She couldn't keep the truth from shouting from her insides.

"Because there was a storm so we couldn't meet," she admitted after an alarming moment of silence. "I was only going to get a book. I *think*…" The tears were sliding down now. "I'm sorry, Michael. I truly am. I wasn't trying to cheat, or do anything *stupid*, it's just…"

How could she say it? How could she state the things she was missing in her spouse, like faith and his presence?

"I just needed that in the moment. Or at least, I *thought* I did."

Pressing the tissue bundled in her hand to her eyes, Lisa let out a shaky breath. "You just haven't been present in the ways I needed."

Lord, please help!

Anger colored Michael's face. "Who is it?" he asked, his voice taut, jaws clenched.

Inwardly, Lisa flinched. Gripping the arms of the chair, she whispered, "Joe."

Michael knew that Joe was the one she had let go of for him. He knew that back then she was even dating them at the same time. His eyes blazed.

"And you're saying *nothing* happened. But you *were* going to meet him?"

Lisa was now strangling the fabric from the chair arm as she quickly nodded.

"It's important that you hear her out, Michael," Dr. Celia intervened. "Understand that your wife has been through a lot and is in a vulnerable season. Even still, you are allowed all of the feelings you're feeling right now and will continue to feel in processing."

Dr. Celia's voice poured between the couple, a river streaming in a desert. Her wisdom and counsel were needed to mend the broken parts.

Michael's jaw was working. His eyes glared down at his paper, and then, something happened. Lisa could see his body exhale before he rubbed his fingers to his temples.

"Michael?" she asked.

"Do you want to share what's on your paper?" Dr. Celia had asked also.

Michael bit his lip. He started smoothing his finger over his paper repeatedly. His knee began rocking.

"Do you want more tea?" Dr. Celia offered, but he shook his head.

"No. It's ok. I'm fine." But nothing more. They all sat there for a few more moments.

"Are you ready now?" Dr. Celia carefully prodded. She had observed him long enough and could see he was wrestling with something. "Do you want to tell us what you've been using to cope, instead of your wife and God?"

Michael kept his eyes low. But then his voice suddenly pierced the air with words Lisa couldn't have fathomed unless she had heard them herself.

"I've been drinking. I've been drinking to cope. I think I'm an alcoholic."

The Heist

CHAPTER 24

The car ride home was filled with crickets. Lisa had so many questions.

Why didn't he tell me he was drinking?

When *was Michael drinking?*

What *was Michael drinking?*

But she was too afraid to launch into an interview when *she* would be in the hot seat herself when it was over. Lisa wasn't sure she even had answers for her *own* behavior. Dr. Celia had said that in this season their marriage had been tested by losses and deaths. It wasn't until their counseling session that Lisa realized just how *much* their relationship had been tested.

The solemn pair made it back to the apartment and went to pick up Michelle from Carol's. Carol had volunteered to babysit during the in-between hours of when Lisa got home and Michelle's school let out. Since her schedule was an open playing field, Carol was all in.

"Michelle and I are going to have *so* much fun!" Carol chirped after promising Lisa that she wouldn't feed her too many chocolate chip cookies. Even if she had, Lisa didn't have many caregiver options, so it just would have been what it was.

"Mommy, I can't *wait* 'til my next art therapy session," Michelle bubbled. She was practically skipping down the hall between Lisa and Michael, her Barbie bookbag swinging at top speed. Last week, Lisa enrolled Michelle in art therapy, given the trauma of finding Sylvia deceased, and, also losing her.

With all this therapy, Michelle better be president, Lisa thought as Michelle gabbed about her new therapist and Michael led them into the apartment. He still hadn't said a word, even when they picked up Michelle. Michelle seemed not to notice though. She was in her usual state of unloading her day to her parents, or anyone who seemed to want to listen.

The evening was smooth enough in spite of how late it was. Carol was a dear and had fed Michelle. Michael said he would make a sandwich. Lisa had no appetite due to the invisible hands obsessively kneading her stomach. Somehow, she managed to do Michelle's hair, listen to her story, and tuck her in by nine o'clock.

"I love you." Lisa kissed her daughter on the forehead. *And if your dad leaves me, at least I have you,* she couldn't help thinking.

"Love you too." Michelle turned over as Snowball snuggled near her feet. The cat was a godsend.

Squaring her shoulders, Lisa walked to her bedroom. Michael was on the bed, clad in pale blue pajama bottoms and freshly showered. He fiddled with his tablet but Lisa couldn't discern by his expression if it was for work or pleasure.

When they finished their counseling session, Dr. Celia provided resources for Alcoholics Anonymous. She also encouraged them to share the rest of their lists, discuss their feelings, and said she would see them next week.

Lisa felt a little overwhelmed. When they first decided to do counseling, she thought it would be more of a check-up, having no idea that *all that* would be dug from beneath the surface.

"Hey," she greeted quietly, gliding to the dresser to remove her jewelry.

Michael responded with a short, "Hey," but didn't look up.

Another ten minutes of silence ensued as Lisa peeled off layers, put on her PJs, then shuffled to the king-sized bed. "Are we gonna talk?"

Finally, he looked at her, "Fine," then cut off his tablet.

Ok. I guess I'll *lead the conversation.*

Sitting cross-legged, Lisa faced him. *Lord, help me with this stone wall of a man.*

"I know *I* was surprised tonight by the things said," she started. "How come you didn't tell me about the drinking?"

Michael's face exuded shock. "The same way you told me about Joe?"

Touché.

"The thing with Joe isn't really a thing," Lisa began, but the conviction of the Holy Spirit nabbed her. So she added, "*Yet*. It wasn't a thing *yet*."

Before elaborating, she stroked her forehead. "I know we have a responsibility to protect our marriage, and I was flirting with that line. I'm sorry, Michael. But, do you really want to know the truth?"

Michael nodded for the first time with something in his eyes other than anger. Blatant fear.

"I genuinely feel I have *some type* of unfinished business with Joe. He was a good friend—*is* a good friend. I don't trust many people. You know that. But I do trust him. I trust his character. When I told him about Lee's death, he gave me some resources that have really helped. That's what I was gonna meet with him about. A book he recommended for dealing with grief."

"And you couldn't get this book at the library? Or Amazon? Or Barnes & Noble?" Michael's eyes were flat as his snarky comments steamrolled out.

Lisa tried hard not to roll her eyes. "Like I said, I feel like I still need to have a conversation with him. So no, it's not just about the book."

There. She had said the thing she was scared to say to her husband. Scared to say to herself.

I feel like I still need to see my ex.

"You know how crazy this sounds? You tryna hook up with some dude you used to date eyons ago even though you're married with a kid? You've moved on, Lisa. What else could be said?" Michael's voice harbored both aggression and the fear she had gleamed ealier.

He needs reassurance, she could sense in her spirit.

Scooting forward, Lisa removed the tablet from Michael's hands and cradled them.

"Baby. There is no one else I want to be with other than you. You are the one I chose and you are the one I'm choosing. I admit, the way I went about things with Joe wasn't right. I was keeping it hidden. Not just from you, but from myself. I'm not making excuses, but I was also in a vulnerable emotional state. I wanted a man who could pray for me. You were running and hiding in work. And now, I've learned, hiding in drinking."

Michael's eyes lowered, but Lisa wasn't trying to point the finger; she just wanted him to understand where she was at.

"I'm in this thing with you," she continued, locking their hands tighter together. "I messed up. Just like you've messed up. But I'm not gonna lie to myself or you anymore. I lied several times. I lied about my doctor's appointment with Dr. Singh. I lied about connecting with Joe. I'm sorry. I'm gonna try harder to trust you. To trust that you won't leave if I tell you the full truth."

Michael grimaced. "I'm not leaving you. I'm never going to leave you. I know you struggle because of your dad. But I'm not him. At least, who he used to be."

Lisa nodded. They had entered several rounds of this conversation a few times over the years, but often, it was hard for the truth to stick. She was still on a journey of healing from her abandonment wounds.

Michael lifted her chin. Lisa hadn't even realized it had dipped downward.

"I'm here, Lisa."

She cried. She couldn't help herself. As many times as she feared him leaving, Michael was still there.

Even after all this.

Her husband reached for her and she let him press her cheek against his chest and rock her. It was the most comforting thing in the world.

"I'm sorry. I'm sorry I didn't trust you enough to tell you the truth."

"It's ok. We're learning," Michael murmured above her crown of tendrils. "We're learning how to be there for each other."

Michael's warmth enclosed Lisa, and she couldn't deny the love they shared. There was no one in this world she wanted more than this man.

~

THE NEXT DAY WAS A SLEW OF EVENTS LEADING UP TO Thanksgiving. To Michelle's delight, Vanessa had flown in, and the Dorises snagged her from the airport.

"I don't think I'll ever fly two days before Thanksgiving *again!*" Vanessa announced, hopping into the backseat. "That holiday crowd is *brutal.*"

Lisa laughed and turned her neck to peer at her mother. "I'm glad you made it, Mom."

They had decided they would make this an annual thing. The plan was for Vanessa to visit for Thanksgiving, and the Dorises would do a week before Christmas at Michael's parents in Maine before popping in on Hank and his family. This year, of course, they would be at Disney for Christmas. Out of everything, the family gathering with Hank made the churning ramp up to high speed in Lisa's gut. Other than a handful of awkward video chats, she hadn't had *any* kind of connection with her half-siblings.

Lord, be with all of us, she threw up in prayer when they made the holiday arrangements.

After arriving home, Lisa and Vanessa got busy in the kitchen and started on some of the side dishes that would take the most preparation. Vanessa agreed she would help Lisa bake a Sweet Potato Pie, fulfilling her sudden desire to bake. During cooking breaks, The Temptations played at high volume while Vanessa taught Michelle 'The Twist'.

"Mom, look!" Michelle cried while shimmying across the kitchen floor in her Christmas socks.

"Yeah! You got it!" Vanessa encouraged.

Lisa grinned.

"I think we need to enroll Michelle in dance class," she murmured to Michael as they admired their daughter from the living room entry.

Michael grabbed Lisa by the waist from behind. "Famous last words, Mrs. Doris," he teased in her ear, and she laughed. But then, still nuzzling her, he grew serious. "Remember that thing you said you felt like you had to do?"

Worry nudged Lisa. It couldn't be what she thought it was. "Umm, the ex-thing?" she said slowly. Her eyes dug into Michelle, making sure she wasn't overheard.

"Yeah," Michael answered softly. Lisa turned to face him. "I was thinking. I trust you, Lis. If you feel like you gotta do it. Then do it."

Whoa. That was the *last* thing she had expected to hear her husband say. "Umm, you sure? Because—"

"I prayed about it," Michael cut her off. He pressed his finger to her lips. "I trust you."

My husband is praying. Wow.

Without a moment's notice, Lisa planted her lips onto his. It was the most powerful word she had ever heard. *Trust.* His trust in her made her know for certain that she, too, could trust herself.

THE NEXT DAY, LISA, MICHELLE, DANITA, AND VANESSA SMOOSHED into a cab dressed in all black.

"Why are we all in black?" Michelle had asked Lisa when they met up with Danita outside the apartment entrance.

"Because, your friend Ms. Danita is a funny lady and wanted us to," Lisa responded with a smirk.

"Because we're going on a heist," Danita declared, rolling her eyes at Lisa before flagging a cab.

"What's a heist?" Michelle looked thoroughly confused.

"It's a top-secret mission to capture something," Danita filled in as they shoved their way into the vehicle.

When Michael gave Lisa the go-to to pick up the book from Joe, she texted him. Turns out Joe was leaving Thanksgiving Day for his sister's and would be gone for a week. Today was the only day that worked, unless of course, they waited until he returned. But, since her mother would be in town, Lisa wanted to capitalize on the support system and have Vanessa by her side. She sent a group text to her mother and Danita and updated them on the situation. Danita was all-in, though she felt like Joe, as safe as he seemed, needed some insurance. That was when she suggested they do "the heist."

"We need a secret code word. If things get dicey, we need to rush in and swoop Lisa," Danita demanded in the group text.

"Christmas!" Vanessa texted back.

"No no. That's too normal. What if they talking about their Christmas plans?" Danita responded.

"Kwanzaa!" Vanessa texted. So, Kwanzaa it was.

Then Danita was adamant that Lisa needed a code name.

"We can't just say, Lisa, it's time to go. We are on a mission. And she needs extra protection so we can save her if necessary."

"I don't need a code name." Lisa typed back while toweling her hair after her shower.

"You need a code name," Danita responded immediately.

"Little bug," Vanessa suggested. **"That was her nickname when she was little."**

"No, Mom," Lisa texted, **"I'm grown."** She laughed and shook her wet head as Michael gave her a strange look. He had just come in to brush his teeth.

"L-Boogie!" Danita texted.

Now, I can't be mad at that, Lisa thought and sent a thumbs-up emoji.

Lisa laughed at her peeps and their loving protection. She also had no qualms about her undercover nickname since it was in homage to her favorite rapper.

Though she was nervous as all get out about meeting Joe, her community's care enclosed her. Their marriage counseling session with Dr. Celia showed how important being transparent about their weaknesses was. That realization motivated Lisa to roll with her crew on this mission.

After the cab dropped them off, the quartet bustled into Devon's. It was swinging in full gear. Holiday garb laced the cafe as "Jingle Bells" blasted from the speaker.

"Hey, Lis!" Denise, the cute young waitress called and swaddled Lisa into a hug. "Haven't seen you in *forever*." She then took in her growing daughter. "Dag! Michelle has to be like 13 now, huh?" Swooping down, Denise bearhugged Michelle, who laughed.

"*No*. I'm only 9," Michelle corrected but it was clear she loved the miscalculation.

Denise pointed to a section in the back. "Y'all want a table? They filling up fast."

Lisa was already scanning the cafe. She could see Joe seated on the opposite side of where Denise was pointing.

"Y'all go get seated, and I'll meet you," Lisa told her mother and Danita, who grabbed Michelle's hands on either side.

Denise looked confused but followed Lisa's body angled in the other direction. Her eyes fell on the back of Joe's head. Though her face said it all, the crafty waitress knew enough not to say anything out loud.

"Just let me know when you're ready to order," Denise tossed over her lock-draped shoulder, and went on her way.

Before she could lose her nerve, Lisa inhaled a breath while marching towards Joe. Standing in front of him, his whole face lit up, and a cozy smile met her lips. Everything about Joe looked the same. Lisa wasn't sure what she had expected. It had only been four years. How much could change in four years? But then, she thought about her life lately.

Shoot, how much can change in a few months?

"Lisa, it's so good see you!" Joe embraced her.

It was a sweet, kind, short hug, and Lisa was relieved that she had no longing for it not to end. Even though she had the okay from her husband, her mother, her friend, and, even God Himself, she wasn't stupid enough to think she couldn't be ignorant of some lurking desire for her ex.

But, as they settled into light chit-chat over coffee and Joe popped out the book he promised, Lisa felt the friendship she was right about. It was just that. Friendship. There were no butterflies. No romantic notions. No missed opportunity that she had somehow forfeited when she chose Michael. It was God just using Joe for that period of time to get her to where she needed to be.

As if Lisa needed any more confirmation of her life choice, Joe blew her away. "I'm thinking about proposing," he confided, and Lisa tried not to choke on her coffee.

Wiping the liquid that drizzled her chin, she said, "Umm. I didn't know you had met someone?"

Joe smiled. "Yeah. We've been dating for a while now. Nina," he breathed. And with that, popped out his phone, showing off a beautiful caramel woman with a gorgeous smile.

Lisa smiled back. *I can't believe he's dating.* Joy filled her. *Insurance!*

That's when Joe shared his Christmas-planned proposal.

"Oh my God, Joe. I'm so happy for you!"

And she genuinely was. There was a burden that lifted. All these years she had been carrying this heavy, fearful dread that somehow, she had made a mistake. And even if she hadn't, that Joe was just out here, this lonely, great guy who couldn't find someone. But he had.

He has.

Joe grinned and updated Lisa on their courtship. How Nina was the first woman God had confirmed to be his life partner. How much she demonstrated an inner beauty in addition to her outward beauty.

"I think it's time."

He asked Lisa to pray because he also felt led to start his business.

"It's a leap of faith because I would never think to try and get married while becoming an entrepreneur. But I feel like God is asking me to trust Him. You know?"

Joe peered at Lisa with those kind, dark eyes that had piqued her interest so long ago. Back then, she didn't have a spiritual relation-ship with God. Back then he couldn't have asked for her to pray for him. But today, Lisa had come so far in her faith journey. She had loved and lost and loved again. She had navigated the tumultuous waters of trials and tribulations. She had trusted God with her husband's faith, saw the restoration of her relationships with her parents, felt the healing balm of childhood wounds and was growing in trust toward her husband. Lisa was now able to pray for Joe just as he had prayed for her so many years ago. And it was this realiza-tion that warmed her heart.

Lisa had grown in her faith.

⁓

AFTER OFFERING QUICK HUGS TO DEVON AND NATALIE, THE LADIES headed to the soup kitchen off 14th Street. Since Michelle desper-ately needed to learn how "the other side" lived, Lisa had signed them up. Instead of complaining, as she had expected, her little girl was excited.

"I love helping, Momma!" Michelle said when Lisa told her they would be serving food to the homeless the day before Thanksgiving.

Yeah, we'll see, Lisa thought with worry. Michelle had never been that up-close and personal to a homeless person.

I hope this child doesn't embarrass me.

"She'll be fine," Vanessa assured when Lisa confessed her doubts.

They entered to find a food line already growing and Michael waiting in a chair on his phone. He was decked in a tan peacoat and scarf, and Lisa's heart sped at the sight of him. Michael was magnificent.

Love squeezed her as she found her way to her husband. Her presence drew his gaze in the way it always did. She saw the ques-tion in his eyes and hurried to answer it. Grabbing both ends of his scarf, she lifted him to his feet, peered up into his light browns, and murmured, "I love you, Michael Doris," then let her lips mount his.

The chatter around them faded and it wasn't until Michelle

begged for them to hurry up and get their aprons on to "feed the needy"—sadly that was exactly what she had said—that the couple parted.

But Lisa didn't let her daughter's colorful words deter her. No. Instead, she let herself wade in the moment. Standing in front of her love, Lisa held Michael's gaze.

"I love you too, Lisa Doris," Michael responded while stroking her cheek.

And all was right in the world.

Epilogue

A group of men and women surrounded them on all sides. One after the other, folks stood, reciting words and stories that had become all too familiar. Welcoming eyes and empathetic nods decorated each attendee. Like any other lot, common characteristics bunched them together, but the dominant one was their stint with addiction. Finally, it was Michael's turn to speak.

Lisa watched him stand and recite his speech. Though he didn't always share, these meetings were probably some of the most vulnerable moments she had ever witnessed from her husband. That was saying a lot, having spent 14 years with the man. AA was peeling back layers in Michael that he didn't even know he had. AA and God that is.

"I'm grateful for the support I have," Michael began. "Grateful for the program that's not just given me space to heal from an addiction, but to heal from the pain I was using that addiction to run from."

Michael ducked his face and rocked a little from side to side, both hands buried in his dress slacks. Lifting his eyes, he continued.

Lisa listened quietly. She knew how much it took for Michael to share. After their second counseling session, he had finally gone into detail about his drinking. He confessed to Lisa that he had been drinking at night while she was asleep. Confessed about the hidden bottles in the trunk of his car. How he was convicted after Vanessa visited but still couldn't stop sneaking Vodka. He even shared that when he had accused Lisa of overdrinking, it was really out of guilt for his own behavior.

"There was so much pain, I feared it would swallow me alive."

Michael gripped the creases of his slacks and Lisa fought the urge to cradle his hand. She was seated next to him, and no matter how many meetings they attended together, it was never easy watching him struggle. But through the program she had learned the necessity for an addict to feel the pain. The pain was reality and the addiction was used to escape reality. Her husband needed to be present.

"I thank God for His grace to have 313 days of sobriety under my belt."

The members smiled and clapped at Michael's declaration, and a wave of thankfulness washed Lisa. Dealing with her mother's addiction was so traumatic that when Michael revealed his struggle, it scared her half to death. But God promised her victory. He told her she wouldn't travel the road she had already been down. Thankfully, Michael was eager for assistance and had readily enrolled in the AA program tucked in Celia's resources. They had been attending weekly meetings ever since.

After the meeting, the Dorises headed home, then stopped by Carol's to swoop Michelle.

"Are you sure you can keep looking after her *and* Tony?" Lisa asked again for the umpteenth time. Her eyes peered adoringly at the baby in Carol's arms. Anthony Robert Johnson flaunted the same baby blues as his momma and the same round peach face. Named after his grandfather, he was bundled in love and coddled in affection.

Carol rolled her eyes, rocking Tony. "Like I've said, Michelle is a *doll*. She *helps* with Tony. Isn't that right, Michelle?"

On cue, Michelle beamed while clutching her bookbag by both

straps. "Yep. I helped change his diaper today," she stated with a proud nod.

"It's giving her plenty of practice." Carol winked and her gaze dropped to Lisa's belly.

Lisa grinned and instinctively rubbed her swollen stomach. "Well. Ok. But just let me know when it gets to be too much. I'm coming out of the office next month for my C-section, so I'll be home full time for a while."

Carol smiled. "Yes. I know. Just like you've told me a *million* times."

"Babe. Our plane is leaving in a few hours. With the holiday craze, we gotta get to the airport." Michael started shooing Lisa toward the door, which was needed, or she would have gotten entangled in conversation with Carol.

Over the last year, their bond had only strengthened, with Carol being her afterschool caregiver and Lisa assisting her with becoming a new mother. Then, when Lisa got pregnant, she had to borrow Carol's faith to believe she wouldn't relive the nightmare she experienced with Baby Lee.

"You're going to be fine." Carol had clutched Lisa's hands in assurance when she shared the news of her pregnancy. Tears slid down Lisa's cheeks. "Remember how David lost his child then God gave him Solomon?" Carol said. "This one is yours."

"I know. I know," Lisa kept repeating. The two continued leaning on each other and attending the virtual *Jesus Calling* devotionals every morning at 4:30 am like clockwork. Sarah Young's writings were truly edifying during difficult times.

Leaving Carol, Michael, Lisa and Michelle, successfully managed to make their flight through the biting cold and throngs of travelers eager to visit loved ones. At Michael's insistence, Lisa had purchased first-class seats.

"I don't want anybody bumping, or shoving you," he growled, deep lines sandwhiching his frown.

Lisa knew her husband was terrified of her flying, but she assured him, "Dr. Swan said flying is perfectly fine up until 36 weeks." She rubbed his hand. "I'm only at 32."

Michael huffed a resigned sigh but was still on guard. Every passenger who shuffled along, looking remotely overweight, he eyed wearily and watched carefully. But, despite his concerns, the flight was more comfortable and smoother than Lisa could have fathomed. It was barely two hours, and the extra cost for the snazzy wide leather seats seemed overkill. But anything to bring Michael comfort. Michelle, of course, loved first class. She stayed glued to her favorite show on Michael's tablet the whole time.

What was actually challenging Lisa's faith and hijacking her peace wasn't the flight but the inevitable face-to-face with her father's family. Particularly her half-sisters. Never before had Lisa been in the same room with them. They had never even breathed the same air.

Lord, this is ludicrous, she recited internally a few times during their commute. While on the plane. When they checked in to their hotel that her father had paid for at The Hilton. Then, again, after they had all taken showers and changed for dinner.

Straight ludicrous!

It was Christmas Eve, and Hank invited them to dinner. "So we can catch up, and you can meet the girls," he had said.

"But, Dad, we'll be there on Christmas Day. And several days after," Lisa had argued, but Hank wouldn't take no for an answer.

"I missed too many days with you. I want as many as I can have," he responded on their video chat. His eyes were pleading, his voice raw with emotion.

So Lisa prayed repeatedly, *Please let this work out,* as they rode the elevator down and traipsed through the lobby in an effort to see her father for Christmas Eve.

"Wait while I get the car," Michael said and headed outside for their rental.

"Mommy, is Ohio fun?" Michelle asked, dancing in her snow boots from side to side, and Lisa laughed.

"It probably depends on what part you're in, just like any other place."

But, Lisa had actually never visited her father's residence, so she really had no clue.

"I read there are farms here. Do you think Papa Hank has horses?"

Before Lisa could respond, Michael texted that he was outside.

"I don't think they have farms in Shaker Heights which is where we're going. Plus, if Hank has a horse, I'm sure he would have said something about it by now," Lisa said, climbing into the all-white SUV.

Michael hopped around to help her in as her belly was its own extra baggage to lift.

The drive was rather uneventful. Much easier driving than in Manhattan. As the greenery covered in snow drifted by, Lisa's phone buzzed. Expecting to see Hank's name, her eyes lit up in surprise.

"Hey, Ma," she answered the video chat with a warm smile.

"Hey, hon. Y'all there yet?" Vanessa piped back.

"We're en route to Hank's."

"Hey, V," Michael said.

"Gramma V!" Michelle leaned forward and propped her chin on Lisa's shoulder to see her grandmother on the screen. Lisa held it directly in front of her to let the two chit-chat.

Lord, please be with us. Anxiety grew with each minute that diminished on the GPS dashboard, notifying that they were even closer to their ETA.

"Baby, give the phone back to your momma," Lisa heard Vanessa direct and pulled the screen away from her daughter.

"I just wanted to wish you a Merry Christmas in case we don't talk tomorrow," Vanessa said. "I know you'll be busy."

"Thanks, Mom. Are you with Janette and Sasha?" Lisa was referencing her mother's friends. In the last year of their growing closer, she had become more privy to her mother's social life and learned the names of her besties.

Vanessa nodded. "Yep. We're heading to a movie, so I'm a let you go."

Lisa shook her head in agreement, but concern must have been etched on her face because her mother suddenly said, "And, sweetie. Enjoy yourself."

Vanessa winked and blew a kiss, the act massaging her daughter's nerves. At that moment, the baby kicked, and Lisa took it as a sign.

"Thanks, Mom. I love you."

They hung up right when Michael pulled into the long driveway of a flat, ranch-style home. It was draped in lights and the whole lawn was garnished in various inflatable Christmas garb.

"We're here!" Michelle announced the obvious and a nervous chuckle oozed from Lisa.

The crew unbuckled their seatbelts and Michael hurried to unload Lisa. Gripping his neck, she stepped onto the ground carefully. Before she knew it, they were in front of a red door with a fresh-looking wreath on its face. It looked handmade.

"There's an elf on the window!" Michelle pointed next to the door where Christmas lights outlined the window. Fake snow frosted the inside edges and a snow elf loomed in the bottom right frame.

"Wow," Michelle exclaimed. "That's so cool!"

Well, at least Michelle's won over, Lisa thought, clutching her child's mittens in her leather gloves.

"Oww. You're hurting me," Michelle cried, and Lisa loosened her grip.

"Sorry," Lisa muttered.

Michael was only able to get one solid knock in before the door flew open.

Hank stood before them, eyes bright, sporting a cute Christmas sweater with Rudolph posing in the center.

"Papa Hank!" Michelle was already in his arms.

Hank lifted her but then hunched over, pretending to be hurt. "Michelle, you got even bigger. I can't pick you up anymore!"

As Hank stooped over, Michelle looked fearful.

"I'm sorry!"

Then a round woman entered the doorway, with roasted umber skin that glistened, and a broad smile. She wore the same sweater Hank did. Lisa had no doubt the twinning was her idea.

"Now, Hank, you better stop all that fuss and not scare this chil'," she reprimanded before her gaze drank in the trio. "Come on and get inside before y'all get frost bit." Eagerly, she flapped her hand inward and the three obeyed.

The group was swarmed with sweet hugs and helpful hands, nudging them out of their winter gear and ushering them into the home. It was toasty inside, not just from the heat but from the eminent love that saturated Lisa's heart. She couldn't deny it.

"You're bigger than what you showed me on that video chat." Hank's eyes studied Lisa's belly, and he hovered his hands around her, pretending to measure her stomach.

"Now, you know ain't no woman tryna hear how big she is," his wife chastised. She winked at Lisa who smiled.

"Amen to that," Lisa spouted, but really, she was grateful for her belly. Having loss made one appreciate annoyances like weight gain and stretch marks. Now her gained weight meant she had a healthy, living, child growing inside.

"Aww, now, come on, Novelle. She know I'm only teasing," Hank replied.

"Candace and Gina will be coming in shortly," Novelle said. "They went out to grab a few last-minute items for me." She led their visitors to their destination in the living room.

Lisa sank down next to Michael and Michelle sat on her other side.

Hank brought mugs on a tray from the kitchen, announcing, "We got hot chocolate!"

The proud look on his face snatched Lisa's heart. She couldn't believe she was sitting in her father's home with his wife, a woman she had barely spoken to, other than a few polite greetings when she lurked in the background during video chats. But watching Novelle was like watching a Hallmark Christmas movie. She was the perfect hostess, making sure they were comfortable and offering homemade cookies with their drinks.

Lord, You do great things, Lisa marveled, munching on a snicker-doodle. It tasted divine.

"I can't believe you have those girls out there in this mess," Hank was saying. He ran to the window and peered out at the snow-covered evening, then turned back around.

"Oh, hush. They fine. They not kids, you know." Novelle shoved a cookie into Hank's hand and drew him back into his leather recliner. Her eyes then caught Lisa's.

"Now, honey. How is the pregnancy going?" Novelle's face exuded concern.

Lisa knew that Novelle was really asking if everything was going better than her last pregnancy. Michael reached for her hand and squeezed it for support, but she was fine. She knew her stepmother was prying out of care.

"I can honestly say it's going well," Lisa shared. "I haven't had any issues. I'm thankful that I have my same doctor, so I have someone familiar with my history and needs. Dr. Swan has been a godsend."

It was lovely to say those words. For a while there, Lisa was just as angry with her physician as she had been with God. When she lost Baby Lee, it felt like Dr. Swan had lied to her. Telling her she had to trust God with her child, only for God to take her child. But once she was able to heal from the anger, she could see that her doctor was right. It was always wise to trust God, especially during the storm.

"Why does He allow these things?" Lisa remembered asking Sylvia. Pain flew across her mentor's features at the question. This woman had lost so much. Her father, her husband, the gift to procreate. But even with all she had lost, she still spoke with such certainty.

"He's with us, even in the storm."

Channeling her mentor's faith, Lisa said simply, "I know that this child is meant to be," and patted her belly.

Michael smoothed his hand along hers on her stomach and Michelle followed suit. The three of them were sitting like that when the door suddenly burst open.

"*Whew.* It is *serious* out there!" A young woman exclaimed, shivering and jumping around the entrance.

"Yeah, next year we need to make sure you have *everything* for this special pie, Ma!" a younger woman cried from behind. This one was such a dead-on resemblance to Lisa that her mouth actually fell open.

It's like Michelle in five years, she thought, blinking and trying not to stare.

The girls both threw their apparel on the coat rack as Novelle hurried to retrieve the grocery bag from the older one.

"Y'all not gone' be complaining once you taste my Nana's Sweet Potato Pie! This here is the secret ingredient," Novelle proclaimed, swinging the bag on her way to the kitchen.

The older girl snorted, "Not so secret if we went and bought the ingredient." She laughed until her eyes fell on their company. "Oh! Y'all made it!" Sporting a huge smile, she hurried to the Dorises as everyone stood.

"I'm Gina," the girl said, but instead of a handshake, she swept each one into a hug.

Lisa was in shock. She had no idea her sister would be so friendly. And then Candace was upon them.

"Come here, Candace. Lisa is you in 20 years!" Gina declared.

Candace rushed to the group, "Let me see!" then stared at Lisa, who couldn't help but laugh.

"Well, if I'm you in 20 years then Michelle is you in five." Lisa rested her hands on Michelle's shoulders who peered up at Candace.

"Yeah. I can see it," Michelle said and everyone laughed.

"Now I have all my girls!" Hank proclaimed. He stood behind the kitchen island peering through the opening, staring at them. A large grin swallowed his face.

The crew chatted about their lives, getting to know one another, but the real revealing of their personalities were exposed in a friendly game of Taboo. They split into two teams. Turns out Lisa's fieriness was shared by Candace who was also an avid competitor. After the game, they broke out a puzzle, spending Christmas Eve working it and listening to R&B holiday songs. By then the hot chocolate had turned to eggnog. Lisa was in the kitchen helping herself to more eggnog when she felt a presence behind her.

Hank said, "Can I touch my grandchild?"

He was so sweet to ask. So many rubbed first and apologized later. Lisa smiled. "Of course."

"And it's a boy," she revealed.

As he rubbed her stomach, Hank's eyes glistened. "Oh! He kicked!"

Lisa grinned even more. "Yeah. Jonathan Hank Doris is a kicker."

Hank's eyes bulged, and he looked at her. "You mean?" and she nodded.

"Yeah. We're naming him after you. At least, his middle name."

Fat tears rolled down her father's cheeks. He dropped his head, trying to remove them. Lisa moved forward and reached for his hand.

"I don't deserve it," Hank whispered.

"None of us do."

Lisa wrapped her arms around her father with the peace of God snuggling her heart. All was healed. All was forgiven. Lisa and her father had finally finished their unfinished business.

About the Author

Nicole D. Miller is a 5x's self-published award-winning author, tenured blogger, and urban fiction novelist who takes immense pleasure in crafting stories that intertwine Black culture and faith. As a serial entrepreneur, she's used her degrees in business to launch her bookkeeping business, ABN Bookkeeping LLC, and hybrid book publishing company, ND Miller Publishing LLC. The latter specializes in assisting debut authors with manifesting their book publishing dreams. Via the vehicle of ND Miller Publishing LLC, Nicole personally provides publishing, ghostwriting and one-on-one coaching services.

Born in Toledo, Ohio and raised in Cleveland since she was five years old, she enjoys covering stories of hope through freelance journalism to positively influence the narrative of Cleveland.

A member of the Greater Cleveland Association of Black Journalists, her articles have been featured in a variety of local news periodicals such as The Land and Destination Cleveland. She guest blogs for several organizations, including Mas Larae, a multimedia production platform.

In addition to her writing endeavors, she is the founder and host for the female-led, panel discussion/podcast, Girl Talk, featuring high-achieving women leaders in the community and beyond. Her servant leadership has also been seen through her mentorship position at Teen Enterprise, who specializes in training inner-city youth to be the next generation's entrepreneurial business leaders.

Nicole's accolades include the 2024 Career Mastered Magazine "Emerging Leader" Award, nomination for the 2024 "Author of the Year" for the Stiletto Boss Foundation, induction into the 2024

Who's Who in Black Cleveland and nomination for the 2024 Cleveland Arts Prize Award.

Additionally, Nicole is the Producer of the Great Lakes African American Writer's Conference, an event held annually that celebrates and promotes the rich literary contributions of African American writers.

Nicole's lifetime goal of uplifting her spheres of influence utilizing a plethora of creative talents has enabled her to flourish in all that she does. Her heart is that every person she encounters will be encouraged and inspired to fulfill their purpose and identity in the earth.

Ghostwritten Books

BY NICOLE D. MILLER

"The HERology of A Woman"- Dr. Shamarah. J. Hutchins

"Hold on Sis, Let Me Take My Wig Off!"- Staci Purpose Kirk

"Sorry for the Weight"-Ariel D. Baker